This couldn't be happening.

"Damn it," he said, striding toward the door.

He glanced at the woman on the steps. "Don't make this situation worse by crying," he said. "I'll not tolerate it." A moment later, he looked back over at her. "I mean it," he added, before turning and pounding on the door.

When no one answered the knock, he turned, frowning down at her.

Now what did he do?

"Will you take me in?" she asked.

When he didn't—couldn't—respond, she smiled tremulously. "My reputation is evidently destroyed. Does it matter if I stay with you?"

"It matters to me. I've no intention of caring for a woman. A silly woman. A woman without an ounce of sense."

"Why are you so angry? I'm the one who's just been tossed out of her home. Not you."

He glanced down at her.

"I felt, for some reason, compelled to rescue you from the events of tonight. I didn't realize that would require finding you a place to live, too."

Romances *by* Karen Ranney

A Borrowed Scot
A Highland Duchess
Sold to a Laird
A Scotsman in Love
The Devil Wears Tartan
The Scottish Companion
Autumn in Scotland
An Unlikely Governess
Till Next We Meet
So in Love
To Love a Scottish Lord
The Irresistible Macrae
When the Laird Returns
One Man's Love
After the Kiss
My True Love
My Beloved
Upon a Wicked Time
My Wicked Fantasy

A Borrowed Scot

KAREN RANNEY

AVON
An Imprint of HarperCollinsPublishers

AVON BOOKS
An Imprint of HarperCollins*Publishers*
10 East 53rd Street
New York, New York 10022-5299

Copyright © 2011 by Karen Ranney
Excerpt from *Eleven Scandals to Start to Win a Duke's Heart*
copyright © 2011 by Sarah Trabucchi
ISBN 978-0-06-177188-0
www.avonromance.com

First Avon Books mass market printing: April 2011

Printed in the U.S.A.

10 9 8 7 6 5 4 3 2 1

To Survivors
And you know who you are. . .
Keep up the good fight!

Chapter 1

Early spring, 1866
London

The damn fools were chanting.

He felt like an idiot, and Montgomery Fairfax wasn't partial to playing the idiot.

The circle of men in their brown monks' robes and cowls were muttering together as if they'd practiced this ritual for months, if not years. He could swear he heard beads clicking together as they shuffled into a circle.

Only two beeswax candles illuminated the drawing room. The candles, accompanied by various incense burners and a large brass statue of a naked female figure, sat on the mantel of a cold fireplace at the far end of the room. The incense was strong, a convergence of scents at once flowery and spicy, mixed with the warmth caused by too many people in too small a room.

He should never have listened to his solicitor.

"I'd recommend you take the mirror to the Mercaii, Your Lordship," Edmund Kerr had said. "They can properly determine its provenance and origin." Edmund had procured him an invitation to this gathering as well as providing him directions to the townhouse.

From that conversation, he had been given to believe

the Society of the Mercaii was comprised of reasonably intelligent men whose purpose was to investigate, then dispel, anything abnormal or irrational.

Instead, he faced a group of chanting monks.

The robe he'd been given to wear was too short and the wool cowl made his face itch. He done what they'd asked, and pulled it close so he would remain anonymous. For that fact alone, he was grateful. At least no one of his recent acquaintance would learn of this idiotic exploit.

He knew enough Latin to recognize it was the language the men were chanting. Their voices were low, melodic, and not one of the so-called monks slipped in his recitation.

The circle parted, forming two half-moons. He clenched his hands, forced himself to relax even as he felt his heartbeat escalate.

He didn't particularly like the unexpected.

A figure separated from the others, walked to the mantel, taking one of the candles. With great ceremony, he lit the candles the other men held in front of them. Because their hoods were drawn forward, he couldn't see any of their faces, even after their candles had been lit.

The chanting grew louder; the flames flickered as a door opened in the opposite wall. A tall, black-robed figure entered, moving to the center of the group.

The man—the leader?—spoke Latin in a deep, rumbling voice. The monks answered him in one voice. The gathering had taken on the solemnity of a religious ceremony, but that wasn't the only reason Montgomery was becoming increasingly uneasy.

According to instructions given him, he should have remained in the anteroom until officially summoned. He would have done so if the monks hadn't passed him, chanting. His curiosity had made him follow, but now he wished he'd stayed in the other room, or even opted to leave.

The damn mirror could have remained a mystery for all he cared.

Another door opened, one he hadn't noticed until that moment. A figure, clad in a blue robe, was supported by two monks and led through the circle to stand before the leader.

Mumbling something in Latin, the man in the black robe stepped forward and pulled the cowl from the supplicant's head, revealing a woman with tumbling chestnut curls.

The crowd surged toward her, the atmosphere abruptly changing from a religious ceremony to one more predatory. A hungry and expectant pack of wild dogs ready to set upon a wounded deer.

He took a few steps to the right, to see the woman more clearly. Her face was pale, her profile nearly perfect. Pale pink lips were curved in a half smile; her eyes blinked slowly as if she had recently awakened.

She didn't belong there but, then, neither did he.

Another brown-robed figure brought a bench into the circle. The woman was made to kneel upon it, and place her folded hands on the small ledge in front of her. A lit candle was placed between her hands, her fingers molded around it when she couldn't hold it on her own.

From the way she was responding, he suspected she'd been drugged. Otherwise, she would have comprehended the danger implicit in the sudden eagerness of the men around him.

"Do you surrender your will to the Society?" the leader said, addressing the woman in clipped English.

She shook her head, then reconsidered when one of the men at her side bent to whisper something in her ear.

"Yes," she said softly, almost too softly for him to hear.

He pushed past the first row of garbed members, ignoring the murmur of protests around him.

The woman was oddly ethereal, kneeling as she was, candlelight illuminating her face. She was looking up at the leader, an expression of solemn wonder on her face, her green eyes clear and guileless.

"Do you submit to the Society of the Mercaii?"

Again, she hesitated, then shook her head as if to clear it.

The leader bent forward, whispered something he couldn't hear.

When she didn't answer, the leader bent forward again. This time, his voice was louder. "Say: I surrender myself to the Society of the Mercaii."

She closed her eyes, her head dropping forward.

Montgomery took another step toward her, knowing he couldn't let the game play out to its conclusion.

The crowd around him pressed closer, evidently eager to see the rest. The men behind the leader parted, revealing a table draped with a white cloth.

He placed his hand against the pistol tucked into his jacket. A four-year-old habit of never going anywhere unarmed would prove helpful tonight. Reaching into his robe, he grabbed the handle of the mirror. If nothing else, the damn thing would serve as a second weapon.

Glancing at the woman, then the door, he calculated the distance. From what he'd seen of the British, they weren't an overly confrontational sort. A Fairfax man knew when to fight and when to walk away.

He had to save the woman, but damned if it made him happy.

* * *

Veronica found it difficult to sit upright, let alone kneel. She was forced to look up, and the position made her dizzy. The flame atop the candle she held was surrounded by a bright white halo.

Perhaps she shouldn't have taken the drink they'd given her.

"It'll take away the chill of the evening," someone said, when she'd entered the house.

"I don't drink spirits, sir," she'd replied.

He'd smiled. "It isn't spirits, my dear, just something to warm you."

The man had been so kind and handsome, with blue eyes reminding her of a summer sky in Scotland. She'd not wanted to appear rude, so she'd taken the cup and finished it.

Had it contained spirits? Would that explain her sudden wish to sleep?

The members of the Society clustered around her. She wished they'd tell her what she needed to know. A happenstance, to have overheard a soft-voiced discussion at the tobacconists, when she'd gone to get Uncle Bertrand's favorite tobacco. Against all rules of decorum, she'd addressed the man before he left the shop.

"We should be happy to have you in the Society," he said, smiling. "We're having another meeting the first Tuesday of next month. Would you be able to attend?"

"I will, thank you." He'd given her the address, and she'd memorized it. She had no privacy at Uncle Bertrand's house.

The days had passed too slowly until tonight, when she'd waited until everyone was asleep before creeping down the servants' stairs and out the kitchen door. She'd made her way to a busy street, where she'd hired a carriage, behavior shocking enough to warrant punishment.

Now, she looked up at the leader of the Society, the same man she'd met at the tobacconist's, and congratulated herself on being there. He would tell her everything she needed to know.

If she weren't so very tired, she would ask him.

He took the candle from her, her palms missing its warmth immediately. She was icy inside, like a snowy winter night in Scotland. Would they give her a blanket if she asked? The words formed, then sat on her lips, falling into nothingness before being voiced.

She raised her hand, then stopped, fascinated by her fingers. All she had to do was think, and her fingers moved. She raised them in front of her face and wiggled each one, feeling the most absurd wish to giggle.

A lady didn't giggle in the middle of company.

"Stand."

He'd given her an order, and she would have obeyed, but her legs wouldn't support her. She waved her fingers, instead. The men on either side of her helped her stand, then moved the bench out of the way. She smiled her thanks, amazed when her lips felt numb.

Both men gripped her elbows tightly, moved her closer to the leader. When they released her, she swayed on her feet. Glancing down, she saw the beautiful crimson carpet and thought it looked like blood pooling at her feet.

Where were her shoes?

The leader—had she ever learned his name?—leaned toward her like a buzzard perched upon a limb, waiting for its prey to die. He said something to her, but the words were lost in the curious fog surrounding her mind.

A chill was spreading through her body. She felt as if

she were becoming slowly frozen. Everything was slower than it should have been, including her comprehension. When the two men led her to a table covered in cloth, a warning bell pealed, but any sense of danger felt distant and obscure.

The leader came and opened her robe, pushing it back from her shoulders. She no longer felt any kindness from him. Instead, he reminded her of something dark and dangerous and sharp: a cat's claws, a parrot's beak, a knifepoint. She took a step backward and realized that both men were standing stood behind her, blocking her escape.

Laughter came from far away. Were they laughing at her innocence or her gullibility? Or for her sheer naïveté to believe something good might come from her foolishness?

She should never have come. She should never have left Uncle Bertrand's home.

A man ran a knife from the top of her collar all the way down her bodice. He cut through each successive layer of her clothing, ruining the expensive whalebone corset she'd inherited from her mother, as well as her only shift, one of the few garments she'd brought with her from Scotland.

When she was naked, she was lifted on to the table. Staring up at the rosette of plaster above her head, she told herself it was a dream. A garish sort of nightmare in which she was imagining horrible things.

People were looking at her. She could feel their gaze. The cloth was cold on her back, her buttocks, and thighs. Could she be cold in a dream? The tips of her toes were frozen, and her nose felt the same.

She heard the sound of laughter again. She was Veronica Moira MacLeod, the daughter of a Scots man of letters and his beloved wife. Her father had always told her that a question was the purpose of a trained mind. Why, then, was she being ridiculed for wanting answers to her questions?

The room was spinning, and the cold was growing worse. Was she dying?

She felt the brush of cloth against her feet and managed to raise her head. He was standing at the end of the table, stroking the back of the knife up her leg. She felt herself tremble, but couldn't seem to move.

His hand was scorching on her skin, parting her knees.

The howl of a wolf startled her into semi-awareness. Wolves didn't live in London. A blur of motion jarred her, made her jerk. She turned her head to see a man wrestling with the leader. He was shouting. Something bright and metallic caught her eye, like a pretty talisman dangling in the air.

Two men joined the fight. Thunder sounded, so close she couldn't hear for a moment. The sky separated, rained down, pieces of it falling on her.

God had come, then, to rescue her. Thank You, God.

Her eyes were so heavy she could barely keep them open to see the struggle.

God was winning, but of course He would.

Suddenly, she was upright. No, not upright, but slung over someone's shoulder. Did God carry a sinner in such a fashion? *Oh, God, I have sinned. Please forgive me.* Something hard was digging into her stomach, dislodging the ice. She wasn't feeling very well suddenly and wanted to warn God.

She was miserably uncomfortable, her stomach lurching, her head whirling. Her bottom was cold.

He set her back on her feet, better for her stomach but worse for her head. The room was spinning again. She reached out and gripped God's sleeve only to realize it wasn't God at all, but a man, a stranger.

She tried to get her balance, realizing she wasn't in the same room. Instead, she was in a hallway, being draped in a scratchy brown robe.

The stranger was gripping her wrist with one hand and pulling her after him. She stumbled behind him, wishing he would stop. They were descending steps, long, steep steps that made her dizzy. She flailed for the banister, heard an oath just before she was upended again.

A black cloud was falling over her, something dark and frightening and overwhelming, stripping her of thoughts and feelings.

She succumbed to it with a sharp feeling of regret.

Chapter 2

Night draped over London as if to silence the noise, a mother's protective blanket over the child of the city. London didn't sleep. Instead, the night was always punctuated by the rhythmic clicking of carriage wheels as they traveled over cobbles laid down hundreds of years ago.

Even in this quiet and sedate square, lights flickered beyond the draperies, indicating that sleep wouldn't visit some inhabitants that night. In the distance was the sound of laughter: a raised voice from a neighboring house, a faint far-off protest, whether male or female, he couldn't tell.

Here, nature didn't quiet to rest; night wasn't surrendered to nocturnal creatures like in Virginia. Or perhaps the cycle of life was present in London as well, except the owls, ferrets, and foxes had been replaced by their human counterparts.

London was not a civilized place, unless civilization meant stuffing all the flaws and frailties of humanity into a few square miles. Amid the impressive architecture and culture of a revered society, a man could purchase an assortment of sordid and carnal acts.

Montgomery glanced over at the woman slumped on

the seat opposite him. For the spectators, she'd been an entertainment, nothing more.

She'd been like a dazed and confused child when he'd dressed her in the robe he'd removed. The material had draped over her hips to puddle on the floor.

She was more victim than woman to him at that moment. Her hair was tangled in the cowl of the robe, but he didn't reach out to free it. Ever since depositing her on the seat of his carriage, he'd carefully avoided touching her.

He'd given the order for his coachman to drive some distance away in case the members of the Society of the Mercaii thought to follow him. He doubted they would since he'd proven he was rash and improvident. A man who possessed those traits, as well as a gun, was someone to avoid at all costs.

The woman's eyes were closed, her face unearthly pale. If he hadn't seen her breathe, he would have thought her dead.

What the hell was he going to do with her now?

Veronica woke with two thoughts. The first was that she was vaguely uncomfortable, sitting up in bed in an awkward position, and her nightgown was scratchy. The second thought was she was cold. She grabbed for the blanket only to find it missing.

Blinking open her eyes, she stared at two men. She was in a carriage, and strangers were staring back at her. One was evidently a gentleman from his attire. The other, holding his cap between his hands, was fidgeting and obviously uncomfortable.

She blinked several times, but the strangers didn't disappear.

This wasn't a dream.

She glanced down at herself to find herself attired in an ugly brown robe, and beneath it, she was naked.

What had happened?

For the first time in her life, she'd no clear recollection of the past hours. Only snatches of images that flew into her mind like pernicious birds.

The man whose blue eyes seemed to bore through her had been at the Society of the Mercaii. He'd rescued her.

His hair was thick and black. His face was strong, his cheekbones pronounced, his chin squared and rather pugnacious. His nose fit his face, proud and Roman. His eyebrows and lashes were thick, shielding eyes as blue as the cushions of the carriage. Lines radiated outward from the corners of his eyes, leading her to wonder if he'd spent most of his time outdoors. Or had pain caused them? Twin vertical lines bracketed his full mouth. She suspected they masked dimples that appeared when he smiled. If the man opposite her ever smiled.

"Sir, can I go now?"

She turned her attention to the man with the cap.

"No, Peter. You're our chaperone."

"Chaperone?" she asked. That one word was amazingly difficult to say. Her tongue felt furry and her mouth too dry.

Her rescuer frowned at her. "If you think I have any intention of being found in a compromising position, you're mistaken."

She licked her lips. "I doubt society would think it proper for two men to keep me company," she said, sitting upright. "Now, if you had thought to procure a woman as a companion, that would be another story."

The man opposite her looked disgruntled.

"You're a Scot," he said.

"You're an American although I've never heard an

American who speaks like you," she said. She laid her head back against the seat but found it didn't help the burgeoning headache. "Your words sound stretched out and coated with honey. How very odd."

"I'm from Virginia."

"Virginia?"

"You don't roll your R's when you say Virginia."

He was correcting her pronunciation? She might have had a rejoinder for him if she hadn't felt so peculiar.

"Go ahead, Peter," he said to the man at his side.

As the coachman left the carriage, the chill of the spring night slapped against her face like a wet cloth. She blinked rapidly, inhaling deeply. The pure cold summoned her back to herself as if, for the last hour or so, she'd been floating somewhere not quite attached to her body.

She'd never been the type for hysterics. However, as she looked down at herself and plucked the robe with two numb fingers, she was close to panic.

How on earth was she to get home? Where was her dress? Her shift? The rest of her clothes?

"I have a robe on," she said.

"I put it on you."

She didn't even want to *think* about that.

"If you'll give me your address," he said, "I'll see you home."

Panic clawed its way up her throat.

She raised the shade with her fingertip, just enough to see the milky whiteness of fog. Nothing but damp, clinging fog.

"Where are we?" she asked. "What time is it?"

Folding her arms over her chest didn't make her feel more clothed, especially when she suspected that this man, the stranger opposite her, had seen her naked.

Once she was alone in her bedroom, she'd allow herself to feel the burn of shame. Till then, she simply had to remain as calm as possible. She must extricate herself from this deplorable situation.

"Past midnight, and in the square outside my house," he said. "I thought it expeditious to leave the Society as soon as possible." He hesitated for a moment. "Do you remember any of it?"

Some, but she wasn't about to admit it to him. Another thing to contemplate once she was inside her room.

"I don't feel well," she said, a salty taste bathing the back of her throat. She closed her eyes, fighting against becoming sick.

"Did anyone make you eat or drink anything tonight?"

She opened her eyes. "I had a cup of something warm when I arrived. It tasted like grapes, but it wasn't wine."

"It was probably drugged."

She'd been a fool to take it, but she'd been so grateful to the Mercaii for allowing her to attend that she hadn't wanted to be rude.

"How long have we been here?" she asked.

"A little over an hour."

He folded his arms across his chest and stared at her coldly. "I've been waiting for you to surface from whatever they gave you."

"I shall not trouble you any further," she said, reaching for the door handle.

He leaned forward and put his hand over hers.

"I'm not about to let you leave after I've rescued you from harm. Where do you live?"

"I didn't ask you to rescue me," she said, pulling her hand free.

"No doubt you would have preferred to be raped in front of thirty men," he said, his voice deceptively mild.

She glanced at him, horrified by his comment. Was that what they'd planned for her?

"Thank you," she said faintly, feeling nauseous. "Thank you for rescuing me, but you needn't do more."

"Where do you live?" he asked, his tone bordering on exasperation.

"I beg you, please do not escort me home. If you do, I'll be found out, and the punishment will be severe."

"You're afraid you'll be dismissed."

Thank heavens, he thought she was a servant.

"Shouldn't you have thought of that before you went to the Society?"

She pulled the robe even closer, gathering the folds in front of her, as if doubling the robe would offer further protection for her nakedness.

"Do you think they'll say anything?" she asked faintly.

"I've no doubt your tale will be bandied about in certain quarters. Whether it comes to the attention of your employers, I can't say." He hesitated for a moment. "What would make you go to such a place?"

That was a question she wasn't going to answer.

"Why were you there?" she asked.

"A bit of stupidity on my part," he said, glancing toward the bag at his side. "I'd thought to learn about the origins of an object."

Curious, she leaned forward, her fingers brushing against the cloth. A tingling began in her fingertips, traveling up her arm. She jerked back her hand, looking up at him.

"What is it?"

"A mirror," he said.

She leaned forward again, daring herself to touch the bag. When she did, and the vibration didn't recur, she wondered if she'd imagined it.

He didn't say anything when she picked up the bag. Surprised at the heaviness of it, she sat back and balanced it on her knees. Slowly, she loosened the string at the neck of the bag, then removed the mirror.

Three indentations on the handle were a perfect resting place for her curved fingers. How many hands had held the mirror over the years? Age had mellowed the gold and softened the trailing roses pattern incised on the handle as well as the writing on the back. The most surprising thing about the mirror was the row of diamonds around its circular face.

Still, for all its adornment, it couldn't be called pretty. She turned it over to see that the glass had turned brown with age.

"Why would you take this to the Society?" she asked.

"Damned if I know," he said, glancing at her. "Someone I know thinks it's magic, that it shows the future." His look revealed what he thought of that.

"I've heard of people seeing the future by staring at a bowl of water," she said. "Never a mirror."

"I wouldn't know. I've never seen anything," he said.

She glanced down at the glass again. As she stared, the brown color faded. In its place was her face, smiling. She was surrounded by people, and although she couldn't see their faces clearly, she knew they were smiling, too. The mirror, held in both her hands, trembled as if was alive. In the reflection, her eyes were soft with love, her smile curving and tender. The feeling of happiness was so deep and pervasive, she felt her heart swell with joy.

She was herself, yet she was not. The woman who faced her in the mirror was different. Was it age, experience? In that moment, she wanted to be the woman she saw more than the person she was.

Abruptly, he held out his hand, and she had no choice but to surrender the mirror to him reluctantly. Once he'd replaced the mirror in the bag, he glanced at her again. A look of speculation lingered there. Or was it compassion?

Dear God, and she didn't think it untoward to petition the Almighty for assistance in this regard, please don't let anyone who knew Uncle Bertrand and Aunt Lilly discover anything about this night.

Uncle Bertrand was set upon advantageous marriages for his daughters, and a future for his sons, none of which would be accomplished if a relative was known to be scandalous. And what could be more scandalous than what had happened tonight?

Surely, the members of the Society would not comment on tonight's actions. To do so would be to admit they were present. Would it matter to any of them? A man was judged by a different set of criteria from a woman, and often exempt from censure.

She, on the other hand, would be seen as shocking.

Attending a meeting of the Society of the Mercaii had seemed worth the risk. They might have been able to answer her questions. But they weren't the learned scholars she'd heard but simply a gathering of men interested in other pursuits entirely.

Either her thoughts were making her sick, or whatever they'd given her to drink was affecting her stomach. Her headache was getting worse as well.

She glanced at the opposite seat, wishing she could look into her reflection again. Had she really been happy? Had she been surrounded by people who loved her? Was that a vision of her true future, then, and not the abysmal one she imagined?

Or had the drug made her delirious, too?

"Give me your address," the stranger said.

"You mustn't take me home. If you do, someone will see."

"I didn't want to rescue you," he said. "Since I did, I'll see it to its conclusion. You won't walk home alone."

Something sounded in his voice, some emotion that summoned her curiosity. For a moment, she pushed it away. Curiosity had been at the root of this disaster. Despite herself, she glanced at him. His returning gaze was shuttered, flat, as if he felt nothing.

People were never without emotions.

She closed her eyes, sent her Gift reaching toward the man opposite her. She stilled, clearing her mind, and immediately felt something. He was impatient and irritated; but beneath both emotions, surging like the tide, she felt his anguish, so sharp it felt like a knife slicing through her.

In that moment, she almost asked why he was so troubled, halted only by the memory of Uncle Bertrand's words. How many times had he lectured her?

"Veronica, you must not tell people everything you feel. They'll label you a candidate for Bedlam. I have my position to maintain, and it will do me no good to have my niece rumored to be daft."

"I'm not daft, Uncle Bertrand," she'd said. "I cannot help what I feel about people."

"Your mother encouraged you too much, girl. There is no such thing as your Gift."

What had she said in response? Something about not wishing to hear anything bad about her parents. Or had she simply remained silent, knowing any rebellion, however small, was simply not worth the effort?

No doubt she was fortunate not to be locked up in a

third-floor attic somewhere, or relegated to an out-of-the-way place, labeled the slightly odd woman who felt the emotions of others.

"Well? What's your address?"

She opened her eyes, slowing turning her head to face the man who, inwardly, was so troubled. Outwardly, however, he was taciturn, impatient, and supremely annoyed at her.

"If I give you my address," she asked, "have I your word you'll simply let me leave the carriage? That you won't feel it necessary to escort me to the door and let my employers know what's transpired?"

He was looking at her that way again, as if he skewered her to the seat with his disapproval.

"When I've determined you're safe, yes."

Resigned, she gave him Uncle Bertrand's address, praying her uncle and the entire family would be asleep.

He transmitted the address to the driver, then settled back against the seat.

In a matter of minutes, they were approaching her uncle's house. She'd had a story prepared before she left this evening should anyone see her returning to the house. She'd simply gone for a bit of air. She missed the solitude of Scotland. Oh, but that was the truth, wasn't it?

One good thing about being a poor relation was that she hadn't had a season, wasn't going to have a season, and didn't venture out often. The only time she did leave the house was to perform an errand for Aunt Lilly or Uncle Bertrand. None of the shop owners lived in the neighborhood. Therefore, the chances of her being seen and recognized were almost nil.

When the carriage slowed, then stopped, she reached for the door. Before she could leave the carriage, her rescuer leaned forward.

"Promise me you'll use a little more sense in the future than you demonstrated tonight. I don't know what they paid you, but no amount of money is worth such degradation."

"No one paid me," she said.

"Then why were you there?"

"I was curious," she said. That was all the explanation she was going to divulge.

"A damn dangerous place to be curious."

She nodded and opened the carriage door. Gripping the too-long robe with both hands, she stepped to the pavement, feeling the cold seep through the bottoms of her feet. What had happened to her shoes?

The loss of her dress would be difficult to explain since she only had three, each of them in the same blue fabric her aunt said wore well. All the female servants were attired in the same serviceable blue serge, a fact that hadn't escaped her. She could always say she'd ruined the dress with a stain. Her aunt would fuss about the expense, as well as question why she hadn't at least torn the dress into rags.

How did she explain losing her only pair of shoes?

"Are you hesitating because you're afraid you'll be discovered?" he asked.

She turned, startled to see that he'd left the carriage behind her.

He was an arresting figure, a tall man with a subtle elegance, almost a predatory intensity. Caution made her take a step back.

"Did you kill him?"

His smile was razor thin.

"So, you do remember."

"A shot," she said. "Did you shoot him?"

"No, even though he deserved shooting. The ceiling was the only casualty."

The night was utterly still and softly beautiful. The only sounds were the horses restlessly stamping their feet. The fog was thick, changing the street lamps to small moons. The slightly sulfurous odor stung her nose and caught at the back of her throat, reminding her that her stomach was still in rebellion.

The robe was thin and the spring air damp and cold. She needed to be on her way, but she clutched her hands together, took a deep breath, and turned to face him.

"It *is* enchanted, you know," she said.

"What is? The mirror?" Impatiently, he glanced over his shoulder at the carriage.

"Would you give it to me?" she asked. "It's all too clear you don't want it."

"It's not mine," he said. "It was delivered to my doorstep in a trunk containing women's clothing. Evidently, it belongs to the previous owner of the house I purchased."

"Will you return it?"

"If I knew her whereabouts, I would." He folded his arms and studied her. "Why?"

"If you gave it to me," she said, "I'd attempt to find the rightful owner."

"Would you?"

She nodded.

"Your sudden interest in the mirror has nothing to do with its being gold or the diamonds around it, would it?"

"No," she said, surprised and a little insulted.

"Then why do you want it?"

She could tell him. If she did, he would label her even more strange than he already thought her. Who truly cared if she was eccentric or slightly dotty? As a poor relation, she'd have no substance. She'd be a shadow in the corner, an afterthought. "Oh yes, that's Veronica, she's lived with us for ages. Has no money of her own, poor thing. A charity case, you know."

The mirror had given her the first taste of hope she'd felt in a very long time.

"I would attempt to find the rightful owner. Truly."

"No."

She considered arguing with him but suspected that this man, once he'd made a decision, could not be moved.

"Thank you," she said again, turning to leave him. "For rescuing me."

He didn't respond, but his look said it all. If she hadn't been so foolish, he wouldn't have had to rescue her.

The townhouse seemed far away, set back from the street to allow a small fenced lawn in the front. Soon, Aunt Lilly would be ordering the planting of flowers. Nothing too garish to attract too much attention but enough to give the white façade a little color.

Her uncle's townhouse was on the corner; it would be a simple thing to slip around to the kitchen entrance. Uncle Bertrand was notoriously parsimonious. None of the servants was permitted up after ten or before six in the morning. In that way, he saved money on lighting and coal. No one would be awake for hours yet.

She hesitated, glancing over her shoulder at her rescuer.

"Are you very certain you won't give me the mirror?"

"Very certain," he said.

At her silence, he smiled thinly. "It's a mirror," he said. "Nothing more."

It was more than just a mirror. It showed the future, or at least she hoped it did. Before she could explain, a voice rang through the night.

"Oh, Father, it's worse than I thought. Veronica's undressed."

She turned to find Amanda standing there, her cousin's golden hair illuminated by the white light of the fog-shrouded lamps.

Amanda's look was one of studied horror. The key to understanding Amanda, however, was never in her expression, but in her eyes. At that moment, they glittered like those of a cat, catching the faintest light and gleaming brightly.

Amanda was amused.

Anything that amused Amanda usually proved to be detrimental to Veronica, a lesson she'd learned well over the past two years.

Beside her stood Aunt Lilly, her hands flailing in the air as if to contain the situation. Aunt Lilly did not like circumstances to overpower her. Behind her stood the other four cousins. Neither Aunt Lilly nor Uncle Bertrand would tolerate their brood being out of doors improperly attired. However, it was obvious that they'd already retired for the night.

Alice's hair was braided, and Anne had already slathered Mrs. Cuthbertson's Cream for Young Ladies on her face. Algernon's jacket was askew, and Adam, for once, did not have his nose in a book.

Of course not, this debacle was more interesting than anything he might read.

Standing in front of them, his expression thunderous, was Uncle Bertrand.

He was a stout figure of a man, his buttons bulging on his vest. The Earl of Conley was fond of his food, and most of life's pastimes, he was fond of saying. At the moment, however, he didn't look particularly fond of her.

"Well, niece? How do you explain this outrage?"

Chapter 3

"**Y**ou foolish child! What have you done? What have you done?"

Aunt Lilly stepped forward and slapped at her. When Veronica wasn't quick enough to dodge, one of the blows struck her on the cheek. She pulled back, both of them momentarily horrified. As angry as Aunt Lilly had been with her in the past, she'd never before struck her. Especially in public. Outside. In front of an audience.

Aunt Lilly shook her head, as if to negate both the action and the rage that fueled it. "See what you've made me do, child? I've never been so humiliated in my entire life."

She glanced behind her, the look one of summons. None of her cousins mistook it and trailed behind their mother like ducklings heading for a pond.

At the top of the steps, Aunt Lilly turned and looked down at her, decorum evidently pushed aside for her anger. "I took you in because you were family," she said. "And because your uncle is a kind and generous man. You are his only sister's only child. But if I had known, on that day, that you would shame us to such a degree, I would have let you starve in Scotland."

"Lilly," Uncle Bertrand said, silencing her with one word.

It was evident, from the look on her aunt's face, that she waged an internal war between anger and obedience. In this rare instance, however, Uncle Bertrand did not win.

"I refuse to have that harlot in my home," Aunt Lilly said, extending one imperious finger toward her.

Aunt Lilly leveled a look of such fulminating hatred on her that Veronica took a step back. She'd always known that family was intensely important to her aunt. She'd forgive her children anything, any slight, any imperfection, any failing. Evidently, her attitude of tolerance did not extend to a niece by marriage.

"You have offended us in the most grievous way possible," she said, her voice lowering in pitch as if conscious that the neighbors might be listening. "Not only have you sneaked out of our house in the middle of the night, but you return naked. Naked!" Evidently, decorum was being mightily trounced by anger. "You have jeopardized the futures of your cousins. If you cannot think of your own lamentable life, have you no Christian charity to spare for those who've done you no wrong? Indeed, everyone in this house has done nothing but welcome you to their bosoms from the moment you became an orphan. You were never alone. Never left to grieve or mourn. You were surrounded by love from the moment you came to this house, Veronica MacLeod. And what do you do to return that great love?"

Aunt Lilly stood upright, her chest heaving, her florid face trembling with emotion. "You have brought shame to us."

They disappeared into the house, leaving the three of them standing outside in the fog-laden air.

"You're not a servant," the stranger at her side said.

"I never said I was. That was your assumption."

"Of course," he said dryly. "One can naturally assume a lady to be at a Society of the Mercaii meeting."

"What sort of meeting?" Uncle Bertrand asked.

The man at her side furnished the details. "They're given to studying oddities of nature, the supernatural. No doubt ghosts and goblins and the like."

Her uncle turned and looked at her in contempt.

"Your Gift again, Veronica?"

She clasped her hands together, feeling the cold seep from her bare feet all the way up through her body. Or maybe her soul had simply turned to ice.

"I merely wanted an answer, Uncle."

"And did giving you an answer require that you remove your clothing?"

She'd never heard her uncle's voice quite that loud. The neighbors were probably enjoying the spectacle.

She'd never thought to be reprimanded on the front steps of her uncle's townhouse. For that matter, she hadn't thought to return home naked, or nearly so.

Dear God, what had she done? Any criticism leveled at her was rightfully earned. She'd been worse than an idiot—she'd been a gullible, naïve idiot.

Her uncle mounted the steps in front of her; but when she would have followed him, he held up his hand.

"Do you think to enter this house with no further ramifications for your actions, Veronica? You are not welcome here."

"While I agree that your niece's actions were reprehensible," the stranger said, "surely banishment is a bit much?"

Uncle Bertrand ignored him, addressing his comment to her.

"You have set upon your own course, Veronica. Continue on with it." He glanced at the man at her side. "At least you found yourself a titled protector."

"You know who I am?"

"Montgomery Fairfax," Uncle Bertrand said. "An American, recently come to England to prove your right to the title of 11th Lord Fairfax of Doncaster. I'm the Earl of Conley, a member of the Committee for Privileges of the House of Lords, sir. I oversaw your application."

"Should I thank you for your decision, sir?"

"It was a fair one. It's an old title and the line of succession was proven successfully, for all that you're an American."

Uncle Bertrand's glance swept up and down Montgomery in a gesture no doubt meant to be insulting.

The man at her side stiffened.

"A fact that might adequately explain your part in tonight's disaster. However, my niece is not exempted by ignorance. She knows what constitutes proper behavior."

She took a step forward, wondering what she could say to soften her uncle's anger. She hadn't undressed herself. The fact that she couldn't remember exactly what had happened was a worry, but was gullibility punishable to such a degree? Surely, he couldn't mean what he said? Did he intend to cast her out, naked, onto the street?

"Please, Uncle. I never intended to harm you or Aunt Lilly, or any of my cousins. I only wanted to know what they thought."

He disregarded her words, turned, and pulled the door open.

She began to shake. She clasped her arms in front of her chest and willed herself not to fall. She would not faint or beg.

But what was left her?

She mounted two steps. "I wanted to know if my Gift was real," she said. "My parents always said it was, but ever since coming to England, I've wondered."

Her uncle halted in the doorway.

"You've always said I was foolish to believe them, to believe in it. I just wanted to know the truth."

"That explanation is supposed to excuse your behavior? I'm supposed to be reassured that society will call you daft as well as wanton?"

She wasn't going to tell him the other reason she'd attended the meeting. Doing so would probably garner her even more punishment. But what could be worse than being sent to live on the streets?

Her uncle gave her a look no doubt meant to chastise her—and succeeded admirably—before closing the door in her face.

Montgomery had seen men paralyzed by fear on the battlefield. They couldn't seem to grasp the fact that war was real, that death was truly imminent. So they stood there and waited to be shot or blown to bits by cannon.

Right at that moment, he knew exactly how they felt.

This couldn't be happening.

"Damn it," he said, striding toward the door.

He glanced at the woman on the steps. "Don't make this situation worse by crying," he said. "I'll not tolerate it." A moment later, he looked back over at her. "I mean it," he added, before turning and pounding on the door.

When no one answered the knock, he turned, frowning down at her.

Now what did he do?

"Will you take me in?" she asked.

When he didn't—couldn't—respond, she smiled tremulously. "My reputation is evidently destroyed. Does it matter if I stay with you?"

"It matters to me. I've no intention of caring for a

woman. A silly woman. A woman without an ounce of sense."

"Why are you so angry? I'm the one who's just been tossed out of her home. Not you."

He glanced down at her.

"I felt, for some reason, compelled to rescue you from the events of tonight. I didn't realize that would require finding you a place to live, too."

At that, her spirit seemed to rise in some contradictory fashion. She tilted her chin up and glared at him.

"I did not ask you to rescue me."

"No," he said, biting off the words. "You'd have preferred being raped in full view of dozens of men."

That shut her up.

What the hell did he do with her?

He didn't underestimate the Earl of Conley's stubbornness, especially since the man had admitted to being part of that insufferable body of aristocrats before whom he'd had to appear last week. They'd been supremely aware of their position in life as well as their exceptionality.

The Earl of Conley might well leave his niece to starve.

Nor would remaining huddled on the front door of her uncle's home do anything to repair Veronica's reputation.

"You needn't frown at me," she said, her voice sounding as if she were trying not to cry.

"I can't say that I'd do any different if you were my niece," he said, barely restraining his anger. "You've been an absolute idiot."

She turned and, without another word, marched down the stairs, down the path, and to the street. He thought she was going to the carriage, but she disregarded it and kept walking.

She *was* an idiot.

He caught up with her finally, grabbed her arm, and twirled her around to face him. "What do you think you're doing?"

"Leaving."

"Do you have a friend to stay with? Or another relative?"

"I don't know anyone else in London," she said, her curious accent making the words sound almost lyrical.

"Then where did you think you were going?"

"Away," she said, looking up at him. "Anywhere. It's quite evident that neither you nor my uncle wants me around."

The fog was lifting, the lamplight glowing like a yellow moon.

He speared his hand through his hair, offered her the unadorned truth. "I haven't the slightest idea what I'm going to do."

"Neither do I," she said primly.

"Get in the carriage," he said.

She shook her head.

"Why not?"

"Because it wouldn't be proper."

He began to laugh. Probably not the right time for amusement, but her comment caught him off guard.

"After tonight? You worried about propriety while you're walking down the street nearly naked? Get in the carriage, Veronica."

"You should address me as Miss McLeod," she said, then evidently realized the foolishness of that request because a fleeting smile graced her lips for a second before disappearing.

She turned and began to walk back to the carriage,

with him following slowly behind. He couldn't leave her there, especially since he was certain her uncle wasn't going to allow her into the house. Nor could he take her home. That would make the scandal worse.

Although standards had relaxed in the last five years because of the war, if he'd been caught with a Virginia girl in his carriage, attired in nothing more than a robe, he'd have been given the immediate option of marrying her or deciding where he'd like to be buried.

If he'd known anyone else in London, if he'd made any friends close enough to drop Veronica on their doorstep, he'd have done so. Unfortunately, he'd only been in the city a few weeks, and during that time, he'd deliberately kept himself aloof. He didn't like London, and he wasn't certain he liked the English. No, after that night, he was dead certain of it.

Now what?

He couldn't drive around London for hours.

Do the right thing. He'd heard Caroline's words as if she'd whispered in his mind. Damn it, he'd done the right thing, only to be punished for it now.

Veronica turned at the door of the carriage.

"Where are we going?"

There was no other answer, was there?

"To my home," he said, feeling the noose of responsibility tighten around his neck.

Veronica did not have a good feeling about this. Not a good feeling at all. She'd been banished from her uncle's home. What on earth was to happen to her?

Her aunt's voice sounded in her ear: *You should have thought of that earlier, Veronica.*

She didn't feel well. What she wanted most to do was

to go to bed, Perhaps draw the covers up around her and stay there for the next year or so. Just then, however, she didn't have a bed. Or a roof over her head.

If dreams were pennies, we'd all be rich—one of her father's sayings.

She was not going to cry.

Really, she wasn't.

Tears are foolish. How many times had Aunt Lilly said that to her?

She turned her head as the carriage began to move, watching the fog-shrouded scenery. The square was quite orderly and lovely in its way. Everything was regulated and precise. The iron gate was never allowed to sag or rust. The trees were trimmed so they had a pleasing appearance.

Nothing was ever amiss in Dorchester Square.

Except for her.

She was the only odd creature in Dorchester Square.

People did not come in one shape or size. People had different colors of eyes, different shades of hair. Some people were tall, while others were short. Some were rotund, while others were scrawny.

Very well, she wasn't like her cousins. She didn't have their blond prettiness. Her hair was an unremarkable brown. Her eyes were the same color as her mother's, a soft green that on some days faded to a brownish color. They had an odd dark ring around them, so they were arresting, whatever color they chose to be for that day. She was not possessed of many social graces, having been reared in an isolated part of Scotland. She was truly amazed by the life she saw around her and wanted to know the answers to a thousand mysteries.

Surely that wasn't considered odd.

Despite being four years older than Amanda, the

oldest cousin, she sometimes felt young and naïve compared to all of them. She knew nothing of the London season, according to Amanda. Nor, according to Alice, could she dance well enough to comport herself properly in a ballroom. She was not, as she'd kindly been told by Algernon, the type of girl who'd attract the attention of the right kind of suitor.

She'd responded she didn't want to attract anyone.

Adam had countered with a reassuring smile, but most of the time Adam had his nose in a book and couldn't be bothered with what was going on around him.

Anne was the nicest of the girls, and only because she was engaged to be married soon and consumed with her own affairs. In the last seven months, Anne had undergone a transformation. She was no longer as flighty, and had taken to having an almost matronly air. Alice said it was because she felt superior to them because she was due to be married and move to Cornwall with her baronet.

One day, Anne had confided to her that she was already planning the names of her children.

"I shall not name them all names that begin with A," she said. "Instead, I think good, biblical names would be best."

Veronica hadn't an answer. Nor did she have any explanation for what she sensed in Anne: a growing dismay, a certain kind of dread like black ink dissolving in water. The longer it remained, the more it spread, until the whole surface of the water itself was gray and no longer clear.

On that day, only weeks ago, she'd wanted to lean over, place her hand on top of Anne's, and ask her what was wrong.

Anne would no more have confided in her than any of her cousins. Instead, she would've laughed gaily and made some cutting remark, such as, "You're being fey again, aren't you? Is it a Scottish thing?"

Sometimes, the impressions she got were so strong she had to make a concerted effort to block everyone out. Otherwise, she couldn't even hear herself think for all the conflicting feelings. The worst part of it was that sometimes she felt as if those feelings—anguish, joy, and fear—belonged to her. When it got to be too much, the only remedy was to close the door on her chamber and seek out the silence.

She was not odd.

Was it wrong of her to want to know what learned men thought?

And even if she were, surely such a quest for knowledge wasn't deserving of banishment.

Dear God, what was to happen to her?

She glanced at Montgomery Fairfax.

He was taking her to his home.

She'd escaped the Mercaii only to find herself in a worse predicament.

What would her uncle say to that?

Chapter 4

Montgomery Fairfax's townhouse was not appreciably different from Uncle Bertrand's home. It was smaller, of course, being in the center of a row of houses, but the square in which it was situated was as proper and well maintained.

Veronica had a brief view of a long corridor and a steep staircase, but that was all she was able to see since Montgomery had grabbed her hand once she'd exited the carriage and marched up to the third floor, nearly pulling her behind him.

Lust was evidently not on his mind, for which she was deeply grateful. However, she didn't like being treated as if she were a package he'd been given, one that belonged to another person and whose disposition was an irritant.

He knocked on a door at the end of the hall, and when it was opened by an older woman, thrust her forward.

"You are to guard her, Mrs. Gardiner. She is not to leave your company. You are not to let Miss MacLeod out of your sight. Do you understand?"

The older woman nodded, her surprise replaced by an earnest expression.

He turned to her, his expression as closed as it had been earlier. "You're to remain with my housekeeper. It's the only chance we have of extricating ourselves from this damnable situation. Is that clear?"

She nodded.

Without another word, he turned and left. Any questions she might have had were buried beneath embarrassment as she and Mrs. Gardiner stared at each other.

Neither of them was properly attired for an introduction. She was in her borrowed monk's robe, and Mrs. Gardiner was dressed for night, her hair tied in dozens of little cloth knots, her pink cotton nightgown adorned with pin-tucking and embroidery wrinkled from bed.

"Please come in, Miss MacLeod."

She nodded and stepped inside the room.

Mrs. Gardiner's quarters were furnished simply. Beside the window was a soft and comfortable looking chair accompanied by an ornate needlework covered footstool and a round table on which a lamp sat. Across the room, a double mattress lay plumped atop an iron bedstead. The comforter had been dislodged, indicating that the woman had been asleep when wakened by her employer.

The housekeeper was not much older than Veronica's mother would have been, possessed of thick brown hair, soft brown eyes, and arched brows that gave her a perpetual quizzical expression. Short and plump, Mrs. Gardiner exuded a warm kind of peace, as if the emotions swirling around her were a faint and pleasant potpourri.

They stared at each other for another moment, words evidently being as difficult for the housekeeper as they were for her. What did she say? How could she explain?

Mrs. Gardiner went to the bed, began fussing with the sheets.

"I couldn't take your bed, Mrs. Gardiner," she said. "If you don't mind, I'll sit in the chair."

"For the night, miss?"

For however long she was going to be a prisoner in Montgomery Fairfax's house. That wasn't quite right, was it? For as long as she was a prisoner of her own stupidity.

In the mirror, she'd been happy, almost joyous. In the mirror, she'd been laughing. What had she seen? Had it been a delusion? Had the drugs she'd been given somehow altered her perception of reality?

She couldn't remember much of what had happened at the Society, a fact that disturbed her. Yet did she want to remember? She'd been given something to make her acquiescent, but Montgomery Fairfax had done nothing to her, only commanded that she stay with the housekeeper. Like an obedient hound, she was doing exactly what he'd told her to do.

The problem with rebellion, however, was that it should be based on principle. She had no guiding cause to inspire her to rebel. In fact, her rescuer had seen to it that she had a roof over her head for the night. If she marched out of his house, intent on independence, where did she go?

No, she was not going to be stupid twice in one night.

When the morning came, she'd find a way back to her uncle's house and beg his forgiveness. If that failed, she'd obtain her lockbox. With it, she might have enough money to buy passage back to Scotland.

There, a plan, albeit an incomplete one.

She sat in the chair beside the window, thanking Mrs. Gardiner for the warm throw the older woman gave her. Tucking her cold feet beneath her, she closed her eyes and pretended sleep. Or if not that, then oblivion for a few hours. Anything but think of the disaster she'd caused to fall on her own head.

* * *

An hour past dawn the next morning, the downstairs maid announced visitors. Montgomery was already dressed and waiting for them. He descended the stairs to where the Earl of Conley stood bundled up in coat, hat, and gloves, accompanied by his two sons similarly attired and wearing identical expressions—righteous anger.

He didn't have a majordomo, but there was no necessity for them to remove their clothing on their own. They wouldn't be in the house that long.

He was damned if he was going to welcome the earl. At the moment, he didn't care if he violated every one of the hundreds of rules of proper British etiquette Edmund Kerr had been trying to teach him.

You might want to hold your temper, Montgomery. How many times had he heard his brother, Alisdair, say that to him in his youth? Too many times not to also recall the disappointment in his tone.

The earl looked up at him, evidently understanding that this was not to be a cordial meeting.

"My niece is here?"

"Yes," he said. "In the company of my housekeeper ever since she arrived."

"You think that's enough, sir? You've only made the situation worse."

"What did you expect me to do? Leave her on your doorstep in the cold?"

The older man straightened, a banty rooster showing his puffed up chest.

"Within hours, all of London will know she spent the night under your roof."

"In the care of my housekeeper," he said.

"I'm not aware of society in America, sir, but in England, our females know how to comport themselves.

The fact that my niece has shown lamentable judgment requires that she be punished."

"How? By turning her out of your house?"

"Refusing to do so would indicate I condone her actions."

"What about familial loyalty?" he asked.

"I believe I am demonstrating that, sir, by refusing to allow my niece to taint my children with her scandal."

"It isn't a scandal unless you make it one," Montgomery said.

He held his temper in check, leaned against the wall, folded his arms, and regarded the three of them.

"I doubt all of London knows she's here. I doubt anyone does. Take her home, punish her if you must, but don't misjudge the situation. Your niece was in some difficulty. I provided her assistance. That's all."

"She returned home nearly naked. Can you explain that?"

He couldn't. Not without confessing Veronica had also been naked in front of dozens of men. He doubted the revelation would better the situation.

"Nothing happened between us," he said. "You'll have to take my word for it."

"Tell that to the rest of society, Your Lordship," the earl said, accentuating the title. A hint, then, that Montgomery had not once addressed him properly.

Nor did he have any intention of doing so. He was tired of jumping through English hoops.

"You've been in London a few months, have you not?"

"Two," he said. "Two months." Two endlessly long months.

"Can you honestly say that you believe there won't be a scandal? Surely you know how quickly gossip travels in London?"

He nodded reluctantly.

"Everyone knows who you are, Your Lordship. Or do you discount that, as well?"

He shrugged.

"I've made inquiries as to the Society of the Mercaii. Are the rumors I've heard true?"

He exchanged a long look with the earl. "Last night was my first visit, and my last."

"Which did not answer my question."

"I don't know what you've heard," he said, "but it isn't a place I'd urge a woman to visit."

"Veronica didn't attempt to hide her identity at all?"

He reluctantly shook his head.

"So there's every chance she was recognized. She's ruined, regardless," the earl said, his tone dispassionate.

He held himself still, waiting for the earl to continue. The other man didn't say another word, the silence measured by the soft ticking of the mantel clock in the drawing room.

Montgomery. Caroline's gentle chiding annoyed him. Had she become the voice of his conscience?

The stark reality was that the Earl of Conley's niece was in a damnable situation.

A ruined girl had no future in Virginia. Her only chance for a normal life was to be sent to a relative in another state, one as far away as possible. A soiled dove rarely returned to her family.

But the Earl of Conley wasn't thinking of sending Veronica away. He was simply going to refuse to acknowledge her. She'd become one of those hopeless women Montgomery had seen often enough on his walks.

He was not responsible for the Earl of Conley's niece. He didn't *want* to be responsible for the Earl of Conley's niece. Look how abysmal he'd already been at protecting a woman.

Do the right thing, Montgomery. Caroline's soft and feminine voice had no business whispering to him.

Damn it, he didn't want to do the right thing. The right thing had never brought him any solace or joy in life. The right thing had separated him from his family, destroyed his future, and brought him to this godforsaken country.

"Why are you here?" he asked. "To fetch Veronica only to leave her at your doorstep? Or are you simply going to dump her in the middle of London?"

The Earl of Conley took a few steps forward, his two sons flanking him.

"I've come to forestall any further scandal. All of London knows who you are, Your Lordship. Whether you believe that or not. Whether you also believe it or not, the situation is demanding to be rectified, by whatever means necessary."

In Virginia society, the quickest and most expedient way to solve the situation would be for the couple to marry. They'd take their wedding journey to a relative's home or perhaps visit the Springs. After a few months, they'd return home, and if a child was born, the old biddies would count on their fingers; but they'd do so quietly, without public comment. What they said in the confines of their sewing circles was another matter.

The problem was, he hadn't done anything to warrant having to take responsibility for Veronica Macleod. He hadn't touched her. He hadn't *thought* about touching her. In fact, he'd attempted to be the only honorable man among dozens.

Perhaps he should have remained in the background and let them do what they wanted to her, but he would have hated himself for his inactivity. He would have been as responsible for her degradation as those who caused it.

Doing nothing would have been the response of a coward, both last night and, regrettably, now.

Doom settled over him, the same cloud of doom he'd felt all night long.

"I see no other alternative, sir," the Earl of Conley said, as if hearing his thoughts.

Neither did he, damn it.

"I'm not prepared to marry," he said.

The Earl of Conley's lips turned upward in a half smile. "Nor am I prepared to have scandal touch my family's name, sir. We'll let it be known that it's a love match. Society is accepting of impulsiveness."

"Just not reason."

The other man inclined his head slightly, an imperious gesture that annoyed him further.

"You have a choice, of course, Your Lordship."

To marry Veronica MacLeod or leave her to her own fate. In that moment, he honestly wished he could. She'd been foolish and improvident, yet she didn't deserve the punishment that her uncle—and society—would mete out to her.

The Earl of Conley nodded, evidently satisfied.

"Veronica will come home with me now. In two days, the wedding will take place. That will give you enough time to arrange for a special license.

"Even if I'm an American?"

"You'll find that money stifles a great many objections, sir. Even in the case of Americans."

He stared at the Earl of Conley for several ticking moments.

The hours before dawn had found him awake, attempting to reason a way out of this predicament. He hadn't come up with a solution. Nor could he standing there.

"I'll marry her," he said. "Damn it, I'll marry her."

Mrs. Gardiner woke her from a surprisingly restful sleep. The sleep of the just, the unrepentant, the innocent, which hardly applied in her situation but for which Veronica was grateful.

"Pardon me, miss, but His Lordship wishes you to meet him downstairs."

She glanced down at the hated brown robe.

"I'll see if one of the maids has a dress you can borrow," Mrs. Gardiner said, correctly interpreting her look.

She shook her head. "Never mind," she said. Montgomery Fairfax had already seen her attire—and more.

"You have no shoes on, miss."

She glanced down at her feet as if just then discovering them bare.

"I've lost them," she said, then smiled at the housekeeper to indicate that it was no great loss. Compared to the loss of her home, security, and whatever future she might have had as a poor relation in her uncle's home, what was a pair of shoes?

She slipped behind the screen, performed her morning ablutions, and, once finished, left the room and descended the steps. Halting at the landing, she stared down at Uncle Bertrand, and behind him, Adam and Algernon.

Uncle Bertrand glanced up at her. She would not make the mistake of speaking first. She might not be as learned as her cousins in the ways of London, but she was astute when it came to people.

Uncle Bertrand liked to be in charge.

He gave her a disgusted glance.

In all honesty, she could not blame him for being

annoyed at her appearance. She'd not brushed her hair, and she was as improperly attired as she'd been the night before.

"Is Mr. Fairfax not here?" she asked, descending the rest of the steps.

"He's the 11th Lord Fairfax of Doncaster, and more properly referred to as His Lordship. And he's given us the privacy necessary for this meeting."

Before she could speak, he waved his hand toward the door.

"You're coming home," he said.

Had he forgiven her?

What had Montgomery Fairfax said to him to bring about this great change?

She clasped her hands in front of her, not about to annoy her uncle with too many questions.

"Thank you for forgiving me, Uncle," she said. The gratitude she felt was tempered by the knowledge that she would, no doubt, have to pay for her uncle's largesse in the future.

"I haven't forgiven you," he said flatly. "You'll remain with us until His Lordship acquires a special license. You're to be married, Veronica."

Stunned, she could only stare at her uncle.

When she made no comment, he continued. "His Lordship understands that, while the situation was in no way of his doing, any other action would be unthinkable."

"Married?" She cleared her throat. "I don't know the man, Uncle."

"You should have thought of that before appearing with him naked."

How odd she couldn't think at the moment.

"You should count yourself fortunate, indeed. His

Lordship is quite a wealthy man. At least you will be well provided for, unlike your mother."

"My father was a well-respected scholar," she said. "A teacher."

"Who had not held a post since before you were born. He dabbled in poetry, Veronica," he said, the depth of his loathing evident in the disdain dripping from each word.

Her father's poetry was beautiful, lyrical, and moving. None of it had survived, however. Yet if she could have shown her uncle, she was sure that he would have appreciated her father's great talent.

"Your mother's inheritance provided a roof over your head."

To that, she had no answer.

He turned and nodded to his sons. Neither Algernon nor Adam had looked directly at her. They only stepped aside so she could precede them, following Uncle Bertrand out the door.

Veronica managed to keep silent all the way back to Uncle Bertrand's home, a feat easily managed since no one in the carriage seemed inclined to talk, least of all to her.

Instead of being a poor relation, she was to be married. Instead of living forever in Uncle Bertrand's house, she was to have a husband.

Not only was she free of Amanda, Uncle Bertrand, Aunt Lilly, and her four other cousins, but she was to have an establishment, a family, of her own.

She wanted to dance. Even then, her feet wanted to tap on the carriage floor. If she'd begun to sing at the top of her voice, Algernon and Adam would have nudged each other and commented about poor daft Veronica, who was making a spectacle of herself. Had the girl no sense at all? Uncle Bertrand would have frowned at her again—or still—since he hadn't stopped frowning.

A husband. She was to have a husband. Not simply any husband, but an American: Montgomery Fairfax.

He was a stranger.

Perhaps she should be more sober, look at the situation with a more realistic view. While it was true he was a handsome man, appearance wasn't as important as other qualities in a husband.

He was kind and evidently possessed of compassion, or he wouldn't have rescued her from the Society.

He hadn't been the least bit happy about it, however. His gaze hadn't revealed any warmth when he'd looked at her. Her Gift had discerned the degree of his pain. Did he mourn for someone? The pain she'd felt in Montgomery had been strong and deep. Did he grieve for a lost love?

Had her uncle pressured him into marrying her? Of course her uncle had used some sort of pressure to induce His Lordship to marry her. He hadn't developed a tendre for her in the few hours they'd been together. Alone, together in a carriage, with nothing more than a thin robe between her and nakedness.

He'd seen her naked.

Heat traveled over her skin.

So much for lust.

Wasn't he supposed to be overwhelmed by the power of his feelings for her? He'd seen a great deal more than her shapely ankles. Yet all he'd done was place her in his housekeeper's company.

What would she have done if he'd made an advance? Of course she would have dissuaded him quite precisely. She would have told him, in no uncertain terms, that she was not *that* type of young woman, her actions to the contrary.

Yet he hadn't done anything. He'd acted the perfect gentleman. She was the one who'd bent every rule of proper behavior.

To be a good wife, she'd have to learn as much about her husband as possible. If for no other reason than to express her gratitude to him for rescuing her twice. Once, from a scandal of her own making, and secondly, from her abysmal future. She hadn't the slightest idea how to be a wife, but she had some experience in watching a loving couple. Her parents had been devoted to one another.

The carriage stopped in front of the house, and her uncle frowned at her. She nodded in response to the unspoken rebuke and waited until Algernon and Adam preceded her before leaving.

She took the stairs quickly, grateful her aunt was nowhere about. That reckoning could, she hoped, wait until later that morning.

Veronica closed her bedroom door behind her and leaned back against it, palms flat against the cool wood.

She walked to the middle of the room, twirled in a circle with her arms spread wide, a dance of utter, complete joy. Twice, three times, four, she spun before collapsing on top of the bed, eyes closed, a smile curving her lips.

Veronica Moira MacLeod murmured a fervent prayer of thanksgiving. Even the worst kind of husband would be better than being a poor relation.

Her greatest wish had been granted.

She'd been saved.

"Were you intimate with him?"

She froze.

Slowly, she sat up to see Amanda standing in the doorway.

"You did what you set out to do, Amanda."

She disliked Amanda intensely, and when they were alone, dropped all pretense of amiability. Over the last two years, she'd tried to like the girl or to at least find some common ground. From the beginning, she'd felt only antipathy from her cousin. Amanda had a quality about her no one else noticed, a certain type of cruelty that repelled her so much she attempted to avoid the girl.

Of all her female cousins, Amanda was perhaps the prettiest, with reddish blond hair and green eyes as sharp as chips of ice. Her features were lovely, and although she was shorter than Veronica, her figure was more fulsome. Amanda was, no doubt, the epitome of female beauty and as far from her cousin in looks and temperament as two people could be.

Since she'd come to live with her relatives, Amanda had made her miserable. Everyone else thought Amanda kind, generous, and genuinely concerned for the welfare of her older Scots cousin. She and Amanda knew the emotions were only pretense.

"It was you who informed Uncle Bertrand, wasn't it?"

"Would you have me lie for you, cousin?" Amanda said. "Especially since I was worried about you. Why ever would you leave the house at night?"

"You could have asked me rather than inform your father," she said.

"It's Father's duty to see to you, Veronica, since you've no one else."

A fact Amanda brought up each day. God forbid she be allowed to forget, even for a moment, that she was an orphan.

Before that morning, Veronica had been doomed to be shunted off to a corner, to be a shadow for the rest of her life, unobtrusive, barely noticed, a figure about whom people commented in passing. "Oh, her? That's Veronica. Pay her no heed. She has no one but us, poor thing."

Instead, her foolishness had been rewarded, not with punishment, but a husband.

Amanda entered the room and closed the door, sitting on the bench below the window.

"You didn't say. Were you intimate with him?"

"Don't I pay you enough to leave me alone, Amanda?"

Amanda only laughed gaily.

"Sometimes, cousin, I think you and I are the only ones who understand each other completely. I need not put on airs around you, and you are free to be yourself with me."

She didn't respond. Silence was safer around Amanda than answering every barb.

Amanda turned and smiled at her, such a beatific smile she might have been fooled by it if she hadn't looked in Amanda's eyes.

Her cousin pointed one foot and studied the tip of her shoe. "I've spent all my allowance," Amanda said. "Every bit of it."

"You should be more careful with your money," Veronica said.

"I believe you're right, cousin, and if I should get my hands on any more money between now and when my allowance is paid next month, you can be certain that I would be very much on your side. You might not be punished severely, after all. Father does listen to me, you know."

She knew that only too well.

"You were very foolish, Veronica," her cousin said, sitting beside her with a cat's smile on her face.

She closed her eyes, feeling the sensations that always overcame her when she used her Gift. A warm wave came first, then the essence of emotion from the other person.

What she felt from Amanda wasn't one emotion but a group of them, mixed to form something that appeared translucent like uncooked fish. It was as if her cousin had not yet decided which way to nudge her spirit, toward goodness or evil. At the moment, Amanda was a little amused, a little excited, a thread of anger woven though her emotions.

She opened her eyes, turning to look at her cousin.

"Why do you dislike me so, Amanda?"

In those next seconds, she watched as Amanda's face changed. The amusement disappeared first, to be replaced by a watchful expression, one she'd rarely seen on her cousin's face.

"What do you mean?"

"From the very beginning, you've disliked me. Why?"

The expression hardened on Amanda's face as she glanced around the room. She was no longer so pretty.

"I would've had this room but for you. It's larger than the others, and sunnier. But, no, Veronica must be given the best room."

"For a room?" she asked, incredulous. "You've disliked me because of a room? Why didn't you say? I would have gladly changed rooms with you."

Amanda's eyes narrowed. "No one would have allowed it. Everyone did everything for poor little Veronica, poor orphaned little Veronica."

Did they? She hadn't noticed.

"I would have more money in my allowance but for you."

She felt the first touch of humor since Amanda had entered the room. "Surely you cannot blame me for your profligate ways, cousin."

"I always had enough money before you came. Now, Father has to plan for you, too."

Amanda stood, walked to the door. "I know you're upset," she said sweetly. "I'll give you a few hours to think about it. Father was very upset with you. I can make life easier for you."

Veronica smiled. "I won't need your help," she said. "You see, I'm to be married."

She stood and went to the door.

"And yes, I was gloriously intimate, Amanda. For the entire night. Hours and hours of scandalous, unbridled, shocking, intimate passion."

Smiling, she closed the door in Amanda's face.

She'd waited two years to do that.

Chapter 5

Montgomery stared at the sheaf of papers his solicitor handed him.

"All of that?" he asked.

"Yes, Your Lordship. Now that your claim has been recognized by the House of Lords, there are many documents you need to sign."

"And when I do, you can go home, is that it, Edmund?"

His solicitor, Edmund Kerr, only smiled faintly.

The man was near his own age, neither a boy nor close to doddering. A good thing, too, since he'd expended some effort to find Montgomery in America. The last two months had been spent navigating through the complex legal maneuvers necessary to have him recognized as the 11th Lord Fairfax of Doncaster. A thankless duty, all in all.

"Do I pay you enough?" Montgomery asked. Since money was no longer an object, perhaps Edmund deserved an increase in his salary.

He studied the man surreptitiously. Edmund reminded him of his brother James. James had worn a full beard as well. Edmund's shoulders were a little stooped, however, like those of an older man. The man's gaze was often fixed on objects, like the corner of his desk, or his fingers rather than looking a man in the eyes.

The one word he would use to describe Edmund Kerr was average. His height was average, the tone of his voice neither deep nor high-pitched. His appearance was neither noticeable nor memory-invoking.

"I thank you for your concern, Your Lordship. I'm very well compensated by the estate."

"I suppose that goes along with it, doesn't it?"

"What is that, Your Lordship?"

"Being Your Lordshipped to death."

Another faint smile. The man retreated into expressions when words would have done just as well.

His housekeeper, Mrs. Gardiner, was the opposite, being as voluble as Edmund was deferentially silent.

She was responsible for the room in which he spent most of his time. The room was decorated in what he imagined was Gentleman's Library motif. Because of Mrs. Gardiner, he'd settled into London with less trouble than he'd imagined. Mrs. Gardiner, and to some extent, Edmund, had furnished the house and installed other creature comforts in his new home.

When the housekeeper had unveiled her efforts to set his library to rights, she'd patted her hands together like a child excited at the idea of a candy, reminding him of Aunt Penny. Aunt Penny, before she'd learned of both her husband's and son's deaths at Antietam. From that day until her death a scant two years later, she'd worn a sweet and somewhat vacant-looking expression. Everyone had understood that Penelope had simply gone away, and only the shell of the woman remained.

A richly patterned carpet in shades of emerald and ivory covered the mahogany floorboards. Thick velvet draperies of a color reminding him of the forests around Gleneagle hung on either side of the two floor-to-ceiling windows. Bookcases lined the wall to his right, while to his left was a large fireplace, its white marble mantel heavily carved with fruits and trailing vines.

Mounted above it were four paintings of English countryside pursuits. Braces of hares were slung over the shoulders of aristocratic hunters while pursuing hounds dodged the steps of prancing horses. Country houses with smoke curling from their chimneys lured the visitor to stand and study the scene.

Opposite the desk where he sat, below the windows, was a long credenza. When he'd first seen the room, a stuffed owl sat there, entombed in a glass case. He'd removed it when Mrs. Gardiner wasn't looking and claimed he'd accidentally broken the dome. When she'd assured him it would not be difficult to procure a replacement, he'd convinced her it wasn't necessary.

Evidently, the penchant for all things stuffed was an English trait.

For all its show of wealth, the room revealed nothing about him. He'd only had one small valise when he'd arrived in London. The sum of what was left of his life, it contained a change of clothing, a letter from President Lincoln thanking him for his service to his country, notes Montgomery had made about his navigation system, a pistol, and two silver brushes, the last physical items to tie him to his home, his past, and his boyhood.

He could not hold a daguerreotype in his hand to fuse the image of a loved one in his mind. He couldn't touch an object his father had collected or his grandfather had prized. Anything he carried was tucked away in his heart, memories of Alisdair and James and Caroline, laughter he recalled at odd moments, love, affection, a feeling of belonging that never tarnished regardless of the passage of time.

The longer he was away from home, the farther away

those times seemed. The separation pulled at him, but it was more than physical distance. Even if he returned to Virginia, walked the earth of Gleneagle within the month, he'd feel the same discordance in his mind, the same yawning cavity of grief.

Nothing would ever be the same.

Montgomery pushed aside memory in favor of a more pressing topic.

"I visited the Society of the Mercaii last night," he said.

"Indeed, Your Lordship," Edmund said. "How did you find it?"

He smiled, the expression not fueled by humor. "Interesting. I'm due to be married."

Edmund stared at him.

"Married, Your Lordship?"

He sat back in his chair and watched as Edmund paled. He'd had much the same reaction to the idea.

"The Society might be interested in the occult, Edmund, but last night they were attempting to indoctrinate, if that's what you want to call it, an unwilling young woman when I intervened."

Edmund sank into a chair in front of his desk. "They were recommended to me as a group that studied oddities, bizarre events, and such."

"The only oddity I saw was the leader of the society attempting to rape a young woman. One thing led to another, and now I'm about to be married."

Edmund stood, walked to the far wall, and perused the titles on the bookshelves. Montgomery had not picked a single volume himself. Mrs. Gardiner, again, no doubt selecting what she considered to interest a peer of Scotland. Or perhaps she'd simply ordered the books by the pound.

The bookshelves contained a variety of books on gardening and husbandry, sheep, cattle, and the occasional novel. He'd been intrigued to find a book by Jules Verne and had set it aside to read when he had a chance.

Edmund, however, was ensuring he didn't have any free time.

"It's imperative you travel to Doncaster Hall, Your Lordship," Edmund said now, turning from his study of the bookshelf, his equilibrium evidently restored. "Will you have time before the wedding?"

"No," he said, sitting back in his chair. "In fact, I require your assistance in obtaining a special license. I've been assured that, despite the fact I'm an American, there will be no difficulty."

Edmund nodded. "Would I know the young woman?"

Montgomery met the other man's eyes. "She's the Earl of Conley's niece," he said. "Is he familiar to you?"

Edmund closed his eyes, then opened them, as if he'd had a file of faces and names behind his lids. "Three daughters," he said. "Two sons. An estate in Hampshire, quite a prosperous one, and a reputation for being a bully in the House of Lords."

"He knew who I was," Montgomery said.

"He would, Your Lordship, being on the committee that approved your petition."

"Your memory's quite impressive."

"I spend some time in London, Your Lordship."

Montgomery nodded, then concentrated on the stack of papers he still had to sign.

"There are many decisions you need to make, Your Lordship."

Carefully, he put the pen back in its holder, sat back, and folded his arms.

"Is that going to go on forever?"

At Edmund's look of confusion, he smiled.

"The Your Lordship business. We've known each other for three months, Edmund. We traveled from America together. You know everything there is to know about my life. Can we not dispense with the title?"

"If I've given offense, Your Lordship, then I apologize deeply." Edmund bowed, another gesture almost as irritating as the constant spouting of his title. "I believe in giving respect where it's due, Your Lordship. You're the 11th Lord Fairfax of Doncaster, and I have a duty to treat you accordingly."

Montgomery knew all about duty. *Duty* was a word that made him do something he didn't want to do. Duty was the hook at the bottom of his conscience dragging him from place to place. Duty gave him courage, a kind of fearlessness that, when viewed in retrospect, was insane.

He was damned tired of duty. Duty, however, had evidently not yet tired of him.

Montgomery nodded, pulling the stack of papers toward him. He reread a clause on one contract written in a type of English that hadn't been spoken in two centuries.

If Edmund hadn't been annoying him so much, Montgomery would have asked him for a quick version of what he was reading, but he stubbornly refused to, stumbling through the passages himself until he realized it was an attainder.

"Doncaster Hall is entailed to my son or daughter," he said, glancing over at Edmund.

"In Scotland, women are not necessarily prevented from inheriting."

"Nor are they in America."

"You'll find there are many similarities between

America and Scotland, Your Lordship," Edmund said. "It is, after all, the mother country of the Fairfax family."

"My grandfather still had the brogue," he said. "I remember wishing I could speak like him."

He made a neat stack of the papers and handed them to Edmund, who took them and placed them in his leather valise.

"Will you be ordering more supplies today, Your Lordship?"

Montgomery had spent the last month ordering bolts of silk, leather ropes, and securing the efforts of a few dozen craftsmen. Edmund, however, had not once asked why Montgomery needed a basket woven in an oval shape, and ten feet long. Nor had he ever questioned why Montgomery had met with a metalworker, spending a few hours in earnest discussions with the man over the design of a fan.

Edmund, evidently, had no adventure in his soul.

What truly surprised Montgomery was that he still did.

"I've only a few more things to see to, but I can do that in the next few days."

"Shall I make arrangements to travel to Scotland, then?"

"Why don't you go on without me? You don't live far from there, do you? Wouldn't you rather return home than forever harangue me?"

Edmund smiled, an expression that didn't quite reach his eyes.

Montgomery had noticed over the past few weeks that, while Edmund might appear friendly, the solicitor possessed a reserve, a distance that he put down to being British.

"I have served the estate for some time, Your Lordship. I live there for many months in the year."

Montgomery remained silent, waiting.

"I would prefer to remain in London, Your Lordship, should you have any wish for me. It would not be unnatural for me to witness your nuptials."

"Suit yourself."

Bowing yet again, his solicitor gathered the signed documents, his leather folio, and left the room.

Montgomery stood and walked to the window. From there, he could see the street, and watched as Edmund got into his carriage.

He felt a great deal like Edmund's charge, as if the solicitor had been given responsibility for him. Perhaps, after the events of the night before, he needed some type of escort. His behavior, while understandable, hadn't been restrained.

Yet of all the men in the room, he'd been the only one to step forward. Had the members of the Society been drugged as well? Or had it simply been a case of the strong victimizing the weak? At least the weak should have a fighting chance.

He could not protect the world. He hadn't even been able to protect his corner of it. Yet by his actions, he'd taken the niece of the Earl of Conley to protect and defend. Not just for a night, but for the rest of his life.

God help her.

Edmund's carriage pulled away, lost in the activity on the street.

A bird perched on the windowsill, then flew away, a metaphor, perhaps, for his secret wish. London was too congested. The city was never quiet, leading him to crave endless stretches of silence punctuated only by the murmuring of nature around him. He missed the sounds of water, the cicadas in the trees, and the gentle sough of the wind around Gleneagle.

What had been almost a providential event was now a millstone around his neck. Instead of being simply Montgomery Fairfax, he was now the 11th Lord Fairfax of Doncaster. People expected him to be wise, prudent, resourceful, and caring.

All he really wanted was to be left alone.

Chapter 6

"**Y**ou look peaked, girl," Uncle Bertrand said to her at breakfast two days later. "Didn't you sleep well last night?"

"I'm fine, Uncle, thank you," Veronica said, staring down at the table.

"I should hope so. Today is your wedding day." He smiled at her, an expression he didn't often send in her direction.

The day before, she'd been the model of decorum. After all, she wasn't entirely certain her uncle wouldn't change his mind and banish her from the house on a whim. From his glowers when she'd encountered him, and from the tense atmosphere in the house, it was all too evident she'd sinned and sinned mightily. She'd dared put the reputation of the Earl of Conley and his family in jeopardy.

On her wedding day, however, all was evidently forgiven.

She concentrated on her breakfast, ignoring both her uncle and the glances from her cousins.

Today, of all days, her parents should be here. Today, her mother should be bustling about with a smile curving her lips. Today, Veronica would return to her room with its white-painted window frames, pretty green curtains, and counterpane of green and pale pink. The vanity and stool had been a present for her sixteenth birthday, and it was there she'd sit and prepare herself for her wedding.

Before the ceremony, no doubt held in the parlor just as this one would be, she'd stand at the window of her second-floor bedroom, and simply take in the sights of the lush glen around her and the mountains sitting like dragons' teeth on the horizon.

Her father would come into her room and hug her, whisper some reassurances, something to make her smile. He might have composed a poem for the occasion and would have to be summoned from his study, so immersed in his work he'd lost track of the time. He might have been persuaded to recite his effort for the assembled guests, or he might have chosen to give the poem to Veronica early, so she could read it alone in her bedroom.

What would he have said? Something about love, no doubt, since it was clear her parents loved each other. Something about forever, the future, the deep and abiding union of souls.

Would her dear father have understood expediency? Or that she was more than willing to trade a well-known prison for an unknown cage?

But if her parents had been alive, she wouldn't be getting married in London at all, and certainly not to Montgomery Fairfax.

Her aunt sailed into the family dining room, took one look at her assembled brood, and beamed at them. Her smile dimmed when she caught sight of Veronica.

"Oh my dear, that won't do at all."

She braced herself, knowing what was coming.

"You've done your hair yourself, haven't you? We have certain standards in this house, and it's not simply enough to grab a hank of your hair and wind it into a bun, Veronica."

A spate of laughter greeted her remark, and Aunt Lilly smiled again at her children.

"Especially today," she added.

"Hester was otherwise occupied, Aunt Lilly," she said, but her aunt disappeared into the kitchen again and paid her words no attention.

Aunt Lilly wasn't a cruel woman. She was a woman with a great many concerns and a great many opinions, most of them acquired from her husband. Her appearance was outwardly pleasant, masking a will of iron. Her face was puffy, as if she were a loaf of bread passed its first rising. She was plump in other places, too, even the fingers normally adorned with an assortment of rings. By afternoon, she would complain her fingers were hurting and remove all her jewelry. First thing in the morning, as now, she was bejeweled, impeccably dressed, not a hair out of place, and expecting everyone else to appear the same.

When Veronica had lived at home, she'd never had anyone do her hair, and her results had been acceptable to everyone.

Her morning had always begun with a smile and a kiss from her mother, and the same from her father. Their conversation consisted of ideas, thoughts, her father's poetry, her mother's garden.

Ideas were not acceptable topics of conversation in her uncle's household. Her uncle decided what everyone thought about politics, religion, or the news of the day.

All of them freely discussed other people, however. What people wore, how they behaved, the things they said were all fodder for conversation. Occasionally, someone uttered a compliment, but mostly the comments were critical.

No one was as good as the fair cousins.

As much as they loved to gossip among themselves, they relished sharing information with their friends. Veronica could only imagine the talk if the real story of what had happened the night before last became known. Or perhaps they'd be too afraid that society would judge them as harshly as they judged others.

Her breakfast finished, Veronica stood. Her aunt returned from the kitchen and regarded her with some displeasure. Yet the emotion Veronica felt from her aunt was not irritation as much as it was resignation. As if she had exhausted all of Aunt Lilly's patience.

"I'll tell Hester to help you dress, Veronica," Aunt Lilly said, the look in her eyes daring Veronica to argue. "If there's time, she'll redo your hair."

Her aunt was going to win the battle because Veronica simply didn't care. She could enter the parlor in little more than two hours naked and clad in the brown wool robe, and she wouldn't care. They could shave her head bald, and she wouldn't care. Nothing could dim her joy. Nothing could alter her gratitude to Montgomery Fairfax.

"Thank you, Aunt Lilly."

"Shall we help as well?" Amanda asked, sending a look toward her mother, a sweet smile curving her lips.

"Thank you, cousin," Veronica said hastily. "I shall manage. In fact," she said, allowing herself to look a little uncertain, a little shy, "I would welcome the moments alone to contemplate."

"As well you should, Veronica," her aunt said, glancing at her husband. Both of them nodded in tandem.

She left the room, praying that the moments raced by, so she would soon be free of that house, her aunt, uncle, and all the cousins.

Stepping behind the screen where the washbasin was located, she knelt and removed the loose floorboard.

Slowly, she retrieved a small lockbox, the only possession she'd brought from Scotland.

She stood, carried the lockbox back to the window seat, and twisted the knob. Although it had always been kept in her father's desk drawer, she'd never known it to be locked. No one in their household would've thought to steal from her father. She couldn't say the same in her uncle's home.

Inside was the totality of her inheritance. If Amanda had known the extent of the lockbox's contents, no doubt her requirements would have been larger over the past two years. As it was, Veronica could afford to pay her cousin some small amounts from time to time in an attempt to be spared Amanda's petty cruelties.

She closed the lid of the lockbox and held it on her lap. This lockbox, along with her two remaining dresses, two pairs of stockings, a robe, two nightgowns, and a spare corset, was the extent of her belongings. Her dress for the wedding was borrowed, as well as her shoes.

Gone was the silver she'd put away in her wedding chest, as well as all those carefully embroidered garments for her trousseau. Her copy of *Mrs. Beeton's Book of Household Management* had been stored in her chest as well, and on nights when she couldn't sleep, she'd pored over the recipes, planning for the day when she'd prepare them for her own family.

Her female cousins had never given any thought to doing such things. They'd been reared to believe they'd always have cooks and housekeepers. Now, so would she.

How odd she'd never given a thought to marrying a peer. Although her mother was the daughter of an earl, she'd married a Scot with no aspirations but to write. They'd lived simply, and happily, in obscurity. Her mother had been content to manage their small staff of four, to spend her days caring for her father, being his audience as he read to her his latest work.

Had they ever discussed Veronica's future? Not in specific terms. She'd known she would wed, but her mother's comments had been geared toward wisdom and maturity. "It isn't always important to understand everything your husband does as much as it is to support it, Veronica." Or, "Kindness is a virtue everyone can afford, Veronica."

If her mother were here, what advice would she give?

Be patient, Veronica. Be understanding. Guard your words. Mind your actions.

Her mother would not have understood the visit to the Society of the Mercaii. A foolish deed performed for a good reason. She'd never had the opportunity to ask the questions she'd wanted to ask. Instead, her entire life had changed, and for the better.

Veronica stood, placed the lockbox in the bottom of her valise, already packed for her departure from her uncle's house, and walked to the vanity. These moments were the last of her spinsterhood. In a little less than two hours, she'd be married, a wife. She would no longer be an oddity among a group, a solitary kitten amid a litter of puppies.

The knock on the door signaled Hester's arrival. But it wasn't the maid at all but her aunt.

"I wanted a little time with you," Aunt Lilly said, sitting on the end of the bed and gesturing that she was to join her.

"Today begins the rest of your life, my dear," Aunt Lilly said. "Tonight, your husband will come to your bed, and you must accept him because it is the lot of all women to do so. God has decreed that we are vessels."

Veronica sat perched on the edge of the bed, hands

folded in her lap, her eyes not quite able to meet those of her aunt.

"You must not move while it is happening, my dear. You must remain silent. Nor must you ever remonstrate to your husband for his cruelty and use of you. These things are simply what God has given woman to endure."

She didn't know what to say to that, so she remained mute, behavior evidently pleasing Aunt Lilly if the pat on her hand was any indication.

"You must think of more pleasant things, Veronica. The Empire. The change of seasons, our poor dear Queen."

In her childhood imaginings, when she was dreaming of her future, she'd never thought of passion or desire. Nor had her knowledge accumulated appreciably over the years. She knew how the act was performed. She wasn't an idiot, after all. The emotion behind it, however, was something she'd never felt from anyone.

Anguish, joy, anger, those were easy to sense with her Gift. Passion must be a little more subtle.

When her aunt was blessedly gone, leaving her to contemplate the sacrifice of marriage, she stared at herself in the mirror.

The formidable Montgomery Fairfax would be her husband.

She'd felt pain and anger from him. The anger had been easy to understand, but why was he in pain?

Now that he was going to be her husband, she'd have ample time to discover, wouldn't she?

Montgomery Fairfax would be her husband.

How odd to watch oneself blush.

Chapter 7

The first time Montgomery saw Veronica MacLeod, he'd noticed her beauty. The circumstances of the meeting at the Society of the Mercaii had, however, overwhelmed any further observations. He'd been too intent on rescuing her to note her hair wasn't truly brown or her eyes weren't really green. Instead, her hair had brown and gold and red in it. Her eyes were a greenish hazel with gold flecks.

She stood quiet and still beside him, dressed in a pale blue dress that didn't flatter her coloring. She smelled of something reminding him of spring, something womanly and fresh. Her face was too pale, however, and her lips nearly bloodless.

If he'd known her better, he would have bent and whispered something nonsensical in her ear to make her smile. He would have commented about any of the many people who crowded into the Earl of Conley's parlor, or told her an anecdote about Virginia. Because he didn't know her, because she was suddenly his wife when he didn't want to marry, he merely stood silent beside her, finding himself amazed that this day had ever come.

In the last hour, they'd been married by an ancient minister who'd taken so long to perform the ceremony Montgomery thought it would never be over.

In the last day, he'd given more than a fleeting thought to returning home, thereby extricating himself from the situation. His honor, however, wouldn't allow him to renege on his word, however grudgingly it had been given.

The parlor in which they stood was filled with bric-a-brac, nonsensical fringe, deep purple and crimson upholstery. The crimson velvet drapery defeated even the bravest sunbeam, but somehow the ferns and plants occupying every available surface were flourishing. The result was a crowded and oppressive room.

He wanted to be away from here almost as much as he wanted to be unmarried.

What would Alisdair and James have thought of this day? No doubt they'd have made some ribald comment about his bride, her beauty, and Montgomery's obvious impatience to be gone from this place. If they'd been alive, he wouldn't have been there at all. Alisdair was the oldest, followed by James. One of his brothers would have been the 11th Lord Fairfax of Doncaster. Montgomery would have remained at Gleneagle, content to be about the business of ensuring that the plantation was profitable or practicing law.

Instead of his brothers standing beside him, he'd been accompanied by his solicitor. Edmund had left after witnessing the ceremony, claiming the press of work, an excuse Montgomery wished he could emulate.

Too many people milled around the small parlor. The air was stuffy with the various scents of perfume clashing with the dried flower arrangements and the aroma of breakfast lingering in the air.

Someone spoke at his elbow, causing him to flinch. He covered the movement as smoothly as he could with a practiced smile. He didn't like people approaching him without warning. He didn't like standing close to another human being. Arm's length was near enough, or even farther. Rifle distance was probably the best.

One cousin or another fired a volley of questions at him. He attempted to answer each in as cursory a fashion as possible.

The British had a strange way of talking. The more elevated a man was in their society, the more precise his speech. In the last two months, he'd been told, on more than one occasion, that he spoke like an American, a comment made with such derision there was no doubt it was meant as an insult.

"How are you finding London?" one of the cousins asked.

"I've learned a great deal since I've been here." There, that didn't give away his antipathy to London, did it?

"Tell me all about America," asked another one of Veronica's cousins. Amanda? Anne? He hadn't paid enough attention to their introductions.

"I'd rather hear about England," he said, forcing a smile to his lips. For the next fifteen minutes, she proceeded to regale him with tales of shops, balls, and her many admirers.

Montgomery had never been so bored.

When Veronica left to change her dress, a task evidently requiring all three of her female cousins, he stood with his back to the wall, away from the other members of Veronica's family.

He couldn't stand it any longer. He had to get away. He couldn't go outside because it was raining, and it would look too much like escape if the bridegroom stood out in the rain and refused to come back inside.

Montgomery moved to the side of the room, entering the corridor and slipping into the Earl of Conley's library. Thankfully, the room was vacant. He walked to the window, stood staring out at the rainy day, wishing he were somewhere, anywhere but here.

You're a married man now, brother. James's voice. *Responsible and mature.*

It's the right thing to do, Montgomery. How odd that, of the three, he could always hear Caroline's voice more clearly. Perhaps guilt had something to do with it.

"Caroline, get out of my mind."

"Who's Caroline?"

He turned to find Veronica standing there. She'd changed into an ugly dark blue dress similar to the one she'd worn to the Society of the Mercaii. It flattered her even less than her bridal gown.

"When can we leave?" he asked.

She looked surprised at the question or perhaps simply the abruptness of it.

"Anytime you wish," she said.

"Now," he said, walking to the doorway, brushing past her in his haste to leave, only to come face-to-face with the Countess of Conley.

"Have we overwhelmed you with our numbers, Montgomery?" she asked. "Here you are, hiding away, when everyone wants to know about you."

The woman's fawning affection was cloying. The whole family was cloying. Within five minutes of his arrival, Montgomery had known he wouldn't be able to bear their company more than an hour or two.

In two minutes, it would be three hours since he'd arrived.

The countess had insisted on calling her husband, "the earl," an affectation he found almost as annoying as the English habit of treating people with titles as if they were religious icons.

"We have to leave," he said, trying to recall some of

the manners he'd possessed all his life. He feigned a smile. "We really do."

"Of course," she said, giving him a coy little smirk. "We shall allow you to settle in, of course," she was saying now. "Before we visit."

He was grateful to see his bride's answering expression was less than enthusiastic. Perhaps she dreaded the idea of being visited by the Countess of Conley as much as he did.

The countess patted him on the arm, smiled at Veronica. "Here we thought our Anne would be the first of the girls to marry."

Evidently, the Countess of Conley had forgotten the scandal precipitating their union.

He exchanged a quick look with Veronica, wondering at the glint of humor in her eyes. It was gone so quickly, he might have imagined it.

"We're leaving London tomorrow," he announced. "My business necessitates it."

"Where are we going?" Veronica asked.

"I'm sure your husband will tell you all you need to know," the countess said firmly. "Do not be presumptuous, Veronica."

He frowned at the countess, then turned to his bride.

"To Scotland," he said. "But now we must be on our way."

The countess looked startled when he passed her. He escorted Veronica to the door, stood impassively as she said her farewells, then walked her to the carriage.

Montgomery nodded to the young man holding the door, waited until Veronica entered the carriage, and followed her, sitting with his back to the horses. She didn't look at him, intent on staring at the house, her family clustered on the steps. Her fingers pressed against the glass; her mouth curved in a small, almost sad, smile as if she couldn't bear to part with them.

If he'd been in her place, he'd have been singing hosannas right about then.

As the carriage slowly pulled away from the curb, her family called out their farewells. She waved, then turned away, facing him.

"Where in Scotland?" she asked softly.

"Doncaster Hall, the house I've inherited along with the title."

Her look of surprise warned him. Evidently, he wasn't supposed to speak of such things, merely pretend he'd always been the 11th Lord Fairfax of Doncaster. He wasn't to mention money. He wasn't to talk about an entire list of things forbidden by British rules.

"I'm from Lollybroch," she said, in the same tone she might have admitted to being royalty.

Was he supposed to know the place?

She tilted back her chin and looked at him. No pale miss, now. She looked almost proud of her heritage. Once, he would've felt the same. Instead, all he felt was confusion, and a share of grief, not only for his country but for Virginia and Gleneagle.

"Are we going to live in Scotland?"

"It will do as well as any other place," he said. He couldn't imagine being as ill at ease in Scotland as he was in London.

She smiled.

If he didn't know better, he would have thought her happy with the marriage instead of feeling like a pawn being moved about on a chessboard by her uncle. Or perhaps it was the prospect of returning to her homeland that pleased her.

What would Caroline have thought of Veronica?

Would she have counseled patience with his new wife? Would Caroline have placed her palm on his cheek, as she often did, staring into his eyes with that intent gaze of hers, giving him comfort with her words, kindness, and the generosity of her love?

Caroline wasn't there to give him advice. He'd have to muddle through this marriage himself.

"I don't love you, Veronica," he said abruptly. "This is not a love match. Or even a political marriage. You were in trouble, and I was forced to intervene. That's all."

Wide-eyed, she stared at him. Her fingers clenched, released, clenched again. She looked down at her gloved hands, then resolutely back at him.

"It's the truth, isn't it?" He settled back against the seat. "The truth should never offend."

She turned her attention back to the window.

"The truth should not be used as a whip, either, Montgomery," she said without looking at him. She took another deep breath. "How can you love me? You don't know me. Yet you needn't say it in such a tone. As if feeling anything for me in the future would be impossible."

"I didn't want a wife. I expect to deal amicably with you if I can ignore you." At her swift look, he added, "If I've hurt you, forgive me. It was not my intent."

"What did you intend, Montgomery?"

She rolled the R in his name, making the name longer, giving it a flavor of Scotland.

When he didn't answer, didn't know what she wanted him to say, she folded her hands together and turned to look at him again, smiling pleasantly.

"To ensure I know my place? How could I not? You and my uncle have made it perfectly clear what my place is. I'm an imposition to be removed, an impediment that walks and talks. If it weren't for Veronica, we wouldn't be touched by scandal. Tuck her away, marry her off, place her somewhere she can do no more harm."

"If you hadn't attended the Society meeting, Veronica, none of this would have happened. Why the hell did you?"

"The Society of the Mercaii was reputed to be a legitimate organization seeking to study the occult," she said.

"The Society of the Mercaii is an organization given up to the study of hedonism and sex."

"I didn't know that at the time," she snapped. "I thought I was going to be engaged in intellectual inquiry."

"Intellectual inquiry?"

"Yes."

She looked away, which just annoyed him further.

"In what? What did you think the Society could do?"

She remained silent for a few moments. Finally, she spoke. "I feel things," she said. "I have a Gift."

He folded his arms, recalling her conversation with her uncle on the steps the night he'd rescued her. "A gift?"

"I feel what other people are feeling. I can sense their emotions. I wanted to know if the Society knew of any other people like me."

"You can sense other people's emotions?" he asked. He wondered if she could *feel* his incredulity.

She frowned at him.

"A great many people mock what they don't understand," she said.

"You'll find that the majority of the world mocks clairvoyance. Most of us are rational."

"I'm not daft. I'm fey, but I'm not daft."

"Then I needn't bother telling you what I think," he said. "Since you can feel it."

"I don't read minds," she said.

"Tell me."

She frowned at him again.

He smiled. Evidently, she was cross when her bluff was called.

"You've been grieving," she said suddenly, her tone as flat as the look in her eyes. "Is that why you're so angry? Because the woman you love isn't here, and I am?"

The question was so unexpected it stole his breath.

Silence ticked between them, marked by the sounds of ordinary life. Another vehicle passed, and the horses seemed to greet each other. Inside, however, each was mute. Neither looked away, as if rooted to this place, this moment, by some tenuous connection.

"I don't know what you're talking about," he finally said.

She smiled slightly, the expression without humor. A simple curve of the lips that meant nothing and conveyed little. She tilted her head, studying him as if she were a curious bird.

"There is such pain coming from you, Montgomery. Even during the ceremony, I felt it. A wave of anguish that almost knocked you to your knees. Even here I can feel it. It's as if you're bleeding."

He folded his arms in front of his chest, staring at her impassively. If he could have simply ignored the circumstances that night at the Society, he wouldn't be here. No, he had to rescue this woman because he'd been unable to save another.

Damn it, he *had* been thinking of Caroline.

Neither he nor Veronica spoke, the atmosphere in the carriage one more suitable to winter than a fine spring day.

Veronica laid her head back against the cushions, closed her eyes, effectively distancing herself from him. Or so he thought, until she started to speak.

"You love her very much, don't you?"

He remained still, not from fascination or interest but because he knew that if he moved, it would be to silence her. He'd reach across the seat and place his hand over her mouth to keep her from speaking.

Abruptly, she opened her eyes, her face going pale.

"She's dead, isn't she? That's why you're in so much pain."

If he could have left the carriage, he would have. Instead, he fixed a look on his bride that she evidently understood because she suddenly went mute.

Soon, they were at his house. When his driver opened the carriage door, Montgomery ignored all the rules of etiquette by leaving the carriage and striding to the front door, unknowing and uncaring how his wife was welcomed to his home.

She followed him into his library.

"I'm sorry I'm not her," she said, continuing their conversation as if he hadn't walked away.

He turned slowly to face her, attempting to regain his composure.

Alisdair and James would be howling with laughter to see what Fate had done. He was married to a woman dottier than Aunt Maddie.

He leaned over, reached for the bell on the corner of his desk, and rang it twice.

"Mrs. Gardiner will show you your room," he said. "Please tell her if you need anything."

"Am I being dismissed?" she asked.

"If I could dismiss you, Veronica, I would. However, I'm afraid that you and I are linked by law."

"Thank you for marrying me," she said, startling him. "Thank you for being a gentleman, and in some ways, a knight. I didn't mean to hurt you, Montgomery. If I did, I'm sorry. I can't help what I feel. It just comes to me."

"You have no control over it, I suppose?"

She shook her head.

"In that, you and I are different. I have control over my life. I don't have to suffer your company."

She flinched as if he'd struck her.

"Feel anything you want about me. I just don't want to hear what you feel or what you think."

"From now until the day we die, Montgomery?"

"I'm not as privileged as you, Veronica. I do not pretend to be able to view the future."

"I don't see the future. I never said I did."

He inclined his head. "That's right, you don't see the future. You can only read someone's heart. You can only feel what he's feeling."

"Yes," she said, nodding. "At the moment, you're wishing you'd never seen me," she added, her voice so faint he almost leaned forward to hear her. "That you'd allowed me to be raped or that you'd simply walked away."

Then his surprising wife turned and left him staring after her.

"It was a lovely ceremony, Mother," Amanda said, helping her mother count the silver.

"I'm afraid it was a very hole-and-corner affair, my dear. Given the circumstances, it was as well done as it could have been." She straightened, slapped her hands together as if to rid herself of the problem of her niece, and smiled at her oldest daughter.

"You can rest assured, my dear, that when your wedding comes along, it shall be a grand and illustrious event."

Amanda smiled. "Veronica will be pleased to live in Scotland again," she said.

Her mother shivered. "Such a barbaric country. I find

it difficult to believe that our poor dear Queen has loved it all these years."

"I think we should plan to visit them."

Her mother looked at her with some surprise. "You have never expressed an interest in travel before now, Amanda."

"She is family, Mother."

Her mother nodded, as if giving the idea of travel to Scotland some serious thought. "If it's good enough for the Queen," she said, "then it's good enough for us." She smiled. "I shall speak with your father about it. We should, if nothing else, ensure that Veronica is living well in Scotland. After all, we're the only family she has left."

"Except for her new husband," Amanda said. "A very interesting man."

"A Lord, for all that it's a Scottish title," the countess said.

"Even so, Montgomery is a handsome man," Amanda said. "How very like our sly little Veronica to have escaped scandal with such a catch."

"Had it not been for you, Amanda, we should never have known."

The fondness of her mother's smile was indication enough she'd pleased her parents.

Yet in telling her parents about Veronica's shocking actions, Amanda had cut off a potential source of funds. She could become quite cross about the entire situation. Veronica had married and left the household. However, her dear cousin had married a wealthy man.

There must be some way to make that work to her advantage.

Chapter 8

Veronica was served her wedding dinner in a small dining room, the meal punctuated by a solicitous Mrs. Gardiner, who insisted upon coming back into the room every few minutes.

"Is there anything I can get for you, Lady Fairfax?" she asked again.

Since it was the third time Mrs. Gardiner asked, Veronica realized the housekeeper was not as intent on being of assistance as she was offering her sympathy.

"Everything is wonderful," she said, forcing a smile to her face. "Thank you for your kindness," she added, finding it odd to be an object of pity on her wedding night.

Mrs. Gardiner nodded, leaving the room after several backward glances. No doubt the poor woman wanted to make some explanation for Montgomery's absence but was constrained by loyalty.

Her new husband was nowhere in sight. Nor had he sent word to her as to his whereabouts or intentions.

After the endless meal, she retreated to the room she'd been given, to be greeted by Mrs. Gardiner and a young girl pulled from kitchen duties to act as a lady's maid.

"I truly don't need any assistance," she told the housekeeper. "I've never had my own maid, you see."

"Yes, Your Ladyship, but you're married, now."

She didn't know what part of that comment was more disturbing, the fact she had just noticed that Mrs. Gardiner had been calling her by her new title or that the housekeeper believed her life had changed.

True, marriage had altered her status from poor relation to rich wife. She was Lady Fairfax, whereas she'd been simply Miss MacLeod a day ago. Montgomery, however, didn't believe in her Gift, which was not an appreciable change in her life. No one had except her parents.

She was as lonely as she'd been for two years.

With the maid's help, she dressed in the present from Aunt Lilly and her cousins, a lovely peignoir of lemon-colored silk that had been in Anne's trousseau. After the girl left, she brushed her hair until it curled around her shoulders, studying her reflection in the mirror and noting the flush on her cheeks.

Would a man consider her beautiful? Would Montgomery? Or would he even see her as she was, avoiding the wedding night as he'd avoided her for the whole of the day?

She was a bride without a bridegroom. A bride, deserted shortly after the ceremony. A bride, left in no doubt of her new husband's antipathy for her.

One thing her marriage had brought her, however, was the freedom of her emotions. She was growing angrier by the moment.

Was she supposed to sit meekly in her room and wait for her husband? Then welcome him into her bed? She'd perform her duty, but she wasn't going to like it.

Or him.

Let him mourn the woman he loved.

I don't love you.

She didn't love him, either.

Was it too much to wish for love? Was it too foolish to wish that someone watched the door in anticipation of her arrival? Or listened to his watch to ensure that time, itself, hadn't caused her delay? Or to have someone stand at the bottom of the steps looking up, his hand on the banister, his eyes lighting up because he'd just seen her?

Was it so terrible to want something so simple, so fragile?

Montgomery's eyes wouldn't light up when she entered a room because he hadn't chosen her. Of all the women in the world, he'd not singled her out to share his life. He'd no choice in the matter.

Neither had she.

She clenched her fists, then forced herself to relax her hands. The bubble of anger wouldn't subside. However much she told herself that resentment had no practical purpose, she felt it, nonetheless.

Was she simply to be a leaf blown by a strong wind? Always acquiescing to everyone's plans for her? She'd been a dutiful daughter. However, it had been more difficult to be a dutiful niece, a companionable cousin. As the months passed, as one year faded into another, she'd found it more and more difficult to remain silent and agreeable.

Now, she was supposed to be a dutiful wife, submitting to her fate, silent when her husband abandoned her not an hour after their wedding.

Her marriage wasn't going to change her life at all.

Yet in Montgomery's enchanted mirror, she'd not been lonely. She'd had a family. She'd felt joy for that second, been surrounded by people who loved her.

How much had she really seen? Or had she imagined it all?

She could look again.

For the first time since she'd left Montgomery's library, her spirit lightened. The mirror was somewhere in the house. Unless, of course, he'd returned it to its rightful owner. Yet Montgomery said he didn't know to whom it belonged.

She glanced at the mantel clock. Where was he? Had Montgomery left for an evening of carousing? She should have taken advantage of Mrs. Gardiner's solicitousness and inquired as to her husband's whereabouts. She'd been too embarrassed, too ashamed to ask.

Removing her wrapper, she replaced it with her worn but sturdier robe, belted it tightly, and left the room, heading for the third floor.

Mrs. Gardiner urged her into her room, after looking both ways down the hall as if afraid the other servants would discover her on the third floor.

"Your Ladyship," the housekeeper said, wrapping herself in a thick plaid robe, "how may I be of service?"

Once in the room, Veronica didn't quite know how to ask.

"I'm looking for a mirror," Veronica said.

Mrs. Gardiner's lined face furrowed even more. "Is there not a mirror in your chamber?"

"A mirror with diamonds around the edge of the glass," she said. "And writing across the back. I think it's Latin."

The housekeeper's face smoothed with her smile. "The Scryer's Mirror," she said. "You know about the Scryer's Mirror?" She studied Veronica for a moment. "Was it a bride's gift, Your Ladyship?"

Lying was wrong. Standing there in the housekeeper's room was, no doubt, wrong in another way. So was being abandoned by her husband.

Veronica smiled. "Do you know where it is?" Not quite a lie, but definitely not the truth.

"I do," Mrs. Gardiner said. "Shall I bring it to you, Your Ladyship?"

"I don't want to trouble you, Mrs. Gardiner. If you'll tell me where it is, I'll fetch it myself."

For a moment she thought the housekeeper wouldn't agree. A hand went to a curl neatly tied in a strip of white cloth. Evidently, Mrs. Gardiner was not too old for a little vanity. She obviously didn't want to be seen outside her room prepared for sleep.

"You've been so kind to me, Mrs. Gardiner," she said sincerely. "I truly don't mind."

The housekeeper studied her for a moment, a look reminiscent of that very room two nights ago, and how Mrs. Gardiner had sat propped up in bed watching her until she'd fallen asleep. She'd taken her duty seriously and evidently her loyalty as well.

Except Veronica was no longer just some girl to be watched. She was Lady Fairfax.

"It's in His Lordship's library," the housekeeper said. "In the credenza. The third door. I placed it there myself."

Before leaving Mrs. Gardiner, Veronica folded her hands together tightly, and asked, "Did you see anything in the mirror, Mrs. Gardiner?"

The housekeeper wouldn't meet her eyes.

"I'm a godly woman, Your Ladyship."

She nodded.

"Do you think the mirror is magic? Is that why you called it a scryer's mirror?"

"Some say that magic is not the Lord's province. It's the Devil's."

Veronica didn't comment.

"Still, it was a pretty sight I saw. All my nieces and

nephews surrounding me, singing." The housekeeper finally looked at her. "How can something so lovely be evil?"

She didn't comment, merely thanked the older woman, and made her way back down the stairs.

On the third floor, the staircase was not as ornate, the balusters more simply carved. As she descended to the first floor, however, the carving became more elaborate, the banister mahogany instead of simple pine.

The steps curved at the landing instead of being squared, and as she reached the well-polished wooden floor, the soft glow of an oil lamp on the table beside the front door illuminated her way.

She'd extinguish the lamp on her way back to her room.

The beeswax and lemon polish used to buff the fine mahogany furniture mixed with the sandalwood from the potpourri pots, no doubt placed in strategic locations to offset the odor of the oil lamps.

Light pooled around the hallway table but not enough to illuminate the library. She stood at the doorway, staring into the room. Shadows enveloped the corners, draped over the desk and chairs.

She entered the room and lit the oil lamp on the corner of the desk. The wick caught flame, the glow expanding beyond the glass globe. For a moment, she watched it to ensure it was burning correctly, then looked around her as she'd not had the opportunity to do earlier.

Turning, she faced Montgomery's desk. A leather-bound blotter sat in the middle of the desk, a pen case slightly to the right. A crystal inkwell rested an inch beyond the blotter. A small, japanned box rested on the left corner of the desk beside a bell.

What kind of work did Montgomery do when he sat

there? Did he write letters home? In his next letter, would he mention her? Or would he keep their sudden marriage a secret from those he loved?

She wished she knew more about the man she'd married. Where was he? Or was that even a question she should ask?

Aunt Lilly had always been solicitous of Uncle Bertrand, but she'd never heard her aunt question her husband. If her uncle volunteered information, Aunt Lilly was content enough. Not once had she ever said to him, at least within Veronica's hearing, "What will you be doing today, my dear?" Or, "With whom will you be meeting? Have you any plans?"

At the same time, her aunt was careful to ensure that her husband approved all her outings, including those involving the girls.

Her parents' relationship had been different. Each morning, they'd discussed their plans for the day. Her mother had neither sought approval for her actions, nor had her father granted it.

How did she create a marriage like that, especially when she knew so little about the man she'd married?

She pushed thoughts of her new husband aside for another task, that of locating the mirror.

A series of bookshelves occupied the far wall, filled with leather-bound books. On the wall beneath the windows sat a long credenza.

The third cabinet, Mrs. Gardiner had said. The light from the lamp didn't extend to the corner, so she was forced to bend down to peer inside but could see nothing. She knelt and stretched out her arm to reach into the back of the credenza. Her fingers felt fabric and she pulled it out. Sitting back on her heels, she opened the heavy drawstring bag and withdrew the mirror.

She laid the mirror facedown, stroking her fingers over the cool surface of the gold. One by one, her fingers measured each diamond positioned around the edge.

Perhaps it would be wiser not to look into the mirror again. What if she'd been wrong? Mrs. Gardiner had seen something, however, so her vision couldn't be an aberration.

Slowly, she raised the mirror, pressing the glass against her chest, holding it there, before bowing her head and saying a short but earnest prayer.

Please, let me see something. Something hopeful.

Would God decree her a sinner if she wanted to see something better than the life she was living now? Was it wrong to want to be happy instead of lonely?

The lamp sputtered. Perhaps that was an answer.

She looked into the mirror. The glass was brown, flecked with spots, indicating its age. When nothing happened, disappointment surged through her. She was in the process of lowering the mirror when the color lightened. Hands trembling, she gripped the handle of the mirror and raised it so she was staring directly into her reflection.

She was surrounded by people, their faces too blurry to recognize. Her own face was clear enough, her expression filled with such joy and animation, she stared at herself in wonder. She was laughing, the image so real she could almost feel joy bubbling up in the middle of her chest.

"Another example of your intellectual inquiry?" a voice asked from behind her.

Startled, she pressed the mirror against her chest and glanced over her shoulder at Montgomery. He was standing in the doorway, leaning back against the frame, his arms folded over his chest. His hair looked tousled as if the wind had played with it. Raindrops glittered on his shoulders, dampened his clothing.

He glanced at the lamp she'd lit.

"At least you didn't attempt to hide your activity, Veronica. Perhaps that's a credit to your favor. Theft, however, is not."

"I wasn't stealing it," she said. "I was just looking."

She slipped the mirror back into the drawstring bag and replaced it in the credenza before standing. His gaze dropped. Her robe had come open, revealing the silk of her nightgown.

"You've seen me naked before," she said.

"The last time I saw you naked, you looked rather pitiable. You don't now."

Oh.

She pressed her lips together, then forced herself to relax. Her heart, however, was beating so quickly she felt breathless with it. She stared at the carpet before, annoyed at her cowardice, she forced herself to look at him.

"Were you outside?"

"I felt the need to take some air," he said. An excuse so like the one she'd devised a few nights ago that she smiled.

"Do I amuse you, Veronica?"

He had a way of looking at her intently, as if he wished to peer behind her eyes to see the soul of her.

Perhaps it was the intensity of his look or her irritation at his desertion that sparked her answer. Instead of demurring, instead of saying something polite and noncommittal, or instead of simply excusing herself and leaving the room, she gave him the truth.

"No," she said. "No, Montgomery, you fascinate me. You confuse me. You worry me. However, I wouldn't say the emotion I feel in your presence is amusement."

She stored away his startled look to enjoy at another time.

"Go to bed, Veronica," he said, stepping out of the doorway so she could pass. "Now."

She stood, clasped her hands together, and walked toward the doorway. As she passed him, she looked up. A muscle in his jaw clenched. She almost raised her hand and cupped her palm around his jaw.

He looked as if he would flinch if she touched him, but that wasn't what she was feeling from him. He was angry and disturbed, but something else was there, something dark and powerful, an emotion she'd never felt.

Perhaps this moment was not unlike the night at the Society of the Mercaii. She felt as if she were drugged, subdued and silent, her surroundings swirling around her.

"Good night, Veronica," he said, his accent coating the words with honey.

The look in his eyes, measuring, and a little dangerous, didn't make her afraid. Instead, she felt warmth spread through her body.

"Will you come to me tonight?" she asked, congratulating herself for her courage in asking.

The seconds ticked by, and he said nothing. Evidently, the absence of an answer was an answer.

"You won't forget to extinguish the lamp?"

He frowned but still didn't speak. After a moment, he nodded.

She walked down the hall, only too conscious of his gaze. At the base of the stairs, she stopped and looked back at him. How handsome he was and how mysterious.

Montgomery grieved with such ferocity that the emotion was almost a living thing, hunkered down on all fours between them like a creature from a nightmare. He stood silent and alone, embraced by shadows.

She wanted to draw his head down so it could rest on her shoulder, enfold him in her arms and hold him, and tell him that grief had a way of becoming more bearable each day. She'd never forgotten her parents. They were always with her, their loss like a wound leaving an ugly scar. She would never be without the scar, but the wound was beginning to heal.

Montgomery, however, would not allow her to comfort him. She knew because he turned and entered the study, closing the door softly behind him, a repudiation without words.

Very well, he wouldn't come to her tonight.

What a fool she was to be disappointed.

She was an innocent yesterday; she would be an innocent tomorrow. For how long? The length of Montgomery's grief?

How long would that last?

Chapter 9

Edmund Kerr sat at the desk and withdrew a sheaf of papers from his leather folder. He'd been empowered to discuss something with Lady Fairfax, a task he found objectionable. That duty should have been performed by Lord Fairfax. Instead, it had been delegated to him. Edmund picked up the bell, rang it twice, then placed it back on the top of the desk, inwardly counting how many seconds passed before his summons was obeyed.

Not only had it been something of a shock to realize that the 11th Lord Fairfax was an American, but Edmund had had to travel to that country to tell the man of his good fortune. He'd also been forced to use the power of his persuasion to convince Montgomery Fairfax to take up the title.

He'd found Montgomery without too much difficulty. The man had been a decorated war hero, and the government of the United States, however much in disarray they might have been after their civil war, was diligent about keeping track of their war heroes.

All in all, it hadn't been that distressing a journey. He'd seen the devastation, of course, but since he knew no one in America, the ruins he'd passed had been more like viewing a daguerreotype than witnessing something personally affecting.

In the first few weeks, he'd thought Montgomery Fairfax would turn his back on his inheritance, refuse it, and go about his business in America. He'd had to cajole the man to England and through the process of being recognized as the 11th Lord Fairfax. Now the man was married, another shock. With marriage came heirs, and it was inevitable that the Fairfax clan would increase in numbers soon.

A depressing thought, but then, he hadn't been appreciably cheerful since discovering that an American would take up the title.

A maid came to the door, finally, a great many minutes after she should have arrived, looking surprised to see him sitting there instead of Montgomery.

"Will you summon your mistress?" he asked.

At her look of confusion, he added. "Lady Fairfax."

She nodded and disappeared, all without a word spoken.

He shook his head and arranged the papers Lady Fairfax would need to sign in front of him. Sitting back, he took a deep breath and prepared himself for the confrontation.

Veronica's breakfast was eaten in solitude, an odd event after living for two years in the cacophony of her uncle's home. Not having to make a concerted attempt to ignore her cousins made for a better mood to start the day.

Her first full day of being a wife. In the previous day, she'd seen her husband for a total of two hours, at the most. She was mulling on how to correct that situation when Mrs. Gardiner entered the room.

"Your Ladyship," the housekeeper said, smiling, "Mr. Kerr would like to visit with you if you've a moment."

"Mr. Kerr?"

"Lord Fairfax's solicitor, Your Ladyship."

"Oh yes," Veronica said. "What could he want with me? Isn't it Montgomery he needs?"

"His Lordship has taken himself off to the import warehouse," Mrs. Gardiner said. "He's buying more silk. Mr. Kerr specifically asked for you, Your Ladyship."

Why on earth was Montgomery buying silk? Why was the solicitor requesting her presence? Just two more questions to add to the pile of them she'd accumulated since her wedding.

As she stood and left the dining room for Montgomery's library, she pushed back her dread. Had Montgomery requested an annulment? She was certainly not underage, but did he think her mentally incompetent? They shared no relationship of any sort. What other grounds could he use?

Dear God, what would she do if he annulled their marriage? Where would she go? Uncle Bertrand would not take her in, that was certain. An annulled wife was almost as shocking as an unmarried girl who'd been ruined. She would really have to take the last of her father's funds and travel to Scotland alone.

But what would she do, once there?

Fear is a wasteful emotion, my dear child. How much better it is to confront an issue than to be frightened into inaction. Her father's words. He would have cautioned her to wait until she'd heard from the solicitor himself before imagining different scenarios. *Never borrow from the future more than you can handle today,* he'd always said.

She stood at the door to Montgomery's library and waited until the solicitor noticed her.

"Your Ladyship," Edmund Kerr said, standing at her entrance.

Mr. Kerr waved her to a straight-back chair in front of the desk.

She took her seat, arranging her full skirts with the dexterity born of years of practice. Finally, Mr. Kerr sat, stacked his papers in front of him, and gave her a toothy smile.

The solicitor's face was long and narrow, his forehead broad, his nose a petite nub. His beard was closely trimmed to his face and extended to his sideburns as if calling attention to his large brown eyes. His ears were narrow, pointed, and lay flat against his head.

Regrettably, Mr. Kerr reminded her of an earnest squirrel, a resemblance accentuated by his habit of tapping his papers with the edges of his palms as if the stack of papers was a nut he'd found.

What she felt from him, however, was not as amusing.

An odd darkness surrounded him, as if he were angry and attempting to hide it. She bent her head, ostensibly arranging her skirts while she concentrated on Mr. Kerr's emotions. Regret? Sorrow? There was something about him that was oddly off-putting.

"Lord Fairfax has instructed me to tell you about the marriage settlement he's made for you, Lady Fairfax. Although this arrangement is normally made prior to the actual nuptials, His Lordship did not want to involve your uncle."

"A marriage settlement?"

"Yes," he said, and named an amount that had her staring at him in shock.

"That's very generous," she said. More than generous. She could live the whole of her life comfortably on that amount.

"Why, Mr. Kerr?" she asked, pressing her damp palms against her skirts.

"Why, Lady Fairfax?" Mr. Kerr's mouth turned down, making him look like an angry squirrel. "I agree, Your Ladyship, it is odd. However, His Lordship was adamant you have enough funds to enable you to live well on your own."

A ball of ice formed in her stomach. "Does he not anticipate being with me, Mr. Kerr?" she forced herself to ask. "Is he annulling the marriage?"

He looked surprised, staring at her without speaking for several moments.

"Have you any knowledge he might wish an annulment, Lady Fairfax?"

She shook her head.

"Then I should not concern yourself with that thought. Especially since His Lordship has made ample provision for your future."

Because of Montgomery's generosity, people would not have to take her in, show her charity. She'd have enough money to set up her own household no matter what happened in the future.

"Is my husband returning to America, Mr. Kerr?"

The solicitor didn't answer her immediately. Finally, after an agonizing minute, he shook his head. "I have not been told that, Lady Fairfax."

"Would he tell you?"

His face settled into disapproving lines. Was he annoyed because she'd asked? Or annoyed at the thought of Montgomery doing anything without consulting him?

"He would have to do so, Lady Fairfax. There are any manner of details that would need to be arranged if His Lordship decided to return to Virginia."

She told herself she should be grateful for the settlement and not delve further into Montgomery's plans. Another example of meekly acquiescing to the future?

"If you'll sign these, Lady Fairfax," he said, "I'll take them to the appropriate authorities. The next time you'll see me will be in Scotland."

"You'll be in Scotland, Mr. Kerr?"

"I live in Scotland, Lady Fairfax. At Doncaster Hall."

She signed where he indicated, keeping her emotions in check. Later, out of Mr. Kerr's presence, she would think about everything he had said and whether to worry about it or not.

Montgomery's errands had been successful, resulting in promises from several companies to expedite his orders to Scotland. London was too congested for his purposes. Edmund had assured him there was room enough in Scotland to do what he wished. He entered the townhouse with his thoughts occupied by the design of the air flow chambers only to be stopped by the sight of his wife.

Veronica was sitting on the steps.

He didn't need any type of clairvoyant gift to figure out she was annoyed.

"You're waiting for me, I see," he said.

She didn't speak, merely stood, walked down the steps, her gaze not leaving his. Instead of approaching him, however, she walked into the parlor, never glancing back to see if he followed.

Montgomery debated going on to his library and finishing the lists of equipment he needed, then discarded that thought. This conversation had been coming since the night before, when he'd decided it would be wiser to remain celibate than to bed a stranger.

Evidently, Veronica was angry about his decision.

That was not, however, the first comment she made when he followed her.

"Are you returning to America?"

He entered the parlor, a plainly decorated chamber, the antithesis of the room in which they'd been married.

The Countess of Conley was given to an over appreciation of her furnishings. Mrs. Gardiner was, blessedly, more restrained in her taste.

"We're going to Scotland."

Veronica clasped her hands together and looked up at him.

"Are you taking me with you?"

"What made you think I was traveling to Scotland without you?"

Relief flashed in her eyes, so quickly that if he'd not made a practice of studying the men in his command in the last four years, he might've missed it.

"When? When are we leaving?" she asked, flattening her hands against her skirts.

"This afternoon," he said, realizing he should have told her earlier. He'd been used to thinking only of himself for so many years, he'd have to become acquainted with another person's needs.

"The train leaves at two. Will you be ready?"

She nodded.

He retreated to the sofa, set at a right angle to the fireplace. Upholstered in a green and flowery fabric, it was a bit too feminine for his tastes. Perhaps an English parlor was a woman's domain.

Veronica didn't sit beside him. Instead, she stood in front of him and repeated her first, surprising, question.

"Are you returning to America?" she asked.

"Why would you ask that?" Caution tempered his words.

She took a step toward him, then another, halting only when she was an arm's length away.

"Why did you give me a settlement?"

When he didn't answer, she frowned at him, standing in front of him as if he were a boy in short pants and she his chastiser. He wasn't particularly fond of being chastised.

He leaned back, folded his arms, and regarded her.

"You've provided quite adequately for me, Montgomery. Is that supposed to make up for desertion?"

"Desertion?" he asked, surprised. "I provided for you, Veronica," he said. "Be satisfied with that."

She studied him for a moment, as if deciding whether to believe his answer.

"You didn't come to me last night," she said, finally, startling him again.

He wasn't used to her straightforwardness. She didn't flirt. She didn't hide behind double entendres. She wasn't the type to hint at anything. Instead, Veronica came right out and told him what she was thinking.

A woman's wiles had no effect on him, but her directness was fascinating. So, too, her voice. With her accent of Scotland, she changed words, made them sound new, as if English were a language he'd just started to comprehend.

How the hell did he answer her complaint?

"I'm not prepared to bed a stranger," he said, giving her the truth.

She blinked at him several times.

Did she *feel* something from him? Oh, for the love of God, was he beginning to believe she actually had a Gift?

"How will we be anything other than strangers if you continually avoid me?"

"I haven't continually avoided you," he said. "We haven't been married a full day yet."

"It's been a full day," she said, glancing at the mantel clock.

"Are you always this argumentative?"

She considered the question. "I believe I was," she

said. "Not lately, of course, but when I lived with my parents. My father liked to debate. I often took the other side of an argument simply to please him."

Before he could comment, she took another step closer. "You've never even kissed me," she said.

"Why do I worry you?"

She blinked at him again.

"Last night, you said I worried you."

"Oh, good heavens, Montgomery, you're an American. You're different from anyone I've ever met. You're a stranger. I'd be a fool not to be worried."

"Yet you still wanted me to come to your bed."

"I'm a bride. You're supposed to come to my bed."

"Am I?"

"Don't you know?" she asked, blinking at him.

He was almost tempted to continue to tease her, to see what she would say. She amused him, and he hadn't expected that.

"A kiss? Is that all you want?"

Without giving her a chance to answer, he reached over and grabbed her skirt, pulling her toward him until she tumbled into his lap. Her hands fluttered in the air for a moment until his arms locked around her waist.

"In what way am I different?"

She was evidently not prepared to answer that question because she simply stared at him.

He tipped her head back, his attention on her face, a face even then coloring under his inspection. He lowered his head.

"I'm a Virginian," he said. "You can't utter a dare to a Virginian and expect him to ignore it."

Her eyes widened.

Amused, he placed his hand over her eyes.

"You're supposed to be overcome by passion," he said,

bending to kiss her lightly. "Or at the very least, over-whelmed by romance."

"I don't think I've ever felt romance," she said against his lips. "Or passion."

Now, *that* was a challenge.

He removed his hand and her eyes popped open. Evidently, their first kiss hadn't impressed her. He lowered his head again, his mouth gently resting over hers.

His tongue traced her bottom lip, coaxed her mouth to open, then thrust inside. She made a sound in the back of her throat. Protest or appreciation? At the moment, he neither knew nor cared.

Kissing Veronica was a surprise. She was trembling in his arms. One of his hands reached around to smooth over her back. The other slid to her bodice, a thumb reaching up to rest just below her breasts.

When his hand moved, she gasped, such a delicate protest he wasn't certain if she was offended or simply surprised. He tested the thought by cupping a breast.

She abruptly drew back, her face crimson.

"That wasn't a kiss," she said.

"You haven't any experience, have you?"

She stared at him. "Any experience? Of course I haven't," she said, sounding shocked. "I think I know how it's done well enough. We had cats and horses. They're not altogether shy about mating."

He wanted to smile but knew if he did, she might interpret his emotion incorrectly. He wasn't feeling humor as much as he was an unexpected tenderness.

His celibacy was suddenly useless and unnecessary. He wanted his wife, his unexpected Scots wife, who was all innocence and ignorance, who spoke of being fey, and who managed to startle him with her directness.

She was like the wind, as changeable as the flow of air itself.

He should stand, excuse himself, and be about his work. Instead, he lowered his head to kiss her again.

"Proper behavior, Veronica, is what separates the upper classes from those who would ape their betters." Aunt Lilly's dictum. "You know nothing of proper society, Veronica." That comment from each of her cousins in turn.

"I don't think it's proper to be kissing in the parlor," she said, pulling back from their last kiss.

From the smile on Montgomery's face, she'd obviously amused him. She didn't have time to think about it because he leaned down and kissed her again.

He tilted his head a little, and the kiss became something different. She felt as if the top of her head were spinning. His breath entered her mouth, and it was the most intimate act she'd ever experienced with another human being.

He deepened the kiss, and she no longer thought about being proper. Besides, compliancy was the mark of a good wife. Until, of course, he started unbuttoning her bodice. She slapped his hand away, but it returned. The second time he did it, she broke off their kiss and glared at him. The third time she slapped his hand away, he shook his head.

"I have no intention of becoming naked in the parlor, Montgomery Fairfax."

"Not naked, Veronica. Just a little, shall we say, loosened?"

"I'm loosened enough, thank you."

"You're a bride, remember?"

He was down to the fourth button, and she placed her hand against the skin he exposed. She suspected he would continue unbuttoning her, but she was already revealed nearly to her waist. She grabbed both sides of her bodice and held them together, a fact that didn't disturb him one whit.

Instead, he reached past her hands and began to work on her corset laces.

That was too much.

"Stop it, Montgomery," she said.

"Very well," he said, and reached up to cup one of her breasts.

Oh dear.

Gently, almost tenderly, his thumb brushed across the tip, and a jolt traveled through her body. She shook her head, as if to negate the sensations, then gripped his wrist with both hands to stop him.

He kissed her again, and it didn't matter.

Her shift was fastened at the front with a tiny silk bow. He pulled one end, slid his hand inside the garment, his fingers dancing across her skin to rest against the outer slope of a breast.

Exactly what part of the Empire was she supposed to think about at the moment? She would think of Scotland, deeply grateful she was returning home, despite the circumstances. She would think of her own little village, Lollybroch, and all the joy she'd felt while living there. She would not think about what he was doing with his fingers.

How could she think of anything when he was kissing her so deeply?

She moaned, reached up, and gripped his jacket with both hands, fisting the material to pull him closer.

His hand came up to touch her cheek, and before she knew what he was doing, his fingers were spreading through her hair, dislodging her careful bun.

Heat was pooling in her body, coming from everywhere

at once. Her cheeks flamed; it was difficult to breathe, and any thoughts of Scotland flew right out of her head.

Montgomery should wear a placard, some type of warning stating he was dangerous. The tips of her fingers tingled, as if they sought to touch the planes of his face and smooth over his jaw.

Was that permissible? Or was it considered wanton? And was wanton the same as common?

Montgomery's hand lingered on her breast, his fingers trailing over her skin. He kissed her until her face was hot, and her lips felt swollen. Her heart was beating fast, and other parts of her body were throbbing in time.

She had never been so thoroughly enchanted.

Her hands rested on his shoulders, and when he moved to kiss her throat, her head dropped back to allow him . . . anything.

When he kissed the base of her throat, she held her bodice open for him. When she heard the fabric of her shift rip, she wished, in a fleeting and forbidden thought, that he'd managed to remove her corset as well. As it was, her breasts were plumped up in a manner that was most assuredly lascivious and thoroughly naughty.

She almost fainted when he kissed her there, and when Montgomery drew a nipple into his mouth, she felt it throughout her body. First one breast, then another, his cheeks hollowing as he sucked on her. Her hands reached up to trail through the hair at his temples, measuring his cheekbones and the angle of his jaw. When he would have pulled away, she kept him in place, pressing her palms against the back of his head.

Oh my.

His hand trailed beneath her skirt, and she shivered when she felt his palm against her thigh. His fingers pulled on the bow of her garter, shocking her further.

Did he think to undress her here?

"Montgomery," she whispered frantically.

"Veronica," he said, his voice soft and smooth and seductive.

"Should you be doing that? Here?"

"No," he said. "I shouldn't."

He did not, however, stop. His fingers began to walk up her leg.

No one had ever mentioned something like this might happen. No one had ever warned her she might be ravished in the parlor.

Montgomery was stroking her skin as if learning every inch of her.

She should have begged him to stop. Instead, she shockingly wanted to be naked so no barriers of corset and petticoats and hoops stood between them.

"Oh, pardon, Your Lordship."

Montgomery froze.

She kept her eyes closed, holding her breath, shocked into immobility. She kept her cheek against Montgomery's. If she couldn't *see* Mrs. Gardiner, then the housekeeper wasn't there.

"What is it, Mrs. Gardiner?" Montgomery asked, flattening his hand against the apex of her thighs. His fingers danced over her skin, horrifying her.

Was he going to continue to ravish her in full view of Mrs. Gardiner?

He placed his other hand against her back, pressing her against him. Perhaps Mrs. Gardiner wouldn't see her bodice was gaping, her breasts visible, her nipples wet from Montgomery's mouth.

"I've prepared a hamper for your journey, Lord Fairfax. Is there anything else I can do?"

Go away. Oh, please go away.

She'd never been so embarrassed in her life.

A moment ago, she was willing to be taken on the parlor floor. Now, she wanted to sink into that same floor and disappear.

"Thank you, Mrs. Gardiner. We don't require anything further."

She still didn't move. He brushed aside her hair to whisper in her ear, his voice sounding amused.

"She's gone," he said.

"She was never here," she said. "Never here, Montgomery."

Brushing aside his hands, she buttoned her bodice herself, noting with some dismay his hand hadn't moved from beneath her skirt.

His fingers toyed with her garter again, and she grabbed at it outside her skirt.

"Stop that!"

"You're right," he said, his eyes glittering, his smile producing the dimples she'd once suspected. "The rest will have to wait, Veronica."

She couldn't breathe again, and that pulsing ache was only growing. She wanted to touch him, stroke her palms up his chest, down his arms.

He should be half-undressed as well.

With some regret, she pulled away from him and stood, straightening her skirt with deliberation, her gaze focused on the action of her hands. She would *not* look at him.

What had happened?

Was that seduction?

Because if it were, she knew why all the warnings had been issued to her and to any unmarried woman. If she'd known, if they'd all known, what seduction was like, they would have fallen, moaning, into the hands of their seducers, begging for more of the same.

Chapter 10

By the time they reached Inverness, Veronica was furious with her new husband.

For hours, she'd sat beside Montgomery in the first-class cabin with a dozen other people, all prosperous citizens. The accent of Scotland welcomed her home, and the closer they got to their destination, the more grateful she was to Montgomery for making the journey possible. Her gratitude did not, however, offset her irritation with him.

Montgomery had been taciturn, if not downright forbidding, for the whole of the journey. Whenever she was tempted to broach a subject, he'd send her a look, and she'd keep silent.

After a full twenty hours aboard the train, they'd finally reached Inverness station in the middle of a storm.

The station was very loud, its tall, pitched roofs and ceiling windows echoing the rain. Dozens of arches led from one platform to another, each of them filled with talking people, purposefully walking toward their destinations.

She waited while Montgomery finished attending to other matters, and when he joined her, they hired a carriage.

"I wanted to meet with the stationmaster," he said, as they entered the carriage. "The trunk containing the mirror came from Inverness station."

"Was he able to tell you anything?"

Montgomery shook his head as he settled opposite her.

Tomorrow, they'd finish their journey to Doncaster Hall, but tonight they'd stay in Inverness, in a hotel, information Montgomery had imparted before leaving London.

Their departure from London had been accomplished with some rapidity, a fact for which she'd be eternally grateful. She'd only had time to utter a hurried thank-you to Mrs. Gardiner before being rushed into a carriage. She had not, blessedly, had to face the woman for long.

Montgomery had no such reserve. He'd thanked the housekeeper, spoken softly for several moments, giving her instructions as to the care of the house, no doubt. Was he returning to London? Were they?

Twice, she almost asked him. Twice, she stopped herself from asking.

As they traveled through the city, Montgomery remained silent.

He was too easy to read, his emotions a combination of grief, irritation, and an odd touch of anxiety. Why was Montgomery anxious? She knew he wouldn't tell her if she asked.

"You were more communicative to me when I was drugged," she said, jerking angrily at the bonnet ribbon before retying it in a perfect bow. She hated bonnets, hated wearing anything on her head. "Is it me? Or are you simply this uncommunicative around everyone?"

Montgomery didn't say a word, didn't even glance toward her.

"I felt my lips move, Montgomery. I know I spoke."

There, that garnered her a glance before he once again stared at the rain-streaked window.

She leaned forward, looking into his eyes. "I was just assuring myself you were awake," she said, sitting back. "Very well, shall we talk of the weather? It's raining again. We've now exhausted that topic." She glanced out the window. "The scenery? It's difficult to discuss the scenery when it's raining so hard. One could say everything looks a bit watery."

They crossed the River Ness on the Black Bridge, the wooden timbers making a hollow sound of welcome.

"Tell me about America," she said. "Tell me about Virginia. Or your home there." She was searching her mind for a list of other acceptable topics when he smiled at her.

"You don't like being ignored, Veronica."

"I have spent the last two years being ignored, Montgomery," she said. "I'm quite used to it. I was not, however, expecting it from my husband."

Especially after he'd seduced her in the parlor.

"My home is called Gleneagle," he said, turning his head and staring out the window at the curtain of rain. "My grandfather was both its architect and its builder, and he named it as well."

"Do you grow tobacco in Virginia?"

He glanced at her, evidently surprised. Both the look and its implication annoyed her.

"A woman can be educated, Montgomery."

"Yes," he said. "Tobacco, as well as a variety of other crops."

Now, what did she say? She didn't want to ask this question, but she did so anyway. "Do you miss it?"

"With my whole heart," he said.

The emotions swamping her weren't difficult to understand. Fear, because she faced the unknown. Would Montgomery remain in Scotland or return home? Regret, because she didn't want to be transported to a strange country, and sadness, because a man should evince that kind of longing for a person, not a place.

Yet what would she have done if he'd mentioned someone?

She wanted, almost desperately, to ask about his grief. For whom did he mourn?

Rather than looking at him, she concentrated on the passing scenery. The rain had lightened a little, enough to see the river. She'd visited Inverness often, and the series of bridges in the city had always fascinated her.

Inverness reminded her of her parents.

"I didn't want to marry you either," she said, a few minutes later. "If I'd had my say, I would've chosen almost anyone else. A stranger on the street, a lamplighter in the square. If he talked to me periodically and didn't look through me as if I were a pane of glass, he'd be a very acceptable husband."

He glanced at her, the corner of his mouth turning up.

"Do I amuse you, Montgomery?"

"Yes," he said, startling her. "You do."

She looked away, uncertain whether to be offended or hurt.

"I had no intention of being rude," he said.

Something in his voice made her turn and look at him again.

"I understand," she said, her irritation banished beneath her compassion. "Truly I do."

He sat back against the seat and closed his eyes.

"Your clairvoyance again?"

"I know Scotland is strange to you. I know what it's like to have everything you'd thought familiar and normal suddenly vanish," she said. "I know what it's like to look around and see that your entire life has changed."

His eyes opened, his gaze intent.

"Is it permissible to ask you about the war?" she asked.

Anything she'd learned about the American Civil War had come from newspapers, and she wasn't certain her information was accurate. She was willing, however, to talk about anything rather than be ignored.

"How did the war affect you?"

He smiled, but the expression didn't have any humor in it.

"How it affected me?" He shook his head a little as if to negate the question.

She lowered her gaze.

"Very well, I'm not to ask about the war. Will you please tell me what I am to talk about?"

"People who don't know anything about war always want to know everything about it. Do you want to know if I got sick the first time I killed a man? Or how I lay on my pallet at night staring up at the stars, wishing I could somehow transport myself home? How, at the end, I didn't care much about anything, even my own survival? I lived because of luck, Veronica, not because I wished it or even wanted it. I lived because I didn't die, and that's how war affected me."

Perhaps it would be safer to distance herself from Montgomery just as he distanced himself from the world. In her case, it would be for protection, to prevent him from hurting her, or fascinating her, or even seducing her.

Was it the same for him?

Still, she wanted to say something to ease him, to take away a little of his pain, but she had no words. She'd tolerated the kindness of people after her parents' death but wanted them gone more than she'd wanted to hear their condolences. So she said nothing, an intention lasting until the carriage halted in front of the hotel.

"Will you come to my bed tonight?"

She clasped her hands together, forced herself to meet his look, refusing to glance away.

"Is it a Scots thing?" he asked. "This directness of yours?"

"I think it's mostly a Veronica thing," she said. "Isn't it better to ask than to wonder? To discover, rather than to guess?"

For the longest time, he didn't answer her, and she wondered if he was going to retreat into silence once more. If he was, she'd follow him. Perhaps, in the future, people would remark on how attuned they were, how they didn't need to converse. They wouldn't know she and Montgomery had simply stopped speaking to one another.

"Please do not tell me we're strangers, Montgomery," she said. "You've had your hand up my skirt and your mouth on my breasts."

She could *not* believe she was saying those things. Her skin was prickling with embarrassment.

"You would have no objection to bedding a man you hardly know?"

"Not if he's my husband."

He nodded. "You're very dutiful."

"Dutiful?" She smiled. "I doubt if it's dutiful. It must be done, and I'm all in favor of doing it. It's what one does, after all, when one is married."

He folded his arms and stared at her as if she were the most unusual creature he'd ever seen. She wasn't certain it was a polite look he was giving her.

Since she'd already revealed herself, probably too much, she continued. "I am told I shall not like it one little bit. I'm supposed to close my eyes and think of the Queen." She doubted that was entirely true, if the experience in the parlor was any measure.

"You're a very well made man, Montgomery. I doubt I'll dislike seeing you undressed. As for me, you'd know only too well what I look like naked. We might as well get down to the act itself."

He still didn't comment.

The carriage door abruptly opened, and Veronica felt as if she'd been saved from the further embarrassment of being unable to stop herself from talking.

She smiled brightly, pasting an expression of such utter bliss on her face that anyone looking at her must surely know she was terrified.

Chapter 11

Veronica had never stayed at a hotel before, but The Royal George Hotel had been visited by the Queen herself, they were told. The manager who made that announcement also escorted them into the building under a wide umbrella before ringing for a chambermaid to escort them to their room. They were given demonstrations on the various amenities, the location of the buzzer to ring for assistance, and directions to the hotel's dining room.

When they were left alone, she was surprised at how much smaller the room suddenly felt.

The iron bed was enormous, taking up most of the space. The mattress looked as if it were double the size of her bed at her uncle's home. A small table, two straight-backed chairs, and a washstand comprised the rest of the furniture in the room. A small fireplace was set into one wall, while two windows on the far wall boasted a view of the river through a curtain of rain. Although it was early afternoon, the day was as dark as night.

The chamber was pristine. The hotel was lovely, the staff amenable. She could find no fault with her accommodations.

The problem was her husband.

"Are you hungry?" Montgomery asked.

She shook her head. They'd eaten the contents of Mrs. Gardiner's hamper during the first part of the trip, and taken tea when they'd arrived at the station.

"Then we'll begin, shall we?"

She glanced at him, her eyes widening.

He walked up to her, brushed aside her hands, and began unbuttoning her bodice. She slapped his hands away, as useless as batting away the sun. He just waited until she stopped before beginning again.

"It's still daylight!"

"Somewhere," he said, unconcerned.

He finished unbuttoning her bodice and moved to her cuffs. Soon, she was divested of her bodice, watching as it sailed across to room to land in the corner.

One of them should behave with some decorum. Shouldn't she? After all, this business of losing her maidenhood was a serious one.

"If you mean to scare me," she said, "I have to tell you I'm not frightened."

He halted in the action of unlacing her corset to glance at her.

"What a hell of a thing it would be if you were," he said, once again concentrating on his task. "Intimidation is equally shared, you know. After all, you've demanded I take your virginity from the moment the ceremony was finished."

She blinked several times, trying to act nonchalant as he loosened her corset and pulled it off. In seconds, it, too, was flying across the room.

"I suppose I have," she said, considering the matter with what attention she could since he was working on the fastening of her skirt.

Something sparkled in his eyes, something she couldn't identify. At that particular moment, she didn't know if she'd made him angry or if he was amused. Nor did she have the concentration to use her Gift.

Bending his head, he pulled her skirt free and watched as it sank to the floor. He extended a hand to help her step out of it.

"Let's just get this done, shall we?"

"It's not a chore," she said, frowning. "Or is it?"

He took her hand and pressed it against his trousers until she felt something very hot and very hard there. He felt as large as a mastiff she'd once seen, trailing after a bitch with his mouth hanging open and his instrument fully erect.

"Oh."

"Yes," he said. "Oh."

"I quite enjoyed what we did in the parlor," she said.

"Did you?" he asked absently.

She was down to her shift, hoop, stockings, and pantaloons.

"Shouldn't you close the drapes?" she asked.

"I would, but I don't want to stop."

"Oh."

"I want to see you naked again," he said, pulling at the tabs holding her hoop. "Have I rendered you speechless, Veronica?" he asked, as it collapsed to the floor.

She nodded as she stepped out of it.

"I shall have to remember exactly what I was doing when that happened."

"I believe I can remember," she said, since he was kneeling before her, reaching up to roll down her stockings. Her pantaloons had a large slit in them to accommodate certain personal needs and were hardly any protection from his eyes.

She looked anywhere but at him.

He pulled the ribbon of one garter free, his fingers

trailing a path of heat from her thigh, over her knee, down her calf, to stroke around her ankle.

Veronica wasn't the least ticklish, but she could feel each movement of his index finger.

She licked suddenly dry lips and wondered when it had become so warm in there. Why wasn't he undressing?

Were they going to have relations with the curtains open?

Her eyes widened at the touch of his fingers on the drawstring of her pantaloons. He was standing in front of her, gently pushing them off her hips. Not simply content to allow them to fall, he was following the garment with his palms, feeling every inch of her.

Her heart was beating so furiously she was breathless, incapable of speech. Incapable, too, of telling Montgomery he really should not look at her in quite that way.

The same way the mastiff had when the bitch glanced over her shoulder at him, slowed, and braced herself in the dirt.

Oh my.

A lock of hair had tumbled onto his forehead. He wore the strangest smile, an expression that was definitely not amused. Intent, perhaps, as if this task took all his focus.

His fingers hooked in the scoop neckline of her shift and began to pull. She slapped a hand over his.

"Please don't rip it. It's my only shift."

"Only?"

She nodded.

He frowned. "The Earl of Conley is a wealthy man."

She bent her head, concentrating on the floor, his shoes, and his trousers. Her gaze crept up his legs, hesitated. If she placed her hand there again, would she feel the same hardness? Or was it possible that he'd gotten even larger?

"Veronica."

Her face warmed as her gaze flew to meet his.

"Why don't you have more than one shift?" he asked gently.

"Uncle Bertrand had not expected to bear the expense of clothing and housing me," she said.

His face changed a little, but the emotions she suddenly felt from him were like tinder exploding in a fireplace.

"Just how many times did he utter that little comment to you?"

She placed her hand against his chest.

"You cannot blame him, Montgomery. I was his sister's daughter, not his own child."

"You're family."

"Should we be discussing Uncle Bertrand now?" she asked. "I'd just as soon we didn't."

He nodded, bent, and grabbed the hem of her shift before pulling it over her head.

She was naked again.

His large hands cupped her breasts, his thumbs brushing against the nipples. His attention was not on the action of his hands, however, but on her face.

Veronica could feel heat rush through her body, pool in the core of her.

What did he want?

Her hands reached up to grip his wrists. Instead of pulling his hands away, she merely kept her fingers there, feeling the beat of his heart at his wrists. A beat as rapid as her own.

Her legs trembled; her entire body shivered, not from the cold or even anticipation. What she felt was something different, something that hollowed out her insides, pushed aside all reticence and shyness.

Anything he wanted, she'd do.

"Will you kiss me?" she asked.

"Now?"

He smiled, an almost wicked smile, one that fascinated as much as it charmed.

"Please."

He leaned forward, placed his mouth softly over one nipple.

That wasn't what she'd meant.

His tongue flicked her nipple, his lips gently surrounding, sucking.

Her hands moved to curve around his shoulders.

"Montgomery," she said. That was all, just his name.

He stepped back, removed his jacket and vest, his eyes never leaving hers. Instead of touching her again, he turned her slowly, wrapped his arms around her, his shirt and trousers gently abrading her bare back.

His arm covered her breasts, one wrist resting against a nipple, while his fingers brushed against the right. His other hand pressed against her stomach, pulled her back against him as he kissed his way down her neck.

She felt cut off from him in that position, distanced, as if he wanted to touch her but didn't want her to reciprocate.

His hand moved lower, his thumb playing across her navel, fingers combing through the soft hair at the apex of her thighs. She laid her head back against his shoulder, and he took advantage of the position to place a kiss beneath her jaw, his lips hot, his tongue tasting her skin as if to measure the frantic beat of her blood.

She felt as if she were melting against him. Her hips wanted to move from side to side, to guide his exploring, intrusive, talented fingers, but each time she did so, he pressed his hand flat against her stomach to still her.

Her skin felt hot, too tight, as if she were growing out of it.

The pleasure mounted until she could think of nothing but the strumming of his fingers. Her breath caught painfully, her hips moving as if he'd set them in motion. He was relentless, seeking another spot with his fingers, rubbing so gently she sighed and surrendered. Her nipples hardened, and a warm rush of heat pooled between her thighs.

How utterly wicked and wanton she was. She wanted to smile, to laugh in recognition of her own decadence. Montgomery was her husband and surely such actions were sanctioned. Even if they were never whispered about, or never discussed.

Reaching up with both hands, she gripped the arm binding her breasts, holding him as he explored her. Her knees felt weak. Her eyes squeezed shut on the feelings: anxiety to excitement, anticipation to pleasure.

She arched against his hand, needing the touch of him, craving the circular motion he'd begun between her thighs. She bit her lip as the pleasure mounted, laid her head back against his chest as the tension built.

"You're so beautiful," he murmured against her ear. "So responsive, Veronica."

She was almost weeping from the pleasure. He pressed himself against her bare bottom. He was hard, his breath ragged.

His fingers brushed against her nipple, then tugged at it.

Her hands dug into his arm, her hips pressing back against him, then against his relentless fingers.

He murmured words of praise, decadent comments that shocked and pleased her. His clothing was abrasive against her skin, the stubble on his cheeks was scratching her hot cheek. His lips were warm against her ear, his teeth sharp against her earlobe.

Nothing existed but Montgomery and pleasure. Nothing but pleasure then, the molten heat of it spreading through her, summoning her keening cry.

She sagged against him, but in the next moment, turned in his arms, pulled his head down, and caught his lower lip between her teeth. She gripped his shirt, wishing he were naked, hoping he'd soon be naked, needing him naked.

A pleased laugh rumbled in his chest as he lifted her in his arms, placing her gently on the bed. She lay there, spent, surrounded by pleasure as if it were a cloud. She watched him, marveling at the body revealed as he removed his clothing. Shirt, shoes, trousers, underclothes all flew into the same corner with her garments.

A moment later, he stood there, naked, the part of him that made him male standing erect. Fascinated, she reached out and touched him, feeling him hard and hot beneath her fingers. She stroked one finger down his length, watching as he quivered at her touch.

How magnificent he was.

What they'd done in the parlor hadn't hinted at this.

What was the proper word? *Coupling? Ravishing?* Thank God she was about to be ravished by this man. Or was *ravish* the proper term since she very much wanted what would come next?

She moved over on the bed, holding her hand out for him.

He joined her, supporting himself on his hands. Leaning down, he kissed her.

This was not a gentle kiss, or one in which he'd held something back. This kiss scorched her lips, sucked her breath, hinted at pleasures she'd never felt. This kiss darkened the room and sent her spiraling out of control.

A sound escaped her as her hands reached up and gripped his shoulders, fingernails digging into his skin.

The throbbing beat was back, hammering at her, transforming shyness into a primitive need as he worked his way across her breasts, nipping at them with his teeth, soothing her skin with his heated lips. She curled her hands around his head, pressing him to her.

His hands were busy, stroking her curves, palming her, fingers splayed, both gentle and intrusive. His mouth was on her again, breasts, shoulders, the inner curve of her arm, the base of her throat. Never leaving, never giving her a chance to recover or become herself again. She didn't know who this woman was but slipped into her heated body without protest, glorying in the sensations Montgomery gave her.

He moved away, and she answered his departure with a sound of protest. He smiled, then the smile faded as he lowered his head to kiss her once more. When he drew away again, she stroked her hands up his muscled arms, rested on his shoulders, and looked up at him, grateful she could see him in the faint light.

His eyes were heated, his face bronzed by passion.

Slowly, he raised himself.

She needed to brace for the pain, close her eyes and think of the Queen. She needed to remind herself that women through time had faced this anguish and survived it.

Her legs widened involuntarily, her hips rose to the exact angle to allow him penetration. He entered her gently, allowing her to accommodate herself not only to his size, but to the act itself. Yet what should have felt so foreign was oddly right, as if she'd been waiting for him to do exactly that. As if her body had patiently waited all those years to experience those very sensations.

He lowered his forehead to hers, his breath harsh.

"Am I hurting you?"

She shook her head from side to side. "It's quite an unusual sensation, isn't it?"

He raised his head.

"Is it?" he asked, his eyes glittering in the semidarkness.

She nodded. "It's like putting on a pair of leather gloves after they've been treated. Snug, but not uncomfortable."

"You're feeling a little snug yourself," he said. "Whereas, I'm feeling pretty damn good."

He drew slowly out as she watched his face. All amusement gone, his expression was now intent.

Her hips rose again as if to entreat him to reconsider. He entered her again, taking his time, deepening the penetration. She felt a slight pinch, but nothing more than that.

Her hips rose when he left her, fell when he returned, repeated the dance with her hands clenched on his shoulders, her eyes wide, her gaze fixed on his face. He braced himself on his forearms, entering her, then pulling out just as gently, a slow, measured, careful seduction.

Her breath caught; her throat unexpectedly closed on tears.

She wrapped her arms around his shoulders, closed her eyes, and held him as the rhythm between them quickened. He reached down between them with one hand, stroking her, coaxing pleasure with his fingers. She shivered where he touched, felt herself falling into darkness, then soaring higher. Her body bowed, arched up to meet his, and she cried out in surprise as pleasure washed through her again.

He buried his face in her hair as his body tightened. A second later, he whispered her name, drawing out the syllables in a voice turned silky, then collapsed on top of her.

She kept her eyes shut, her hands smoothing over his shoulders and the broad planes of his back, reveling in his body lying heavy on hers as if he claimed her still.

Too soon, he rolled over, his forearm over his eyes.

Was he disappointed in her? For long moments, they remained like that, neither speaking, or moving toward the other. Had she done something wrong?

"I was not supposed to move," she said in the silence.

He turned his head.

"A proper wife simply endures," she said.

She glanced at him in the gray light. "Is it proper to couple in the middle of the day?"

"It's not the middle of the day," he said, turning away from her.

Did other women feel the same as she did? Her lips were swollen, her cheeks chafed by his emerging beard. Her breasts were different, somehow, as if they were larger, more sensitive. Beyond the physical sensations, she was filled with both contentment and confusion.

Were other women as amazed?

"Have I done something wrong?" she asked, steeling herself for his cutting reply.

She told herself what they'd just experienced was mating, pure and simple. It had not been a spiritual joining or a deepening of their understanding of each other. They'd not become lovers; they'd merely consummated their marriage.

"Was it your aunt?" he asked. "Or your mother?" He turned his head and regarded her. "The person who told you that you shouldn't enjoy the marriage bed?"

"My aunt."

He nodded as if he'd suspected it.

"You did nothing wrong, Veronica," he said, sitting up on the other side of the bed.

He didn't say anything further, but she had the decided impression he could have filled volumes with what was left unsaid.

Montgomery moved from the bed to the washstand behind the screen. His trunks had been sent on to Doncaster Hall, so he went to his valise, where he'd packed enough clothes for the stopover in Inverness.

He believed in planning.

Planning had kept him sane.

Planning had kept him alive.

Planning had gone to hell the day he'd met Veronica MacLeod. Veronica Fairfax.

He didn't like confined places, and the room was just small enough to qualify. The other reason for wanting to escape lay in the bed, hair tousled, lips well kissed, a flush coloring her cheeks, a lambent look in her eyes.

She'd managed to seduce him when all he'd wanted was to consummate his marriage.

He'd lost himself in her. Exquisite pleasure had taken over his mind, his memories, and any anxiety he felt about coming to Scotland. Even with the memory of their lovemaking barely faded, she tempted him.

He left the room without looking at Veronica again, knowing if he did, he'd probably return to the bed. Passion was an opiate stronger than drink. He wanted her again and after that, probably again.

Outside the hotel, the air was balmy, almost soft to the touch, reminding him of summers at Gleneagle, when heat boiled up from the ground, and the breeze off the river cooled his skin.

Carriages and pedestrians forced him away from memory for a time, into an appreciation of the wooden bridge stretching across the River Ness, and a sky turning purple with dusk.

At home, when he was restless, he'd stroll from room to room at Gleneagle, or spend some time reading the newspapers he'd ordered from Washington. If his mind wouldn't settle, he'd leave the house and walk down the hill to the river. Occasionally, he'd take the road to the church that had once been at Gleneagle but had been relocated where it had found a larger congregation.

Sometimes on his walks, the moon was high and full, casting shadows and bluish white light over the fields. Sometimes, like now, the moon hadn't yet risen, and only a softly scented night greeted him.

Occasionally, either Alisdair or James would accompany him, as if his older brothers knew when he needed company. Trained for the law, he was not prepared to be a planter, but he'd handled his duties as well as he was able, stepping in when his family had needed him.

"You need to marry, Montgomery," James had said one night. "Your wife would keep you home and in bed."

James had been the tallest of the three, whipcord lean with broad shoulders and black hair. His angular face was covered by a beard, but his mouth was wide and habitually curved in a smile. His eyes were intense blue, the Fairfax eyes. They all had them.

"Ah, but you've stolen the best of the available women, James," he'd answered. "Why should I settle for second-best?"

"Caroline has a sister," James said. "You'd be doing

me a big favor if you'd consider courting Ethel."

He'd only sent James a look. Ethel was a petite blond with a habit of simpering and giggling. "One night with Ethel, and I might start walking and never stop."

"Well, it was worth a try," James said. "We're going to Richmond to visit Caroline's family before the unpleasantness starts."

"You just wanted company for future visits."

"Good Lord, yes," James said.

They hadn't spoken for a few minutes, and whatever they'd said after that he couldn't remember. Something one brother would say to another, a comment not meant to be recalled.

The unpleasantness had started, especially between the brothers. Alisdair and James had fought for the Confederacy. Montgomery had no choice but to join the Army of Northeastern Virginia. Ethel had stopped giggling and become a nurse, an example of selfless dedication. She'd died of a fever she contracted while caring for her patients.

And Caroline? He didn't want to think of Caroline.

On this wet and balmy spring night in the middle of Inverness, his brothers felt especially close. If he turned quickly, would he see James leaning against one of the bridge supports? Or Alisdair, staring off at the distance, transfixed by the view of Inverness, glittering in the near darkness?

What would they have thought of this journey of his?

They'd talked of coming to Scotland, to see the place where Magnus Fairfax had been born and raised. He'd never thought to make the journey without them, but then he'd been forced to do many things without family.

What would James have thought of Veronica?

She certainly didn't giggle, but she did act oddly from

time to time. Claiming she was clairvoyant, for one. Being a virgin who took to lovemaking like it was water and she'd been thirsty all her life, for another. Not that he would have told his brothers either fact.

He nodded to a few people, surprised at the friendliness of the Scots. The brogue of Scotland flowed around him, reminding him of his grandfather. It was one of the reasons he hadn't wanted to come. He'd not wanted to be reminded of Magnus Fairfax. He'd been closer to his grandfather than even his father, and his grief felt fresh here in Scotland.

The child he'd been had always thought his grandfather's rumbling voice sounded like thunder. He heard it then in his imagination.

"You're thinking dour thoughts, lad, when it's spring. It's time to think of the earth. Planting. Life."

Magnus Fairfax had always been so much a part of Gleneagle, it was odd to think he'd never walk the fields again, never look to the sky for rain.

A spring in Virginia was a busy time, filled with planting, readying the earth. Long, exhausting days measured the progress of the season. When they hit the beginning of the summer, they had a little respite from the sheer physical labor of planting time, not to mention the record keeping.

Montgomery leaned back against a support, watched the river flow beneath the bridge. Sometimes his heart was so filled with Virginia, he couldn't see anything else around him.

Inverness, and maybe Scotland, was tapping him on the shoulder and reminding him that it was the birthplace of the Fairfax dynasty.

A dynasty with only one member remaining.

His grandfather had been born here, had lived and left

for something new and better and more rewarding. Yet Scotland had locked itself into Magnus's heart. When his grandfather told a tale of Scotland, there'd been longing in his voice.

Tomorrow, they'd reach Doncaster Hall, and Montgomery would assume the responsibilities that circumstances had labeled his. Magnus wouldn't be with him. Nor would Alisdair or James.

He was the last Fairfax. The last member of his family, and it was somehow fitting he return to Scotland where it all started.

The question was, did he stay in Scotland?

Have I done something wrong?

Even here, Veronica's voice found him, plucked at his conscience. He wasn't comfortable talking to people, especially one who disturbed him as much as his wife.

Not only had the Fairfax family come full circle, but so had his thoughts.

What was he going to do about Veronica?

What was he going to do about Scotland?

Chapter 12

"**W**e should reach Doncaster Hall soon," Veronica said the next morning.

"Did you speak to the coachman?" he asked, surprised.

Edmund had, with his usual competence, arranged for a coachman from Doncaster Hall to be waiting at the hotel the next morning. The comfortable carriage they traveled in now was Montgomery's, the coachman his employee, and the woman sitting opposite him his very annoyed wife.

She didn't look at him when she answered, but she hadn't looked at him the whole morning. Even their breakfast had been a restrained affair, with Veronica deliberately focusing on her meal.

"Doncaster Hall is not far from where I used to live," she said.

"You never told me that, Veronica."

"If you recall, Montgomery, I've not been encouraged to converse."

In that, she was correct, but it annoyed him she refused to do so when he wished her to.

"Tell me about your home," he said.

"No," she said, glancing over at him. "I don't think I will."

"You didn't do anything wrong," he said gently. "Quite the contrary," he added, fascinated by the dull red flush sweeping over her face.

"Tell me about your home," he said.

"No," she said again.

She stared out the window, leaving him no recourse but to frown at her.

"Then tell me about Doncaster Hall."

"You'll see soon enough for yourself," she said.

"Are you angry with me? Because of yesterday?"

She still didn't look at him.

"I thought it was quite wonderful," she said, finally. "However, I don't wish to discuss that, either."

"I didn't hurt you, did I?"

She stared down at her hands, smoothed the leather over the backs of her gloves.

"Yesterday. I didn't hurt you, did I?"

"As I said," she said, raising her face to look at him, "I thought it quite wonderful. Didn't you?"

None of the women he'd bedded had ever asked him that question. He should have expected it of her. He didn't know if he was disconcerted or embarrassed.

"I was quite pleased," he said. What the hell did she want to hear? That he'd been astonished at her passion? That, even now, watching her work at her gloves, he wanted to pull her across the seat and make love to her? Or engage in a little play as they had in the parlor?

"Enough to do it again?" she asked.

No, it wasn't embarrassment he felt, but heat.

"I'd be a fool to say no, wouldn't I?"

She kept jerking her gloves tighter on each finger. He couldn't help remember what she'd said about his fit. He found her actions so arousing he had to turn and focus on the scenery.

He'd not expected the mountains around him, their scraggly peaks still capped with snow. The soil was barely a thin layer over a base of rock, as if the Almighty had sprinkled it over the Highlands as an afterthought.

As they traveled farther west, the earth began to sprout green, turning from rock to undulating glen. In the distance was the glimmer of a lake surrounded by a forest of pine. For a time, the road followed a glistening silver river before the rolling hills hid it from view.

He liked Scotland, and it surprised him that he did. He liked the mountains surrounding him, the scent of the air, different from Virginia. His home was young and vibrant. A seed dropped in the ground would boast a budding plant within days. This ground was harder and older. Any coaxing would be done with oaths and threats.

They stopped for a drink a few hours later at what Donald, the coachman, told him was the Well of the Phantom Hand. The water was cold, crystal clear, and welcome, as was the respite from the silence in the carriage.

When they resumed their journey, it was with the information they'd arrive at Doncaster Hall within the hour.

The hills varied in shape and size, some large, some smaller, all in varying shades of green from olive to emerald. The far-off glint of water hinted at the river they'd followed for a time.

The slope of one hill ended where another began, almost like interlocking fingers. The packed-earth road, wide enough to accommodate two wagons abreast, wound up and over each incline. Two deer looked out from behind a cluster of boulders, curious about the strangers.

"We're nearly there," Veronica said, as they crossed a

wide planked bridge, the wood darkened to a rich umber.

A glen, shaped like an arrowhead, opened up before them. On either side, the tree-covered hills seemed to point the way to another hill, one carpeted in emerald grass and topped by a sprawling house. A river, now wide and placid, sat like an engorged snake beside the home of the Lords Fairfax of Doncaster.

The breath stilled in his chest.

Before him, as if it had been magically transported from Virginia, was Gleneagle. Two long red brick wings jutted from either side of a center structure boasting a tall pitched roof. White-framed windows glittered in the morning sun. The river flowing around the base of the hill might have been the James, and the mature trees, some looking to be well more than a hundred years old, might be those he'd played in as a boy.

He closed his eyes. For a long moment, he kept them closed, fighting against a spurt of longing so intense it threatened to unman him. Then he tested himself again and opened them to find the scene unchanged.

"What is it, Montgomery?"

He forced himself to glance over at Veronica.

"Nothing," he said. How could he explain the rush of memory? Or the sudden awareness his grandfather had built Gleneagle as a reminder of all he'd loved in Scotland. How could he tell her that the ghost of the old man was beside him now, patting his shoulder in approbation?

He would sound as odd as she did when speaking of her Gift.

She remained silent, kindly allowing him his lie.

As they approached the house, the past surged up to welcome him. The circular drive to Doncaster Hall was the same as Gleneagle's. He half expected, when the carriage stopped in front of the door, to see all the people he'd loved rushing out to greet him. His brothers, Caroline, ghosts who had never seen this place, and never walked this ground.

The silence remained unbroken for long moments.

Finally, he gripped the door handle, pushed it open, and stepped down. He half turned toward Doncaster Hall as the front door opened, the yawning cavern revealing nothing for a moment. In that second, he held his breath, waiting. Was this heaven? Had he somehow died on the voyage to England? Had God rewarded him for his minuscule good deeds by conveying him to this place, this mound of earth so resembling the home of his heart?

Instead of Magnus or James, Alisdair, or even Caroline, the man who opened the door was a stranger to him, followed immediately by Edmund Kerr, his solicitor.

He turned, extended a hand to Veronica, and clasped hers too hard as she stepped down from the carriage. His wife then did something odd. She stood on tiptoe, one hand on his shoulder for balance, and kissed him on the cheek.

Before she pulled away, she whispered, "I'm here, Montgomery."

He was startled to see a look of compassion on her face. Was he so transparent she could tell what he was feeling?

"Welcome to Doncaster Hall, Lord Fairfax," Edmund said, striding to the carriage.

He turned to face his solicitor, conscious that Veronica had slipped her arm through his. Who was supporting whom?

"You made good time," Edmund said, smiling widely.

How odd that his solicitor had lost his dour appearance and now appeared almost jocular.

He nodded, still uncertain if he could speak.

Edmund gestured with a hand toward the house. "As you can see, this is Doncaster Hall."

Montgomery made a great show of patting Veronica's hand and studying the gravel before following Edmund up the path.

The wind surprised him. Soughing through the trees, it was almost a welcome, a greeting in some native Gaelic. He'd learned some of it from his grandfather, but not well enough to speak it without prompting. The sounds of the birds, however, fit into his memory of Virginia, as well as the sight of the eagles soaring overhead. This, too, was another facet of his home he suddenly understood. His grandfather had named the house in Virginia for an eagles' aerie in Scotland.

His entrance into Doncaster Hall was accompanied by the same odd feeling that he was in two places at once. Stretching up for three floors was an oval staircase, wide and dramatic, and carpeted in emerald wool. At the top of the staircase was an oval ring of Corinthian columns, each column a floor high. The view from the ground floor as well as the top was an ornately designed ellipse.

"The oval staircase, Your Lordship," Edmund said. "Designed by Adam himself in the last century. It leads to the public rooms. Would you like to have a tour now?"

He shook his head. "I think my wife and I would like to be directed to the family quarters," he said, turning toward the left wing. "They're through here, are they not?"

"Yes, Your Lordship," Edmund said, looking confused.

"The second floor," he said, testing himself. "The first door leads to the state bedroom, then a series of smaller bedrooms and dressing rooms and, finally, the owner's bedroom."

"The state bedroom was converted to His Lordship's bedroom," Edmund said. "A dozen years or more, sir." The man hesitated. "Have you been here before, Your Lordship?"

"No," he said.

"Yet you know the layout of the house."

He only nodded. His grandfather couldn't have known about the changes, but everything else about Doncaster Hall had been replicated at Gleneagle.

"I've heard about it," he said, an answer that evidently placated Edmund.

He glanced at Veronica, who was looking at him with a studied gaze. He hadn't fooled her. He needed time to understand what he was seeing before he discussed it with anyone.

Magnus had been a Scot, through and through, but he'd left the Highlands with bitterness under his tongue.

"The land couldn't support us, Montgomery. Not with all those sheep. It's why I'll not have the devils on my land." Magnus had ruffled his hair, then. "I'm raising a fine family of Scots here in America, boy. Men who are Highlanders in their hearts."

His grandfather had died before the war, before seeing his family torn in two. He'd died and been buried in the churchyard down the road before knowing what had happened to Gleneagle.

Now, Magnus Fairfax was here, his ghost as companionable as those of Alisdair and James and Caroline. Gleneagle was here, sprung forth from the land to welcome him in Scotland.

Who was being fey now?

"The staff would like to greet you," Edmund said. "They're arranged in the Round Parlor, Your Lordship."

The last thing he wanted to do was play Lord Fairfax,

but he waved Edmund toward the other wing of the house. He glanced at Veronica. She'd not released his arm, and, as they turned, she squeezed it, a wordless gesture to indicate her support.

"Shall we go introduce ourselves?" he asked.

She nodded, and he couldn't help wonder if she felt as dazed as he, albeit for different reasons. He decided to push his thoughts away until he could deal with them. Nothingness was easier.

They followed Edmund through double doors and into the River Wing, the side of the house facing the River Tairn. Although its dimensions were the same, the Round Drawing Room was different from its twin at Gleneagle, a fact Montgomery found to be a relief.

The room overlooked the sloping banks of the river and featured views of the rolling glens. Was this room used like the one at Gleneagle: a place for visitors to be greeted and impressed by the view, or impressed by Gleneagle itself? The power and the influence of the Fairfax family were evident once a visitor had been welcomed to their Virginia home.

Above him, the ceiling was festooned with ornate carvings, complete with plaster ribbons trailing from a center bouquet to each corner, where a dimpled cherub held one end. He was grateful to note that the mania for fringe and crimson dominating the living spaces of London hadn't reached Scotland. Instead, the walls were covered in a pale green fabric, the gilt furniture arranged in such a way that guests could walk close to the windows, or perhaps utilize the door to the left to wander to the terrace outside. A trio of sofas, accompanied by the requisite number of tables and lamps, were arranged in front of the massive white stone fireplace.

Arranged in a line from the windows to the door were

the men and women who comprised the staff of Doncaster Hall. An impressive number of people—short, tall, portly, slender—each attired in what were probably Fairfax colors, pale blue and white. Each woman and man bore a singular expression, one of sincere welcome that would have been flattering had he not felt as if the last quarter hour was out of time and place.

He forced a smile to his face and greeted each person, nodding as Edmund introduced them. Ralston was the majordomo, an older man with stiff, broad shoulders and boasting a thatch of white hair tamed in a leonine fashion. Mrs. Brody, the housekeeper, in turn introduced the rest of the staff, from Cook to the gardeners. He heard Veronica murmur greetings beside him, grateful she, at least, had been suitably trained in such details.

What the hell was a Virginian, schooled in the law, forced into war, and interested in an odd avocation, doing playing at being a lord of Scotland?

Veronica had never felt such blistering pain from anyone. The sight of this place, this house, had opened a door in Montgomery, emotions she'd only fleetingly felt earlier. Grief, mixed with despair and longing, rolled in waves from him. Even without her Gift, she would have seen the anguish in his eyes.

She gripped his arm tighter, just to let him know he wasn't alone. She was here, and she'd help in whatever way she could to banish that look in his eyes and the set, frozen expression on his face.

His responses were proper, if distant. His greetings were polite and a little cold. The warm welcome on the faces of the staff faded to caution. Here was a master who would not be as benevolent, their eyes said. Here was someone who would not care for their welfare as much as the 10th Lord Fairfax of Doncaster.

She tried to add what warmth she could in her smile, in her comments, but she was more concerned with the stiffness in the arm she held, an iron control she suspected was hard-won.

When they were done, the staff still stood at attention, as if expecting a speech from Montgomery. The man of an hour ago could have done it, but she didn't know if this man could push back the pain long enough to make the effort.

Montgomery surprised her, however, by striding to the windows, then turning and facing the group.

"Thank you for your welcome for me and my wife," he said, glancing at her.

She smiled in response, the perfect expression for such a situation. Thankfully, she'd been privy to many of Aunt Lilly's lectures on the decorum expected of the daughters of an earl. With any luck, the lessons would translate well to being the wife of a lord.

"I look forward to our continued cooperation in the months ahead," he said.

The staff smiled and nodded, but she saw more than a few confused glances. Why had Montgomery said months and not years? Had he decided to return to America after all? She pushed back the thought, keeping her smile firmly moored in place as he strode ahead of her, Mr. Kerr at his side.

"Shall I see you to the family quarters, Lady Fairfax?" the housekeeper asked.

She slowed, allowing her pace to match that of the older woman. It was just as well, she'd lost sight of Montgomery.

Mrs. Brody was older, with the confidence of someone

who knows she does her job well. Her hair was closer
to silver than white, arranged in a coronet at the top of
her head. An almost militaristic arrangement, as if she
cowed any stray tendrils into obeying. Her face bore a
few faint lines, especially around the corners of her eyes
and mouth, giving her the impression that the woman
smiled more than the role required.

"If you would, please, Mrs. Brody."

"You've the voice of Scotland," the housekeeper said
in surprise.

She nodded. "My home was not far from here," she
said. "Lollybroch."

The expression on the housekeeper's face changed
from polite interest to genuine delight. "I know the village well," she said. "We've hired several girls from there
over the years."

For a few moments, they discussed people each might
know. Veronica didn't explain her father's studious habits,
or the fact her mother had followed his lead. As a family,
they hadn't socialized, but she did add she hadn't been
home in more than two years.

"Once a Scot, always a Scot," Mrs. Brody said, reaching over and patting her arm in a gesture that would have
garnered a remonstrance from Aunt Lilly. In Scotland,
however, the lines between servant and master were often
blurred.

"Your husband, though, he's from America."

She nodded. "He is. Virginia."

"We've had a number of ours gone to America," Mrs.
Brody said. "It's a sight for one to come back."

She wasn't certain Montgomery was here to stay, another comment she didn't make to the housekeeper.

"Shall I tell you a little about the house, then?"

What she really wanted to know was why it had such

an effect on Montgomery, but she nodded. Otherwise, the housekeeper would no doubt complain to the majordomo, and the tale would slowly filter down to all the staff that the mistress had no interest in the house itself.

The corridor in which they traveled was filled with portraits, all done in the same style. A three-quarters pose, painted in front of rows of bookshelves, the subject staring out at the River Tairn.

"A tradition," Mrs. Brody said, noticing her glance. "Each of the lords has had his portrait painted in the Grand Library."

The men arrayed in the gallery did not bear much resemblance to Montgomery. No distinct familial traits were revealed in each successive portrait. No large nose or widely placed eyes, or ears that stuck out too much. No one had the distinctive blue eyes Montgomery possessed. Nor were any of the prior lords as handsome as her husband.

They mounted a set of stairs nowhere near as ornamental or magnificent as the oval staircase. Still, the banister was polished mahogany, and the balusters were ornately carved and dusted with gilt.

At the second-floor landing, she halted.

She'd not expected as much rich detail in the family suite as she saw. The emerald carpets were a perfect backdrop for the brass and crystal chandeliers. The walls were covered in a pale green patterned damask, while white vases and urns were placed throughout the hallway and on two long mahogany tables. Someone had filled the vases with spring flowers. The effect was not only welcoming but warm.

"We have the Best Bedroom here," Mrs. Brody was saying. "And the dressing room that goes with it. Then there's the Lady's Private Room next to that, and the Lady's Bedroom."

Mrs. Brody walked down the hall, gesturing with her hand toward the end of the hall. "That staircase leads to the nursery wing," she said. "Shall we go there first?"

"If you don't mind, Mrs. Brody, could you just show me the Lady's Bedroom? I find I'm extraordinarily tired from our journey."

A little lie, but surely one for which she'd be forgiven. She didn't want to see the nursery wing just then, didn't want to think of the future when it was so uncertain.

The housekeeper looked aghast. "Forgive me, my lady, of course you're tired."

She opened the third door in the hall, then stood aside for Veronica to precede her. "If you'll note the poppy seed heads in the plasterwork detail, Your Ladyship. That dates from the time the house was first constructed."

"It's quite a lovely room," she said, looking around her. The bed was smaller than she'd expected, more space being given up to the two armoires and vanity. The wallpaper, ivory with gold flowers, was lovely. The floorboards were covered in an ivory carpet with the same flowers replicated at intervals. A room fit for a Scots princess.

She was, at least, a Scot.

Mrs. Brody opened the door to the Lady's Private Room, which turned out to be three rooms: a bathing chamber and lavatory, a dressing room, and a small sitting room connected to the sitting room adjoining the Best Bedroom. Evidently, if a wife wished to communicate with her husband, she needn't leave her chamber and walk down the hall to do so.

"What an unusual arrangement," she said.

Mrs. Brody nodded. "Doncaster Hall has many secret corridors as well, Your Ladyship," Mrs. Brody said. "I would be more than happy to show you those as well. Shall we say tomorrow?"

She nodded her agreement. Doncaster Hall was like something out of one of her novels, complete with a handsome prince and hidden passages.

Clasping her hands together, she turned to face the housekeeper.

"It's a lovely suite, Mrs. Brody," she said.

"Perhaps you would like to join me in the attic tomorrow, Lady Fairfax. We've stored a lot of the furniture there. If you'd prefer something more to your taste. Of course, we employ carpenters as well. Or you might wish to have something brought from Lollybroch. Or even London. A great many of our furnishings have come from London, Edinburgh, and even Paris," she added proudly.

"I wouldn't change anything," she said honestly. "Not one thing."

After Mrs. Brody left her, she walked back into the sitting room. The wallpaper in the room was a blue-patterned silk, while the furnishings were overstuffed in a pale blue fabric, similar in hue to the shade the servants had been wearing. Was it called Doncaster Blue?

She stood at the window, gazing at the green sloping banks leading to the River Tairn. A gray horizon hinted at a coming storm. She'd missed a Highland storm.

She'd missed everything about her home, from the sound of the language, to the winds of the Highlands, to the feeling of belonging. Her accent wasn't unusual here; she shared a common ancestral history. She felt about this land the same way her countrymen did, as if there was something magical in each hillock, in each gentle swell of glen.

In a few months, all the surrounding trees would drop their leaves and prepare for the long winter but not before a dazzling display of autumnal color. The river would grow slower, then one morning it would boast a layer of ice. There'd be frost on the hills first, followed by snow. Spring would come gradually, creeping up on winter unawares. The air would grow warmer, then the green shoots and leaves would appear.

This was Scotland, her home.

This house could be her home as well.

On their quarterly visits to Inverness with her family, she'd seen Doncaster Hall from the main road. She'd been intrigued by the sight of the great sprawling house and thought it had looked unbearably lonely.

Yet the moment she'd walked into Doncaster Hall, she'd felt welcomed, as if the house hadn't been lonely at all, merely waiting for her. As if this place, in all of Scotland, was just where she should be.

Amazingly, she was the chatelaine of Doncaster Hall. She'd gone from being a poor relation to the wife of the man who owned this magical, wonderful house.

She was to live here, to share her life with a complicated, mysterious man who was beginning to fascinate her. She was invariably curious, but never more so than about Montgomery Fairfax.

Would any of her questions about him be answered? Was it even wise to want to know more?

Chapter 13

Montgomery headed for the hallway door beneath the first soaring arch of the oval staircase, Edmund following. If he was correct, the library was at the end of the corridor, overlooking a series of terraced gardens.

He smiled as he entered the room, with its deep-set mullioned windows and recessed ceiling. The walls were covered with floor-to-ceiling bookcases, and each shelf stuffed with well-worn volumes. Stucco medallions adorned the ceiling, and incised scrolls had been carved into the white mantel and fireplace surround.

The room was almost identical to the one he'd known so well.

The desk was different, of course, larger and older, the mahogany surface scarred from years of use; the blotter stained with ink. An oil lamp sat on the corner, adjacent to a silver pen holder and silver inkwell, both revealing a patina from decades of service.

He turned, leaned back against the front of the desk, folded his arms, and faced Edmund.

"My grandfather knew this place."

"It's quite possible he may have been employed here, Your Lordship,"

He leaned against the desk, folded his arms, and studied Edmund. "Explain."

"The 10th Lord Fairfax was very kind to many people in his family, sir," Edmund said stiffly. "He paid for their education. His father was equally generous. It's quite possible your grandfather worked for the 9th Lord until emigrating to America. It's equally possible the 9th Lord paid for your grandfather to do so."

If that were true, then his grandfather's accomplishments were even more amazing. Barely twenty years after he'd arrived in America, Magnus Fairfax had built Gleneagle.

"What happened to the 10th Lord's family? I know his children predeceased him, but what about his wife?"

"Unfortunately, Your Lordship, the lady was sickly ever since the death of her children. She died ten years before the 10th Lord."

"So he lived here alone?"

Edmund nodded. "For many years."

"You worked for him a long time?"

"Since leaving school," Edmund said. "Would you like to see the ledgers now, Your Lordship?"

"No, not now. Later is soon enough," he said, turning and staring out the window, an effective dismissal for Edmund.

Thankfully, his solicitor took the hint.

When he was alone, he walked around the desk and sat.

What the hell did he do now?

Something other than sit here, surveying his domain.

He should have felt some sense of triumph, returning to Scotland bearing a title Magnus had never thought to wear. Instead, all he felt was sadness for the boy who'd so loved a place he'd built its twin in a faraway country.

Standing, he left the library, taking the back stairs, that were exactly where he'd expected them to be, and left Doncaster Hall.

* * *

"I do think we should visit poor Veronica at the first opportunity," Amanda said, taking the packages from her mother. The Countess of Conley did not like to be encumbered with her purchases.

She truly liked these outings with her mother; it was one of the few times they were alone. Otherwise, one of her siblings was always trailing about, listening or talking.

"You didn't purchase the embroidery thread you wanted, Amanda," her mother said, signaling their coachman. He inched forward on the crowded London street, and her mother headed toward the curb, leaving Amanda to follow.

"I changed my mind," she said. Her financial situation was such that she had only a few coins left until her quarterly allowance in two months. Her parents expected her to use her own money to purchase those items she wanted rather than needed. Did they realize how very expensive new gloves could be? Or that perfumes from Floris were almost ruinous in price?

Her mother looked askance at her. "Have you forgotten, dear Amanda, that Veronica is newly wed? I would not be so gauche as to interrupt those first tender weeks of marriage."

"Nor would I normally suggest it," she said, handing the packages to her maid. "If we were well acquainted with Montgomery. He's an American. He's a stranger to us although not much of one to Veronica." She allowed her voice to trail off to a sigh that garnered her another sideways look from her mother.

"They were married because of scandal, Mother. However inappropriate it may be, however, I can't help think it would be wise to see, for ourselves, that Montgomery is a good husband." She pressed her hands together, almost prayerfully. "Marry in haste. Repent in leisure."

"There is that," her mother said, preceding her into the carriage. "Why are you so set on visiting Veronica?"

Amanda felt a fluttering deep in her stomach, a feeling too like fear to be comfortable. "I have my own reputation to consider, Mother. If Veronica will do anything to shame us, as a family, I would rather be forewarned."

"Whatever do you mean?"

"She might return to London," Amanda said.

"Why on earth would she return?" her mother asked. "She married a lord. Granted, it's only a Scottish title, but, nonetheless, she's a Lady."

"If her marriage is an unhappy one," Amanda said, "where could she come but back to London? After all, we're the only family she has left. What other recourse would she have?"

"She wouldn't think of doing so," her mother said, but her expression left no doubt the idea was worrisome.

"Unless, of course, Mother, you've already instructed her such behavior would not be tolerated." She settled in next to her mother, smoothed her gloved hands over her skirt, and frowned at the maid who tripped over her own feet. "Which I'm sure you did."

"Of course," her mother said. A moment later, her mother spoke again. "Do you think she truly would? Return to London? How utterly shocking that would be."

She only glanced at her mother and smiled weakly. "Veronica has already behaved in quite a shocking manner. To return home . . ." She withdrew her handkerchief and pressed it to her mouth as if she couldn't quite manage the rest of the words.

"A few weeks would not be too intrusive," the Countess of Conley said. "After that, a young couple should be receiving visitors. Even an American and a Scot should know how to comport themselves."

Amanda sat back, pleased. Her financial problems might soon be solved.

Thunder raged and bellowed against the walls of Doncaster Hall. Rain sheeted the glass, added weight to the leaves until the branches of the trees hung low. No soft and gentle downpour here. This was the land of God's tantrums.

Veronica stood at the window of her bedroom, studying the dark gray sky, her mind filled with thoughts of Montgomery.

She hadn't seen him since he'd left her earlier. Was she supposed to go in search of him? Was she supposed to wait meekly until he noticed her again?

After yesterday, she'd thought they were to be husband and wife. After being abandoned for the day, his behavior mirroring their departure from London, she had the suspicion that being Montgomery's wife would not be a simple matter.

Was she supposed to go to him with her daily decisions? Her mother had always gone to her father, but in a spirit of cooperation rather than submission. Aunt Lilly's behavior around Uncle Bertrand had been different. She handled most things unless a domestic crisis erupted. Then Uncle Bertrand's word always took precedence. His decision was law.

Thunder rumbled again, announcing the arrival of a firestorm of lightning. She moved back from the window, standing in the middle of her new room.

She felt as if all her emotions had been contained in a leather cup and spilled on a tabletop. She could find sadness well enough because it was larger than the other pieces. Excitement? That, too. Confusion was there, as well as uncertainty, and gratitude. She was, above all, conscious of her overwhelming good fortune. Her husband was handsome, titled, and rich, and could bring her passion and pleasure so effortlessly it had felt like magic.

Turning, she studied the three trunks in the corner and sighed. She needed to unpack. The sooner she began, the sooner she'd finish.

She was halfway done with the first trunk when a knock on the door interrupted her.

Mrs. Brody stood at the door, accompanied by two maids.

"Your Ladyship," Mrs. Brody said, bobbing a curtsy, "I've brought you Millicent and Elspeth. They're both good girls, good workers, and have a wish to advance themselves in the world. You've the choice of either one."

Before she could speak, Mrs. Brody drew both girls into the room. "For your maid, Lady Fairfax. Your lady's maid. His Lordship said you'd no time to hire someone in London. I'm certain either girl would do well for you. You've only to interview them yourself. And if neither of them pleases you," she said, eyeing both girls severely, "then I can certainly find other candidates for the position."

She drew Elspeth forward. The girl had light brown hair, soft blue eyes, and a shy smile. She looked down at the floor when Mrs. Brody introduced her.

"Elspeth has been with us for a year now, and has served as the upstairs maid. I'd trust her with any of the finer furnishings in Doncaster Hall. In addition, she's shown great talent in removing stains and arranging flowers."

Millicent was strikingly lovely, with brown hair, brown eyes, and a wide mouth that would have been more attractive had it been arranged in a smile. At the moment, however, it was curved into an expression reminding Veronica too much of Amanda's sneer. Although Millicent was a young girl, lines were already forming above the bridge of her nose and beside her mouth, giving her the look of someone who disliked most of what she saw.

Millicent, who'd not appeared happy during the recital of Elspeth's talents, didn't wait for Mrs. Brody to introduce her.

"I've been here five years, Lady Fairfax. I began in the kitchens, then the laundry. I was a downstairs maid for a year before Mrs. Brody promoted me to the upstairs position. I'm in charge of caring for the public rooms, Your Ladyship. I'm quite good at hair, as well," she said, eyeing Veronica's hair with some disdain.

Elspeth still had not spoken. Her hands were clasped in front of her, and her gaze was on the carpet rather than staring defiantly forward.

Veronica instantly knew why she'd been given the choice. Mrs. Brody evidently did not want any more problems with Millicent than she'd already suffered. Veronica couldn't help wonder if the girl's transfer from position to position was due to Millicent's growing abilities or simply because she'd made everyone in her vicinity miserable.

She smiled at both girls. "I'm sure you can understand how difficult this choice is for me," she said. "Just as I'm certain both of you would be excellent in the position. However, there can only be one person serving as my maid." She glanced at Elspeth. "I could very much use your help."

The girl looked at her finally, and smiled, a particularly sweet expression. Millicent, on the other hand, frowned at both Veronica and Mrs. Brody, turned on her heel, and left the room before another word was spoken.

Mrs. Brody looked relieved.

"Elspeth," she said, addressing the young girl, "be about unpacking Her Ladyship's trunks. And putting yourself to good use, then."

Mrs. Brody closed the door behind her, leaving them alone. Before she could speak, however, Elspeth stepped forward.

"Mrs. Brody said I should not mention it to you, Your Ladyship. I think it would be wrong of me not to bring it up when it's on my mind so fiercely."

Elspeth hesitated, as if waiting for permission.

She nodded.

"I have a half day off on Sunday, and I was wondering if I could make that a half day off on Wednesday, instead. It's because of my Robbie, you see. He has a half day off on Wednesday and if we had the same half days, we could go home and visit his family in Lollybroch." She twisted her hands. "We're married you see, only a few months now, and his mother is ailing."

"Lollybroch?" she asked. "What's his family name?"

Elspeth frowned, then smoothed her face of any expression. "Cadell," she said.

"He's a blacksmith?"

"His father was," Elspeth said, her frown remaining in place. "Robbie does the same here. Work at Doncaster Hall keeps him busy, not like Lollybroch. How did you know, Lady Fairfax?"

"I grew up in Lollybroch," she said.

The frown was replaced by a look of surprise. "The village is not all that large, Your Ladyship. Robbie would have mentioned."

"We lived outside the village," she said. "On the other side of McNaren's Hill."

Elspeth had such a revealing face. Her eyes were swimming in compassion.

"Are you the MacLeod girl, Your Ladyship?"

When she nodded, Elspeth smiled. "I've heard tales of you. Robbie's family will be pleased to hear."

"Give them my greetings," she said. "And my best wishes to his mother. She was always very kind to me when I was a little girl."

"I'd heard you'd gone to London, Your Ladyship. How strange you married an American and come home. And now you're Lady Fairfax." Elspeth's smile was so bright it could have coaxed the sun out from behind storm clouds.

"Wednesday is fine with me, Elspeth. Would you like me to talk to Mrs. Brody for you?"

The girl looked relieved and nodded.

She and Elspeth spent the next hour finishing the chore of unpacking her trunks and arranging her belongings. After her trunks were unpacked, Elspeth showed her how to work the taps in the bathing chamber.

"We have our own boiler," Elspeth said. "The old lord was all for us taking a Saturday night bath for services on Sunday. Will the new lord be leading the services, Your Ladyship?"

She hadn't any idea and wondered if Montgomery knew of that duty.

After they'd finished, she sent Elspeth to her dinner after Mrs. Brody arrived with a tray Veronica had requested. She'd take time with her meal and try not to wonder about Montgomery.

A task she set for herself, and one in which she knew she'd fail.

Chapter 14

The night was crisp, cool, and oddly clear, as if the thunderstorm earlier had washed the air. The damp grass glittered in the moonlight, raindrops sparkling like stars.

Montgomery slowly took the path through the trees.

He felt a twinge in his right knee brought about by the dampness of the night. The accident resulting in his injury had been a foolish one. He'd landed on the roof of a church, but at least he hadn't tumbled to the ground.

By such small things were his life measured.

If he'd read between the lines of Caroline's letters, he would have found a way to go home. Caroline would have lived, and he'd be at Gleneagle.

If a trunk hadn't been delivered to his house, he would never have gone to the Society of the Mercaii. Veronica MacLeod would have been ruined. She might have ended up on the streets, a gentlewoman spurned by her family.

Instead, she was his wife.

If he hadn't read one particular article in the newspaper, he would never have begun a correspondence that led to his avocation, and in a way, his survival.

Shielded by the overgrown oaks and aspens of Doncaster Hall, he stood and listened to the droplets of rain falling from the leaves. A discordant melody having no rhyme, meter, or pattern. A reminder, perhaps, that he'd lost his own patterns in the last five years.

Once, the seasons had measured his life: planting, harvesting, drying tobacco being the framework for everything else. Now, he didn't have that. Gleneagle and Virginia society had provided structure. Both had been a testing place for his manners, his charm, and his abilities.

Few of the great families were left; the stunning beauties were pale, wan, and ravaged by war, and wealth had disappeared. Any opportunities had bled into the earth along with the lifeblood of most of Virginia's proud young men.

Here he was, though, a lord in a country he'd never considered home, heir to an estate and a fortune that made Gleneagle's once not-inconsiderable affluence look paltry in comparison. He was steward of an empire requiring his participation and interest.

How was he going to be what Edmund decreed he should be, what Veronica no doubt deserved? How was he going to manage to be a proper Lord Fairfax, a decent, caring husband?

His nightly walks were commonplace to him now. In London, he'd almost welcomed the danger of them, even being so incautious as to head toward the center of the city, daring someone to accost him. No one had, and he'd been curiously disappointed.

He took the path down the hill to a shallow brook, tinted silver by a looming moon. He climbed to the top of a nearby hill, surveyed his gray-white kingdom, and felt loneliness pull at him as if it was a carrion bird pecking at his innards. At times, he wanted simply to dissolve into nothingness, or grip something tight and hold on to it in desperation.

Would the wagons arrive tomorrow? He'd already spotted an outbuilding he could convert to a work space. The structure had once been used to make whiskey, he'd been told, and was unsuitable to house animals. All he wanted was a tall, steep-roofed structure, with space enough to work on his navigational designs. The building, still referred to as the distillery, would fit his needs perfectly.

He kept walking. The night air was cool, but not so much he was uncomfortable. In the last five years, he'd endured worse conditions.

Montgomery, are you well?

"Caroline," he said softly, and she appeared in the night like a creature crafted of moonbeams.

He knew she wasn't real. None of the ghosts who visited him from time to time were real. Nor were they frightening. They didn't come to castigate him or offer blame. They came to ease his heart, to numb the pain because he missed them so desperately he'd created them to make life bearable.

Walking through the Scots night, he acquainted himself and his ghosts with the terrain, the feel of the curving earth beneath his feet. He headed toward an outcropping of stone, only gray shapes layered over black, and listened to the sound of the river.

"It's not the James," he said. His ghosts didn't answer.

You're a lord, Alisdair said, a note of amusement in his voice.

"You would have been," he answered. "If you hadn't died." Silence greeted that announcement.

He felt, rather than heard, Caroline's disappointment. She never understood that brothers had a duty to aggravate one another.

Your wife knows you're in pain, Caroline said.

He turned toward a lighter patch of tumbled rock. If Caroline were there, she'd be standing in the most prominent place. She liked the attention, always had a bit of drama about her. Was that why he'd ignored her? Because he'd no patience with histrionics?

You should tell her about us, Montgomery, she said.

He smiled. "That I see you? That I hear you?" he asked, facing the river, speaking to them in the silence of his mind.

You don't, you know, she said, softly, so much compassion in her voice his heart felt as if it were being sliced in thin little strips.

"I want to," he said.

Only the wind answered him, blowing his hair back, catching his coat, and billowing it around his torso. He closed his eyes, feeling the sharp bite of pain, the endlessness of it.

A little while later, he retraced his path back to the house, knowing sleep would come late that night, if at all. He'd become accustomed to his sleeplessness, accepting it as part of the price he paid for survival.

He'd known some poor souls who'd suffered head injuries in the war. They'd never been the same. Some had stared off into space as if seeing the past or the future. One or two had simply retreated into himself, arms wrapped around his knees, rocking back and forth as if trying to capture the time when he'd been a babe in his mother's arms.

His war injuries had been slight: a piece of shrapnel lodged in his thigh from cannon misfire, a scar on his right knee from a bad landing. Memories that never left him.

In the next few days, he'd have something on which to concentrate, an occupation bridging his past and present. He needed something familiar, and his airships would provide that.

As he stood staring at the main part of the structure,

lights greeted him from the family wing. He knew Veronica was still awake.

A silhouette stood at the window. Could she see him? If she did, what did she think about the strange American she'd married? Should he confess to her that he was still angry about their marriage? That he'd not wanted to be her savior and had become so reluctantly? What would Veronica say if he told her she annoyed him, confused him, and intrigued him too much for his peace of mind?

He could still feel her on his palms and the tips of his fingers, hear her soft moans, see the shocked awareness in her eyes as her body climaxed.

In her arms, he'd found intense pleasure.

Only a fool would resent that.

A few minutes later, he entered the house, took the stairs two at a time to his bedroom, passed through the lavatory to the sitting room, and opened the connecting door.

Veronica was standing there, still staring out at the night, a look he couldn't quite decipher on her face.

"I thought you'd be asleep," he said, walking toward her.

She turned to face him.

"I was waiting for you," she said, surprising him. "Have you been walking the grounds?"

He nodded.

She didn't ask what made him so restless, only reached out her hand to touch his arm. A gentle, wifely touch, one of reassurance and comfort. She'd done the same earlier, when he felt as if he were being pummeled by memory.

As he looked into her eyes, he wondered what, exactly, she felt from him. If he believed in such things.

He reached down and picked up her left hand. The back of her hand was soft, the tips of her fingers rough. Surprised, he examined her palm, and when she curled her fingers rather than allow him to see, he pulled her hand back.

"Why do you have scars on your hand?"

She looked away, and when he tried to uncurl her fingers, she pulled them back, wrapping her arms around her waist.

"Veronica," he said gently. "It doesn't matter to me. I merely wanted to know how you hurt yourself."

She glanced quickly at him, then away, but didn't answer.

He placed his hands on her arms, rubbed them slowly up and down, then gently pulled her into his embrace. Reluctantly, it seemed, she sighed and laid her head on his shoulder.

Surprisingly, he felt the cold hard center, that had been there since first viewing Doncaster Hall, begin to melt. Maybe this was what he needed, communion with another human being, the ability to touch someone, to feel her warmth.

Her breath tickled his neck, and he smiled. He turned his head a little, and kissed her forehead, the softness of her skin an attraction for his lips. His mouth trailed down her nose, over the edge of her jaw, and up to her temple.

His hands flattened on her back as she wound her arms around his waist, anchoring him there. He closed his eyes, breathing the scent of Veronica: warm woman and roses. Comfort and welcome, soft curves and passion: a lure he didn't want to ignore.

He released her from his embrace, but only enough to unfasten the buttons at her cuffs. She didn't speak, didn't question his actions. Slowly, he began to unbutton her bodice. Her eyes followed his progress, but she remained silent. He pulled her bodice free of her waistband and began to work on her skirt.

She stood, completely proper, yet about to become unveiled an inch at a time. Her bodice was open, but only a small square of skin was revealed. He bent to kiss that spot above her corset, feeling the increased pulse rate.

Although he would have liked to continue kissing his way down her body, he attended to his task, that of loosening the waistband of her skirt and freeing the tapes of her petticoat and hoops. If he'd been profligate, he would have simply sliced through them with a knife. He gave more than a passing thought to doing just that, with the reasoning he was wealthy again. What was money for if not to use it to one's advantage? He could certainly afford a few dozen petticoats and hoops, but just as he was at the point of leaving her in search of a knife, the knot loosened in his fingers. Slowly, he allowed the hoops and petticoats to drift to the floor, along with Veronica's skirt.

He slipped the bodice from her shoulders and watched as it slid down her arms, the material catching on her elbows. With a shake, Veronica loosened it, and it fell to the floor.

She was a Botticelli Venus. Instead of emerging naked from a shell, she stood straight, clad in her corset, shift, pantaloons, and stockings.

"Women wear entirely too many clothes," he said.

She didn't reply, but a look passed between them, one reminding him of yesterday.

He bent, pushing aside the frothy mountain of her garments to unfasten each shoe.

"Step up," he said.

Veronica put her hands on his shoulders for balance, lifted her foot so he could remove her shoes, one at a time.

She sighed, and he glanced up to see her eyes close, a smile curve her lips.

"Your shoes don't fit properly," he said, wondering why he hadn't noticed yesterday.

She looked down at him. "They aren't actually my

shoes," she admitted. "They belong to my cousin, Anne."

He sat back on his heels. "You don't have shoes?"

"I lost mine at the Society, remember?" she said.

"Along with your spare shift?"

She nodded.

"But I gained a husband," she said, before he could speak. Her glance encompassed the sitting room, the view beyond the darkened window. "And a palace in which to live. What's a pair of shoes?"

"Gleneagle had its share of seamstresses," he said. "No doubt Doncaster Hall does as well."

"And cobblers?"

He nodded.

Her garters were next, lacy little bits of silk. He untied them, pulled them from her legs, slowly pushing down her stockings one leg at a time. Only then did he stand, to see her face had flushed, reminding him that his bride, despite her response to him, was only one day removed from her virginity.

She flattened her hands against her thighs and fisted them.

Her knees were so perfectly formed that he stroked his hands over each, his fingertips delicately tracing a pattern behind them. She moved her leg, and he looked up, to find her lips curved in a smile.

"Ticklish?" he asked.

She nodded.

His palms made a leisurely path down her legs to the delicate curves of her ankles, fingers playing across the top of each pretty foot. Her toes clenched in the carpet, inciting him to smile. He rubbed his fingers over the red spots on her toes, wishing he had noted her ill-fitting shoes before this.

Sitting back, he allowed his gaze to travel up her

body, taking in the sight of Veronica being seduced.

Reaching up, he pulled at the drawstring of her pantaloons, then stripped the garment from her. The shift was entirely too modest, coming almost mid-thigh. He wanted her naked.

Without standing, he reached up and tugged at each corset string, grateful this knot, at least, was easily untied. When the corset was loosened, he grabbed it, hefted it in his hands, wondering why he hadn't noticed a day ago how heavy it was. Her shift was a well-washed linen, so sheer he could see the red marks around her waist. Standing, he pulled her shift over her head, tracing each line the corset had made.

Her breasts were perfect globes, with large coral areolas surrounding beautiful long nipples.

Bending his head, he kissed an angry-looking mark trailing from the center of her breasts to just above her navel.

Her swift inhalation of breath made him smile.

Her eyes widened, and her color mounted as his hand trailed down to cup her gently. Her lips parted as she made a movement against his hand. The fluid slide of his fingers was enough to make her tremble. He turned his head, kissed her softly on the temple, and murmured her name. Her hand gripped his arm, and he stilled the action of his hand, waited to see if she would pull away. She remained where she was, her eyes closed, lips parted, and a pink flush coloring her cheeks.

He didn't say a word, merely bent his head to kiss her lips lightly. Her mouth opened as she leaned toward him. He indulged himself in another kiss before pulling away. He had other things planned first.

He took her hand and walked her through the sitting room to his chamber. She pulled away at the door, returning to her room and extinguishing the lamp on the table before returning to his side.

Grabbing her hand again, he walked her up the steps and to the bed atop the dais. Only then did he release her, long enough to lift her in his arms and place her gently in the middle of the bed.

There she lay, a feast for him, her legs spread to reveal the glistening heart of her.

She was delicious, and he was so damn aroused he would have begged if she'd denied him.

He dragged off his shirt, his shoulders arching. He toed off his boots, watching her. Not once did she shield herself from him. Her arms rested at her sides, her hands flat against the coverlet. Her eyes were beginning to deepen in color, as if passion were heating her inside.

He wanted to explore every part of her. He wanted to taste and touch every inch.

Unfastening his trousers, he pulled his clothing off impatiently. Lowering himself to the bed, one hand traveled from her wrist, up her arm, across her shoulder, then down.

She sighed when he cupped a breast, teased the nipple. Slowly, his eyes still on hers so she'd have no doubt of his intent, he bent and took her nipple into his mouth. As he gently pulled with his lips, her hand came up to rest against his cheek.

His lips smoothed over her skin, teeth scraping against her curves as if to mark her as his. He was suddenly desperate to mate, urgent in a way he'd rarely been.

His fingers slid over her, into her as she flowed around him, liquid and soft. The feel of her was almost too much. Not yet. He wanted her panting and wanting before he entered her.

Her skin was flushed, felt hot; her eyes were closed as

he drew small circles around her softness, moving faster, then slower.

"Montgomery." His name was a siren call, a sweet, crooning sigh.

He raised his head, met her eyes, before moving down her body. When his mouth touched her, she gasped aloud in shock.

He placed his hands on each of her thighs, smoothing his palms against her heated skin as he spread her open. His mouth feasted on her as she made a sound in the back of her throat. Both of her hands flailed in the air, then gripped the coverlet. He felt her fingers dance across the top of his head, then her hips arch against him as he flicked his tongue across her.

She twisted in his grip as he tasted her, until she shuddered against him. and he was drenched with her passion.

He rose, looked at her. She lay splayed across the bed, her legs spread, her arms outstretched, her breasts heaving.

Her taste was on his tongue, the need for her a pounding beat in his blood.

He slid into her, bracing himself on his forearms, playing with the damp tendrils of hair at her temples. He moved over her like a shadow, a promise. She moaned, called his name as he rocked back and forth until he'd seated himself completely in her. He could feel her clench around him, almost came at that moment, the pleasure crawling up his spine and shivering through his body.

Her fingers dug into his shoulders, her eyes opened, dazed, alarmed, and pleased all at once. He wanted to fill her, lose himself in her, bury himself in the sweet heat of her body.

In her, he sought both forgiveness and forgetfulness.

Veronica gripped his shoulders, pulled him to her

with the tyranny of the aroused. Her eyes closed, and she peaked again, her surprised gasp of pleasure summoning another of his smiles.

A tear slipped down her cheek, and he closed his eyes at the sight of it, buried his face in her hair, and felt himself erupt in a gushing flood.

She wrapped her arms around his neck, held him tight. He moved to the side and pulled her atop him. She tucked her head against him, her breath against his neck. Her heartbeat mirrored his in its frenetic race. Her skin was damp; his hand stroked over the curve of her bottom possessively.

Words failed him. He couldn't think of a damn thing to say. Not only was he physically sated, but he felt almost at peace, as if this act, this woman, had the power to reach deep inside and ease all the wounded places inside him.

A few moments later, she raised her head, propped her chin on her folded hands, and studied his face.

What did she see there?

Uncomfortable with her wordless inspection, he moved her away from him, suddenly hoping she wouldn't speak.

When she was a little girl, Veronica had thought the world a magical place, where people like her, possessed of special gifts, were welcomed and understood. Maturity had left her with the knowledge people would never truly understand her Gift, and it was foolish to consider the world enchanted.

Yet, now, she wondered if she'd been wrong. What she'd felt with Montgomery had been nothing less than magic.

As he left the bed, she sat up, feeling self-conscious for the first time since he'd arrived in her sitting room. He went to where his trunks were stacked along one wall and unerringly chose the second to the last, opened it, and withdrew a robe. She'd thought he meant to wear it, but he returned to the bed naked, evidently feeling no shame about the state of his undress.

Why should he? He was so magnificently constructed that even then, when her body still thrummed from the pleasure he'd given her, she wanted to run her hands over his arms and legs, curve her palm around his shoulders, stroke his chest, and admire the man Providence, and her own impulsiveness, had made her husband.

He gently pulled her to her feet, placed the robe around her shoulders, helping one arm, then the other, into the sleeves. The robe felt like silk, sliding against her skin in a whisper of coolness. He folded one lapel over the other, wrapped the belt around her twice, then tied it in a bow in the front, as if she were a precious package.

She didn't know what to say to him. What words were proper? Should she even have any comments about what had just transpired between them?

Raising her hand, she placed it on the side of his face, her fingertips brushing against his night beard. Although he was clean-shaven, unlike most of the men of her acquaintance, his cheek was bristly.

They exchanged a long, wordless look, one that might be interpreted any way she wished. She gathered the material of the robe in one hand so she wouldn't trip and stepped down from the dais.

She halted at the door and looked back at him. He was standing there, still naked.

When Montgomery didn't speak, she left him, doing so with the sense that perhaps he'd have spoken if she'd only had the words or the wit to coax his thoughts free.

Chapter 15

Streaks of clouds in shades of orange, gold, and pink stretched across the sky like scarves tossed into the air. Veronica stood at the window of her bedroom, captivated by the sight of dawn in the Highlands.

Elspeth knocked on the door and entered, smiling brightly.

"Good morning, my lady," she said. "Isn't it the most glorious day?"

She wasn't certain what kind of day it was going to be, and wasn't that a pitiable thing?

The rumble of wheels prevented her from having to respond. A caravan of wagons, each piled high and covered with a canvas tarp, rumbled up the road and disappeared behind a nearby hill.

"What is that?" she asked.

"I suspect something His Lordship ordered," Elspeth said, coming to the window. "They've been coming for hours. Would you like me to go find out, Lady Fairfax?" Elspeth asked.

"No," Veronica said. "I'll go see myself when I'm dressed."

She flew through her morning ablutions, the only difficulty coming when Elspeth attempted to detangle her hair. Finally, she asked her new maid to simply gather it and cover it with a lace snood. No ringlets or elaborately styled hair softened her face. Her eyes looked too wide, their shade an unremarkable hazel. Her face was pale, her lips a little swollen, and softly pink.

Her maid was looking at her oddly, her head tilted to one side, her eyes narrowed slightly.

"What is it, Elspeth?"

"You look different, Your Ladyship, but I can't quite decide what it is that's different. Did you sleep well?"

Hardly at all, not a comment she'd make to her maid. She could feel warmth creep up her cheeks as she stood and grabbed her shawl.

"Mrs. Brody asked what time would be convenient for you to meet with the seamstress."

She turned. "Seamstress?" she asked, although she already knew. Montgomery had made arrangements to augment her clothing.

Elspeth nodded.

"I'll find Mrs. Brody myself," she said, leaving Elspeth to set her rooms to rights.

Twice, she turned left when she should have turned right, and was given directions by a smiling maid. She waved away an offer to lead her to the housekeeper, saying she'd rather find her way. After all, she was to live here. The sooner she learned Doncaster Hall, the better.

The Blue Drawing Room was the first of the public rooms she investigated. Here, the walls were hung with a blue damask fabric that focused the eye on the delicate plasterwork of the ceiling and the white mantel, with its frieze design of lions and thistles. A larger drawing room was next, a room she privately thought of as The Picture Room, taking up the whole of the east side of the second floor. Paintings of ships and men attired in naval uniform adorned one of the crimson walls. The other walls were covered in landscapes of Doncaster Hall and portraits of previous Lords Fairfax with their wives.

Other art treasures sat on tables and credenzas, evidently placed to display them at their best advantage. She wasn't an expert on porcelain, but the statue of a shepherdess looked valuable, as did the Chinese vases colored the same crimson hue as the walls.

On the top floor, she discovered a ballroom, its inlaid floor shiny with wax, a series of couches and chairs arranged along the sides of the room for weary dancers to rest. The musicians could either perform on the stage at the far end of the room or from the gallery above the dance floor.

As she walked through Doncaster Hall, the magnificence of the house called to her. She suspected there would be charm even in the scullery.

The nursery occupied the whole of the third floor, consisting of adjoining suites for nurse, governess, and tutor, and bedrooms for older children. She stood in the doorway of a room designed for an infant, the large fireplace carefully screened, a comfortable chair in the corner adjacent to a reading lamp. A carved bassinet sat in the opposite corner, ready for a new mattress and an occupant.

Resolutely, she pushed any thoughts of the future from her mind and continued her search for Mrs. Brody.

She was lost for a good ten minutes before she found herself in a wide corridor leading to the public rooms. She opened a door she thought was the dining room, one that would lead to the kitchen.

This wasn't the dining room at all, but a strange room with curved walls, one covered in weapons. Worse, Mr. Kerr was seated at a table in the middle of the room.

She stepped backward, hoping the solicitor hadn't

heard her. Her hopes were dashed when Mr. Kerr raised his head and pinned her with a look.

"Can I assist you, Lady Fairfax?" he asked.

"No," she said, stepping back. "I'm simply exploring Doncaster Hall. I apologize for the intrusion. I didn't mean to bother you."

"Without a guide?" he asked, putting down his pen.

"Do I need a guide, Mr. Kerr. In my own home?"

When he stood, she took another cautious step backward.

"Are you afraid of me, Lady Fairfax?"

She stared at him for a moment, uncertain how to answer. The solicitor wouldn't understand the confusion she felt in his presence. His emotions felt restrained and blanketed as if he hid his feelings even from himself.

Something about the solicitor disturbed her, an odd feeling that grew stronger each time she met him. Perhaps it was the fact that he had an air of barely suppressed superiority, but then, she would have expected that if he knew the story behind her marriage to Montgomery.

"No, Mr. Kerr, I am not. Do you want me to be?"

"Indeed not, Your Ladyship. It's just that you seem hesitant in my presence. As if you fear me, somehow."

"This is quite an unusual room," she said, looking around rather than responding to his comment.

"The Armory is one of the more famous rooms of Doncaster Hall. The 3rd Lord Fairfax purchased the weapons from the Office of Ordnance. It's said he nearly stripped the Tower of London of its collection of swords, pistols, and other weapons."

"Why?" she asked.

He looked surprised at the question. "To have them, of course."

She looked around the room. One particular sword

boasted a blade with a dark red stain. She sincerely hoped it was rust and not dried blood.

Mr. Kerr walked to the curved wall. "Twenty-five chests of weapons were delivered to Doncaster Hall, along with two men from the Tower who were skilled in their use. Now, they're displayed here."

"And you've chosen to work here." She simply could not envision Mr. Kerr as a warrior. Perhaps a warlike squirrel, brandishing a nut as a weapon, but hardly more.

"Since the Armory contains an area for the cataloging and maintenance of the hundreds of weapons stored here, I've chosen to use this desk, yes."

"A reminder of England's bloody past," she said. "And Scotland's."

Added to the English weapons were those from Scotland: enough Highland dirks, cudgels, two-handed claymores, and basket-hilted broadswords to outfit a good sized army.

"The majority of Fairfax men were not of a warring mentality, your husband excluded."

Had she heard correctly?

She glanced at him.

"Your husband fought in the American Civil War. Did you know, Lady Fairfax?"

She nodded.

"Quite a brave man. Decorated for it."

"Why do you sound so disapproving, Mr. Kerr? Surely courage is a virtue?"

"He killed a number of men, I understand."

"Have Fairfax men never killed, Mr. Kerr? Not in defense of their land or their freedom?"

"The 11th Lord Fairfax is a borrowed Scot, Your Ladyship," he said, the words tinged with something she couldn't quite name. Bitterness? Envy?

"I must leave you," she said, pretending a cordiality she didn't feel. Two years of living with Uncle Bertrand and Aunt Lilly had prepared her well for the sin of prevarication. "With my apologies for having disturbed you."

"It is no bother, Your Ladyship," he said, waiting until she reached the doorway before sitting once more. "If you need anything of me, you need only send your maid."

She studied him for a moment.

"Why are all those wagons arriving?" she asked.

"I imagine they're the purchases your husband made in London, Lady Fairfax."

She waited for him to continue, but he said nothing more.

Finally, she left him, found the housekeeper, and arranged for a time to meet with the seamstress and her assistants. In addition, she and Mrs. Brody decided on an hour each day to meet to discuss those items that required her decision.

Thank heavens Aunt Lilly made her trail behind her most days to be of assistance. At least she knew what was required to keep a large household functioning. Although the townhouse in London could easily fit into Doncaster Hall a dozen times, the principle was the same. Procure, prepare, and preserve food, ensure that the servants knew how to, and were, performing their chores, and ensure that all who lived at Doncaster Hall had their needs met and were healthy.

Duties she would have to grow into, she suspected. If they were to remain in Scotland.

Inside the distillery, the bricks were blackened from decades of wood fires boiling under copper kettles. The air was strangely sweet, as if the aroma of whiskey still wafted through the building. Once, there might have been boards beneath Montgomery's feet, but only packed earth remained. The roof, supported by several brick pillars, possessed a half dozen holes, allowing shafts of sunlight to illuminate the space.

He strode out of the distillery, in search of Ralston. The older man was directing the uncrating of the bolts of silk he'd purchased in London.

"Are there any carpenters at Doncaster Hall?" he asked.

Ralston nodded. "We've got two lads who can build anything, Your Lordship."

"Then I'll keep them busy for the next couple of weeks. I need at least six worktables. First, the roof needs repair."

Ralston looked up. "That it does, Your Lordship. When we stopped making whiskey, there was no other use for the building."

"Why did you stop making whiskey?"

"Maybe I misspoke, Your Lordship," Ralston said with a smile. "We haven't given up making whiskey. We've just given up making whiskey *here*. There's a large Fairfax distillery outside Glasgow now."

From what Montgomery had learned in London, the Fairfax wealth came from fisheries, mines, shipbuilding enterprises, and various other industries. Unlike the American branch of the Fairfax family, the Scots branch did not work the land.

He walked away from Ralston, ignoring the activity behind him for a moment. Perched on the hill in front of him was Doncaster Hall. The emerald leaves of the trees were dusted with sunlight, some leaves frosted white by the glare. Dark brown trunks arrowed up from an undulating earth carpeted in lush green grass. The river glinted silver in the sun.

A peaceful view, nothing out of place or garish, as if the scene before him had matured for generations.

At home, it was time for planting. The young seedlings would not have been brought out from the sheds yet, but there would be furrows as far as the eye could see. From dusk until dawn, people would be walking the roads, while mules and wagons carried supplies to Gleneagle's farthest acres. The air would be heavy with animal sounds, conversation, and song.

Standing a half world away, Montgomery could almost imagine the dampness of fecund earth, sweet mimosa, and the musky tang of crabapples.

Birds burst out of the trees surrounding Doncaster Hall like cannon shots, circled in formation, and returned again. A signal he should be about his tasks. Thoughts of the past, and Virginia, would have to wait until later.

Veronica asked one of the men on the path about the arriving wagons. He pointed her to the distillery, located some distance away.

Doncaster Hall was perched on top of a knoll, larger than a hill, smaller than a mountain. In the back of the house, an approach not seen by visitors, were various outbuildings. The land sloped to a valley intersected by the River Tairn and spanned by an arched bridge of weathered gray stone.

Across the bridge were several buildings. The largest, of the same weathered gray brick as the bridge, stood alone, two wagons parked in front of its large open doors. The rest of the vehicles were taking the long way around, down the valley to where a wider wooden bridge allowed wagons, carts, and carriages to cross. She watched them from the top of the walking bridge, hesitant to go any farther only because Montgomery was directing the wagons.

As she stood there, the most curious melancholy flooded her. He was the only person with whom she'd ever been intimate. Yet she and Montgomery might as well be strangers. Only the unexpected passion they shared bridged their ignorance of each other. Perhaps she should be grateful for that. Was it something every married couple experienced? Would she trade their passion for the ability to talk to Montgomery?

Why couldn't she have both?

The skirt of her dress was too full, the fabric felt stiff and shiny as if it had been starched. She pressed her hands against the material, and it almost bounced against her fingers. Elspeth was very diligent in her tasks.

At the moment, however, she wasn't as concerned about her apparel as she was her appearance. Would Montgomery think her pretty? Vanity had never been one of her flaws. How odd to experience it at this point.

She followed the path from the bridge to the distillery, hesitating as a wagon rolled in front of her.

Montgomery saw her, acknowledging her presence with a nod. At least he didn't banish her. Neither did he stop directing the wagons and their drivers.

The first of the wagons was already being unloaded, and several men she recognized from the staff greeting were assisting in the process. Numerous crates and barrels were revealed when the canvas tops were taken off the wagons. One huge crate, nearly six feet square and almost as tall, required six men, including Montgomery, to carry it.

She could hear his voice as he shouted instructions to the men.

"Be careful of that one, it contains a burner." A few

minutes later came another order: "We need another pair of shoulders over here, lads."

Even the majordomo was being pressed into service. She would not have been surprised to see Mrs. Brody and all the upstairs maids there as well. However, this endeavor, whatever it was, was evidently a masculine pursuit.

As they disappeared into the yawning abyss of the distillery, she circled one of the wagons, staring at the huge basket inside. It looked like one of the structures she'd seen at the Crystal Exhibition in London. Uncle Bertrand had been quite pleased to get special tickets for that day and had taken his entire family for an outing.

"Is it a balloon?" she asked, when Montgomery emerged from the distillery and drew near.

"That one is, yes. How did you know?"

"The Crystal Exhibition," she said. "Mr. Green's balloons. I saw one of them tethered there."

"It's what I did in the war," he said, answering her unspoken question. "Before the war. I've always been fascinated with flight."

"Isn't it dangerous?"

"Breathing in and out is dangerous," he said, his expression tightening. "I don't feel required to solicit your approval, Veronica."

She truly was surprised. She began to smile.

"Have I said something amusing?"

"No one has ever sought my approval for anything, Montgomery."

Without saying another word, he turned and walked back into the distillery.

Veronica stepped back to view the contents of other wagons.

Two baskets were lined up, side by side, next to a tall

pole. At the top of the pole was a flag, fluttering in the afternoon breeze. Scores of crates were being opened, revealing pipes, metal plates, and parts that looked as if they belonged to the inside of a boiler. Another set of crates was being carried into the distillery by two young men.

She wondered if Montgomery had commandeered them from the stable or from the house itself. Either way, no doubt working on a balloon was more eventful than their normal chores.

The most amazing sight was on the far slope of the glen. There, long stripes of blue and green silk lay on the grass. Next to it was an oval gondola, and a crate marked HANDGRIFF SORGFÄLTIG.

Montgomery came out of the distillery, heading directly for her. She wondered if she was to be banished for her curiosity. She clasped her hands in front of her and attempted to smooth her face of any expression.

"You grew up around here," he said, reaching her.

She nodded.

"What's the weather like?"

"The weather?" she asked, surprised.

He folded his arms and regarded her with impatience. Was she supposed to just answer his questions as if she were in a schoolroom?

She folded her arms and regarded him just as impassively.

"It rains. When it doesn't rain, the sun is shining. At night, it's dark."

The corner of his mouth quirked, and might have become a smile, but it disappeared too quickly to tell.

"Is it windy?" he asked. "I understand there are periodic gusts."

"In early spring more than now."

"The area's not prone to storms?"

"Periodically," she said. "Like the one yesterday, but not overly so."

"What about birds? Have you noticed any odd patterns in their flight?"

"Are you ever going to answer any of *my* questions, Montgomery?"

When he didn't answer, she unfolded her arms, frowned at him, and gripped both sides of her skirts.

"No," she said, a touch of exasperation in her voice, "I've never seen any odd patterns in the flights of birds. They simply fly."

He studied the ground as if he were taking all the information she gave him and putting it into a mental book.

"Why do you want to know? Is it because of your balloon?"

He turned and walked away without answering her.

She followed him to the entrance, but Montgomery only glanced at her as if her presence surprised him.

"What is it, Veronica?" he asked impatiently.

She took a step back. "Nothing, Montgomery. Absolutely nothing."

He disappeared into the distillery, leaving her standing there.

She turned and began to walk back to Doncaster Hall. The façade in place since the day she became Montgomery Fairfax's bride was in danger of crumbling. If it did, all her fears would come spilling out to be met, head-on, by all her doubts.

Until that moment, her marriage had had a hint of promise to it. She thoroughly enjoyed the marriage bed, whether or not she was supposed to, and anticipated spending nights in Montgomery's arms. She'd thought they might be able to establish some sort of relationship, some friendship as well.

Evidently, she'd been thoroughly naïve.

He'd made no secret of wanting to return to Virginia. He wanted to go home. He wanted to surround himself with people who loved him, who understood him. God knows she didn't understand him, and as far as loving him?

Who could love Montgomery Fairfax? He was arrogant, impossible, secretive, and silent.

Yet didn't they both want the same things? He wanted to be home, and so did she. She wanted to stay there, in her country, not far from people who'd once known her. She felt tied to the land, to the history, to the people.

She didn't want to go to Virginia. She'd no wish to travel to America. She didn't want to be surrounded by strangers. Living with her uncle Bertrand's family had been bad enough. She'd only met them twice before going to live with them, both events being strained visits between her mother and her brother, and barely tolerated by the two spouses.

When she reached the top of the arched bridge and glanced back, it was to find Montgomery standing in the doorway, watching her. A borrowed Scot, Mr. Kerr had called him.

A man so filled with pain she could feel it even from here.

Chapter 16

*Y**ou were unkind, Montgomery.* Caroline's voice censured him.

She'd said the same when he'd ignored one of her cousins, a girl with a braying laugh who'd come to spend a few weeks at Gleneagle. He'd found almost any excuse to avoid her. Caroline had had fond hopes, of course, and he'd already warned her about trying to pair him with one of her many female relatives.

The woman he was watching, however, wasn't one of Caroline's cousins. Nor did Veronica have a braying laugh. She was, however, stubborn. No doubt a Scots trait. What about her disconcerting ability to disturb him? He suspected that was something only Veronica possessed.

Her eyes were warm, too compassionate and caring. He didn't believe she could feel his emotions. Yet she always seemed to know when to touch him, when to lend her support.

She surprised him with both her curiosity and her passion. He suspected there'd be no sensual limits between them, and that was an arousing thought, one that momentarily took his mind from the tasks at hand.

He turned, walked back into the distillery, and tried to occupy his mind with something other than his wife. Veronica, however, refused to disappear that easily. She was as determined a ghost as Caroline, for all that Veronica was alive.

He'd have to apologize.

What did he say? That he was as uncertain of himself as he'd ever been? That he felt out of place? He hadn't yet formulated a goal, a reason for waking every morning.

The only thing in his life that was familiar and comforting was his airship.

Resolutely, he began an inventory of the items being uncrated, pushing thoughts of Veronica away. Thanks to the fortune accompanying the title, he'd had enough money to order items he couldn't afford since before the war: two envelopes of silk, one in an inverted teardrop, the other in an oval shape, a burner, made in Germany and boasting a paraffin oil reservoir, and three woven basket-like gondolas, two square, and one in a larger rectangular shape.

He'd utilized enough of his own fortune before the war to know how expensive it was to operate an airship. Nor had he flown in one since the War Department disbanded the Balloon Corps.

Six years ago, he'd amused his family with his love of all things aerial. He'd corresponded with the giants in the field and created an area not far from Gleneagle where he experimented with and launched his own design. The day he took Alisdair and James up in a tethered balloon and seen the expressions on their faces was when he knew they'd never ridicule him again.

Nor had they.

Two years later, he was flying high above Confederate forces, using his airship to spy on the enemy. An enemy comprised of his family and friends, people who no longer existed.

If a man lives on through the memories of others, then the whole of his family would perish when he, too, died. There would be no one to remember all his aunts and uncles, his parents, or his brothers. No one who'd known Magnus. No one would remember their names or even that they'd lived in a place called Gleneagle in Fairfax County, Virginia.

He turned to look toward Doncaster Hall again. The house had remained standing for hundreds of years, proof the Lords Fairfax existed, walked the earth. Some of the lords had performed deeds that would be forever remembered. Most simply lived ordinary lives in the house now standing as a monument to their family's continuation.

Montgomery was one of them now, whether he wished it or not. Even if he returned home, he'd forever be known as the 11th Lord Fairfax.

The future was like a silk envelope before an influx of hot air. Nothing was destined, nothing determined. He might become anyone he wanted. He might be a despot or beloved for his kindness. He might remain aimless or possess a fire for achieving a goal yet unknown.

And happiness? How, then, did he become happy?

No one greeted her as Veronica opened the front door. She regarded the oval staircase in front of her. Such beauty, such magnificence, was wasted on a house built for only one family. Such architectural genius should have been saved for a public building, perhaps. Something that could be viewed by more than just a few people.

Two of the maids nodded to her as she passed. In England, they no doubt would have curtsied to her, at which point she would've felt embarrassed and unworthy of such obeisance. In Scotland, however, the lowest member of the clan was equal to its chief. Her father had taught her never to look at another human being as if he were subservient.

We are all here to strive and to learn, Veronica, he often said. *Some of us are in different stages of our education.*

What would he have said of Montgomery? Would he have been angry on her behalf? Or would he, more likely, have counseled patience on her part?

She didn't feel exceptionally patient at that point. Yet what other option did she have?

"Your Ladyship, you're back," Elspeth said, peering around the landing. "Mary said she saw you in the ballroom earlier. I was wondering if you were doing a tour of the house."

"Only my own," she said, forcing a smile to her face.

"So Mrs. Brody didn't take you, then?"

She shook her head.

"You'll not have seen the secret passages, and the dungeon as well," Elspeth said, joining her on the stairs.

"Dungeon? You didn't say anything about a dungeon."

"I didn't mention the ghosts, either," Elspeth said with a twinkle. "A drummer boy plays when anything bad is about to happen to one of the Lords Fairfax. It happened when the 10th Lord died. Granted, he was an old man, but one of the maids heard the drummer, all the same."

"The very last thing I choose to worry about, Elspeth, is whether or not someone hears the sound of a drum. We'd be in a constant state of alarm."

Elspeth nodded. "I agree, Your Ladyship. Plus, the girl who heard it was a silly sort anyway."

"We'll put off the tour of the secret passages and the dungeon for later," she said.

"If it's all the same with you, Your Ladyship, I'd rather

not see the dungeon, and the secret passages give me the shivers. The 10th Lord was all for the maids using the passages to go from room to room, but Mrs. Brody put a stop to that when one of the girls forgot how to open the door in the study. You could hear her scream through the whole of Doncaster Hall."

"Mrs. Brody sounds like an eminently practical woman."

Perhaps she should emulate the housekeeper and become more practical herself. Dismiss the notion she could feel the emotions of others. Banish the thought, too, that she'd seen anything in Montgomery's magic mirror.

In the next three hours, she met with the seamstresses and was then given a comprehensive tour of Doncaster Hall, including those rooms she'd already seen. She didn't mention her earlier explorations. Nor did she tell Mrs. Brody, when the housekeeper asked if the Family Dining Room would be suitable for their dinners, that she was certain Montgomery would avoid her if he could.

From now on, she would either take a tray in her sitting room or do without dinner altogether. Too much pity was, well, simply too much pity.

Three lanterns illuminated the interior of the distillery, with another lantern on each end of his makeshift worktable providing enough light despite the hour.

It's that damn airship again, James said, repeating a refrain he'd uttered often enough in life.

Montgomery checked the barrel of paraffin oil next to the wall and performed a final inspection of all the empty crates.

I would have thought you'd get bored with that.

He had no intention of arguing with a ghost. James

had been an irritant when he was alive. Why should death render him silent?

This time, however, he also heard Alisdair's comment, one his older brother had made numerous times.

He'll give it up once the newness wears off.

He thinks he can fly like a bird. James flapped his arms.

"Am I supposed to be amused?"

They never answered him. He'd be shocked if they did. His ghosts were remnants of memory, plucked from the past and set among his present moments. Perhaps his mind did so in an attempt to ease him, to remind him he'd once been surrounded by people so intrusive he'd wished for solitude.

Veronica could soften his loneliness. Veronica, with her ability to make him smile, her surprising passion, and the comfort he found in her arms.

He owed her an apology. Would she see his appearance as that? Or as weakness, that he couldn't resist her?

Damned if he cared at the moment.

After dinner, Veronica took a bath, dismissed Elspeth, and retired to her sitting room. For long moments, she sat there, trying to calm herself. The emotions coming from others were sometimes easier to decipher than her own feelings. Was she simply angry? Or hurt as well?

Montgomery could touch her, and her will melted. Her body knew his, craved his. Outside their bed, he wanted nothing to do with her. He wouldn't talk to her, wouldn't spend any time with her.

She was a wifely concubine.

She stood, walked to the connecting door, and hesitated. Was he inside? She heard no sounds to indicate he'd returned. She opened the door and stared into Montgomery's room. Being there was, no doubt, violating some marital rule. A wife was not supposed to transgress against her husband's privacy or dare too much. Theirs was not any ordinary marriage, was it?

Where would he have put the mirror?

She moved to his armoire, feeling a tug of conscience for violating Montgomery's privacy as she opened the doors. She found the drawstring bag in the bottom of the armoire, grabbed it, and returned to her chamber.

Montgomery was standing in her bedroom.

She took a step back, acknowledgment that he was a formidable man. Not only was he extraordinarily handsome, but he was filled with all sorts of emotions she wished she could understand.

He glanced at the drawstring bag in her hand.

"Should I be surprised that you've violated my privacy again?"

"How do you do that? How do you walk so quietly, or enter a room without my hearing you?"

"How do you manage to invade my privacy so often?" he asked, spearing both hands through his hair. "If I give you the damn mirror, will you give me privacy?"

"I don't know," she said.

"You don't know? What the hell does that mean?"

"I don't know what you mean by privacy. Am I to leave you alone all the time? Am I never to talk to you? Am I never to share a meal, a conversation?"

When he didn't answer her, she looked down at the bag. Was the mirror worth an argument? She should give it back to him, walk away, and pretend they were in perfect accord with each other.

Years of pretense, however, grew tiring.

"Take it," he said, finally. "It's little enough payment."

Stung, she watched as he walked toward her.

"Payment for what?"

"If I want to bed you, I will."

He pulled the drawstring bag out of her hands and tossed it on her bed. Only then did he grab her hand and pull her back into his room, shutting all the doors and latching the one to the hallway.

"If I want to bed you, I will," he said again.

"You needn't pay me for it," she said.

Beneath the surface of Montgomery's calm, she could feel the carefully cloaked and civilized rage. She couldn't reach either his grief or his anger. Something dark lived in Montgomery, something skittering away from the light, and she wasn't certain she was courageous enough to face it.

What compelled her, then, to place her hands on his face and look up at him? What made her think she might heal him with passion?

His kiss was hard, startling, and hot. He pushed the robe from her shoulders, made an impatient sound against her lips when he encountered the belt. Perhaps she should have said something, but heat crawled up her spine, warmed the icy ball of anxiety in her stomach until she felt as if she were boiling inside.

She gripped his shoulders, then lost that grip when he nearly threw her on the bed.

Quickly, she raised herself on her elbows, watching him, stunned by the speed at which everything was happening. This was not the gentle lover, the man who'd brought her such bliss yesterday and the day before. This was a man who scowled at her as he jerked off his clothes, who threw his boots to the other side of the room, barely missing the pier glass. This was a man empowered by an emotion stronger than any she'd ever witnessed.

Her belly clenched as heat filled her.

An instant later, he threw himself on the bed, covering her, ripping the nightgown from her until their skins rubbed against each other.

"Damn it, I need you," he said, in such a harsh and grating tone she wouldn't have recognized his voice if she hadn't been looking at his face. "I need to be in you."

Her arms locked around his neck, and her mouth answered his assault with one of her own. She inhaled his breath, bit at his lip, heard him swear as he stroked her breast before replacing his hands with his mouth. Her palms pressed against his hollowed cheek as he suckled her.

His fingers, his hands, danced across her body in a furious ballet of passion, measuring the curve of her breasts, the slope of her hips, sliding between her legs to stroke her. He murmured praise as his fingers slid through slick folds, swallowed her soft exclamation, and urged her higher.

They fought with each other and soothed each other. She nibbled at his shoulder; he sucked her nipples. He palmed her wetness; she scraped her nails across his buttocks.

She moaned. He swore.

His fingers were inside her, measuring her response, her willingness, her need. She shivered, and he pressed harder. Not a gentle request but a demand. She willed her eyes to open and watched him watching her.

"I have to be in you," he said, his voice rough. "Do you understand?"

"Yes."

Her hips lifted off the bed, and suddenly he was there, filling her. Pleasure wound through her, around her, laced her to this man, this act, this fierce joy.

Gripping his hips, she demanded a rhythm of him,

set him into motion like a pendulum while he kissed her breathless. She bucked again, her whole body pressing up to take more of him. Greedy, she wanted more. She wanted everything.

Shuddering, she watched the shimmer of pleasure wash over his face as his eyes closed, and his throat arched. He tensed and held himself tight, pouring himself into her.

Her palm cradled his head, her thumb brushing his cheek as he rested his head on the pillow next to her.

In a moment, he would leave her. His face would close, his expression unreadable, but she would feel a hint of the pain leaking through his control.

When he would have spoken, she placed her fingers against his lips, turned her head to kiss him, willing him silent.

What the hell was that?

Montgomery moved, rolled on his back, away from her.

Pleasure wasn't a strong enough word to describe what had happened, but he couldn't think of another at the moment. He wasn't sure he could think at all. He wiggled his toes to make sure they were connected to his feet and the feet connected to his legs. He knew his left arm was still intact because that was over his eyes. Experimentally, he flexed his hand, surprised to find it was still working.

He thought his lips might be numb but knew his manhood was still firmly intact. Everything he was feeling radiated outward from that one spot.

He'd seen Veronica dressed in her blue wrapper, and beneath, a nightgown so diaphanous he could see the curves of her breasts and the darkness at the apex of her thighs. Lust had taken him unawares. Instant, raging lust, as if he were some rutting beast. He had to have her, and reason or rationale or thoughts of an overdue apology hadn't stopped him.

Thank God Veronica, his surprising wife, hadn't allowed herself to be forced. Nor had she succumbed. She'd demanded. She'd been as wild as he. He had a bite mark on one shoulder to prove it. And possibly some scratches on his buttocks.

What the hell had come over him? Over her?

He slitted open one eye. Veronica had her eyes closed, her face upturned. He wished he knew what to say to her. Did a husband thank a wife? Did he especially thank her for being a virago in bed?

She'd urged him on, as he recalled, and he doubted he was going to forget that anytime soon. The memory of this night, every night with her, might well live on until his deathbed.

God, he felt good.

Veronica should get up and go back to her room. Tonight, he'd sleep. He might be hard-pressed to stay awake until she left. Except she wasn't leaving. She was turning toward him, her hair spread over the pillow, marking it as hers.

He should speed her on her way, say something to her that he could apologize for in the morning. A statement to get her out of his room.

Instead, and counter to everything he thought wise, he rolled over, pressed a kiss to her temple. She opened her eyes and quickly closed them again, avoidance in a gesture.

"Stay," he said softly. "Please."

Without waiting to hear her answer, he drew the sheet over them.

What the hell was he doing?

* * *

When Veronica awoke, it was dawn.

Montgomery was dressing, and she watched him for a few moments from beneath half-closed lids. He was so handsome it was a pleasure simply to look at him. Each action, from drawing on his shirt to fastening his cuffs, was done with deliberation. He didn't look at himself as he dressed. Instead, his gaze seemed focused inward, as if mentally ticking off a list of things he needed to do.

He sat, pulling on his boots, and remained there a moment, both hands on the arms of the chair, head bent, as if he'd been given a problem requiring a weighty decision.

Veronica closed her eyes and tried to sense what he was feeling, but all that came to her was a cloud of confusion, colored gray and black.

She heard him walk to the door, then pause. She pretended to be asleep, not from shyness as much as reluctance. They dealt so much better with each other in the act of passion than when they tried to talk. She didn't want her questions left unanswered, or see the flat expression in his eyes or the set look on his face.

Better to love the lover than try to talk to him.

When certain he was gone, she opened her eyes again and rolled to her back. A moment later, she sat up on the edge of the mattress, found her wrapper lying neatly at the foot of the bed, and dragged it on. Gathering the remnants of her nightgown in case one of the maids found it, she bunched the fabric in a ball in her hands and left Montgomery's room. Once in her bedroom, she tossed the ruined nightgown into the rubbish, hoping Elspeth wasn't all that curious.

At least the seamstresses were preparing a few more nightgowns for her.

She walked to the bed, picked up the mirror where Montgomery had tossed it the night before, and pressed the drawstring bag against her chest. If she were truly courageous, she'd open the bag, examine the mirror again, and look at the image she'd seen there.

Instead, she went to the bureau, placed it in the bottom drawer, and slowly closed it.

The present was confusing enough.

Chapter 17

The morning she'd awakened in Montgomery's bed marked the beginning of a pattern. Veronica rarely saw her husband during the day. Whatever Montgomery did in the distillery with his airship was a secret shared only with Ralston, the majordomo, who was found more often working with Montgomery than at his post, and the other men from Doncaster Hall.

Nor did Montgomery join her for meals. Every morning, she sat at the family dining table, staring across the expanse of the grand mahogany table, set with a white damask tablecloth, two place settings, and an assortment of fine china. On the sideboard was a selection of chafing dishes, all filled with more food than she could possibly eat. Dinners were taken alone in her sitting room. Sometimes, after dinner, she'd wander down to the library and select a few books to read, including one of the history of Doncaster Hall and the Fairfax dynasty.

Only at night did they come together, sharing a passion that never failed to surprise her.

She'd discovered she liked being touched. She especially liked being touched by Montgomery. His hands were expertly talented at doing just that. His kisses were drugging, intense, and she found herself craving them.

The previous night, he'd not come to her, and it was

the first time he'd ever stayed away for two full nights other than the time she'd had her monthlies. She'd wanted to go to him. She'd even left her bed and entered her sitting room, staring at the connecting door.

If they'd only shared themselves a little more, she might have knocked on the door to see if he needed her. Not her physical self as much as her emotional one. Did he need comfort? Was he in pain?

Why did he walk the grounds of Doncaster Hall? Every night, no matter the weather, he walked, taking the same route. No doubt the servants thought themselves haunted by a dark specter, a shadowed man. Not a drummer, but a warrior, home from war and evidently still pained from it.

They didn't communicate, and other than their kisses and the pleasure he gave her, they didn't share anything else.

As the days passed, she became more and more desperate to fill them. She decided to devote herself to good works, perhaps visit all the nearby villages to see if anyone needed assistance from the Fairfax family. Once, she'd written poetry. Perhaps it was time to take up that interest again. She might even plan a visit to those people at Lollybroch who'd been so kind to her a few years earlier. Or take up her needlework again.

She might begin cataloging the precious objects in the Blue Parlor or the Long Drawing Room, ensuring the records of those possessions were as detailed as the weapons in the Armory. Altogether, she could find occupations for her time, none requiring Montgomery's approval, assistance, or presence.

If she tried, she might be able to block all thoughts of him from her mind during the day, thereby replicating his attitude toward her. He didn't tell her what captured his attention in the distillery. Nor did he ever discuss his airships. The only comments she ever heard were from Elspeth about the laundry maids fussing at the oil stains on his clothing.

This morning had been the same as each of the previous mornings for the last three weeks. She met with Mrs. Brody to discuss what needed to be addressed by the lady of the house. Mrs. Brody was expert at her position. The housekeeper managed to feed them all well, and for less, Veronica suspected, than most great houses. The maids worked diligently; the supplies required for the upkeep of Doncaster Hall were purchased with an eye to cost.

In other words, Veronica wasn't needed.

She halted on the staircase, the wood warm beneath her fingers. How much of this was she expected to endure? The rest of her life? Her spirit rebelled at the thought of spending hours each day attempting to find a purpose for herself. Better she should simply find her own way, her own purpose in life.

She would treat Montgomery exactly as he treated her, as an ornament, perhaps. A prize for a good day's work. Passion would be a reward, a sweetmeat. The mutton of her life would have to be discovered on her own.

Montgomery stared at Edmund Kerr, annoyed that the solicitor had interrupted his work.

The carpenters had provided the six tables he'd needed with remarkable speed, and they'd been set up in a U shape in the middle of the building. Now, Edmund was standing in front of one of the tables, looking at Montgomery as if he were found wanting.

"You do not wish to tour the factories in Glasgow, Your Lordship?"

"I can't imagine a greater waste of my time," he said, glancing down at his notes.

He wanted to fix the propeller to the steering wires, a delicate task requiring his concentration. He'd have to wait until Edmund left.

"Or the fisheries?" Edmund asked.

"Do they require my presence?"

He'd spent hours today bending the fins of the propeller into shape. Converting his written plans for a steering mechanism into a prototype had been easier than he'd imagined. For years he'd worked on this design. Being able to build it and fit it to the top of the envelope was cause for celebration.

He didn't have anyone to tell.

He'd never divulged to anyone other than his superior officers in the War Department that he was attempting to devise a way to steer a balloon. Doing so would enable them to command the air currents rather than be at their mercy. No longer would they have to remain tethered in place.

He'd never discussed his plans with Alisdair or James. Neither of them would have been interested. Nor would they have understood. Caroline was the only person with whom he'd ever discussed his ideas, and that conversation had taken place only because she'd discovered him working late one night in Gleneagle's library.

Success without an understanding audience was still success, however.

If he opened a baffle on both the port and starboard sides of the ship, he could have a positive airflow, enough to give him more control over altitude. He made a notation about tilting the fins just a few degrees before glancing over at Edmund.

"Is that all?"

"You don't care about Doncaster Hall at all, do you, Your Lordship?" Edmund asked. His voice held a befuddled amazement, robbing the words of their sting.

He glanced up from his notes and focused on the other man.

"No, I don't."

"May I ask why not, sir?"

He smiled. "No, you may not."

"Is it that you have no intention of remaining in Scotland, Your Lordship?"

He regarded the man steadily until Edmund took the hint, turned, and left the distillery.

"Those that board with cats may count on scratches, sir," Ralston said from behind him.

He turned to see his majordomo, now budding Balloon Master, staring at Edmund's back.

"I take it you don't like the solicitor, Ralston."

"I've no fault with him, sir. He thinks like a lawyer. What cannot be helped must be put up with."

He decided not to tell Ralston that he, too, had studied law with every intention of practicing. Life had interfered, however.

"He's got good intentions, sir," Ralston said. "But he's all for the estate. Never mind that people are more important."

He doubted Edmund would see it that way. From the moment he'd met the solicitor, it was evident Edmund was devoted to Doncaster Hall and him, but only because Montgomery was the 11th Lord Fairfax. It was the position he revered, not the person.

Damn it. His concentration was broken. He stared down at the plans in front of him and cursed the solicitor.

"I'm nearly ready to take the balloon up, Ralston," he said. "To test the air currents. Care to accompany me?"

Ralston shook his head.

"It's not as bad as all that."

"Better be a coward than a corpse, sir," Ralston said, grinning.

"I'll have to get you to change your mind," he said, deciding to end his work early.

"You can certainly try," Ralston said, walking beside him as he left the distillery. "It's only fair to warn you, sir. The habit of stubbornness is bred into a Scot."

He knew that only too well, being married to a stubborn Scot. Yet any comment he might have made was lost in amazement at the scene before them.

Doncaster Hall had a staff of forty, equally divided between men and women. Most of the men were arrayed on the sloping lawn in front of Doncaster Hall, forming three lines, while his wife stood at their head. In front of each line of men was a bucket of water.

When Veronica raised her arm, the first man grabbed the bucket, passed it to the next man, who passed it again, until the bucket reached the last man in line who threw its contents on a pile of flaming straw behind them.

Evidently, Veronica was timing each group, and when the winner was announced, the men in the middle line raised their arms in triumph.

"What's she doing?"

"A fire brigade, sir," Ralston said. "Lady Fairfax has insisted upon it."

"Has she? Why?"

"I'm sorry, sir, but I've no idea. The lads have been at it since noon."

She was wearing a dress he'd not seen before, something in a green stripe he liked.

He strode up the hill, advancing on his wife. Veronica saw him coming and addressed the men.

"You've all done very well. Remember the colors of your units, and we'll practice more next week."

"Colors?"

She didn't answer him, merely turned, and placed the buckets in a stack.

"Veronica."

"Montgomery," she said, still not looking at him.

"Why have you begun a fire brigade?"

She turned and faced him. "Are you returning to America?"

"What?"

"Why do you walk every night?" she asked.

"What's wrong with you?"

She lowered her voice. "Why haven't you come to me in the last two nights?"

He frowned at her.

"What are you working on in the distillery?"

When he didn't speak, she matched his frown with one of her own.

"I'm not answering *any* of your questions," she said, "until you've answered *some* of mine."

With that, she grabbed the buckets, turned, and marched away, leaving him staring after her.

Veronica took the stairs to the second floor, hoping Elspeth wasn't in her room. She was perilously close to tears and didn't want anyone to witness them. She'd always been protective of what she felt, probably because she felt the emotions of others so keenly.

Entering her chamber, she was grateful to find it empty, and closed the door behind her.

After taking the mirror from the bureau, she walked into the sitting room and sat on one of the comfortable chairs near the window. Slowly, she withdrew the mirror from its protective bag but kept the brown glass facing away from her. Did she want to see a glimpse of her future again? Was it even the future? Perhaps it was only her deepest wish given form. Perhaps she wouldn't see happiness at all. Instead, she might witness Montgomery returning to Virginia alone.

She held the mirror up, then turned it, forcing herself to look into the reflection. The brown glass remained dark and murky. All she saw was the faint reflection of her face, her eyes too wide and almost fearful.

Had she imagined what she'd seen?

In the carriage, after the meeting at the Society the Mercaii, she'd still been suffering from the effects of whatever drug they'd given her. On her wedding night, she'd seen something, but Montgomery had interrupted her before she could study the reflection completely.

At the moment, she wanted to see her future. She wanted to see something more hopeful than what she felt.

The glass didn't change.

She heard Elspeth come into the bedchamber, and it gave her enough time to compose herself. Before she could put the mirror into its bag, however, Elspeth peered around the doorway.

"What is that, Your Ladyship?"

Her heart sank when Elspeth walked to her side, reached down, and picked up the mirror. The other woman didn't look into the reflection. Instead, her fingers fingered the diamonds on the edge of the mirror.

"It's the Tulloch Sgàthán," Elspeth said, her voice amazed. "I haven't seen it since I was a little girl."

"The Tulloch Sgàthán?" she asked, motioning to the adjoining chair. Elspeth took a seat, smiling down at the back of the mirror.

Veronica was vacillating between disappointment she

hadn't seen anything in the reflection and a surge of excitement that the mirror had been identified by Elspeth, of all people.

"Although I can't remember all these bright stones," Elspeth said. "It may not be the same one." She glanced over at Veronica. "It belonged to my grandmother, Mary Tulloch."

"You're not looking in the mirror, Elspeth, why?"

The other woman smiled, looked down at the back of the mirror before handing it back to her.

"It's the Tulloch Sgàthán," Elspeth said, as if that were enough of an explanation.

"Does it tell the future?"

Elspeth smiled. "My granny said the mirror showed a woman a path. It was up to her whether to take it. So, I guess it does tell the future in a way."

She stared down at the mirror.

"The stones are a new addition," Elspeth said. "It didn't have them when I was a child."

"Have you ever looked at it?"

"I did, once, when I was a little girl. I saw myself as I am now, only a little older." Elspeth's smile broadened. "I had two little ones with me. It was enough of a look for me."

She kept the mirror face down on her lap. "I can't see anything anymore."

Elspeth reached over and patted her on the knee, a curiously maternal gesture.

"If you can remember anything she might have said about it, please let me know."

"You might ask her yourself, Your Ladyship."

Startled, Veronica stared at her. "Your grandmother is still alive?"

Elspeth nodded. "She was on my last visit home. One

of my brothers or sisters would have let me know if she'd died. She's very old, but she's spry. She lives outside Kilmarin, near Perth, where I was raised."

"I thought you were from Lollybroch."

Elspeth smiled and shook her head. "No, that's my Robbie's family. My own comes from Perth, and it's homesick I am from time to time."

"I know how that feels," she said, remembering the two years in London.

"How do you come to have the Tulloch Sgàthán?" Elspeth's cheeks flushed. "Begging your pardon, Your Ladyship, it's not my place to ask."

"It was by way of being a wedding gift," she said, stretching the truth a bit.

"Have you never seen anything in it, Lady Fairfax?"

"I did, once," she said. "Not now." She placed the mirror back in the bag, pulling the drawstring tight. "I think, perhaps, for me it's just a mirror."

The other woman didn't say anything. What could she say? That Veronica was being foolish? Or would Elspeth say, if she'd felt the freedom to do so, something like the expression often quoted by her father? The worth of a thing is known by the want of it.

Veronica wanted, very much, to see something in the Tulloch Sgàthán, and for that reason, it was priceless.

Chapter 18

Montgomery hadn't slept well for years. The only time he could remember sleeping deeply was after he'd been with Veronica, a fact that annoyed him.

She wasn't a drug to be taken when he couldn't sleep.

He'd stayed away from her for two nights to prove he could. Good, he'd won that battle; he needn't continue to avoid his wife.

A physician had suggested, a year or so ago, he use laudanum, but he'd decided against it. There'd been too many times in the last year when he might have been tempted to take too much of it. He wasn't a coward.

He could hear the River Tairn gurgle in its triumphant passage through the glen, pausing to rest in pools and, once rested, babbling over rocks. The air was clean and almost icy at Doncaster Hall, reminding him of being aloft. A curlew sounded mournfully from a nearby tree, accompanied by the hiss of the wind through the pines. He thought he saw the shadow of a deer peering out from the junipers, but in a moment it was gone.

The pines growing in stunted profusion around the base of the mountains were not the pine trees of home. Here, they boasted a reddish brown bark, their shaggy branches growing only at the top of the tree.

Even the oaks were different. The massive gray trunks

stretched up forty feet or more, the gnarled branches thick with emerald leaves. These Highland oaks looked resilient enough to endure any season and had done so for centuries.

In winter, the winds would howl, snow that even now capped the distant mountains would form drifts across the glen. The hardy Scots sheep, expected to subsist year long on a diet of Highland grass, would become indistinguishable from the snow.

He wasn't certain he'd be here, then.

In the last few weeks, he'd learned the topography around Doncaster Hall well enough that he could walk the paths and the hills without the benefit of a full moon. Tonight, he'd walked for nearly an hour before retracing his steps to halt in front of the house.

The façade of Doncaster Hall reminded him so much of home that he could imagine himself there, five years ago, the sound of music carrying into the garden. The occasion was the first party they'd given since their parents had died of fever two years earlier. The first party, and the last, because plans had already been made. He was due to work with Thaddeus Lowe with his balloons, a decision garnering its share of ridicule from his brothers.

"He hasn't given up thinking he can fly." He could hear Alisdair's voice so clear in his mind it was as if he stood there beside him.

"He's not a bird," James had said. "He's a bat, and he's going to hang upside down by his feet."

He'd taken their good-natured ribbing in stride, knowing it concealed worry. His decision to join the Balloon Corps had made his defection marginally easier. His brothers were going to fight for Virginia while he was going to join the Union Army.

That night had been warmer than this one, the scent of

honeysuckle so thick in the air, he'd suspected his clothes would forever smell of it. Besides the smell of the night and the swell of the music, he could remember laughter.

They'd all been so damn happy five years ago. Happy to be young, to be wealthy, to be going gallantly and magnificently off to war. He'd been the anti-soldier, the one person in the ballroom who hadn't bragged of his division or his newly bestowed rank.

Only the four of them knew he was about to be a traitor to everything he'd known. Yet every time he remembered, he knew his decision would have been the same.

He glanced up at Veronica's window, now darkened. If he went to her, she'd welcome him into her arms and grant him some sort of peace. Perhaps he didn't deserve peace, after all. Perhaps he was destined to walk the night forever to pay for all his many sins.

Even so, he knew he was going to her.

Veronica stepped back from the window, grateful she'd extinguished the lamp. Montgomery couldn't see her.

She pressed her fingertips to the glass, wishing she could call out to him or send comfort to him somehow. He would say she couldn't be fey or possess her Gift. Yet even with distance separating them, she could feel his isolation and his pain.

Every night, for the last three weeks, it had been the same. Montgomery walked around Doncaster Hall, taking a solitary route down to the river and up to the hills. When he was done, he came to her.

What troubled him so much that he walked every night? What demons pursued him? Did memories of the war keep him awake? Or was Caroline the source of the deep and profound sadness she felt from him?

How very foolish to be jealous of a ghost. Yet she was.

She removed her wrapper and got into bed, tucking the covers around her and staring up at the ceiling.

How did she fight a ghost?

She was here and alive, willing to be a wife in all ways. Why, then, did Montgomery ignore her? Why was there only passion between them and nothing else? They never spoke or shared thoughts. They never planned for the future. Doncaster Hall was so large she could exist in it for weeks without seeing him.

Was that what he wanted?

She wanted more.

She wanted what her parents had had, a communion, a deep understanding she could feel from one to the other. She wanted passion, but she also wanted to be able to look across a room, meet Montgomery's eyes, and know what he felt without using her Gift.

A noise halted her thoughts.

He must have eyes like a cat to be able to walk through the darkened room with no need for a light. All she could see was a black shadow standing in the doorway. Was he trying to frighten her?

She was beyond fear but well into anger.

The shadow halted just beyond her footboard as she sat up.

"You needn't come any closer," she said. "I'll not welcome you into my bed."

"You're my wife."

"You might as well say, 'You're my dog. Or you're my horse.' Would you talk more to me if I were your dog or horse, Montgomery?"

"You're angry."

She punched her pillow into place, then leaned back against it, glaring at him.

"Yes, I'm angry. I'm very angry. Go away."

Instead of leaving the room, he walked to the side of the bed.

"Why?"

Instead of just sitting there waiting for him to pounce, she slid from the other side of the bed.

"You might have a legal right to be here," she said. "You don't have a moral one."

"What the hell does that mean?"

She walked around the end of the bed until she neared him.

"You don't talk to me, Montgomery. You don't say a word to me all day long, and I'm supposed to welcome you into my bed as if I'm grateful for your attention? Any attention?"

"I have to talk to you?"

He sounded so astonished, she poked him in the chest with her finger.

"Yes. You have to talk to me."

"What do you want me to say?"

"I want you to answer my questions," she said.

"Take off your nightgown."

"Did you not hear a word I said?" she asked.

"Take off your nightgown, and I'll answer your questions."

She knew what happened the minute she was naked around him. She shook her head. "No. You answer one question, and I'll unbutton my nightgown. One button."

He folded his arms and regarded her, a black shadow that was probably frowning at her. She didn't care. She wasn't retreating.

"One question? One button? That's a little steep, isn't it?"

"Then go back to your bedroom," she said. "I'm not changing my mind."

He moved to the bedside table and lit the lamp. The

sudden yellowish glow in the room made it as bright as day. She wished he'd allowed them to remain in the darkness.

"Ask," he said. "Be prepared not to like the answer."

Any answer had to be better than endless silence.

"Are you returning to Virginia?"

"I don't know," he said.

"You don't know? When will you know? When you do, will you bother to tell me?" The man was maddening.

He shook his head. "That was one question, Veronica, and I answered it. A button, please."

"That's hardly fair, Montgomery. That was part of the whole question."

He leaned closer. "Then you'll have to be more careful of your questions in the future, won't you?" Surprisingly, he continued. "This isn't my home," he said. "Scotland might have been the home of my forebearers, but I'm a Virginian."

"I'm a Scot."

He didn't have a response, only pointed to her button. Slowly, she unfastened it.

"Would I like America?"

"Another button, please."

She grudgingly unfastened one more button.

He considered the question for a moment. "I don't know," he said. "Virginia is certainly warmer."

"I don't want to go to America," she said, her attention focused on her hands rather than at him. "I belong here, Montgomery. I know that sounds selfish," she added. "Aunt Lilly says a woman has no right to question her husband."

"Is this the same woman who gave you advice about your wedding night? Must you pay any attention to her words at all?"

She shook her head, smiling.

"Why do you walk at night?"

"Another button."

This was not going well. Soon, she'd be naked.

He smiled at her. Montgomery was so handsome, her throat closed when she looked at him. She wanted to banish the game entirely, reach up and kiss him and begin another sport.

Instead, she unfastened the button, wondering if she dared to ask the questions that most troubled her. Would he leave her if she did?

The placket extended to the middle of her breasts, and she had four more buttons. Four more questions if he allowed her to ask that many.

"Why do I walk? I like the solitude."

She knew he was lying, and from his look, he was aware she knew it as well. Rather than press him for more of an explanation, she moved her fingers back to the placket.

His attention was fixed on the actions of her fingers, his gaze warming her blood.

"What is your middle name?"

He looked startled at that question, then smiled at her again, the expression deepening the dimples on either side of his mouth.

"Alexander. And yours?"

"Moira," she said. "Did you own slaves?"

His face stilled, the smile fading. "Have you wondered that all along?"

She nodded.

"Are you an abolitionist, Veronica?"

She hadn't expected him to ask her that. "I think I am, yes," she said, placing one hand flat on the placket.

He didn't answer her question, time ticking by achingly slow.

"You're not," she finally said.

"I'm like my grandfather," he said. "He refused to own another man." He smiled again, but this smile was sadder, wreathed in memory. "My grandfather used to say we have dominion over the earth and over the seas, but not over other men."

"So Gleneagle had no slaves?" she asked.

"I didn't say that."

He turned, moving to the window, pushing back the drapes until he could see the view of the glen darkened by night.

Should she take back her question?

Before she could do so, he turned, his back to the window, the heels of his hands braced on either side of him on the windowsill. He stretched out his legs, studied his boots, then the interior of her bedroom, taking time to answer the question.

Perhaps she really should take it back, but curiosity kept her silent.

"You're a Fairfax now. You deserve to know the history," he said. "My grandfather purchased slaves. Growing tobacco takes people. The moment a man was brought to Gleneagle, he was freed. He was under contract to work for five years, and after that, could leave or stay, as he wished."

She remained silent, intent on his words.

"When my grandfather died, my father stopped the practice. Maybe he was greedier. I often wondered if it was the influence of my mother's family. They openly ridiculed my grandfather's actions, seeing it as fiscally unsound."

He folded his arms in front of him and studied the carpet.

"Evidently, economic expediency trumps moral certainty," he said.

"The English abolished slavery more than thirty years ago," she said.

He nodded as if he knew.

"It was the one issue separating my brothers and me," he continued. "They followed my father's example. I took my own path."

"Which was?"

He turned and faced the window again. "To walk away from all that my family held dear. To choose my conscience over my kin."

"Your grandfather wouldn't have approved of what your father or brothers did."

He glanced over his shoulder at her. "No, he wouldn't have."

"But I think he would have approved of your being the 11th Lord Fairfax of Doncaster," she said.

He smiled but didn't respond.

"It must've been very difficult for you," she said softly. "Disagreeing with those you loved."

"Have you never disagreed with those you loved?" he asked, his attention on the view from the window.

She thought about those years with her uncle's family in London. She'd been miserable, not finding very much of a common ground with anyone. She'd felt a familial tie with them; her uncle was her mother's brother, after all. But had she loved them? Not the way she'd loved her parents.

"I cannot imagine disagreeing with my parents," she said.

"As you said, it was difficult. After a while, the difficult becomes commonplace."

"Are they dead? Your brothers?"

He didn't answer for a moment, but when he did, his answer was not unexpected. "Yes," he said simply.

She came to stand at the window beside him. What she felt from him defied her description of it. Pain was there, yet something else, a memory of joy, a bittersweet longing. She suddenly understood how much he wished to be home. But home was not just a place for him, it was more. To be surrounded by the familiar, the beloved, those people who'd made up his life.

Could Montgomery ever truly go home?

For now, they'd leave the past behind.

"So you found yourself a lord," she said, pasting a smile on her face, "came to England, and became a husband. Enough difficulty for one man, I would think."

"And you, Veronica?" he asked, turning. "You found yourself wife to a stranger, an American. Enough difficulty for one woman, I would think."

She didn't answer him.

"I try to stay away. Somehow, I always find my way here."

His honesty startled her.

She unfastened the rest of her buttons.

"No more questions?" he asked.

"No," she said, as honest as he'd been. "It's foolish to pretend. You come near me, and I want to make love to you."

At that, he was the one to look startled.

"You're the most amazing woman."

"Am I?" She smiled. "Amazing enough that you'll continue to talk to me? I know nothing of you, Montgomery."

"On the contrary, Veronica, you know a great deal about me." His smile was slightly wicked.

"I'm not talking about how you look naked,

Montgomery. I'm talking about what you do all day in the distillery, or what your plans are for your balloon."

She stood in front of him, placed her hands on his arms, and allowed her fingers to trail from his upper arms down to his wrists and back, needing to touch him. He'd taken off his coat, but his shirt was in the way.

"We won't talk about the past. Can we talk about now? Or what might come in the future?"

His eyes stayed fixed on her face. Yet he gave her no hint of his thoughts as silence stretched between them.

She closed her eyes, reached out, and tried to feel the emotions coming from him. Heat. Desire. Need. A loneliness so acute it mimicked her own.

"Veronica."

Her eyes flew open at the sound of his voice. Low and soft, it had the effect of causing her skin to pebble.

"What price do you demand for a kiss?" he asked, gripping her waist with both hands and pulling her close.

"I'll give that to you as a gift, Montgomery."

He pulled her up until she was standing on tiptoe. Her arms wound around his neck, and his lips were on hers. It felt like a lifetime since he'd kissed her.

When he released her, she laid her forehead against his chest, breathing hard.

"What else do you want to know, my inquisitive wife?"

She wanted, desperately, to ask about Caroline, but suspected he would leave if she did. She took another moment to compose herself, then asked, "What do you do in the distillery?"

"I'm developing a navigation system for my airship. It's in the early stages yet."

She pulled back and looked up at him. "Why?"

"Come to the distillery next week, and I'll show you."

He'd never welcomed her there, and on the few occasions when she'd strayed to the building, had been annoyed at her appearance.

"I'm not taking off my nightgown yet," she said.

"I'm answering your questions."

How many women in America had he charmed with that smile? How many women had nearly swooned at his appearance?

He placed his hand on her left breast, gently cupping the linen. His thumb stroked against her nipple.

She closed her eyes at the sensation. A moment later, she opened them again as a thought occurred to her.

"Would you prefer I didn't feel anything when you touched me?"

He lowered his head until his lips brushed her temple.

"That's a question too foolish to answer."

"I can't help feeling things when you touch me," she said.

"We'll keep it a secret between us," he said. "I'll never divulge you're a harlot in the bedroom and a lady in the parlor."

"I wasn't very proper in the parlor, either," she said, trying to concentrate when he was gently squeezing a nipple. Heat pooled between her thighs. "Have you visited many harlots?"

"I don't think that's a question I'm going to answer. If I do, I will demand something quite large in return."

"What would that be?" she asked. When had she become so breathless?

His hand had not moved, and two of his fingers were plucking at her nipple. The soft linen magnified the effect of his touch, sending a spear of heat down through her body.

"The entire nightgown," he said. "All at once. I want you naked, Veronica."

The game had become a tug-of-war between them, something almost forbidden, and therefore even more exciting.

"I think not," she said.

His lips began to trail down her throat, and she tilted her head back to give him better access. He was cheating, in his way, but it felt so delicious, she didn't challenge him.

"How did you become so adept at lovemaking?" she asked, feeling his lips curve against the tender spot just below her chin.

"Is that a proper question for a wife to ask?"

"No," she corrected him, "I'm a harlot at this moment. Not a wife. Not a lady."

"Then you should definitely be naked."

"I'm a very expensive harlot, Montgomery. A man must earn the right to bed me."

"I've answered all your questions," he said, bending to kiss her.

She reached out with both hands and gripped the material of his shirt. Her fingers scraped against his fabric-covered skin. She wanted to feel him, feel her skin against his, the friction of damp flesh against damp flesh. She wanted him inside her, bringing her release, coupling with her in a dance of pleasure and passion.

If she were playing the harlot, she should excel at her role. She stepped back, took his hand, and led the way to her bed. She stripped off the nightgown, extinguished the lamp, and slid beneath the covers, reaching for him.

In seconds, Montgomery was naked and joining her.

She trembled when he touched her, reached out a hand and closed it over his hard length and guided it to her wetness. If it were possible to need too much, then she did. She wanted the connection, ached for the pleasure.

He drove into her. Her body, pierced by pleasure, arched in response. Her fingers clenched on his shoulders before reaching down to grip his hips.

Her skin was slick, her heart pounding. She wanted to experience it all, the feel of Montgomery, the wildness of his passion, the strength of his body, the sound he made when his head arched back, and his face tightened.

They were separate people, each strangers to the other. They came together in passion, though, didn't they? If that was the only way they could communicate, then so be it.

It would do for the moment.

Chapter 19

Montgomery may have answered some of her questions, but two remained uppermost in Veronica's mind. Who was Caroline and did Montgomery still grieve for her?

Nor had his response about leaving Scotland appeased her. *I don't know.* Hardly a satisfactory answer.

She hadn't lied to him; she didn't want to go to America.

She could close her eyes and hear the timbre of the speech of the maids and know herself home, feeling a closeness to her parents she hadn't felt in London. The sheer beauty of the mountains surrounding Doncaster Hall and the undulating flocks of sheep declared her in the Highlands, and this was where she wanted to stay.

A borrowed Scot, that's what Mr. Kerr had called Montgomery. Did the solicitor know something she didn't? Had Montgomery been more candid with him? He'd professed to know nothing in London, but had something changed once Montgomery reached Doncaster Hall?

"Lady Fairfax."

She nearly jumped at the sound of the solicitor's voice.

"Mr. Kerr," she said, placing her hand flat against her chest. "You frightened me." Especially since she'd just been thinking of the man.

"Forgive me, Your Ladyship, it was not my intent."

The solicitor stood at the base of the stairs, looking up at her.

Slowly, she descended the steps, halting when she was two steps above him.

"You met His Lordship at the Society of the Mercaii, did you not?"

She nodded. Montgomery's solicitor must know of the circumstances of their meeting. Did he know the entire story?

"Doncaster Hall is experiencing many temporal disturbances, Lady Fairfax. It's my intention to attempt to contact the spirits and calm them."

She descended the next step, coming so close to Mr. Kerr that she could reach out and touch him.

"I didn't know you had an interest in the occult, Mr. Kerr."

"I assume, Your Ladyship, by your attendance at the Society, you share my interest."

She didn't answer, merely waited for him to continue.

"Would you care to assist me in a gathering?" he asked.

"You're going to talk to the dead, Mr. Kerr?"

He nodded.

She could feel his thrumming excitement. If he'd been a squirrel in truth, he'd have been standing on his hind legs, his paws scrabbling in the air and his nose twitching frantically.

She wondered if she'd misjudged him. Or was it simply the idea of contacting the dead that inspired her to smile at him, matching his toothy expression? She might solve the mystery of Caroline's identity on her own.

"Yes, Mr. Kerr," she said, "I would very much like to assist you."

* * *

Montgomery hadn't gotten any productive work done all day. Every time he tried to concentrate on the design, he thought of Veronica's words.

Did you have slaves?

He could hear the barely veiled horror in Veronica's voice when she'd asked that question.

Gleneagle had been left to all three of them equally. One brother had no more say than another, despite his birth placement. However, two of them could outvote the third, and he'd found his wishes being overridden by Alisdair and James.

In an action that, even to this day he couldn't accept, his brothers had continued the practice their father had instituted. Gleneagle had been no different from any other James River plantation. Everything Magnus Fairfax had believed in, everything he'd taught Montgomery, everything Montgomery had come to accept was right and moral, had been pushed aside.

His decision to join the Union Army hadn't been an easy one. Nor had it been simple to explain why he did so to his family. His brothers hadn't understood and decided it was his airships dictating his decision. He'd allowed them to continue to believe that.

If he had it to do over, he'd tell them the truth. Even now, he sometimes wished his ghosts were real. If they had been, he'd address Alisdair first, as the oldest. Then James, waiting until his brother's mischievous twinkle sobered.

Would it have changed anything? No, but at least he wouldn't have been left with this feeling that he'd not been honest.

"I'm stopping," he said to Tom, who, until a week ago, had been more than happy to work in the stable. In the past week, however, the boy had gotten a touch of airship enchantment and was checking all the seams in the balloon Montgomery would take up in a few days to test the air currents.

"You can give it up for the day, Tom," he said, guessing that if the boy had his wish, he'd keep working.

"If you don't mind, Your Lordship," he said, "I'll finish what I've started."

He nodded, approving of Tom's work habits. All the people employed here were the same, leading him to wonder if being industrious as well as capable were traits of the Scots, or if they were reserved for those who worked at Doncaster Hall.

Gloaming had settled around Doncaster Hall by the time he entered the front door. Ralston wasn't at his post, but that in itself wasn't unusual since Ralston had, for the last several weeks, been absent, devoting himself to errands necessary for the care and maintenance of Montgomery's airships. Yet when he went in search of Veronica, he couldn't find her, either.

He wondered if he'd missed dinner again and consulted his pocket watch to ensure he hadn't. Mrs. Brody, always assiduous in her duties, sent a maid to the distillery with provisions each day, in case he grew hungry or thirsty while working. Therefore, hunger was never a distraction.

Mrs. Brody, also, was not to be found.

He strode toward the Armory, intent on asking Edmund if he knew the whereabouts of the inhabitants of Doncaster Hall, only to be halted at the doorway by the sight before him.

One of the tables had been moved from another room, covered in a white cloth, and placed in the middle of the Armory. Five chairs sat around the rectangular table, several of them occupied by people he sought.

Edmund sat at the head of the table. To his right was Veronica, with Elspeth beside her. Mrs. Brody and a young woman he didn't recognize made up the rest of the group. The wall sconces had been extinguished. The only lighting in the room was a lone candle in the middle of the table.

No one noticed he was standing there, so he moved into the shadows, folded his arms, and leaned against the wall. He knew what they were doing. His Aunt Penelope had conducted numerous séances in an effort to reach her son and husband. No one had attempted to stop her since she seemed to gain some comfort from her spiritualistic sessions.

What he couldn't understand was why Edmund was leading the group.

Something caught his attention, a black space where there should have been a wall. He walked to it and realized part of the wall was ajar. Doncaster Hall evidently had some secrets. He peered inside and could see the shadow of a step.

"Please don't shut it," Veronica said.

He glanced back at her to find she was still staring intently at the candle.

"You need to be very quiet, Montgomery. We're summoning spirits."

"Why?" he asked. "Who?"

Edmund startled him by turning and sending him an irritated glance.

"There have been a variety of disturbances at Doncaster Hall, Your Lordship, ever since you ascended to the title. We are trying to contact the 10th Lord Fairfax to see if he is displeased."

"Does it matter if the 10th Lord Fairfax is displeased? The 10th Lord Fairfax is dead, buried in a crypt."

Elspeth evidently thought that was amusing, because he glimpsed a wisp of a smile before her face assumed a more sober expression. Veronica, however, was still staring at the candle and not looking in his direction at all.

"Do you contact the dead often?" he asked Edmund.

"Alice says she has heard footsteps in the secret passage, Your Lordship," Edmund said, inclining his head toward the girl Montgomery didn't recognize.

"The 10th Lord Fairfax liked us using the secret passages, Your Lordship," Mrs. Brody said. She gestured with her chin toward the open passage door. "That particular one leads to your chamber, sir."

Not after he nailed it shut. Why the hell hadn't anyone told him about the secret passages? It made him wonder if his grandfather had replicated those as well. If he had, surely he'd have let his grandchildren know. What greater exploration could there have been for three curious boys?

Or perhaps Magnus hadn't known all of Doncaster Hall's secrets.

"Maybe the 10th Lord is hard of hearing," he said dryly.

Mrs. Brody turned to Edmund. "He was quite aged when he died, Your Ladyship. Perhaps we need to speak louder."

He'd been jesting, but each person at the table took his comment seriously.

Perhaps you should tell them you talk to ghosts yourself, Montgomery.

He smiled at James's voice. "There's one difference between us," he said mentally. "I *know* you're not there."

Maybe one day you'll think we're real, Alisdair said. *Once, you did.*

He was delirious and ill, Caroline said.

Caroline was always coming to his defense, even in her imaginary state.

He pushed away his ghosts to concentrate on what Veronica was saying.

"We are here if you wish to speak to us. Or let us know if you're unhappy."

Montgomery couldn't believe she was serious.

His solicitor nodded as if he approved of Veronica's comments. "Ask him if he's trapped between the living and the dead, Your Ladyship."

"Stephen," she said, addressing the 10th Lord Fairfax by his given name, "show us a sign you can hear us."

Montgomery looked around the room, knowing the others expected one of the weapons to fall off the wall or the candle to sputter out. Nothing happened. Not even a gust of wind from the secret passage.

Perhaps he should speak in an elderly whisper, just to give them some excitement.

"I don't think he's upset," Veronica said to Edmund after moments of silence. "Could someone else be haunting us?"

"There's a girl who came to a tragic end a hundred years or so ago," Mrs. Brody said. "We call her the Green Lady because she's always wearing a green dress."

"Perhaps she's changed her dress since then. That is, if ghosts feel the need to change in the hereafter," he said.

Veronica glanced over at him. He regarded her steadily. Her chin tilted up, and she narrowed her eyes.

She was taking this much too seriously.

"Someone has disturbed the atmosphere, Your Lordship," Edmund said, glancing at him again.

"No doubt," he said, deciding he'd leave them to their insanity. He wasn't going to contribute to it.

Even if he did talk to ghosts.

Chapter 20

Veronica watched Montgomery leave the room, then turned to Mr. Kerr.

"Can we try to contact another spirit?"

Mr. Kerr nodded. "Who, Lady Fairfax?"

"Caroline," she said, speaking the name in a whisper. She didn't explain. Nor, to her surprise, did Mr. Kerr ask about Caroline's identity. Again, she wondered if Montgomery had divulged more to his solicitor than he had to her.

Mr. Kerr held out both his hands. Veronica grasped his right hand while Mrs. Brody took his left. They were linked by their joined hands, as each of them stared into the flickering candle flame.

"Come forth, Caroline," he intoned, then repeated the request a number of times. As before, no sign appeared of the requested spirit.

If Caroline had chosen to appear, what would Veronica have said to her? *Who are you to my husband? Why does he grieve for you so? Or finally, and more important: will you go away and leave him alone?*

"The spirits are not willing to listen tonight," Mr. Kerr announced nearly an hour later. They disbanded, with some discussion of meeting again at a more propitious time.

To her surprise, Montgomery was outside the Armory and escorted her to the family dining room, where they were joined by Mr. Kerr.

"Have you finished communicating with the dead?" Montgomery asked.

She nodded, hoping Mr. Kerr didn't mention Caroline's name.

"Any revelations?"

"No, they weren't in the mood to communicate," Mr. Kerr said, his look making her wonder if he blamed Montgomery's entrance for their failure.

"Do you really believe in such things?" Montgomery asked.

"It has been scientifically proven," Mr. Kerr said, his voice prim, as if he resented Montgomery's doubts.

"The dead don't speak," Montgomery said.

The remainder of the conversation between the two men consisted of Mr. Kerr enumerating the many tasks he'd amassed for Montgomery to perform and Montgomery's utter disdain for each one.

Montgomery didn't seem to like being Lord Fairfax at all, given his disinclination to participate in any activity honoring him. He outright refused to attend the summer celebration held by Doncaster Village or the crowning of the Summer Queen in Lollybroch.

When she excused herself from the table, Montgomery was still ignoring Mr. Kerr, who was refusing to be silenced. She darted into the kitchen to thank Cook for a lovely meal, spoke to Mrs. Brody, and released Elspeth for the night.

She returned to her chamber, surprised to find the door to her sitting room open.

Montgomery was sitting there in the dark.

He turned his head when she entered and lit the lamp.

Slowly, she closed the door behind her and turned to face him.

His fingers curled against his chin, finger resting on his cheek, pointing to his temple. A contemplative pose, one of judgment, as if he studied her and found her wanting.

She sat on the adjacent chair, conscious her insides trembled. Why was he waiting for her? Had he discovered she'd summoned Caroline after all? She prepared herself for his anger, surprised when he didn't say anything.

Gradually, the silence became peaceful, as if he were simply content with her presence.

"Do you pretend I'm someone else?" she finally asked. "When you lie with me, Montgomery, is Caroline on your mind? When you touch me, is it her you feel? When you kiss me, do you pretend it's her?"

She bowed her head in an agony of waiting. When he didn't speak, remaining silent, she dared herself to look over at him. He was staring at her.

"How do you know about Caroline?"

"You were talking to her on our wedding day, remember?"

He looked stunned by her answer.

"All this time? You've never said anything?"

"Would you have answered me?" she asked. "You never speak of her," she said. "Yet I can feel her in your heart. You never talk about what saddens you, but it's there, Montgomery. It's there and as real as if you'd painted a sign on your forehead."

"Sometimes, it's better just to forget the past, Veronica."

She nodded. "You're right, of course. Forgetting has been so easy for you. That's why you walk every night, why you look so haunted sometimes, why you hold on to me in your sleep as if I'm your anchor."

His eyes went from hot to cool in the space of a breath, but she didn't relent.

"Whoever she is," she said, "you still love her."

"How do you know that? Your Gift?"

She smiled. She was familiar with people ridiculing what she knew to be true.

"Is it to be like this for the rest of our lives, Montgomery? Me, wanting to know, and you, hiding every one of your secrets?"

"Isn't that why they call them secrets?"

She stood, moved into the bedroom, extinguishing the lamp before returning to the sitting room.

"Why are you here, Montgomery? To bed me?"

"Are you sending me away, Veronica?"

"You know I won't," she said softly. "I can't."

He stood, reached out, and cupped her shoulders with his hands, slowly drawing her toward him.

She tilted her head back and stared at him, wishing he wasn't quite so tall. Yet her female cousins had remarked, many times, on how tall she was compared to them, how dull her appearance.

Abruptly, she asked, "Would you prefer if I had blond hair?"

Was Caroline blond?

He shook his head slowly, as if uncertain where her question would lead.

"Or if I had blue eyes?"

Were Caroline's eyes blue, like yours?

"Why are you asking that?"

"Do my looks displease you?"

"You're a beautiful woman, Veronica."

She felt a glow of pleasure but pushed it aside for another question.

"Then what is it about me that displeases you?" She forced herself to meet his gaze. "Is it my Gift?"

He studied her for a long moment, and she had the

feeling he was treading carefully, walking barefoot on gravel.

"Is it that I'm not an American? We have a heritage in common, Montgomery. Your family is from Scotland as well as mine."

He gripped her upper arms so tightly she had the feeling he wanted to shake her.

"Nothing about you displeases me," he said, and it sounded like the truth. "When we make love, there's no one else on my mind. How could there be?"

Yet he could not love her. He had no more love to give another woman.

Wasn't she foolish to want more when she had him?

He couldn't stay away, yet every time he was with her, she pulled a little more from him. As if he were a knitted garment, and she was unraveling him bit by bit, wrapping him around her finger. The only way to silence her, and ease himself, was to love her, long and hard, until she was too damned tired to question him.

Either bed was suddenly too far away. In one smooth move, he sat and pulled her onto his lap, dove beneath the mound of skirts and petticoats to find the slit in her pantaloons.

She made a sound, a soft little gasp that aroused him further.

He swore, half to himself, half to her, need rising without his conscious volition. She was there; he wanted her, as elemental as day and night. He wondered if she knew how damn helpless he was around her, how much he thought of her, how easily she could arouse him. She smiled, and he wanted her. She frowned, and he wanted her. Whatever emotion she was feeling, whatever she was wearing, whatever she was doing, he wanted her.

"Montgomery," she murmured in that sensual Scots accent of hers. She might have been fussing at him, but he found it seductive as sin itself.

"Open your legs," he said, wondering if she would.

She widened her legs just the smallest bit, so his fingers could play there.

They were a pair, cautiously circling each other, besotted by desire, desperate to mate. He'd never felt this way about any woman, wasn't certain what to call it, then uncaring as she made another sound at the back of her throat.

If someone entered her sitting room, they wouldn't see his fingers stroking her wetness, teasing that soft and delicate opening.

She moaned, such a demure little sound it might have been from any cause, not his finger stroking her, then entering her a moment later.

He was so hard he hurt.

"Are you thinking of the Queen?" he asked, his voice rough.

Her eyes fluttered shut. "No."

"Bad Veronica," he said, and pulled his hands away.

Her eyes opened, and she blinked a few times. "I'll try," she said, her voice thick.

He returned his fingers to her, gently touched each swollen fold, then placed both hands on her thighs to lift her.

"Widen your legs."

She did, and he unfastened his trousers, slid home in one long, smooth movement.

Veronica gasped.

"Don't move," he said, leaning his head against the back of the chair, lost in the feel of her.

How the hell could he think of another woman? Hell,

he could barely hold on to any thought at the moment.

She leaned forward, at precisely the perfect angle, as if she'd done this before and knew how to drive him insane.

"You feel so damn good," he said, his voice a rasp. "Don't move." God, please don't move.

She sat erect, in that same posture, her hands folded on her lap. He was inside her, buried to the hilt, her heat and tightness threatening to end this interlude before its time.

He moved her hair away from the nape of her neck, trailed his fingers over her skin to her collar, properly buttoned. He smoothed his hands down her bodice, feeling the fabric over her cinched waist, his thumbs running back up each seam as if to test the propriety of her attire. His right hand flicked at a fold of her skirt, his left was at her hip to keep her in place.

Her dress covered his legs and most of the chair. He pressed down on the mass of the fabric between her back and his open trousers, his fingers dancing up her clothed spine.

Her breath was fast, her lids half-shut, a becoming flush turning her cheeks rose. She'd caught at her bottom lip with her teeth. Because of his position, he couldn't reach her mouth. He surged up just once, to punish her for making him want to kiss her.

She turned her head slightly, her eyes bearing a lambent gaze of arousal coupled with awareness. The lady hadn't been replaced by the harlot. Instead, the lady knew the strength of her own allure, the price he'd pay to drive both of them to madness before this was finished.

Anything.

"You're perfectly dressed and proper, Veronica," he said. "I wish Elspeth would enter now and see us sitting together in such accord."

He could feel her thighs clench at the thought and

moved a little in reward. His restraint was nearly at the breaking point, and they'd just begun. She was motionless, hot, and wet, so tight that even her breathing was an unbearable friction.

His hands dove beneath her skirts again, pulled on both sides of her pantaloons until they ripped apart. He reached for her, trailing a circle in the wet between her thighs, her moans driving him mad.

She pressed both palms flat against her bodice, just below her breasts, her breath coming fast.

"You want me to touch your breasts, don't you, Veronica?"

She nodded.

"That wouldn't be proper."

She shook her head.

"Even asking me to suck on your nipples would be wrong."

She nodded, caught up in the game. "Very, very wrong."

His thumbs met, stroked softly as her eyes closed.

He wanted to move, was nearly desperate to move, but he remained where he was, solid and hard inside her. She was so damn hot, he felt scorched by her heat.

"Are you thinking of the Empire?"

"Yes," she said, breathlessly. "All those ships."

"Sailing around the world."

"All those very tall masts," she said, leaning gently to the side and accompanying the movement with an inward squeeze.

He grinned at her talent, drew his hands from beneath her skirts and placed them on both sides of her clothed waist, and lifted her up, then down. A reward, then, for her wholehearted participation in this game.

"Such strong, thick masts," she murmured, clenching

him again. This time, she placed both hands on the arms of the chair and levered herself up slowly, then just as slowly down.

"You're not being the least proper, Veronica Fairfax," he said, when he could breathe again. "I shall have to punish you."

"Please," she whispered. "No."

She turned her head again; the look they shared was one of lovers.

"Don't leave," she said. "Please."

As if he could leave her.

She'd turned the game neatly on its head, overpowering him by simply enjoying herself. Her face and neck were flushed, her lips full as if he'd kissed them swollen, her eyes wide and hinting at green. She began a rhythm between them by planting her feet full on the floor and lifting herself up and down and to each side, using him.

He was so damn pleased with her he could have laughed.

Instead, he placed his hands on her hips and urged her higher, raising up when she lowered herself, glorying in each of her soft moans.

"You aren't being proper at all, Veronica," he said, before leaning forward and scraping his teeth against her throat, breathing into her ear.

"I know," she said, turning her head. Wicked delight showed in her eyes.

"Faster."

"Yes," she said, a sibilant murmur of need. "Yes."

He wanted to tongue her, taste her, bite her nipples, and suck her into his mouth. All he did was sit there, allow himself to be taken, used, drained. He felt himself gush into her, the exquisite pleasure so powerful it stopped at the barest edge of pain.

Her climax was announced with a keening moan. When she was done, when her rhythmic contractions eased, and her breathing was long and slow, he lifted her and carried her to his bed, staggering a little, but feeling as if he'd conquered the whole damn world.

When dawn woke him, Montgomery watched Veronica as she slept, the rising sun casting an orange glow over the room.

Passion was wrapping a net around both of them, yet he had no intention of fighting free. From the beginning, he'd been startled by her complete surrender to him. Now, he was beginning to know the woman herself, and knowledge of Veronica only bound him closer.

She knew a little about his past but not the whole of it. The truth was a tale filled with tragedy and stupidity, and wasn't a story he wanted to tell.

He had a feeling, however, she wouldn't rest until she'd heard all of it.

What would she say? Would the knowledge change her response to him?

Her hair was mussed around her face. Her lips were pink, her complexion was rosy.

What is it about me that displeases you? Why had she felt so lacking?

She knew about Caroline. Yet in the past weeks, she'd never said a word.

He reached out and placed his hand on her arm, feeling the warmth of her skin beneath his palm. Even in sleep she was alluring. Or perhaps she was simply as elemental as air currents to his ship. He needed her.

Her eyes blinked open.

"Come flying with me," he said, feeling as shy as a boy.

"Flying?" she asked, stretching. "When?"

"Tomorrow." He amended that comment after a glance at the window. "Today."

She looked worried.

"There's no need to be afraid," he said. "I'm taking the balloon up to test the air currents."

"I'm not afraid," she said, but he suspected she was. Veronica had a core of stubbornness to her, one that would refuse to admit any fear.

He waited, patient, tracing a pattern on her arm with one finger.

Slowly, she nodded.

"Is that a yes?" he asked.

She nodded again, accompanying the gesture with a smile.

"If for no other reason than to prove to me you're not afraid," he guessed.

Her broadening smile was worthy of a kiss.

"Passion becomes you, Veronica," he said, pulling back. "Your cheeks are pink, and you look well loved."

He pulled her into his arms again, and any further conversation was lost beneath a tide of pleasure.

Chapter 21

When Veronica awoke in Montgomery's bed the next morning, it was to find herself alone and the morning well advanced. She rang for Elspeth, dressed, then walked to the distillery, her stomach fluttering with excitement.

She saw the balloon before she reached the arched bridge. Constructed of blue and green silk stripes, it was a remarkable sight, one that looked to have attracted most of the inhabitants of Doncaster Hall as well.

Montgomery was standing in a square basket below the tethered balloon. He didn't wave to her as she stood on the arch of the bridge, but he followed her progress with his gaze.

Her body heated, and her heart began to race. He could do that to her with a look.

When she grew closer, he leaned over the basket and extended his hand to her.

"Have you changed your mind?"

"No," she said. Her voice came out as a squeak, a fact that annoyed her.

His smile faded. "I wouldn't put you in danger, Veronica. That I promise."

"I've never been up in a balloon," she said, glancing up at the huge expanse of silk.

Below the throat of the balloon, supported by four wooden dowels, was a metal box.

"Is that your navigation device?" she asked.

"No, that's the burner."

"It's very loud," she said.

Before she realized what he was going to do, Montgomery put both hands on her waist and simply lifted her into the basket.

She was already feeling a little queasy, and when he released her, she kept her hands on his arms. "I think I am afraid," she admitted.

"That's when you feel the most alive, Veronica," he said softly. "It means nothing if you go through life without being afraid. What's important is you've stared fear in the face."

"I'm not entirely certain I'm ready to do that, either."

He smiled. "You already have. You faced the Society of the Mercaii alone."

"That wasn't fear. That was foolishness."

He smiled at her honesty before moving back and making an adjustment on the burner.

She dropped her hands but didn't step away. She would have gripped Montgomery around the waist and buried her face against his chest if she could have. She didn't have a dislike of heights. Nor was it that she lacked any trust in Montgomery. This was a balloon. A balloon, so gigantic it seemed capable of carrying them to the moon.

Montgomery signaled to Ralston.

"Are the riders in position?"

"Yes, Your Lordship," Ralston said.

"Riders?" Veronica asked.

"I'm going to try to return to Doncaster Hall," he said, "but if the wind currents are too strong, and we're blown off course, the riders will be able to pinpoint our landing site. Each has a wagon with him."

"To carry our unconscious bodies?" she asked in a feeble attempt at humor.

He smiled reassuringly, as if knowing her throat was closing and her stomach trembling. Not to mention the fluttery feeling in her chest that made her wonder if she were going to faint at any moment.

"No, for the envelope and the gondola. And our conscious bodies."

"We're not going to be tethered?" Veronica was exceedingly proud of her voice since she no longer squeaked.

"Where's the fun in that?" He turned and faced her. "If you want to wait here, I'd understand."

This morning was the first time he'd ever willingly sought her company outside the bedroom. She wasn't about to leave.

She shook her head, pasted a smile on her face. "I'm looking forward to a new experience," she lied.

Montgomery glanced at her, amused, and went about his duties.

She wanted to sit down, curl herself into the smallest ball possible, and wedge herself into the corner of the woven basket. Instead, she stood frozen to the spot, terrified any movement might cause the balloon to carry them into the air before Montgomery was ready.

Dear Lord, she was going to be flying in only seconds.

"Montgomery," she said, about to beg him to help her out of the basket. He glanced over her shoulder at her, smiled reassuringly, and she changed her mind. She shook her head, and he signaled to the men holding the mooring ropes.

One by one, they began to walk closer to him. The

balloon ascended, and Veronica held on to one of the supports of the gondola as it gradually rose. Her stomach seemed fixed on the ground below and was refusing to make the journey.

Montgomery began to pull the mooring ropes back into the basket until they were tethered only by the strength of two men holding one rope. He leaned over the basket, an utterly foolhardy move in her opinion, and shouted to Ralston.

The men released the last rope, and they were aloft.

The balloon sighed, fell some distance, and began to sway in the air. Montgomery pulled the rope into the gondola as they ascended still higher.

She closed her eyes, grabbed the support with both arms, and pretended it was all a dream.

The last time she'd asked for divine intervention because of a decision she'd made had been the night she'd attended the Society of the Mercaii meeting. She was in the same situation again. No one had forced her into this basket. No one had made her take this adventure unless it was her foolish pride.

"You have to open your eyes," he said, his tone amused. "Otherwise, you might just as well be sitting in your drawing room."

"At the moment," she said between gritted teeth, "I wish I were."

"Veronica."

She opened her eyes to see him looking down at her, a smile on his face.

"There's your Scotland," he said, extending his hand as if offering the panorama to her.

She looked up, which was easier than looking down. A bird flew by, looking as startled at the sight of them as she was to be so close to him.

She was flying, improbably and impossibly, flying. She might as well look.

Her hands came up in the air, fingers splayed as if to press against an invisible barrier as she edged to the side.

He laughed and grabbed her around the waist with one arm, pulling her closer to him.

"You're safer here than you would be walking on a London street. Or in a train."

"That's not exceedingly reassuring," she said. "Since we aren't walking through London or in a train at the moment. We're very, very high up."

With one hand, Montgomery reached over, increasing the flame.

"What are you doing?" she said, panicked.

"I'm ensuring that we'll stay aloft," he said, looking down at her.

"How do we get down?"

"See that rope?" he asked, pointing to a tightly wound rope on one of the gondola supports.

She nodded, careful not to do so vehemently. Even her breathing was cautious.

"It's connected to a baffle on top of the envelope. I can release some of the hot air, which will allow us to land."

"Softly, I hope."

He only smiled.

She parted her feet a little, the better to combat the balloon's swaying sensation, and looked over the side again.

They passed over Doncaster Hall, and she was startled to note the many chimneys, as well as the steep pitch of part of the roof. It seemed as if every person living at the Hall waved to them, and she held up one hand in greeting, feeling as if she were a queen greeting her subjects.

The world lay before them, a panorama of incredible

beauty. The sun, a blurry disk behind a shelf of clouds, was to their left as they headed west.

She'd never thought to see the world from this perspective and was so fascinated she lost her fear after the first few moments. Granted, it helped that Montgomery had pulled her back against him, and his arms were wrapped around her waist. She tipped forward to see the sprawling countryside beneath her, slowly passing, as if they were still, and the world was on some sort of tumbrel.

In the distance, three long mountain ranges stretched like indolent maidens, their limbs pointing toward Doncaster Hall, their heads in the north. Atop them was a mantle of white, a soft and downy blanket, warning of the winter to come.

The River Tairn, an engorged silver snake, coiled back on itself, wrapped around Doncaster Hall and slithered through emerald glens. The sparse tufts of grass near the flocks of sheep became a lush green carpet and the sheep themselves no more than black faced clouds. The air was crisp and cold, as if winter had not yet folded over to spring.

She was giddy with delight.

Peace radiated from Montgomery instead of the horrible pain she'd felt from him for so long. Peace and something else, perhaps joy. For that, alone, she'd come up in his balloon again. To share his happiness was worth any type of fear.

She wrapped her arms around her waist, her hands gripping Montgomery's wrists. She relished his warmth but almost forgot he was there in the wonder she saw before her.

The only sound was the noise of the burner and the thump of her heart. Otherwise, the world was still and perfect.

They crossed the road and several more glens. A farmer, in his wagon, stopped his team of mules to stare up at them. A carriage on the road halted as well.

"Does everybody stare?" she asked.

He leaned close, spoke near her ear.

"They're fascinated. Wouldn't you be?"

She nodded. "And a little envious," she admitted. Yet she was the one in the balloon, experiencing it all, seeing it all.

A few cottages sat together, like a frightened clutch of geese. She knew, suddenly, where they were, traveling northwest, toward Lollybroch. She wanted to close her eyes, to block out the sights so familiar to her. Yet, at the same time, she couldn't quite deny herself the recollection of all of those warm and lovely memories.

Near the main road in Lollybroch was the Presbyterian church, its spire unassuming as if afraid to call too much attention to itself.

"I didn't know we had a village so prosperous this close to us," he said.

"That's Lollybroch," she said.

"Your home."

She nodded, surprised he'd remembered.

"Where did you live?" he asked, leaning forward to look at the cottages tucked into the rolling glen.

"There," she said, extending her arm and pointing toward McNaren's Hill. "On the other side."

She took a step away from him as if to distance herself from her memories. For several long moments, she didn't say anything, afraid she couldn't speak over the sudden constriction of her throat.

"Must we go there?" she finally asked, glancing over her shoulder at him. "I'd rather not," she said softly. "Please."

"I'm working on a way to guide my airship, Veronica," he said. "Until then, we're at the mercy of the wind."

She nodded her understanding, facing forward again. This time, when he came to stand behind her, he didn't wrap his arms around her. She stood alone, watching the approach of McNaren's Hill, feeling herself grow colder as they neared her home.

Whether or not she saw her house, that night was forever emblazoned in her mind. All she had to do to relive it was allow herself to think about it. Normally, she pushed away the memories the moment they came. Otherwise, she'd be immobilized by pain.

There, the lane leading to the house. Another signpost, the tree struck by lightning when she was seven. The creek, the grove, all landmarks she'd known from her childhood.

The only sign a two-story house had once stood in that spot was a soot-darkened brick half wall and the remnants of the kitchen fireplace. Saplings poked up through the blackened earth, as if the forest was attempting to reclaim the spot, healing it with new growth.

A swift breeze skittered across her face like an icy hand.

Veronica closed her eyes, forcing herself to breathe calmly, slowly, deeply.

"What happened?" Montgomery asked.

She didn't open her eyes.

"A fire."

She would have stepped away from him had the gondola been larger.

He didn't speak, didn't pry, granting her the privacy of her past she'd denied him. They hovered over the site until a gust carried them eastward. In those moments, it felt as if God were testing her. As if He wanted her to feel everything she'd successfully hidden all this time.

Because she'd been so insistent that Montgomery share his secrets with her, could she do otherwise?

"My father woke me," she said, pushing the words free. "He was shouting. He put his strongbox in my hand and said something, I never did understand what. Then he went back inside to get my mother."

Montgomery remained silent.

"They never came out. I tried to get to them," she said, glancing down at the scars on her palms. "I couldn't get the door open. I stood there and watched as the house burned, and I couldn't do anything."

She'd stood there for hours and hours, waiting for her parents to appear. They never had, and when the roof had fallen, she'd known they were dead. When three of the four walls caved in, she'd remained there, clutching the strongbox tightly as if her father's spirit were trapped inside. Finally, a few of the villagers had urged her to come away, and she had. She'd seen to it that they were buried in the churchyard only days before Uncle Bertrand had arrived to take her to London.

Her heart felt as if it had been carved open by a spoon.

Montgomery put his hands on her shoulders, moved closer.

She didn't want his pity or even his comfort. If he was kind to her, she'd begin to cry. Everyone had wanted her to be so strong, and she had been. Her uncle considered excessive emotion a character flaw, announcing that tears would not honor her father or her mother.

At her uncle's house, there had been few opportunities for her to give in to her grief. But seeing what was left of the house nearly overwhelmed her.

She lowered her head.

"I'm sorry, Veronica."

She nodded.

He squeezed his hands on her shoulders. She closed her eyes on her tears, felt the sway of the gondola in the wind. God Himself might have been cradling her in apology for His earlier test.

"My parents died of fever," he said. "I still miss them."

She nodded, wanting to thank him for sharing that information with her. The reason he did so wasn't hard to understand. He'd seen her grief and wanted to ease it. But it wasn't just grief she felt.

"It was Cook's half day," she said, her voice flat. "By afternoon, she still hadn't returned. I wanted a cup of tea, so I put the kettle on. I don't remember if I took it off the stove."

He nodded, his chin brushing against her hair. "So all this time you've thought you were responsible for the fire."

She nodded.

"You'll never know, Veronica."

She nodded again.

"We all feel guilt for something," he said. "Regret for acts done or undone. Or for a word spoken in cruelty or kindness."

He extended his arms around her again, and she laid her head back against his shoulder, trading her view of the land for that of the sky.

She wanted to thank him for his attempt to ease her grief. Thank him, too, for the gift of this day, this perfect experience of flying.

"The sky is darkening toward the south," he said, after a few moments of silence. "It might be an approaching storm. We should put down."

Montgomery reached up and grabbed one of the ropes. A second later, the gondola lurched to the left.

She closed her eyes and began praying.

"It's all right, Veronica," he said, amusement threading through his voice. "It's nothing unusual. It's just the air leaving the envelope."

She opened her eyes, looked up at him. "Then I shall attempt to be a little more courageous. You'll tell me if anything goes wrong?"

He nodded. "What do you think of your first voyage?"

"It's been wonderful," she said, and meant it.

"Does that mean you'll go flying with me again?"

"I should like to, very much."

"You're a constant surprise," he said, smiling at her, dimples leading the way to his beautiful blue eyes.

She was stunned by the feeling suddenly sweeping through her. She'd never considered that love might slip up on her unawares, that she might feel her heart open in the span of an instant.

He frustrated her, worried her, and could make her angrier than anyone, including Amanda. She'd felt ecstasy in his arms, and now excitement in his balloon. But she'd never thought to love him as easily as this, as instantly as this.

"What is it?" he asked.

She shook her head and moved to stand beside him. He extended an arm around her shoulders and pulled her closer, and she wrapped one arm around his waist, surveying Scotland spread before her.

When she was a little girl, she'd loved gloaming, the time just before darkness bathed the earth. The air grew misty, as if seen through gauze. This morning, turning to midday, was even more perfect.

Saturated with emotion, nearly giddy with it, she laid her cheek against Montgomery's chest as they began to descend.

"We've visitors," he said, his tone suddenly cold.

She peered over the edge of the gondola to see three carriages, each of them horribly familiar, and felt her heart sink to her toes. Three carriages: one for Uncle Bertrand and the boys; one for Aunt Lilly and the girls, and the third for all their trunks.

"Uncle Bertrand," she said.

"And the entirety of your family," Montgomery added.

She turned helpless eyes to him. "I'm very much afraid you're right."

They exchanged a glance.

"Can't we just stay up here?"

His mouth quirked in a smile. "For a little while, but we have to land eventually. We might as well face them."

"I would much rather stare fear in the face, Montgomery," she said. "Than the whole of my family."

Chapter 22

"**Y**ou need to discipline your staff, Veronica," Aunt Lilly said. "One of the maids actually had the temerity to smile at me this morning." She lifted the lid of each of the chafing dishes, frowning. "What is this penchant the Scottish have for oats?" she asked. "A good dish of herring is what's needed in the morning. Don't you agree, my dear?"

Veronica knew better than to assume the last statement had been directed toward her. Uncle Bertrand looked up absently, then nodded.

Her father hadn't liked oatmeal, either, and it had become a loving jest around their house. *If you don't finish weeding the garden today, Veronica, you'll have porridge for supper.* Her mother used the threat against her father: *If your father isn't done with his writings in an hour, I shall give him a porridge instead of this lovely stew.*

She didn't share that story with her aunt. Neither Aunt Lilly nor Uncle Bertrand liked to speak of her parents, as if not mentioning them would somehow erase them from her mind.

Montgomery, seated on the other side of the breakfast table from her uncle, glanced at her. She didn't need any sort of Gift to know what he was thinking. Her relatives annoyed him.

At least he was there, at breakfast, preventing her from having to suffer through a meal with her family alone, a gesture for which she was exceedingly grateful.

"I'm sorry you don't find anything to your satisfaction, Aunt Lilly," she said. "Perhaps if you would let me know what you'd prefer, I'll inform Cook. Tomorrow morning, we'll be better prepared for you."

Dear God, how long were they staying?

"A good hostess is prepared for all contingencies, my dear," Aunt Lilly said, returning to the table. For someone who hadn't found anything palatable, she'd certainly filled her plate.

"Why, exactly, have you decided to grace us with a visit?" Montgomery asked.

She glanced at Montgomery, then Aunt Lilly. If she'd made that remark, she'd have been chastised for the effrontery of it. With so many people at the table ready to castigate her for one gaffe or another, it was a miracle food hadn't curdled in her stomach.

Aunt Lilly only smiled at Montgomery.

"We are not simply visitors, my dear boy. We're family. I didn't realize we required an invitation to feel welcome in your home." She smiled again. "But then, we didn't know that you would be engaged in . . ." Her hands fluttered in the air as her words trailed away.

Her family had been shocked to see the balloon, so much so that they'd stared at Montgomery all during dinner as if he were some sort of winged creature invited into the drawing room. Breakfast didn't look to be any better.

Of the two episodes—flying in Montgomery's balloon and welcoming her family to Doncaster Hall—she much preferred flying.

She stood before Aunt Lilly could say anything further.

"Of course you're welcome at Doncaster Hall, Aunt Lilly," she said, signaling Montgomery with a glance. She then did something she'd never had the courage to do in London.

She left the room.

Montgomery met her outside the family dining room.

"How could they simply appear?" she asked. "Am I to hear her criticisms until they leave? And when are they leaving?"

"Since they're your relatives, I couldn't venture to guess," he said. "Have you considered asking them?"

"She'll just pat me on the head, tell me not to worry, then proceed to order the kitchen staff about. The only reason breakfast was halfway bearable was because my cousins decided to take a tray in their rooms. Five trays, Montgomery. We don't have an infinite number of staff. Every maid was pressed into service this morning. Even Mrs. Brody was ferrying trays up and down the steps."

"You had no idea they were coming?"

"I had *no* idea they were coming. And if we don't do something now, Montgomery, they will continue to come. Every few months. And stay."

The look on his face mirrored her inward horror. Emigrating to America was almost preferable to endless visits from Uncle Bertrand and his family.

"Can you imagine a repeat of dinner for the next two weeks?"

Dinner the night before had been a higgledy-piggledy affair, with Mrs. Brody's careful menu thrown out due to the unexpected arrival of seven relatives and their three servants. They'd cobbled together a meat course, a fish course, a vegetable course, and pudding, but Uncle Bertrand and Aunt Lilly had not ceased complaining, along with Adam, Amanda, Alice, and Anne, about the paucity of the food and its quality. The only person who hadn't ventured a negative opinion was Algernon, because he was feeling ill and had remained in a hastily prepared guest chamber.

"Perhaps if I was exceptionally rude," Montgomery said, "they'd leave earlier."

She shook her head, feeling panic rush in. "On the contrary. Aunt Lilly would take it upon herself to instruct you on proper manners. She'd stay longer."

They looked at each other. For the first time in their married life, they had a shared goal as well as a common enemy.

"You could come and help me with the balloon," he said.

"Are you asking because you're feeling sorry for me? Or because you genuinely wish my assistance?"

"I'm asking because I haven't any other idea how to spare you your aunt's attentions," he said, holding out his hand.

"I should warn Mrs. Brody," she said. "Tell her to pay Aunt Lilly no heed."

He nodded.

"And warn Ralston as well," she added.

He only smiled.

"We should be a good host and hostess."

"We should," he echoed. "But Mrs. Brody and Ralston will simply have to fend for themselves. As will your family."

She placed her hand in his, allowing him to lead her to the servants' stairs. By the time they reached the arched bridge, they were running, like children escaping the schoolroom.

At the top of the bridge, he placed his hands on her waist, twirled her around until her skirts were swirling above her ankles. She began to laugh, teased into merriment by the look in his eyes and the smile on his face.

Who knew that Montgomery had a mischievous side?

He hadn't been speaking in jest when he said he would put her to work. He gave her a leather apron and directed her to several crates stacked in the corner.

Tom, one of the stableboys who'd come to work with Montgomery, was to assist her. Tom was young, and shy, a fact she discovered when she smiled in his direction. His face flushed, he ducked his head, and he mumbled something she couldn't hear. Rather than ask him to repeat himself, she took pity on the boy and looked away.

"What is it, exactly, you want me to do, Montgomery?"

She glanced over her shoulder at him, startled to notice he'd taken off his jacket and rolled up his shirtsleeves. She'd never noticed how well developed his arms were. Even fully clothed, Montgomery was arresting.

He'd remained in his room last night, and she'd stayed in hers, feeling a little odd about her entire family being in residence and in rooms down the hall. Instead of feeling reticent, she should have gone to him.

Their gazes locked, and she flushed.

"I'm looking for the blades of a fan," he said. "I thought I'd unpacked it but couldn't find it. It's time I unpacked everything, I think."

He gestured toward the six crates, and she nodded.

Tom used an oddly shaped iron tool to pry off the lid of the first crate. By the third crate, she was ankle deep in wood shavings and sneezing periodically, as ladylike as she could. Tom, on the other hand, was enjoying himself immensely, as evidenced by his broad smile each time they discovered something new and unusual.

She'd unearthed an oval crystal object Montgomery identified as a thermometer. Something else that looked like a weathervane incited a word of praise from him. He strode across the distillery, took it from her, and held it up in front of him.

"I wondered where that was," he said. "I ordered it from Italy, you see, and hadn't thought it was here yet."

Without telling her exactly what it was, he strode back to his worktable. Her gaze followed him, watched as he perched on the stool, and smiled at the weathervane-like object as if it were a well-cherished friend.

The air was filled with dust, and the temperature was rising in the distillery to almost an uncomfortable warmth. She didn't know what she was doing yet she couldn't remember a time when she'd been happier.

After her adventure the day before in the balloon, she was more than willing to go up again. Even eager, a comment she made to him when the last of the crates was unpacked and the wood shavings piled into a barrow for use as kindling. He smiled at her, as if pleased at her enthusiasm.

When she saw one of the maids on the arched bridge, carrying Montgomery's lunch, it was a clear signal she needed to return to the house to ensure that her relatives weren't ordering everyone around.

"Is there anything I can do to convince you to accompany me back to Doncaster Hall?" she asked.

He kept his attention on the mass of metal parts arranged on a workbench. For a moment, Veronica was certain he was unaware she'd spoken. A second later, however, he proved her wrong by glancing at her and smiling. He set the tool he was using down on the workbench, wiped his hand on a cloth, and met her in the middle of the building.

Sunlight speared through the door of the distillery, bathing him in a bright light. She walked closer, stopping only when the toes of her shoes met the toes of his boots.

Since the day before, she'd been filled with an effervescent feeling of excitement, an emotion that even the appearance of her relatives couldn't destroy. She tilted her head back and looked up at him, blinking against the light. Placing both hands on his chest, she could feel his heat, and the steady and certain beat of his heart.

"Regrettably," she whispered, "good manners dictate I'm a lady in the parlor at the moment."

"Pity," he said. "I would much prefer a harlot in my bedroom. Or the old distillery," he amended.

He covered her hands with his, a tender touch, and something he'd never done. Nor had he ever lifted her hand and kissed her palm, sending a spear of heat to her core.

The maid placed Montgomery's meal on the table beside the door and spoke to Ralston for a moment. Tom made a comment, Ralston answered him, all commonplace sounds, and all of them an intrusion on the moment.

She wanted, almost desperately, to be alone with her husband. From the glint in his eye, Montgomery felt the same.

"Ralston," he said suddenly, turning to the older man, "I've an errand for you." He left her, went to his worktable, and took a piece of paper from it. "Take this list to Mr. Kerr. It's supplies I need to replenish." He glanced over at Tom. "Take Tom with you."

The older man, bless his instinct for tact, didn't ask one question. All he did was incline his head, nod slightly, then gesture toward Tom. In moments, the two men were gone.

He turned toward Veronica once more.

She brushed her hands against her apron, smiling quizzically at him as he approached.

"Where did you send my helper?" she asked.

"To perdition for the moment," he said, reaching her. Slowly, he untied the leather apron, allowing it to fall to the dirt floor.

She tilted her head, a look appearing in her eyes that fascinated him: curiosity, delight, excitement, and perhaps a little doubt.

"I'm hungry," he said softly.

"Are you?"

She looked toward the door, which Ralston, bless the man's intuitive heart, had had the sense to close.

"Mrs. Brody has sent a tray," she said faintly.

"What Mrs. Brody sent is not what I'm hungry for," he said, his lips curving in a smile.

"Oh?"

Veronica took one cautionary step away from him, but he remedied that by simply gripping her wrist and gently pulling her toward him.

She cleared her throat. "In the distillery, Montgomery?"

"I've been thinking of possible places," he said. "Not on the ground. There's the pile of shavings, of course. I doubt we'd be able to return to the house in any sort of order if we used them as a mattress. You might get splinters on your delectable bottom from the worktable. Unless, of course, I fuck you fully clothed."

She looked away, her face delightfully flushed.

He began unfastening her bodice. "I like this dress," he said, his gaze fixed on the row of buttons. The fabric was royal blue, but the white piping on the cuffs and collar rendered it pretty rather than plain. "Is this one of your new dresses?"

She nodded, looking down at his hands.

"Do you have any new shifts?"

She nodded again, catching her bottom lip with her teeth.

"A few dozen, I hope," he said, spreading the bodice open. A delicate pink bow held her shift closed. A gentle tug, and it was open.

He rubbed his knuckles over her fully erect nipples, pleased at the sight of her breasts plumped up by the corset. He bent his head, trailed his tongue across one nipple, smiling at the sound of her gasp.

She was always so damn responsive.

With one hand, he grabbed the hem of her skirt, raised it, and slid a hand through the froth of her petticoat.

"Thank God you didn't wear a hoop," he said, his lips against her heated cheek.

She shivered, turned her head, and rewarded him with a soft, chaste, kiss.

"It's a very small one," she said demurely. "Suitable for at-home."

He slid his fingers across her thigh, smoothing little circles over her skin, hearing her breath catch as he drew closer to the slit in her pantaloons.

Drawing back, he watched her as she lifted her head. Her eyes were beautifully green at the moment, wide, and filled with desire. Her breath was coming in shallow pants, her heart beating so fast he could see the pulse of it in her throat. He loved seeing her aroused, second only to the look on her face when she climaxed.

His hand trailed between her thighs. She was dampening for him, legs widening as he cupped her, then slid a finger through her folds.

She was his.

"You're wet. Show me how wet you are. Open your legs wider."

An involuntary growl escaped him as she did.

Veronica startled him by pressing her hand against his trousers, feeling his erection, clasping it possessively.

"You're as hungry as I am," he murmured, kissing the edge of her jaw. A delicate kiss that didn't reveal his raging need.

"Montgomery," she whispered. "Anyone might come in."

"Up on the worktable," he said.

"What about splinters?"

"Kneel."

Her eyebrows rose, but she did as he asked.

In moments, she was kneeling on his worktable, fully dressed, the skirt hiding her from his view. His cock was still trembling in its fabric prison and, when he released it, pointed at her as if seeking its home.

Slowly, he raised her skirts. There she was, hidden in the cave of cloth, her dampness evident to him even then. He ran one finger from her bottom through her pink and swollen folds to slide inside her.

Her back arched, then she lowered her head between her shoulders, a small moan escaping her.

"You're beautiful," he said. "I want to put my mouth on you."

Her head turned, her face aflame. Desire and hunger flared in her eyes.

"Spread your legs wider," he ordered, smiling when she did.

"Now, move closer."

She backed toward him. The perfect angle, the perfect height. He ripped her pantaloons, bent his head, and gently bit one of the beautiful globes of her bottom.

Her breathing was raspy, her hair tumbling over her red cheeks.

"I'm going to come in you, now."

Her back dipped; she supported herself on her forearms.

Then, before he spilled his seed from the sheer sight of her, he entered her in one smooth movement, closing his eyes as she sighed his name, her nails scraping the wood of the worktable.

"Now, if anyone comes in, they won't know."

She shook her head, not allowing him that sophistry. Anyone could tell, from her face, exactly what he was doing to her.

He pulled her skirts down over both of them, gripping her clothed hips with both hands, jerking her back onto him. Wondering, as he did so, how much of this he could take.

She was trembling, her body a furnace gripping him possessively. He was in deeper than he'd ever been. A dozen thrusts, and she was rocking back against him, milking him of his seed, moaning with each movement. A dozen more, and she cried out. He joined her seconds later, feeling himself explode into her.

For long moments, neither said a word. He didn't move. No doubt he had a stupid smile on his face. Beneath the satisfaction was another emotion, one that troubled him.

He couldn't keep his damn hands off his wife.

Not only that, but he was beginning to want her in his bed. To roll over and be able to touch her, to feel her warmth. To smell roses when he dreamed, to know the scent meant Veronica was near.

She rose a little, looking away, then back at him, her expression a little difficult to decipher. She was satiated; he knew that much from the pulse beats still pounding against his deflated cock. She was a little embarrassed; not all the flush on her face was due to arousal. Yet she was also a little proud if he wasn't mistaken, as if she'd done something for which she deserved acclaim.

She'd fucked him stupid, and he, for one, was damn glad of it despite the warning bells clanging in his brain.

He moved back.

What the hell did he say now? Stay with me? Or help me, I don't know what the hell is happening?

He helped her from the workbench, occupied himself with putting himself to order, then helping her dress, his trembling fingers fastening each button much more slowly than he'd unbuttoned her.

Lust had made him gallop for the end of the race. Caution slowed him now. Did he apologize for his haste? Attempt to explain he couldn't control himself around her? He was damned if he knew how to handle it.

"Go and be a good hostess for us, Veronica. I'll make it back for dinner," he said, bending his head to kiss her. He held her for a few more minutes, longer than was wise because she cuddled against him. Even her soft sigh was enough to make him want her again.

He walked with her to the door and kissed her again after opening it.

He hadn't wanted to be married and had made little secret of that fact. He hadn't wanted to rescue anyone, but he'd been compelled to rescue Veronica from the Society of the Mercaii. For that, he'd been rewarded with a marriage to the most confusing, fascinating, desirable woman he'd ever known.

She'd never spoken of her parents, and yesterday, he'd discovered that she had her own deep well of grief. Today, she'd been a cheerful helpmate, even charming Tom. She'd worked tirelessly for hours, then effortlessly been a siren he couldn't ignore.

As he leaned against the brick doorway and watched

Veronica walk back to Doncaster Hall, he suspected he wasn't the same man he'd been before coming to Scotland.

Why was he suddenly so damn happy?

As she crossed the arched bridge, Veronica pressed her hands against her skirts, feeling a flush when she remembered Montgomery had done the same. She could almost feel him still inside her, stretching her, claiming her, a memory that brought another rush of heat. He touched her, and she melted. He looked at her in a certain way, and her body grew moist. She heard his voice, and she recalled all the deliciously decadent things they did together.

Passion was a word she'd never used before her marriage. *Pleasure* was a word limited to innocuous pursuits and inane occupations. She felt pleasure when she finished a difficult cross-stitch. She wiggled her toes in pleasure when her shoes didn't hurt.

Montgomery had changed those words. He'd changed *her.*

Right at the moment, she was feeling so wonderful she didn't want to see her relatives. Yet it was her duty to ensure that their needs were met, so she continued to her room, needing to wash and change before the confrontation. Her aunt and cousins would find fault with the state of her dress, and she was determined to give them no further reason to criticize her.

During the noon meal, she'd find some way to ascertain exactly how long her relatives intended to remain. She'd also take time to speak with Mrs. Brody and insist no changes be made to Doncaster Hall because of her aunt's dictates.

Hopefully, the housekeeper was still speaking to her.

Elspeth was in her chamber, arranging her new dresses

in the armoire. Her expression was mutinous, however, and even before she spoke, Veronica knew Elspeth's mood had something to do with her cousins.

"There you are, Your Ladyship," Elspeth said, forcing a pained smile to her face.

"What is it, Elspeth?"

"I am your lady's maid, am I not, Your Ladyship?"

She nodded.

"I am to care for your belongings, bring cut flowers into the room, and straighten up if necessary. Although, I must say, Your Ladyship, you don't leave your things lying about."

Elspeth twisted her hands together, evidently made some sort of decision, and began to speak rapidly.

"It was a great advancement for me, Your Ladyship, and I'm very proud to serve you. Millicent is still angry about it and gives me cold looks. But I must know when you send someone to order me about. Otherwise, I don't know if they have your best wishes at heart. How am I to know you've directed them to do something, and if I argue with someone, Your Ladyship, you'll become angry at me, and I'm not wanting to lose my position."

Veronica moved to the chair beside the window, composed herself, and gestured to the bed.

"Come and sit here, Elspeth, and tell me what happened. Slowly, please."

Elspeth sat on the edge of the bed, dangling her feet, watching them for a moment before she spoke.

"About an hour ago, Your Ladyship, I was bringing your newly laundered dresses back. That stain on the front of the blue stripe came out, you'll be happy to know."

She nodded, trying to be patient. "Someone was in my room?"

"Yes, Your Ladyship. One of your cousins, I believe. She was going through your armoire. She said she was looking for something you sent her for, that I was to leave the room immediately."

"I take it you disagreed," she said, feeling warmth for Elspeth's loyalty.

Elspeth nodded. "I refused to leave, Your Ladyship. She finally did, saying she'd see me dismissed before nightfall."

She was shocked to see tears in Elspeth's eyes.

"I didn't send anyone for anything, Elspeth," she said, standing. "I don't know what my cousin was doing here, but it wasn't at my behest." Although she already knew, she asked the question anyway. "Who was it?"

"I believe it was Miss Amanda."

She placed her hand on Elspeth's shoulder. "Thank you, Elspeth. You did exactly what you should have done. There'll be no repercussions."

"I'm not dismissed, then?"

"Indeed, no," she said. "In fact, I shall visit with Mrs. Brody to see if you and Robbie could get an extra half day for your loyalty."

"Your Ladyship, I don't know what to say." Tears clung to her lashes, but Elspeth's smile reminded her of times when the sun came out in the middle of a storm.

Veronica opened the drawer at the bottom of one of her armoires and checked the lockbox. All her father's money was still there. That was not the only valuable item in the suite, however. She walked to her bureau, pulled out the bottom drawer, and stared at the empty space.

The Tulloch Sgàthán was gone.

Chapter 23

Montgomery looked up as Edmund entered the distillery. He didn't stop what he was doing, intent on putting away his work so he could make himself presentable and join Veronica and her family.

Edmund, no doubt, had another dozen or so papers for him to sign or decisions to make, none of which interested him in the least.

"Your Lordship," his solicitor said, coming to stand in front of the worktable.

He inserted the tool into the leather sleeve before placing both hands flat on the wooden surface of the table.

"What is it now, Edmund? Give the servants a raise, order more provisions for Cook, hire a dozen more maids. Better yet, see my wife about the domestic duties."

"You would give Her Ladyship authority, sir?"

Edmund looked so stunned Montgomery almost smiled.

"Indeed I would. My sister-in-law managed my home in Virginia quite ably. Without my being involved, I might add."

Edmund nodded as if the thought had some merit, but he still didn't move.

"You're not here for a domestic concern, is that it? What is it? Something gone wrong with the looms in France, the sheep, the mines?"

"You have many interests, Your Lordship," Edmund said stiffly.

He glanced at the man. "I realize that, Edmund, and I'm suitably grateful. I'm just not interested in their day-to-day operation."

"Sir, there are people who depend upon your conscientiousness. Whose livelihood is contingent upon your interest."

He stared straight ahead, to the brightness of the afternoon beckoning beyond the door. He wanted out before Edmund began to lecture him on duty again. He'd been a Colonel with responsibility for five hundred forty-two men, leading them into battle for more than a year. He'd buried his family, been steward of their land, borne the burdens of every damn one of his decisions in the last five years, and still, it wasn't enough.

Now, the Fairfax wealth was a cannonball he was supposed to carry around and discount its weight.

"Say what you have to say, Edmund." *Then get the hell away from me.*

"I was interviewed, sir, and I feel it incumbent upon me to tell you."

"Interviewed?" He lifted an eyebrow, waited.

"The Earl of Conley, sir. He was very intent upon knowing the exact amount of your fortune."

"Was he?"

"I believe I erred, sir, in telling him of your largesse in regards to Her Ladyship. He was quite interested in the details."

He didn't know who angered him more at the moment, Edmund, or the Earl of Conley.

"When was this?" Montgomery asked, wiping his hands on a cloth.

"Less than an hour ago, sir. I came directly from our

meeting." Edmund hesitated, then evidently summoned his courage to ask. "What shall I do, Your Lordship?"

"Nothing," Montgomery said. "I'll handle it."

He strode toward the door, turned, and faced his solicitor. "For your information, Edmund, I don't want my business discussed with anyone. At any time, with anyone."

Edmund stared down at the dirt floor. "I've truly erred, Your Lordship. I shall never do so again."

"You live in Inverness?"

Edmund nodded.

"I think it's time you went home, Edmund."

The solicitor looked stunned. "Sir? Who will look out for your interests?"

The cannonball was growing heavier and heavier. He wanted to throw it at Edmund Kerr.

Edmund took a few steps toward him. "Lord Fairfax, I'm sorry. You have my profound apologies. The moment I realized my error, I came to you."

"So you did," he said. "And for that, I'm not dismissing you, Edmund. Yet I think it's time for you to visit your home. At least for a little while. Don't you agree?"

His look dared Edmund to offer an objection. "Yes, Your Lordship. Perhaps it is time."

Anger propelled him across the bridge, over the path, and toward Doncaster Hall. He made it to his room to wash and change before going in search of the Earl of Conley, or to pummel the man, whichever he deemed appropriate.

Elspeth helped her change her dress and fix her hair. Veronica washed her hands, then attempted to cool her face with a cold compress, but it was no use. Her cheeks were bright red, a sure and certain sign her temper was at a boiling point.

By the time she marched into the formal dining room, their numbers being too great to be accommodated in the smaller family dining room, she was shaking with fury.

"It's common to be late," Aunt Lilly said, reaching for one of Cook's scones. "I thought you better schooled in manners."

Veronica halted in the doorway, took a deep breath, and forced herself to calm a little.

The dining room walls were covered in pale yellow silk, the deep cornices leading the eye to a frieze of fruit and vegetables carved on the ceiling. Three chandeliers hung over a mahogany table large enough to accommodate twenty people.

Uncle Bertrand sat at the head of the table, Aunt Lilly at the end, with her cousins making themselves at home wherever they chose. Evidently, her place was to be somewhere in the middle, relegated to poor relation status even here, in her own home.

For the moment, she ignored both her aunt and uncle, and walked to the side opposite where Amanda sat. Her cousin smiled at her across the expanse of the table. Her expression was sweet and charming if one didn't notice the gleam in her eyes.

"Where is it?"

"Where is what, Veronica?" Aunt Lilly said. "Do sit down, girl."

"Where is the mirror?" she said, never moving her gaze from Amanda's face. "You'll not steal from me in my own home."

"Veronica!" Aunt Lilly looked aghast. "What are you talking about?"

"You stole the mirror. Where is it?"

Amanda patted the corner of her lips with her napkin. "I don't know what you're talking about."

"I gave you money of my own free will in London. I'll not give you the mirror."

Amanda turned to face her mother. "I truly do not know, Mother, what she is talking about. Please make her stop saying such vicious things about me."

"Veronica," Uncle Bertrand said, "you cannot simply accuse someone without proof."

"My maid is proof," she said. "She saw you in my room, Amanda."

Aunt Lilly stood, threw down her napkin, and walked to stand behind her daughter. "Amanda is no thief."

"I merely wished to see your suite," Amanda said. "You disappeared this morning, and we've not seen you since."

"Another rudeness, Veronica," her aunt said.

"I doubt, countess," Montgomery said from behind her, "that rudeness should be the topic of this conversation."

Veronica glanced at him to find him staring at her uncle. "You and I need to talk. Now."

Montgomery didn't look like the man she'd left an hour earlier. His voice was decidedly icy, his expression so filled with rage she would have flinched had it been directed at her.

"I trust you will discipline your wife, Montgomery," Aunt Lilly said, going back to her chair, her attention on her meal once more. "She was excessively rude to Amanda."

He glanced at Veronica.

"She's stolen the mirror. She came into my room and stole the Tulloch Sgàthán."

He studied Amanda for a moment, then allowed his gaze to encompass the entire table. To their credit, the other four cousins didn't meet his eyes, looking as if they wished to be anywhere but there. The only people who appeared supremely unaware of Montgomery's rage were Amanda, Uncle Bertrand, and Aunt Lilly.

Montgomery moved to stand slightly behind her and to the left. His right hand reached out, gripped her waist, and pulled her gently toward him, a picture of a couple united.

Aunt Lilly frowned at both of them. "She was extremely discourteous to Amanda, Montgomery. It is only civil for her to apologize."

"It's you who owe Veronica an apology," Montgomery said, before she could speak. "You're occupying her chair." He turned toward the Earl of Conley. "Nor did I give you leave to take my place at the head of the table, sir. Or to question my finances or those of my wife."

Montgomery nodded toward one of the maids. "Ask Mrs. Brody to step in," he said, before turning to Amanda. "Now's the time to tell the truth. Did you take the mirror?"

Amanda's face almost matched her father's in florid color. The look she gave Veronica was so filled with hatred it was almost a living thing.

Mrs. Brody arrived less than three minutes later, but the intervening time was spent in an uncomfortable silence, Montgomery's glance almost daring anyone to speak. Thankfully, no one challenged him.

"Where have you placed our guests, Mrs. Brody?" He turned his head to look at Amanda.

"The young lady is in the Green Room, Your Lordship."

"This is your last opportunity," Montgomery said.

"You cannot think to ignore my word," Amanda said, standing.

"Amanda." Her mother's admonitory tone was almost lost in her daughter's incipient hysteria.

"I've never been treated so abysmally in all my life," Amanda said. She looked to her father for assistance, but the earl, other than a rising color, didn't indicate he was aware of his daughter's discomfiture.

Montgomery turned and held out his hand for Veronica. Fingers entwined, they left the dining room, followed by the Earl of Conley, his countess, and Amanda, who was beginning to cry. Behind her trailed the other four cousins, two maids, and Mrs. Brody.

All they needed was a piper to make it a grand procession.

At the door to the Green Room, Montgomery halted, turned, and looked at Amanda. "One last time. Did you take the mirror?"

"I wish we'd never come here," Amanda said, tearfully.

"I agree," Veronica said.

Montgomery squeezed her hand and released it, turned the handle of the door, and pushed it open. He glanced at Mrs. Brody and summoned her forward with a gesture of his hand.

"Mrs. Brody, if you would, please."

"The mirror is gold and about this large," Veronica said, spreading her hands a foot wide. "The outside of it has a ring of diamonds."

Mrs. Brody nodded and entered the room.

"I must insist," Amanda said. "This is the most horrendous and vile intrusion, Father. You can't think to allow him to behave in such a manner. Not only is it uncouth, but . . ." Her voice trailed off.

"No doubt an American trait," Montgomery said. "Is that what you were about to say?"

She glanced away rather than answer him.

His gaze turned to the earl. "In Virginia, a gentleman would not inquire as to another man's business. Not unless, of course, he had reason to believe the man was a thief or a bounder. Do you think those things of me?"

Uncle Bertrand looked as if he had swallowed something the wrong way. He coughed a few times, his color still florid, his gaze lighting on anything but Montgomery.

"I refuse to stand here and allow my family to be so dishonored," Aunt Lilly said.

"Then I suggest you begin to pack," Montgomery said. "I don't like guests, or relatives, who steal from me."

He held out his hand, and Mrs. Brody walked to stand in front of him, extending the mirror.

"I'll expect your departure within the hour," Montgomery said.

"We have just now arrived," Aunt Lilly said. "A journey, I might add, of more than two days. You cannot expect us to turn around and leave."

"Not only do I expect it," he said, in the coldest voice Veronica had ever heard, "but if you've not gathered your things in the time I've given you, you'll find yourself in the carriage without your possessions. A fact, I can promise you."

She truly expected him to turn around and simply walk away. Instead, he reached out, grabbed her hand again, pulling her with him. She had to race to keep up with him, and as she did so, realized he was heading, not back to the distillery, but to his chamber.

Once inside, he closed the doors so forcefully it sounded like a gunshot.

He handed her the mirror he'd taken from Mrs. Brody.

"There is one thing worse than having no family," he said. "That's having too much of one."

"I honestly don't think of them as my family," Veronica admitted. "We're simply related."

"What did you mean earlier? Has Amanda stolen from you before?"

She looked down at the carpet. How odd she'd never noted it was blue and white, woven in an elaborate pattern that looked faintly Grecian in design.

Montgomery didn't speak, move, or urge her to confess. Instead, he stood silent and patient.

"She didn't steal from me," she said finally. "I paid her to leave me alone."

"Paid her?"

She glanced up. Montgomery was frowning, the expression more than a little disconcerting. Her family was still at the Hall, and if she didn't couch the words just right, she'd no doubt Montgomery would search Uncle Bertrand out again.

"I think she was concerned about my shaming the family," she said. "She was always reporting me to Aunt Lilly or Uncle Bertrand. I didn't finish this chore. I was bad at a task. I was acting oddly. She was a burr in my shoe, and it was easier to pay her to be silent."

"Is she behind our reception the night of the Mercaii meeting?"

She nodded.

"Why did you go, knowing there was every possibility you might be discovered?"

His frown had disappeared and, in its place, was a look she'd seen more than once. As if he were regarding her with curiosity laced with incredulity.

"Because I wanted to know more than I feared being found out," she said.

"About your Gift?"

Perhaps it was time she was honest about that, as well.

"Not just that," she said, twisting her hands in front

of her. "I wanted to know if it was possible to talk to the dead."

He didn't say anything for a moment. When he spoke, however, it wasn't to criticize her. Instead, his comment surprised her.

"I didn't like your cousin from the day we wed," he said.

"Everyone likes Amanda."

"Label me a contrarian, then. She flirted with me."

"Amanda flirts with every man," she said.

"I thought it was inappropriate for her to do so with a groom on the day of his wedding."

"She did it just to annoy me," she said.

"Why?"

"Because Amanda is sly, selfish, and spoiled. She doesn't care about anyone else except for what they might give her in the way of attention or gifts. If she sees something she wants, she gets it."

"Evidently, even if it means stealing it."

She nodded.

"Why her antipathy toward you?"

She shrugged. "I don't know. Have you ever met someone who took an instant dislike to you for no reason? Or for no reason you can determine?" She glanced up. "Or has everyone been charmed by you from the first moment they met you?"

"Hardly," he said. "My brothers were the charming ones. I was the wayward brother."

"I'd ask you about them, but you'll get that look on your face."

"What look?" he asked, frowning at her.

"That one," she said. "The look that says you aren't ever going to talk about your past. That Virginia is a closed topic I should never bring up or be curious about."

He studied her for a moment, then seemed to come to a decision.

"My grandfather built Gleneagle to look exactly like Doncaster Hall," he said suddenly.

She blinked at him, surprised.

"Exactly?"

He nodded. "Down to the wallpaper," he said.

That's why she'd felt so many conflicting emotions from him, including an overarching sadness.

"No wonder you miss Gleneagle," she said. She tilted her head and regarded him. "What do you regret, Montgomery? In the balloon, you said everyone regrets something. What's your regret?"

He studied her in silence for a moment but didn't answer. A moment later, he was gone, turning and leaving the room without speaking another word.

She stared at the open door, wondering if she should follow him. Instead, she opened the connecting door to her suite, closed it silently, and retreated to her chamber.

She wanted to talk to the dead. The moment she'd made the remark, Montgomery knew exactly why. The same reason he found himself imagining Alisdair, James, and Caroline. Sometimes, being with them was easier than missing them so acutely.

He always found himself telling her more than he'd intended. If he'd stayed with her, he'd have wrapped his arms around her, shelved his chin on the top of her head, and told her things he had no business telling anyone. He might even confess to his past.

Or he could love her again, a not-uncommon action around Veronica.

The moment he felt sated, the need built again. Perhaps he should just carry her around with him, kiss her when he wished, and feel the silky softness of her skin against his, her hands sliding over his body. She was learning him, and doing so with such delight and eagerness, that one look from her aroused him.

On the way out the door, Ralston stopped him.

"Your Lordship," the majordomo said, bowing slightly.

He clamped down on his impatience, turned, and faced the other man. "What is it?"

"The sheep need to be moved, Your Lordship."

"Then move them," he said.

"It isn't as simple as that, Your Lordship, I understand," Ralston said. "I believe you need to pick a location where they should be moved."

"What do you think I know about sheep?"

"Your Lordship, you're the only one to make the decision."

"Pretend I wasn't here," he said. "Who would make the decision in my absence?"

"Mr. Kerr, sir. He has always done so since his first day at Doncaster Hall. But I believe Mr. Kerr has left, sir. On your orders."

He bit back an oath. "Edmund is a solicitor. What does he know about sheep?"

"Mr. Kerr has always served as the steward of Doncaster Hall, sir," Ralston said.

"If, for some reason, Edmund was unavailable, who would make the decision then?"

Ralston looked confounded by the question. "Your Lordship, Mr. Kerr has always been available."

Of course, he would have to have the one solicitor in all of Scotland and no doubt the British Empire, who was so determined to fulfill his duty, he didn't miss a day.

"There's also the matter of cleaning the river, Your Lordship."

He braced his back against the doorframe and folded his arms. After his confrontation with Veronica's relatives, he was dangerously close to the limit of his tolerance.

"Cleaning the river?"

"The river narrows, sir, on this side of Lollybroch. If the rocks and boulders aren't removed every spring, the river could dam and back up, flooding the land. We make a party of it, Your Lordship. Invite the inhabitants of Lollybroch to assist us."

"When does that take place?"

"Normally before now, Your Lordship," Ralston said. "Many details were delayed to accommodate Mr. Kerr's journey to America."

"How fortunate he found me," he said dryly.

"A revelation of his character, sir, that he could do so with such assiduousness."

"What does that mean?"

Ralston looked uncomfortable again. "Did you not know, sir? Mr. Kerr is a Fairfax. He would have been in line for the title had it not been for your grandfather."

As Montgomery stared at him, Ralston continued. "His mother was a Fairfax. The title is allowed to travel through the women of the family, but only after all the male heirs have been considered."

"My grandfather."

Ralston nodded.

"Are you certain, Ralston?"

"About Mr. Kerr's ancestry? Of course, sir. The 10th Lord Fairfax paid for his education because he was a Fairfax."

You need to pay more attention to your inheritance, sir. Being a Lord Fairfax of Doncaster is a great honor. Edmund's words spoken to him in London. All the solicitor's endless harping at him made sense now.

Edmund no doubt thought he would have been a better heir.

"Will you be inspecting the stable, sir, and the changes made to the stalls?" Ralston asked.

"Must I?" he asked.

Ralston wore a look of commiseration. The man knew, only full well, that it was more interesting working on his airship than being the 11th Lord Fairfax.

"Set up a time, Ralston," he said, resigned to his duties. For the moment, however, he would escape to the distillery.

Chapter 24

Her aunt, uncle, and cousins left within the time limit Montgomery had given them. Neither Veronica nor her husband was at the door to bid them farewell. No doubt, at the first opportunity, Aunt Lilly was going to send her a scathing letter detailing all of Veronica's foibles, failings, and flaws. When that was done, Aunt Lilly would waste no time regaling everyone she knew with tales of the abysmal treatment she had received at the hands of her niece, that ungrateful chit.

Nothing she did, from this time forward, would ever be enough to make up for the disaster of the last three hours. Her aunt would never forgive her for exposing Amanda as the thief she was, and Uncle Bertrand would never forget the slight to his dignity.

How sad that she could feel nothing but relief.

She stood at the window of the Oval Parlor, watching until the carriages slipped out of sight. A few minutes later, Mrs. Brody arrived in the doorway.

"They've gone, Your Ladyship."

She nodded. How odd, she felt as if she'd aged twenty years in the past day.

"I had Cook prepare baskets for their journey to Inverness."

"Thank you, Mrs. Brody," she said faintly. "I never even thought of it."

Mrs. Brody smiled, the expression having a touch of compassion to it. "It's my duty, Your Ladyship."

Duty. What was her duty?

She ate dinner in her sitting room but found she hadn't much of an appetite. After dismissing Elspeth for the night, she readied for bed, turned off the lamp, and stared up at the ceiling. If it were possible to will oneself to sleep, that was exactly what she did, only to wake three hours later, wide-awake.

Perhaps she should look in the Tulloch Sgàthán. What if it remained blank again? Worse, what if it showed her a future filled with misery?

She rolled to her side, wishing she'd opened the drapes before she'd settled for the night. The room was too dark, the mantel clock shrouded in shadow. After leaving the bed, she walked through her suite in the darkness, stopping at the connecting door to Montgomery's room. Perhaps he was asleep. She leaned her forehead against the door, feeling the wood cool against her forehead. She doubted she'd sleep for the rest of the night, but her inability to do so was not reason enough to wake him.

Still, she rapped on the door.

When he didn't answer, she pushed down the handle and peered inside. Montgomery wasn't in his bed. Either he was taking one of his nightly walks again, walks he never discussed, explained, or even admitted. Or he was still working.

Before she could talk herself out of it, she dressed, deciding to wear only one petticoat. Anyone abroad at this hour would not be concerned about her attire.

The night was cool, with a hint of chill in the air, as if the child of spring relinquished its winter parent with reluctance. A waning sliver of moon, as delicate as a fingernail, sat high in the sky. She halted as she left Doncaster Hall, staring up at the heavens.

When she was a little girl, her mother had told her the stars were angels looking down on the earth.

"Pick one," her mother had said, "and choose your guardian angel."

"I want the brightest, Mama."

"Then you shall have it, my darling daughter."

She looked up at the sky and said a prayer for her parents. Instead of a star, what better guardian angels could she have than the two people who'd loved her so much?

She took the path along the river, but Montgomery was nowhere to be found. Crossing the lower half of the glen, she headed for the arched bridge. From there it was simple matter of keeping the distillery in sight. A flickering light in the back of the building told her Montgomery was, indeed, working.

Halfway to the bridge, she wished she'd worn her heavier shoes. She could feel each individual pebble through her slippers.

She halted in the middle of the path, startled by a sudden sensation that she wasn't alone. The distance between the distillery and the house wasn't all that great, but it was sufficient to make her feel isolated. With the trees so close, and deep caves of shadow facing her, unease skittered over her skin.

How foolish. She was at Doncaster Hall, not in some unknown place. All she needed to do was shout, and someone would come running. Even at that hour, people were working in the stable or the smithy or the other outbuildings not far away.

Was the rustle of leaves simply the wind? Or was someone standing there, watching her?

Her imagination was furnishing the sound of soft footfalls behind her. Or was someone truly there, following her? She'd brought nothing with her, not her reticule, or anything she could use as a weapon. She hadn't even wanted a lantern, since the light would alert others she was going to the distillery.

Suddenly, she wished she'd waited for Montgomery to return to Doncaster Hall.

She thought of running but decided against it because of her slippers and the darkness. She could barely see the path before her. Although her heart was racing, she kept her pace sedate, trying not to look over her shoulder.

As she climbed the steps of the arched bridge, she placed her right hand against the stone, grabbing her skirts with her left. At the top, she stopped, daring herself to turn around. Only the shadowed landscape met her eyes. No one followed her. No stranger hid, watching her. Or, if someone did, it was with such stealth she couldn't discern a shape from the bushes, trees, and the winding path leading back to Doncaster Hall.

Her skirt swung around her, the fabric catching on the rough stone. She jerked it free, caught a movement out of the corner of her eye, but when she looked in that direction, nothing was there.

She was allowing herself to be frightened by the wind.

Resolved to be more courageous, she approached the distillery.

"Montgomery?" She hesitated at the door and called his name again. When he didn't answer, she took a tentative step inside. The light she'd seen earlier had been extinguished. Was he standing there in the dark, waiting for her to leave?

"What are you doing here, Veronica?" he asked from behind her.

She jumped, her heart nearly bounding out of her chest.

"Have you been there all this time?" she asked, wondering if it was Montgomery she'd sensed earlier.

"What are you doing here?" he asked again.

Surrounded by shadows, kilted in night, he might have been a creature of myth and magic, a Highlander come to exact revenge, a brownie intent on mischief.

The idea of going in search of him had been so reasonable, standing in her bedroom. Now, it felt idiotic.

"I wanted to thank you," she said.

"Thank me?"

His voice was icy, devoid of emotion. How did he do that? How did he bury himself so completely behind his restraint?

"I realized I hadn't. Thanked you, that is. For believing me." She took a deep breath. "Thank you for marrying me. You saved me from being a poor relation in my uncle's household. For that, I will be forever grateful."

He didn't respond. Perhaps she should kiss him, instead. They'd had no difficulties communicating when they loved each other. Earlier, in that very building, they'd shared an elemental passion.

"You've been very kind," she said, finally, feeling inept and more than a little foolish.

"I haven't been kind," he said. "For God's sake, Veronica, don't label me with that."

"Montgomery," she said, taking a chance, "if you'd share your grief, perhaps the burden of it might be lightened. I know I felt better for telling you about my parents. Grief shared is sometimes more bearable."

She took a step toward him, then another. "People aren't meant to feel such pain as you feel, Montgomery."

"Perhaps pain is payment, Veronica," he said softly.

"What have you to pay for? What could you have done that is so terrible?"

His hand reached out, fingers brushing the edge of her jaw. "Perhaps it's better if you don't know, Veronica."

She half expected him to leave her, to stalk away in the darkness, silent, arrogant, immovable. Instead, he took a step toward her, his hands resting on her shoulders. With a gentle tug, he pulled her toward him. She stepped into his embrace, resting her cheek against his chest.

She wrapped her arms around him and curved them to lie flat against his shoulder blades. She was so close she could feel his chest rise and fall with his breathing. If it were possible to do so, she would have inhaled his sorrow, rid him of it, and given it another home in which to live. Anywhere but in Montgomery's heart.

For long moments, they remained locked together in the darkness, holding one another.

Perhaps she'd been right to seek him out after all.

"You should go," he said finally, stepping back and releasing her.

"Will you come with me?"

"I have to go over some last-minute preparations. I'm taking the airship up tomorrow."

"May I go with you?"

"No," he said. "I'm testing the navigation baffle."

"Is it dangerous?"

He didn't answer, only reached out and touched her cheek with the back of his hand.

"Go back to Doncaster Hall," he said. "It's chilly, and you're not dressed for walking at night. I'll be there when I can."

She turned and reluctantly left him. The journey back to Doncaster Hall was made easier by the thought Montgomery was within the sound of her voice.

Later, she awakened to the touch of his hands sliding over her skin, long, fluid strokes measuring the curve of her waist, her breasts. Without a word spoken, he seduced her, bent his head to capture a nipple between his lips, drawing softly.

Her heart opened. Her blood raced. Her body heated. She placed her hands on his hips, raised her head for his kiss, and urged him into her. As dawn lightened the room, they moved together, each seeking comfort, each receiving it.

Her hands slid from his back to fall lax on the mattress. Inside, her body thrummed, a beat fast and sure, echoing pleasure even as it faded. Her heart slowed, and her breath eased, the drawstring around her lungs relaxed.

She cherished the weight of his body against hers.

Those silent moments at dawn felt almost like a vow, a ceremony more blessed than their wedding.

Chapter 25

"It's going to be fine, Norma," Veronica was saying, patting the girl on the back.

The young maid, one Montgomery had seen around the house, continued to sob, her face buried in a handkerchief, her shoulders shaking. Veronica reached for a cup, poured tea into it, and made the girl take it.

Sunlight, streaming through the broad windows behind them, danced on Veronica's hair, touched it with gold and red.

He halted in the doorway of the Rose Parlor, wondering if he could disappear before he was seen.

Too late. Veronica looked up to see him. The slight shake of her head indicated, to his great relief, that he wasn't required at the moment. Or possibly wasn't even wanted.

It was that thought that kept him just beyond sight, listening.

"How did you know, Lady Fairfax?" the girl was saying. "Even Mrs. Brody doesn't know, and she knows everything."

"I felt your fear," Veronica said simply.

He laid his head back against the wall, staring up at the ceiling of the corridor. His ancestors had painted

vignettes of Scotland's history on several squares, he'd
been told. The one he was looking at portrayed a battle
about to take place, as men were aligned on separate
hills, their leaders facing each other on horseback.

He was damned tired of war, even in art.

"It doesn't matter," Veronica said, as if the girl had
sent her a questioning look. "What's necessary now is to
plan for the future. Can you go home to have the child?"

The girl began to weep in earnest, but his curiosity
kept him in place.

A moment later, Veronica spoke again. "Then we shall
just have to find a home for you, Norma. Have you any
friends or other family?"

"A cousin in Glasgow, Lady Fairfax."

"Then we'll write her, Norma."

"I don't want to be a burden to her, Lady Fairfax."

Several minutes passed in silence, making him
wonder, exactly, what was happening in the room. He
peered around the doorway to see the girl had wrapped
her arms around Veronica, and she was returning the
hug, patting Norma on the back.

Evidently, the girl had found herself with child and
was going to be sent away to live with relatives. Not an
unusual arrangement. What Veronica said next, however,
was not commonplace.

"You'll not go to them penniless, Norma. I'll see to
that. You'll have funds of your own. That way, you won't
be a poor relation."

She'd said something like that the night before, something he'd dismissed without paying it much attention.
Now, he could only wonder what kind of future Veronica
might have had without marriage.

The longer he was around her, the more he learned. He
knew, now, why she'd been at the Society of the Mercaii,

why she was always so careful to extinguish a lamp, and why she'd begun a fire brigade.

What would he learn tomorrow?

"Oh, I couldn't, Lady Fairfax," Norma said now, pulling back and blotting at her eyes. "It wouldn't be right."

"It wasn't right for your William to leave you in such a condition and disappear."

"He's a good man, Lady Fairfax. He was just frightened."

"He wasn't a man, Norma," Veronica said firmly. "Men don't run away from problems. They face them. They're not afraid of them."

That wasn't entirely true. He'd been afraid numerous times in the last five years and wanted to run like the Devil was chasing him. Circumstances, and perhaps pride, had kept him rooted in place. What he wanted to do and what he was compelled to do were often different, fear be damned.

When he entered the room, Veronica shook her head again. He ignored her that time and approached Norma, awkwardly patting the girl on the shoulder.

"Was William a Doncaster Hall lad?" he asked.

Norma not only looked horrified at his presence but was evidently incapable of answering him.

He smiled to reassure her and kept patting her.

She blinked rapidly, curved her lips into a determined smile, and stared up at him. "No, Your Lordship," she finally said.

He nodded and patted her one last time. "Tell Mrs. Brody I've given you the rest of the day. Go to your room and rest, Norma. Everything will be all right."

She slowly stood, nodding. "If you say so, sir." She offered the crumpled handkerchief to Veronica, but his wife merely closed Norma's hand around it.

"Everything will be all right," she said, repeating his words. Norma looked a great deal more convinced when Veronica said it.

When the girl left the room, he turned to Veronica.

"You felt her fear?"

She nodded, her face expressionless. Her eyes, however, bore a wary look, one he'd seen before.

"You're afraid I'll ridicule you," he said.

She looked surprised at his assertion. "You haven't made any secret of what you think of my Gift," she said.

Had he been that intolerant of her?

"Are you feeling something from me right at the moment?"

She regarded him with more than a little suspicion.

"I want to know," he said. "Truly."

"Contentment, perhaps, but excitement, too." She tilted her head to the side. "You're flying today, and I expect you're always excited to be flying."

Surprised, he nodded. "I am. I've come to get you. Everyone else is already in place, waiting for me to fly."

"You're very certain you'll be safe?"

He decided now was not the time to tell her about the other mishaps he'd had when piloting an airship. No flight was ever truly safe. Man was not a bird, after all, however much he might want to be.

They walked out of the house, and as they approached the arched bridge, he nodded to the people of Doncaster Hall. Most of the young men had asked to be part of the rope brigade, but the women were congregated near the bridge for the best view of the airship. He walked Veronica to Elspeth's side.

Ahead, fully inflated, was the oval envelope of his airship, nearly three times the size of his balloon. The ship was the equal of the distillery behind it, the blue silk trembling in the faint breeze as if it were anxious to make its maiden voyage. A new burner, specially constructed for an envelope of this size, sat beneath its throat, roaring in excitement.

Veronica's eyes widened, but she didn't say anything further—no words of encouragement or caution or even curiosity. He stood in front of her and waited until her head tilted back, and her eyes met his. Only then did he realize she was trembling, too.

"Don't be afraid, Veronica," he said softly, then bent his head and, in full view of the crowd, kissed his wife.

She swayed against him, placing her hands on his chest.

Whenever he touched her, she took flame, as combustible as the burner on his airship. She was so responsive to him, she would have let him grab her hand, pull her into the distillery, and love her for the afternoon, to hell with their audience outside.

The temptation engaged him for more than a fleeting moment.

He ended the kiss, brushed his knuckles against her flushed cheek, and smiled.

"I'll be fine."

She didn't look as if she believed him.

He hesitated, then walked toward the distillery. Sometimes, actions could demonstrate what words failed to convey.

"Today's the day, Ralston," he said, approaching the gondola. He nodded to the ten men holding the ropes. The envelope was still shivering, anxious to be gone from earth like a winged thoroughbred.

"That it is, Your Lordship. That it is."

Both men stared up at the huge blue silk envelope. This ship differed from the one in which he'd taken Veronica. The first balloon had been launched to test the air currents. This ship would master them. The envelope was larger, oval, with a pointed nose. The gondola was rectangular and much longer than the basket for his balloon.

The main difference between the two vehicles, however, was that he could control the direction of the airship. At the top of the envelope were several baffles controlled by wires fed down through the balloon to a control panel in the gondola. In addition, he'd created vents on either side of the ship to direct airflow and a set of fins on the rear and the front to control direction.

If his design proved as successful as he hoped, he'd petition the United States government to reestablish the Balloon Corps. A balloon had a practical application beyond that of spying on the enemy's troop movements in time of war.

"I'd ask you to accompany me," he said to Ralston, "but you've already indicated how you feel about flying."

"And if you'd asked me, I'd just have to tell you no, Your Lordship. I'm Scots by birth, British by law, and a Highlander by the grace of God, but I'm no eagle."

Montgomery laughed, entered the gondola, and began his last-minute checks on the burner.

Ralston surprised him by producing a bottle of wine with a flourish. "I trust you'll not object, sir, but I've taken a bottle from the cellar to christen your ship."

"To do that, I'd have to name her, Ralston," he said.

Ralston looked crestfallen. "Is that not done, sir?"

"Indeed it is," he said, thinking of the two ships he'd piloted in the war. The *Freedom* had gone down in 1862; The *Union* had been retired a year later.

"Have you any ideas, sir?"

"The *Intrepid*," he said, thinking of Veronica.

"A good choice, Your Lordship," Ralston said. "Fearless."

"Or audacious," Montgomery said.

Ralston handed him the uncorked bottle of wine. Montgomery poured a little over the corner of the basket. "Should I say something, do you think?"

They stared up at the envelope, then at each other. The corner of Ralston's mouth twitched.

"I've no knowledge of christening rituals, Your Lordship. Not for airships."

"What about sailing ships? I'd think it would be similar, don't you?"

Montgomery poured a little wine on the grass outside the gondola. "I christen thee the *Intrepid*."

"A good choice, Your Lordship."

"A good idea, Balloon Master."

Ralston grinned, the unexpected expression banishing twenty years from his face.

He donned his gloves, turned the burner on full, and saluted Ralston.

"Best of luck, Your Lordship!" Ralston shouted over the increasing noise of the burner.

"Let it go, Ralston," he called out.

Ralston gave the nod to the four lines of men holding the mooring ropes, and slowly they began to walk toward the gondola.

The inhabitants of Doncaster Hall cheered as the airship began its slow ascent. He smiled, pleased by their reaction, and waved. A moment later, however, he was involved with the details of flight: checking the burner, testing the navigational paddles as well as the wires to the baffles.

As always, the first twenty feet made him feel as if his stomach were dropping to his knees. Then the surge of excitement sent his blood racing and his pulse pounding.

Whenever he flew, he didn't have to remember. The scenery wasn't as important as the freedom he felt, untethered, and alone. Every flight, after that first adventure six years ago, he'd felt the same. Being airborne, the sensation of being poised between earth and heaven, was almost like taking a drug. Being in his airship made him feel both insignificant and powerful.

There, he could forget Virginia, could push back the specters of the last five years. There, even Alisdair, James, and Caroline did not follow.

As he hovered above the waving crowd of Scots, he realized he wouldn't be alone. Not as long as people from Doncaster Hall were watching: anxious, excited, and amazed.

He was their laird, their leader.

They'd welcomed him, all the people of Doncaster Hall, with a great deal more grace than he'd accepted being there. Not once had he heard any grumbling. He was the 11th Lord Fairfax, and they'd simply acknowledged that circumstance had made him, temporarily to them, an American.

The hills around Doncaster Hall were so deeply green they appeared almost blue, the lushness appealing to the planter in him. Too many damn sheep grazed on the far hills, clinging tenaciously to the rocky ground at the base of the mountains. Had it not been for sheep, his grandfather would have remained in Scotland. Had it not been for sheep, Montgomery might have been a crofter himself. Or employed at Doncaster Hall, serving another Fairfax.

He should ask Edmund about the other employees at Doncaster Hall. What kept them here? The clan system was long gone. Or did they simply have a feel for the land, the country, the place?

Veronica felt the same tie.

I'm a Scot, Montgomery. I belong here.

The time had come to test his navigational design. He was hovering between Doncaster Hall and Ben Wyliss. If his prototype worked, he would be able to direct the ship back toward the house. If it didn't, he'd basically be at the mercy of the winds, like a balloon, and his landing would be accomplished by releasing the heated air from the envelope.

He began his first pass, hearing the cheering and feeling like shouting himself as he guided the ship over the house. Damned if his design didn't work! The second turn was as effortless as the first, and his smile felt permanently affixed.

The sudden sputtering sound caught his attention. Montgomery glanced up, saw the flame go from bright blue to orange to nothing. Reaching up, he fired the burner again, but the flame didn't catch.

At least no one was shooting at him.

The last time he'd experienced a problem with a burner had been over Fort Monroe. On that occasion, they'd gone down in the Elizabeth River, a descent that might have killed both him and his helper if it had been over land.

The burner didn't catch again, but the ship would still stay in the air for a few minutes, long enough for him to coast to a landing somewhere level. He wasn't panicked; years of training had equipped him to think of all contingencies in a hurried yet orderly pattern.

Everything would have been fine if he hadn't been too close to the damn mountain.

Of all the idiocy, to survive four years of war to die on a beautiful day in the Highlands.

Chapter 26

One moment, Montgomery's magnificent ship was silhouetted against the sky, an enormous man-made blue cloud. Her throat closed, her heart swelled with pride. Montgomery had done this. All on his own, he'd harnessed the air, become a god in the machine he'd devised.

As if to demonstrate how talented he was, the airship veered to the left, circling Doncaster Hall. The crowd around her shouted, arms waving in pride and excitement.

Veronica stood where she was, smiling, thrilled at Montgomery's achievement. How proud he must be. His navigation system was working.

If he could steer his ship, then they wouldn't have to have outriders following them. He'd know where they were going to land, not too close to the River Tairn like last time.

She studied the envelope as it passed the second time, wondering if she was imagining what she saw. Wrinkles were appearing on the smooth surface of the silk. The oval shape of the ship changed as she watched, became rounder, like the inverted teardrop of Montgomery's balloon. Seconds elongated to hours as she watched him, the silk growing more puckered as time elapsed.

Around her, the crowd began to murmur, the pride of earlier moments transformed to worry, then fear.

Montgomery was on the far side of Doncaster Hall, no longer flying in a circle. If he didn't change direction, he would head directly for Ben Wyliss.

A woman in front of her screamed as the bow of the airship abruptly dipped.

A second later, the ship fell from sight.

There was no time to think. His hands automatically performed the duties learned over years. He tried to fire the burner, but nothing was happening. He let go the last of the emergency ballast bags, but that didn't lessen the speed of his descent.

In the end, all he could do was brace himself against one of the supports and prepare for the impact.

The ground was hurtling up to meet him. The only thing he could hear was the rush of the wind, as if God had taken pity on him and muffled the sound of his own racing heart. The river was too close, but even that landing place would have been a blessing next to crashing into the mountain. A sudden gust of wind seemed to toy with his mortality, sending the gondola nearly perpendicular to the sagging envelope.

He'd wondered about that moment often enough, ever since he'd first challenged himself to fly. What would be his thoughts if he knew he was going to die? He'd been in difficult situations before, but none as risky as this. Would he feel regret? Yes—well, that was a question answered. And sorrow. He felt such acute sorrow that it startled him.

He didn't want to be a ghost in Veronica's life.

Damn it, he didn't want to die.

Montgomery had disappeared.

The crowd surged forward as Elspeth pulled at her sleeve. Veronica shook it off. She saw Elspeth's mouth moving, but couldn't understand her words. A dull roaring noise flooded her ears, as words struck her like bricks.

"Falling."

"Disaster."

"Dead."

The world began to slow, each separate movement taking place in air suddenly gone syrup-like and thick. She was oddly cold. Her hands felt frozen, the tips of her fingers without sensation. A curious fog slipped over her like a gray blanket.

Her thoughts were sluggish as if she were new to the process of thinking. She should join the others, but she couldn't move. She should say something. How odd she'd lost the power of speech.

Mrs. Brody passed her. "I'll get the basket, Lady Fairfax." Yes, the basket. The basket Mrs. Brody used whenever one of the staff was ill or suffered an injury.

She closed her eyes, tried to remember to breathe. Breathing was necessary, wasn't it? There, she was breathing again. She opened her eyes to find Elspeth looking at her oddly. The maid's hand was on her arm. Aunt Lilly wouldn't be pleased. A servant never touched an employer. It didn't matter anymore.

I can't do this again.

Had she said that aloud? She must have, since Elspeth was looking at her with sympathy. That was even worse, wasn't it? Aunt Lilly would be lecturing her for laxity in dealing with the servants. Yet Aunt Lilly would be calling for her smelling salts about now.

Montgomery had fallen.

I can't lose someone I love again.

She could not love Montgomery Fairfax. He was an annoying American who believed that nothing was quite as good as Virginia. He had a bad habit of keeping silent when most civil men would have spoken. He rarely revealed himself, and when he did, it was to expose a level of pain or anger she couldn't reach.

Yet he'd introduced her to passion and accompanied her on every journey to bliss. She wanted him to touch her all the time, even when it was vastly improper. She thought about him constantly, blushing when alone, imagining their loving even when she was surrounded by others.

She could not love him, but she did.

He might be dead.

I can't do this.

She couldn't move. She was planted in the ground as firmly as the heather. The wind plucked at her hair, blowing tendrils across her face. Her heart, stubborn to the last, continued, one stolid beat at a time. She felt as if she were dying by degrees.

I can't do this.

She couldn't go to him. She could not kneel beside his broken body. She could not cradle his head on her lap and brush his thick black hair away from his beautiful face. She could not whisper last words to him, words of love she'd never said, never had the courage to say.

What had he said? Something about facing her fear. How could she do that?

Montgomery.

In the instant before impact, Montgomery's thoughts went to Veronica. Not to his brothers or Caroline, but the woman who'd fascinated, amused, and charmed him since first meeting her at the Society of the Mercaii.

The wind carried the gondola, turning it over until he was almost tipped out. Just as he thought he was certain to be smashed into the side of the mountain, the gusts played with him again like a cat with a ball of yarn. The impact zone changed, suddenly. He was no longer facing a mountain but coming closer to the trees that surrounded Doncaster Hall.

He grinned. He might just escape disaster.

He heard the screams below him, wanted to wave his arms to reassure them, but he'd be a fool to give up his grip on the supports, especially since the wind showed no sign of gentling. A few seconds later, he was thrown into the ancient oaks as if God and the wind had abruptly tired of using him as a plaything.

The only sounds were the breaking of the branches around him, the groans as the gondola caught, slipped, then caught again.

Gradually, however, he became aware of shouts and screams below him, altered in nature. Instead of panic, there was excitement and joy in the voices he heard. He peered over the edge of the gondola, grabbed a nearby branch for support, and waved.

Ralston was among the first to arrive, followed by some lads from the stable. All of the first-floor maids arrived together like a gaggle of geese. Elspeth's husband, Robbie, the members of the red and blue fire brigade, Tom, all appeared below him.

Where the hell was Veronica?

Shouldn't she have been there? Shouldn't her voice have been the first he heard? He pushed aside his thoughts for the very real need to exit the gondola before it slipped from its precarious perch.

"Your Ladyship?" Elspeth said, patting her arm.

Veronica blinked. "Yes?"

"Do you not want to go to Lord Fairfax?"

"Of course," she said, calmly, each of the words enunciated perfectly and clearly. No, God, she could not do this. She could not see him hurt. She could not bear it.

She picked up her skirts. How perceptive she'd been that morning to request Elspeth lace her loosely. She could breathe easily.

Give me strength, God.

Once before, she'd been alone when everyone around her stared at her, wondering if she'd dissolve into tears. Once before, she'd stood in dry-eyed silence, watching as her world crumbled in front of her.

Everyone was there. Everyone at Doncaster Hall had already moved toward the trees. All she had to do was reach out her hand, and they would part silently, urging her onward, creating a corridor to reach Montgomery. She remained where she was, at the fringe of the crowd, marshaling her courage where she had none.

How could she do this?

Suddenly, the crowd cheered. Veronica heard the sound, but it didn't mean anything. The wind meant nothing. Her heart meant nothing. The alarmed squawking of the birds meant less than nothing.

Montgomery might be dead.

She took a few steps closer, halted on the path, closed her eyes, and again prayed for strength.

"Lady Fairfax?" Mrs. Brody's voice.

She opened her eyes to see Mrs. Brody standing in front of her. The housekeeper's coronet of braids had slipped and was askew, her face flushed and sweating. In her arms she held the basket containing all her unguents and bandages, scissors and potions.

"Are you all right, Lady Fairfax?"

She nodded. She thought she said something, but the words simply didn't matter at the moment. Mrs. Brody moved ahead, the crowd parting for her as if she were a force of nature.

Veronica focused on Ralston. The majordomo stood at the base of a venerable oak in his shirtsleeves, head bowed as if he were praying. Then he looked up, as if to solicit God's help from the sky itself.

She felt as if she might faint. Her heart was choking in her throat, and a heaviness slithered through her stomach. Elspeth was at her side, evidently refusing to leave her.

"Hurry with the ladder!" Ralston yelled, a command accompanied by a bright smile.

She abruptly halted in the middle of the path, enraged at his humor.

A boot fell from one of the trees. Then a second boot joined the first.

She pressed both hands against her chest as she looked skyward. The envelope had fully collapsed, sagging among the treetops and blocking out the afternoon light. The gondola was hanging in a space between two mature oaks, almost like a child's swing.

Speechless, she watched as Montgomery climbed out of the gondola, grabbed one thick branch with both arms, and began to descend the tree.

"Praise be," Elspeth said from beside her.

Relief began to heat the ball of ice in Veronica's stomach.

The crowd greeted Montgomery like a hero. Tom clapped him on the back. Ralston did the same, then surreptitiously wiped his eyes. Most of the maids fell behind Mrs. Brody, even Millicent, adding their words of relief.

He was one of them, their laird, their Lord Fairfax.

Montgomery glanced in her direction, made his way through the grove of trees, accepting the words of those who pressed close.

He reached her, stood in front of her, bits of leaves

still clinging to his hair. She wanted to reach forward and brush them loose, but she'd lost the power to move.

They stood looking at each other, only an arm's length separating them. The distance might as well have been miles.

The breeze blew around them, tousled his hair, and swept one leaf off his shoulder. The crowd around them grew silent, no doubt interested in their conversation.

Or their lack of it.

He didn't say anything, but neither did she. Moments ticked by like sluggish snails. The sun beat down on her head since she'd dispensed with a bonnet. She smoothed her hair back from her forehead, looked away, then back at him.

"Where were you?"

"Where was I?"

"Yes, madam, where were you?"

She hadn't raced toward him; she hadn't rushed into his arms. She hadn't laughed with delight at his safety. She hadn't screamed his name. Instead, she'd stood on the fringes of the crowd, calm and unaffected.

She had nothing to say, no explanation to offer him even as he waited.

Abruptly and insanely, he wanted to hurt her. He wanted to wipe that half smile off her face, bring misery into her eyes. He wanted her to feel the depth of betrayal he felt at this moment.

"Should I apologize for surviving?"

She blinked at him. Just that and no other reaction. As if she were so cold that the heat of his anger could not melt her.

She was hot enough in passion. Was that the only way to reach her? Had he been a fool to think that she might have cared for him?

He *was* an idiot to have felt so vulnerable around her, to have confided in her. He *was* an idiot to think that passion could lead to something greater, something more.

They were no better than rutting animals. He'd be her stag, her stallion, her boar, taking her when he wanted. But he'd be nothing else. Not companion or confidant or love.

He glanced at Elspeth, an unspoken request. The maid nodded and slipped away.

"Very well, Veronica. We'll use each other and fuck each other. But I'll be damned if I ever tell you another secret, and I sure as hell won't ever trust you again."

Veronica took a step back, her fingers resting at the base of her throat. He wasn't going to let her escape. He stepped forward, leaning close so only she could hear his words.

"I could almost believe that you had something to do with my crash. Do you want to remain in Scotland so much you'd make yourself a widow?"

"You think I had something to do with your accident?" she asked.

"Was it an accident?" he asked, his voice cold. "You were in the old distillery last night. What were you doing there?"

"I wanted to talk to you," she said. "I told you that."

"Did you touch anything?"

She shook her head.

He studied her for a few moments, wishing she'd say something, hoping she'd offer up a word, an explanation, an excuse. When she remained silent, he turned and walked away, motioning for several of the men to follow him.

She had the time to comfort a maid, but she'd no time for him.

* * *

Rage had rolled off him with such force that she felt it physically. He wasn't angry at his airship, or the trees, or whatever had caused his crash. Instead, he'd focused all his rage on her, as if she were responsible for what had happened to him. As if he *wanted* her to be responsible.

When had he ever trusted her?

She felt oddly heavy, as if she weighed twice what she had that morning. Her movements were slower, as if she'd also aged since then.

She tried to take a deep breath, but it felt as if her chest were constricted or the air too thick to draw into her lungs.

Her hand rested at her throat, fingers playing with the cameo she'd pinned there this morning. She knew the face carved on the surface by touch. Could imagine even the cameo turning to stare at him incredulously.

She felt a tear spill over and trail down her cheek, but she didn't move to brush it away. Instead, she turned and began to walk back to Doncaster Hall, Elspeth falling into place beside her. The distance back to the house seemed immeasurable, the path littered with broken glass.

Every inhabitant of Doncaster Hall looked at her with shock in their eyes. Everyone but Elspeth, who didn't speak, merely glared at them.

Veronica's hands tightened into fists. She released them with some effort, straightening her fingers. Take a deep breath. Wipe away your tears. Go home.

Doncaster Hall was suddenly not home. She had no home. Not one anchor existed. No bulwark. No lodestone. She was as alone as she'd ever been.

She wanted to be gone from there so desperately, she began to think of all the people in the world who might take her in, offer her sanctuary.

She had no place to go.

Norma had a more hopeful future, for all she was expecting a child out of wedlock. She might be shunned by her relatives, cast aside by her friends, and made the subject of a moral lesson in Kirk. In a few years, people would forgive or forget. She'd have her child and a future substantially brighter than Veronica's.

How could Montgomery think she would harm him?

The crowd that had been so effusive in their relief fell silent as she moved through them. Elspeth was the only one who accompanied her. Elspeth, who would be, she suspected, loyal despite any circumstance.

"Tell me about the Tullochs," she said.

Elspeth glanced over at her, a look of concern still on her face. "What would you like to know, Your Ladyship?"

"You're certain your grandmother would know the origins of the mirror?"

"If it's the same, Lady Fairfax. It doesn't look like it did when I was a child, but the diamonds might be new."

"How far away is Kilmarin?"

"By train? A half day, perhaps." Elspeth looked at her curiously. "Have you a mind to go there, Your Ladyship?"

"Yes," she said, glancing back toward the grove of trees. "We'll leave this afternoon."

"We will?"

She turned to look at her maid, forcing a smile she didn't feel to her face. "Didn't you say you had family nearby?"

Elspeth's look of confusion turned to joy. "There would be time to visit with my family?"

She nodded.

Elspeth looked as if she might begin dancing.

At least someone was happy.

Chapter 27

A cool whispery breeze bid them farewell from Doncaster Hall, fluttering the leaves as if the trees were waving goodbye. The soot-colored sky heralded an approaching storm. The perfect Highland morning had disappeared. In its place were rolling gray clouds and the scent of rain in the air.

The brisk breeze from the open window blessedly dried the hint of tears in her eyes.

Veronica closed the window, heard it snap shut with a click. She would have liked to draw down the shade as well, but that would necessitate an explanation to Elspeth.

She was much too close to weeping, and once she started, she wasn't certain she'd be able to stop.

Sitting back against the padded leather, she took off her bonnet and placed it on the seat opposite her. At the moment, she cared less for fashion than she did comfort.

Some conversation was called for, and she scanned her mind for a list of acceptable topics. Her aunt would say servants were to be ignored, treated as the furniture, to be used but given no thought. One did not converse with one's servants, especially during public outings. However, it occurred to her that the same woman who'd helped her on with her stockings could be spoken to when the chore was done.

Besides, she was no longer going to use Aunt Lilly as an example of propriety.

"How long have you been married, Elspeth?"

"Almost a year now, Your Ladyship."

The girl did not chatter. She answered a question but never volunteered any additional information. Nor did she ask any questions in return. Such traits no doubt made her a perfect servant but a terrible conversationalist.

"Where were you married?" she asked.

"In Perth, Your Ladyship." Elspeth tilted her head to the side and regarded her with some curiosity. "Why do you ask, Your Ladyship?"

Should she confess to a need for conversation? If she were talking, even of mundane things, even of someone else's business, she wouldn't be thinking of Montgomery.

He'd thought her capable of harming him.

With some difficulty, she pushed that thought away.

"I'm simply curious," she said. "I apologize if I've offended you."

Elspeth shook her head. "You haven't, Your Ladyship. It's just that no one's ever asked before."

Veronica gripped the material of her skirt. She released her hands, smoothed the fabric, and forced herself to remain placid on the surface.

"Are you happy, Elspeth?"

No, that was not a question she should be asking. She knew that without Aunt Lilly's coaching. Elspeth turned in the seat to face Veronica. Her eyes sparkled, and the dimples in her cheeks deepened by her smile.

"Oh, Your Ladyship, yes. My Robbie is . . ." Her voice halted mid-sentence as her face flushed. "Yes, Your Ladyship, I'm happy."

Envy bit through Veronica like a hungry snake.

No, this was not an acceptable topic of conversation at all.

"It looks as if we shall get some inclement weather," she said, glancing up at the boiling clouds. There, the weather was always an acceptable topic.

Elspeth nodded but didn't comment. For an instant, they'd been simply two women. But the roles were firmly back in place.

She laid her head back against the leather. The carriage wasn't the same one they'd used on their journey to Doncaster Hall all those weeks ago. The interior of this one smelled musty, as if the carriage had been in storage and not often used. However, it was immaculate. Not a touch of dust was visible on any of the surfaces and the pale blue cushions looked as if they'd been brushed recently. Did a coachman do such duties? Or did a maid? How odd she didn't know. If she truly cared, that would be a topic of conversation she might broach to Elspeth. Elspeth would know.

She'd chosen well that first day. Elspeth had been a blessing. Millicent would have colored the days gray with her grim attitude. She'd have complained from dawn onward about some slight or problem.

How like Millicent she was becoming. Right at the moment, she could only see the darkness in her life. The approaching storm mirrored her mood so perfectly, it was as if God Himself had sent it to her to complement these hours.

She had a right to be dour. Her husband had just accused her of trying to kill him.

No, she didn't love Montgomery Fairfax. She didn't much like her husband right at the moment.

Veronica had just stood there, toward the back of the crowd, her face frozen in a calm, expressionless mask.

She hadn't looked as if she'd given a damn that he'd nearly been killed.

Montgomery stared down at the burner, now arrayed in pieces on his worktable. Twice, he'd tried to start it, and twice, the flame sputtered and died.

She'd stood there instead of rushing to his side. She hadn't asked if he was all right. She hadn't expressed any fear. She'd hadn't said a damn word. Not one.

Nor had she denied his accusation.

It could have been an accident. She could have done something and not realized it. She could have been too fearful to admit it.

No, *fearful* was not a word he'd use to describe Veronica MacLeod Fairfax.

With the help of most of the men at Doncaster Hall, he'd managed to get the gondola out of the trees. The envelope would take a little longer, since the silk had been shredded and hung in tatters from the branches.

He'd stared up through the broken oaks, realizing how fortunate he'd been that his ancestors had planted that particular grove. Without the trees to break his fall, he probably would have died.

Would Veronica have cared?

Again, he examined every part of the burner. There had to be a reason it had failed. He didn't believe in accidents, especially since he'd checked everything at least a dozen times himself.

He stood, flattening his hands on the wood surface of the worktable and frowning down at the reassembled pieces of the burner.

Only one thing left to be tested.

He opened his book of notes, selected a blank page toward the back, and tore it free. Grabbing the paper, he strode to the corner of the distillery where the blue-and-white barrel of paraffin oil was stored. After taking off the lid, he dipped the paper into the oil, holding it over the barrel for a moment. Once it stopped dripping, he took the paper back to his worktable.

After allowing the oil to evaporate completely, he walked to the doorway, holding the page up to the sunlight. He brushed his fingers across the paper, dislodging the tiny flecks of green and what looked to be dirt.

Someone had contaminated the paraffin oil.

Not an accident, then, since the barrel was kept securely fastened at all times.

Someone wanted him dead.

Was it Veronica?

From the beginning, she'd eased him with passion, seduced him with her surrender. He slept, deep, besotted sleep next to her, his arms wrapped around her, his cheek cradled against her hair.

Did he really believe she wanted him dead?

He'd said the words rashly, in anger. That morning, her calm acceptance of his fate had disturbed him. Worse, he'd felt betrayed. No, something deeper than that, an emotion he didn't want to face at the moment.

She hadn't seemed concerned. Yet she'd been as stoic when viewing the ruin of her home.

He walked back to his worktable, balling up the paper.

The women of his acquaintance had been strong and resolute, but saw nothing wrong with a man witnessing their tears. He'd suspected, more than once, they'd used tears the way a man might use a sword.

Veronica didn't.

Nor did she share herself easily. Yet she wanted all his secrets.

If he'd divulged his past to her, would she have done

the same with him? Were they destined to forever misunderstand one another except in their bed?

He could recall the exact moment he'd seen her, standing on the edge of the crowd, her face pale, Elspeth standing beside her. She hadn't cried. She hadn't rushed to him. She hadn't expressed any joy he'd survived.

Hell, yes, he'd tried to hurt her, a just payment for what she'd done to him.

Ralston stepped into the distillery, looking apologetic. The man had been at his side most of the day, called away when three wagons had arrived earlier.

"The newly loomed carpet is here, sir. Mrs. Brody needs to know if they should remove the furniture from the Long Sitting Room today?"

The only expertise he had, besides his airships, was growing tobacco. The Lords Fairfax had not cultivated any arable land for decades. Instead, they farmed endless, undulating masses of sheep. He didn't know a damn thing about sheep, and now he was expected to know about carpets?

"Is my wife not prepared to answer some of these questions?" he asked. "Especially questions to do with the house itself?"

Ralston looked discomfited by the question. "I would be more than happy to appeal to Her Ladyship, Your Lordship," Ralston said. "However, she is not here. She left a few hours ago."

He turned and faced the older man. "What do you mean, she left? Where did she go?"

"I'm afraid I have no idea, Your Lordship," Ralston said.

Whenever Ralston was embarrassed, or uncomfortable, he repeated Montgomery's title excessively, a trait Montgomery had noticed over the past several weeks.

"Begging your pardon, Your Lordship."

He turned. The smith stood there, pulling off his cap. He was young, tall, with well-developed arm and shoulder muscles, a sparse beard, and wildly bushy sideburns. Montgomery had him working on rebuilding part of the burner damaged in the accident.

"They've gone to Kilmarin, Your Lordship," the man said. "Elspeth and Her Ladyship, that is. Her Ladyship promised Elspeth she'd have a chance to see her family."

Ralston stepped forward, and whispered, "Elspeth's husband, Your Lordship."

"Where the hell is Kilmarin, and why would my wife be going there?"

Ralston answered before Elspeth's husband could. "I know where it is, Your Lordship," he said. "South, near Perth."

Montgomery addressed the young man. "Do you know why they've gone?"

The man twisted his cap between his hands. "Elspeth didn't say, sir, but then she wouldn't. Loyal as the day is long, she is. All I know is they're taking the train in Inverness."

"How long ago did they leave?" he asked.

"A few hours ago now, Your Lordship."

"Did she tell you when they're returning?"

"Elspeth didn't know, sir."

Anger was not an unfamiliar emotion. The rage sweeping through him, however, surprised him with its intensity and suddenness. For some unknown reason, she'd taken her maid, his carriage, and left him.

Perhaps she'd tried to kill him after all. What reason would she have, otherwise, for leaving so peremptorily?

Guilt? He'd accused her of wanting him dead, and instead of remaining there, she went haring off to Perth.

She wasn't going to leave him that easily.

He slapped his hands down on the worktable, annoyed at Veronica, at himself, at the entire situation.

His airship was damaged, perhaps beyond repair. He had the original balloon, but he'd cannibalized parts from it. He'd damn well have to follow her in a carriage.

He motioned to Elspeth's husband.

"Come with me," he said, striding toward the door.

Damn it, if Veronica wanted him dead, she'd just have to tell him to his face.

Less than a quarter hour later, Montgomery was in the stable, his inquiry whether another carriage was available being met with an incredulous look from the stablemaster.

"We've three carriages, Your Lordship. The fourth is being refurbished, but the upholstery is nearly done."

"I only need one," he said, giving instructions to the coachman before he and Robbie entered the carriage.

Neither of them had packed a valise. They wouldn't be gone that long.

The sky was a bluish gray, the air thick with rain. Even the trees were a dull green, the river a flat pewter color. How much of the scenery was his mood and how much was the weather?

Doncaster Hall's bricks turned a persimmon color in the rain, the house distinct against the backdrop of a gray sky. In Virginia, he would have welcomed a storm. The rain would have been a blessing for the crops.

Raindrops hung pendulous from the frame of the window, then streaked the glass, obscuring his view of the house. He wasn't at Gleneagle but Doncaster Hall. Not Virginia, but Scotland.

"I'm a smith, Your Lordship," Robbie said, from the other side of the carriage. He still looked terrified. "I don't understand why you want me to come with you."

Montgomery turned his head and regarded the man. "Have you always worked at Doncaster Hall?"

"Only in the last two years, sir. I was apprenticed to Old Darby, but he took sick with the gout and had to lie about most of the day." Robbie bit his lip so hard it turned white, then evidently gathered his courage. "Are you angry with Elspeth, sir? She's a good girl and loyal, too."

"I'm sure she is, Robbie."

A moment later, he took pity on the man. "I've a mind to fetch my wife. Since yours is with mine, it was natural to invite you along."

Robbie nodded, but the gesture didn't appear relieved. "Yes, Your Lordship."

"I'm an American, Robbie. I was an American long before I was a lord. Every man is as good as another in America."

"We've our share of pride in Scotland, sir."

"Good, then you won't object to calling me Montgomery."

Robbie looked at him in shock. "I'll not be calling you that, sir. It wouldn't be respectful."

"While I would take it as an insult to be forever called Your Lordship. I'm tired of it, Robbie."

He laid his head back against the seat and closed his eyes.

"Is it that Her Ladyship didn't ask permission, sir?"

He opened his eyes and regarded the smith.

"Is that why we're going after them, sir?"

Damned if he knew how to answer Robbie.

He didn't like the feeling he was getting, the one crawling up his spine and chilling his skin. Shame wasn't an easy acquaintance, and never more than at that moment, when accompanied by a perfect recall of everything he'd said to Veronica.

However he tried to fit her into the role of selfish, manipulative murderess, she refused to fit. She was, however, impulsive, obstinate, passionate, and secretive.

Secretive? Or protective?

He remembered the look on her face when her uncle had ridiculed her, the pain quickly covered by an expressionless mask. She'd looked the same that morning, when he'd asked her why she'd been at the distillery the night before.

He'd hurt her.

Damn it.

She'd hurt him.

Damn it.

He closed his eyes again, but images of Veronica were still there. Veronica, staring at the ruin of her home. This morning, at dawn, when he'd loved her. Every time he loved her. All the past weeks when she'd been obstinate and relentless in poking and prodding at him until he felt his heart creak open.

You've been a fool.

A woman's voice, one he hadn't heard in nearly two years. Once, he would have said he'd forever be able to identify Caroline's voice. This time, however, she sounded too much like Veronica.

Damn it, Montgomery. You've been an idiot.

Either brother would have made that comment.

A good five minutes after Robbie asked the question, Montgomery answered him.

"I need to know why my wife left," he said.

Thankfully, the smith remained silent.

What the hell could Robbie possibly say?

Chapter 28

The rain slowed their progress to Inverness, the storm growing so fierce that Veronica signaled the driver to pull off on the side of the road and wait it out. An hour later, they were on their way again, the stormy skies giving way to a lovely day. Fortunately, that section of road was paved, so they didn't have to contend with muddy ruts.

According to the coachman, the Highland Railway ran regularly between Inverness and Perth, a journey of some four hours. She'd planned to stay at an inn tonight, but in Perth, not Inverness. With the delay, they might well be traveling through the night.

At the moment, however, she wanted to stand in front of a roaring fire and savor a cup of hot Darjeeling tea. She closed her eyes and could almost feel the heat warm the tip of her nose. Perhaps a little toast as well, or Cook's scones. They'd turned out to be almost as good as her mother's.

Thankfully, Elspeth was a good traveling companion. The other woman was not disturbed by the storm, lightning, or even hunger.

"Have you a large family, Elspeth?" she asked.

"I've four brothers and three sisters, my ma and dad,

of course, and Old Mary, plus a score of nephews and nieces. Although there might be even more as it's been a year since I've been home."

"A year?" she asked, surprised.

"It's a fair distance from Perth, Your Ladyship." Elspeth glanced away, obviously embarrassed. "And the fare by train . . ."

Unspoken was the comment that the cost was beyond what Elspeth could afford. Perhaps it was time Veronica investigated how much the servants at Doncaster Hall were paid. She added that to her mental list of things to discuss with Montgomery.

If Montgomery ever talked to her again.

She'd thought there might be hope for her marriage. Instead, she knew it was doubtful he would ever feel anything but lust for her. Once, that might have been enough. Now, she wasn't so certain.

They arrived, finally, in Inverness, only to discover they'd missed the most convenient train. The next was not due to leave for another three hours.

"Will you go back to Doncaster Hall?" she asked the coachman.

He shook his head. "I can wait here for you, Your Ladyship. Otherwise, you'll have to hire a carriage to take you home."

She nodded, then handed him some of the money from her reticule. "Will you need more, do you think?"

He glanced down at his hand. "This is very generous, Your Ladyship. I've friends here, plus Mrs. Brody has given me a list of supplies she needs."

"I doubt I'll be longer than a day or two," Veronica said.

They arranged for him to meet her at the station tomorrow, and the following day if she wasn't on that train.

At that, he touched the brim of his hat, nodding to her, and left.

After an hour of waiting on an uncomfortable wooden bench, they were escorted to the first-class car and told they could wait there until the train was due to leave. She couldn't help but wonder if the deference afforded her was because of Elspeth's reference to her as Your Ladyship within the station manager's hearing.

"Tell me about Kilmarin," she said. Thinking of Montgomery only made her sad and angry in turn.

"What would you like to know, Your Ladyship?"

"Anything," she said.

Elspeth frowned. "It stands on a hill, Your Ladyship, and it's quite a large place. I've never been inside, but you can see it from just outside Perth. Everyone knows about Kilmarin. And the Tullochs. Everyone near Perth, that is."

"Tell me about the Tullochs."

"I always thought I'd be married to a Tulloch, but my heart only saw Robbie, come to visit a relative, and one glance was all I needed."

Elspeth's face glowed with love.

Why was it some people loved easily and well, while others had to struggle at it? Some people didn't suffer any hills and valleys in their relationships but experienced, instead, a calm ocean.

She felt passion for Montgomery, but would she ever feel placid? She sincerely doubted it. Parts of his character rubbed against parts of hers, and the friction was sometimes annoying, often exciting, but never peaceful.

"Everyone for miles around is a Tulloch," Elspeth said, smiling. "It's like being a Fairfax," she added. "If you aren't a Tulloch, then you're married to one."

"What do you mean like being a Fairfax?"

Elspeth smiled. "Well, not everyone, Your Ladyship. Just everyone at Doncaster Hall. Robbie's uncle was a Fairfax. Most of the maids have a connection to the family. Even Mr. Kerr."

"Mr. Kerr?" she asked, surprised.

"His mother was a Fairfax. Didn't you know?"

She shook her head.

Elspeth suddenly sat up straight.

"Your Ladyship," Elspeth said, peering out the window with a very odd expression on her face. The view was of the interior of the station. Not a particularly pleasant vista, but little to alarm the girl.

"What is it?"

"Lord Fairfax just entered the station," she said. "He doesn't look happy." She turned to stare at Veronica. "And my Robbie's with him."

A dozen thoughts tumbled into Veronica's mind, none of them coherent.

"Are you very certain, Elspeth?"

Elspeth nodded.

She clasped her hands together so tightly they hurt.

A few minutes later, the door at the end of the car opened. Montgomery stood there, taking up all the space. Behind him was Robbie, looking as if he'd rather be anywhere but here.

Montgomery stepped aside, and Robbie entered the car. Veronica stood, moved to the front, allowing Robbie to sit beside Elspeth. At the moment, blessedly, the car was empty except for the four of them.

"Wife," Montgomery said, his gaze locking on her face. To the casual observer, his face might have appeared expressionless. She could feel his rage, however. Not to mention that his blue eyes were as cold as shards of ice.

"Husband," she said, in a tone equally frigid.

Montgomery stood with feet apart, hands clasped on either side of the doorframe. Steam from the engine tugged at his jacket, tousled his hair.

"We need to talk, you and I."

Conscious of the curiosity of the couple behind them, she made her way out of the car, consenting to go only as far as the landing. No one was boarding at the moment, but the location wouldn't remain private for long.

Montgomery didn't speak, annoying her even further. She was truly tired of his silences, tired of his eternal, ever-present, restraint.

She folded her arms, determined to be as stubborn.

Montgomery had more practice at stoicism, however.

She unfolded her arms and glared at him. "I didn't try to kill you," she said.

"I'm willing to be convinced."

"No." She shook her head. "I'm not willing to convince you. Think what you want."

"Why did you leave?"

Her eyes widened.

"Did you expect me to stay at Doncaster Hall after you accused me of trying to kill you?"

"You didn't deny it."

Words failed her as she stared at him. If she'd had something handy, she would have thrown it at him.

"I didn't deny it," she said, slowly as if he were devoid of wits, "because I couldn't believe you said it. Now I shall. No, Montgomery, I didn't try to kill you." Each word was enunciated slowly, so he would have no problem hearing and understanding it.

She turned and would have left him had Montgomery not grabbed her arm and held on. "Where the hell are you going?"

"Anywhere. Anyplace. Anywhere you aren't."

"Veronica," he said softly, "I knew the moment I said the words that I was wrong."

Only slightly mollified, she turned to face him.

"How could you think that of me?" she whispered.

"I didn't," he said, slowly pulling her close. "Forgive me," he said, brushing a light, almost passionless kiss over her lips.

"It was a horrid thing to say."

"Yes, it was," he said.

Still, she wasn't ready to forgive him. She pulled back.

"I've put up with a great deal from you," she said.

One of his eyebrows rose. "Oh?"

"Your eternal silences, for one."

"You've had your share of silences, Veronica. You didn't tell me about your parents, the fire, or Amanda."

She thought about that statement. He was correct.

"I don't talk to anyone about my parents," she said, looking down at the landing. "It's been two years, but sometimes, it feels as if it were just yesterday. If I talk about it, it's real, and I don't want it to be real." Her gaze flew to his. "Is that why you don't talk about Caroline?"

Was that why Montgomery remained silent? Because the loss of her was as real and new to him as her sorrow for her parents?

All those weeks, she'd pecked at him like a chicken, an annoying chicken, who'd insisted he spread his heart open for her to examine it. Just when she was about to apologize, he said something that threw her into confusion.

"Guilt is the reason I don't talk about Caroline," he said.

"Guilt?"

The landing where they stood connected two railway

cars. The window showed the car ahead filling with people. This was neither the time nor the place for such a confrontation, but she didn't say a word or move to return to the car.

"Is that the price you'll extract, Veronica, to forgive me for my words? All my secrets?"

She studied him for a moment, understanding Montgomery more in the last five minutes than she had in the last five weeks.

"No," she said, her answer evidently surprising him. She didn't want to peck at him anymore. "No, Montgomery, keep your secrets."

He studied her for a moment, then said, "Caroline was my sister-in-law. James's wife. I wasn't in love with her. I loved her like a sister. I had since I was a boy. We grew up together, you see. Her family lived down the road from Gleneagle."

He glanced toward the station. The billowing steam, excited chatter from the passengers, and a variety of mechanical noises should have made conversation difficult. Yet, strangely, she could hear him easily.

"My brothers went to war together. James died first, at Fort Donelson. Alisdair was next, a year later. By the third year of the war, I was the only one left of my family. Caroline was home, at Gleneagle, trying to keep everything together."

He speared one hand through his hair, glanced down at her. "My brothers went to war to keep everything just as it was. None of us knew, at the time, that life would never be the same again."

He folded his arms, leaning against the other car, his gaze fixed, again, on the distance. She knew, however, he wasn't looking at the interior of the Inverness Station but at the past.

"I received two letters from Caroline when I was in Washington. She tried to tell me how things were at Gleneagle. I told myself she was used to being sheltered and viewed any deprivation as a hardship. I knew she was grieving for James, and I thought she was craving attention."

He moved restlessly, finally meeting her eyes.

"She was like that. She lived life fully. She laughed often and cried often. There wasn't any middle ground for Caroline."

He looked away again. "I didn't know she was starving."

She bit her bottom lip.

"I didn't want to return to Gleneagle. I didn't want to go home, and I did so grudgingly, months after I should have. When I did, it was to find Caroline dead. Gleneagle was gone. The house had been razed, put to the cannon, and the fields set on fire. The Army of the Potomac had leveled my home because it was owned by a family who'd fought for the South."

He unfolded his arms, standing with feet braced apart, his hands at his back. "After that, I didn't much care what happened to me," he said. "The Balloon Corps was disbanded, I was assigned to a regiment. When the war was over, I eventually went home to Virginia. That's when Edmund found me."

She didn't know what to say.

"There's nothing in Virginia but memories, Veronica. Memories of my culpability, my pride, my guilt."

"Why didn't you come back when she wrote you?"

"My airships," he said, his smile self-deprecating. "At first, I was enthusiastic about the idea of being able to use them in war, to show the generals how intelligence could be gathered behind enemy lines without endangering anyone. Then I got caught up in the politics of it. There was talk the Corps was going to be disbanded. I spent weeks arguing with people, writing letters to the generals I'd worked with, trying to convince anyone, attempting to get funds for the Corps. In the end, it didn't matter."

Silence stretched between them, but when he would have escorted her back into the car, Veronica shook her head, placed her palm against his jacket, right over his heart.

"How do you know you could have saved her if you'd returned to Gleneagle?"

"What do you mean, how do I know?"

"Every day, for months, I replayed the night my parents died. If I'd insisted on going with my father to save my mother, I might have saved both of them. If I'd awakened, checked the lamps, made sure the stove wasn't overheated, then perhaps the fire would never have happened. I don't know, Montgomery. Perhaps we're only supposed to deal with what we know, what's already happened, not pretend it might have been different."

"Life isn't a choice."

She smiled. "Yes, it is. What would you choose, Montgomery? To see only bleakness and despair? Why shouldn't we choose a little joy, a little happiness?"

"That's not life, Veronica."

"Oh, Montgomery, it *is* life, just not the one we've known for the last few years."

He looked startled by her words.

"I wouldn't take away what's happened to you, Montgomery. I know that sounds cruel, but it's made you the man you are, the kind man you are. You treat others with dignity and respect. You planned financially for me so I would never be in the same position as Caroline. I understand that, now. Yet, at the same time, what's happened to you has made you stand apart from life, to be uninvolved. Your life will happen whether or not you participate in it, Montgomery, I know that only too well."

She dropped her hand. "Is Caroline a vengeful ghost?"

He smiled. "She's not really a ghost at all."

She nodded, expecting him to say that. "Then she doesn't condemn you for what you did."

"It wasn't what I did I regret, Veronica, but what I didn't do."

"I didn't check the lamps. I didn't ensure the wicks were trimmed."

He frowned at her.

"Caroline could have told you. She could have come out, and said, come home, Montgomery. We're starving. We need help."

"She wasn't reared to be as direct as you," he said.

"So you were supposed to guess what she meant? You were supposed to infer all her thoughts and wishes? I have a Gift, Montgomery, but even I could not have done that."

"You ridicule my past, Veronica."

"No," she said, shaking her head. "I don't. I can understand regretting your actions, Montgomery. But how can you regret something that never happened? Besides," she added, "Caroline wouldn't have wanted you to."

"And how do you know?" he asked, the beginning of a smile curving his lips.

"Because you feel her. Because her thoughts are with you. Because you loved her, and she loved you."

"That's enough? Love?"

She nodded. "Of course, Montgomery. Of course it is."

He would have said something, but a passenger

abruptly appeared at the base of the steps. Montgomery moved aside, grabbed her elbow, and whispered in her ear. "Come back home."

"I've an errand to perform," she said, and told him about Elspeth's grandmother.

"That damnable mirror."

"Had it not been for the mirror," she said, "we wouldn't have met."

He smiled, the expression deepening his dimples.

"We would have met, Veronica. Something tells me that. Fate would have made certain of it."

She couldn't be certain he said what she heard next, because it was such an odd remark for Montgomery to make.

"Or maybe my ghosts sent you to me."

Chapter 29

The peaks of the Highlands gave way to the hills of Perth, as if this part of Scotland were older, the mountains worn to nubs. Kilmarin, the home of the Tullochs, was located atop the highest of these hills, the only approach up a winding mountain road. The stolid Scots fortress, at least four floors tall, was constructed of deep red stone and didn't look the least welcoming.

"Granny's cottage is a ways from Kilmarin proper," Elspeth said. "Granny never did like people much." She glanced at Montgomery, embarrassed. "Her cottage gives her a good command of the road. Like Kilmarin," she added, staring up at the castle. "She's been known to throw things down on people who get lost and take the upper road."

"Perhaps it would be best if you go ahead," Veronica said.

"Oh, she won't know me," Elspeth said easily. "Her eyesight is going, too."

Montgomery glanced at her, a faint smile haunting his mouth. "Your Granny sounds like my aunt Maddie," he said.

Veronica turned to look at him.

"My mother's sister," he said, "who took to wearing her shift outside her clothes."

She pressed a hand to her lips.

"It's all right, she would have been pleased to make you laugh. She delighted in being eccentric and shocking my father." He smiled. "One of my childhood memories is watching my father storm after her when she put a live chicken in his library." He smiled. "She wanted to annoy him, and she succeeded."

"What happened to her?" she asked, then immediately wished she hadn't. The last thing she wanted to do was to make Montgomery sad again.

His smile faded. "When I was thirteen, she took one of the boats out on the river and drowned."

She lifted his hand and linked her fingers with his. "I'm sorry."

"I used to go and visit her grave and talk to her. I always had the feeling she could hear me." His smile was self-deprecating. "One of the reasons I miss Virginia."

"For the graves?"

He studied their linked fingers.

"For the memories."

"Memories are in your heart," she said softly. "My parents are there. Not in that black spot of earth we saw."

Both Elspeth and Robbie looked uncomfortable, and she couldn't blame them. She'd not meant to reveal so much. Nor had Montgomery, from his quick look at her.

The journey from Inverness had taken longer than she'd planned. They'd traveled at night, but halfway to Perth, they'd stopped on the siding and remained there for hours. She'd slept with her head against Montgomery's shoulder. Consequently, their arrival in the city had been at dawn, and after a hasty breakfast, they'd opted to travel to Elspeth's grandmother rather than rest in one of the city's hotels.

The hired carriage made the steep climb with some

difficulty and, more than once, she wanted to simply change her mind about this errand and return to Doncaster Hall. The carriage wouldn't be able to turn around on such a narrow road, however, so she simply sat back, gripped Montgomery's hand tightly, and focused on what she was feeling from the inhabitants of the carriage.

Both Elspeth and her husband were radiating contentment. The love she felt from each of them for the other was uncomplicated and direct. She had no doubt the happiness Elspeth had seen for herself in the Tulloch Sgàthán would come true. As for Montgomery? As always, she felt a confluence of emotions from him: curiosity, relief, irritation, and a happiness so unexpected that she smiled.

Thankfully, they turned to the west, traveling away from the fortress for a few moments until the carriage stopped.

She stared out at the scenery, unsurprised to see a lone cottage in the middle of what looked to be a plateau. As if the top of the hill had simply been scraped flat and Old Mary's home placed in the center of it. Not quite a cottage but more than a hut, the structure reminded her of an upside-down cup. The walls curved outward, no doubt because of the volume of thatch on the roof.

As they left the carriage and slowly walked toward the house, she counted three birds' nests in the middle of the thatch. A red squirrel crossed their path, rose on his hind legs to chitter angrily at them, then disappeared.

"I'll go ahead, Your Ladyship, if you don't mind," Elspeth said. "Warn her she has visitors."

Veronica nodded. After a whispered conversation, Robbie retreated to the carriage. Montgomery looked as if he would like to do the same, but he resolutely remained at her side.

"You needn't stay," she said. She wasn't sparing him

as much as wishing privacy with Old Mary. She'd never mentioned the vision she'd had in the mirror and was a little embarrassed to do so now.

"Are you certain?" he asked.

She nodded.

He didn't argue the point, evidently grateful to escape a meeting with a wisewoman. What else could Old Mary be? She watched as he retraced his steps. Instead of joining Robbie, however, Montgomery veered left, heading for an adjacent hill.

"Lady Fairfax?"

She turned to see Elspeth peering out the door at her. "Granny is ready for you."

She took a deep breath and entered the house.

Montgomery strode to the top of the nearest hill, looking over at Kilmarin and its surroundings. He needed not only the exercise but the solitude. At the top, the vista before him was awe-inspiring.

Cool blue skies topped deep green hills, accented by a sliver of river sparkling in the distance. This land, with its beauty and its history, didn't shine with the promise of a new country or reveal the still-bloody wounds of its growing pains. Scotland endured, as if it were filled with a quiet acceptance of all that had come before and would probably come again.

The strength of the land appealed to him; the stalwart nature of its people impressed him. When disaster occurred, they simply began again, resilient and resigned.

Could he do the same?

He closed his eyes, deliberately summoning his ghosts. James appeared dressed as he'd seen him last, a man intent upon his duty, excitement overlaying the look of worry in his eyes. Alisdair was next, dressed as a prisoner, a role Montgomery had never witnessed but that his imagination furnished only too easily. Alisdair was thin, his beard scraggly, stubbornness gleaming in his sunken eyes. Caroline, darling Caroline, was next, her image that of a girl newly married, desperately in love with James, her laughter trilling up and around the oval staircase of Gleneagle.

Forgive me.

He sent the entreaty to those he'd loved and, for the first time, he felt as if they did forgive him, that they always had. Perhaps only his guilt had fleshed in his ghosts.

What if Veronica were right?

He'd always thought he should have returned to Gleneagle when Caroline had first corresponded with him. He could have read between the lines, understood the dire circumstances, and known they were down to their last resources. He could have left Washington, taken food and supplies. Perhaps his presence would have altered Gleneagle's fate.

As he stood there, looking at Scotland, Montgomery realized he'd believed in his own omnipotence for years. He could have been captured on the way home. Or killed on the journey. Perhaps he couldn't have saved Caroline or Gleneagle. Instead, he might have simply been the last Fairfax brother to die.

As it was, he was the only survivor of Gleneagle, the only one of his grandfather's grandsons, the lone Fairfax brother. He, and he alone, carried the hope of his family.

What had he done with it?

He'd not moved forward, that was certain. He'd played with his navigation system but nothing more. The innovations he'd made could revolutionize the use of airships. He'd not taken responsibility for the Fairfax fortune. He'd not been a good husband. Lust had sent him to his wife, but he'd been too involved in his own misery to discover as much about her as he should have from the beginning.

He'd been a fool. A selfish fool more intent on looking backward than in living his life.

This was an old land. For thousands of years, people had warred over it. Generations had laughed and cried here. Men had gone off to war, and women had stayed behind.

Women like Veronica, with her stubbornness and resilience, with her courage. Veronica, with her impulsive nature, her trust, and her wholehearted passion. Who believed in her Gift regardless of how many time she'd been ridiculed.

What had she said? People mock what they do not know.

How many times had she been mocked? How many people—besides himself—had underestimated her? He'd originally seen her as a foolish girl. The passing days had revealed how wrong he'd been.

He had the most curious thought. Veronica Moira MacLeod Fairfax would never stop being exactly who she was. Another thought, one that startled him in its certainty. Veronica would never abdicate the responsibility for her welfare or that of people who depended on her. She would not give that responsibility to anyone else but would assume it herself.

She would not wait to be rescued.

Two things struck him, then. Somewhere along the way, he'd fallen in love with his wife.

The second thought was he was damned if Edmund Kerr was going to take his future from him.

* * *

Old Mary lowered herself to a chair with a series of gasps. "I'm old, child," she said, when Elspeth hovered at her side. "Not crippled."

Elspeth exchanged an amused look with Veronica.

"I've waited all this time," Mary said, turning her head toward Veronica. Her pale blue eyes, so light it seemed as if they had no color at all, speared through her. "Wondering if the mirror would come back to me. It's time for it to return," she said. "I'm nearly done."

"Oh, Granny," Elspeth said, falling to her knees beside the chair. Tears sparkled in her eyes, earning her a caress as the old woman smoothed her withered hand over Elspeth's hair.

A moment later, Mary reached for the drawstring bag, withdrew the mirror, tracing the line of diamonds with a withered finger.

"It's an ugly thing," she said, "but someone tried to give it beauty." She smiled, the expression deepening the furrows on her face. Her hair, thick and black, belied her age, revealing not one touch of gray.

"It's come full circle. I gave it to a woman who'd lost a love, and a woman who's found a love brought it back to me."

"Have I?" Veronica asked, startled.

Old Mary smiled. "Have you not looked in the mirror?"

"I have," she said.

"Is it that you didn't like what you saw? Or you didn't believe it?"

She leaned forward, placed her hand on top of Old Mary's. The elderly woman's skin was soft, the veins on the back of her hand engorged and blue. The hand she clasped was cold, however, as if Mary's body had already begun to prepare for the grave.

"Does it tell the future? Or does it just reveal something you want to see?"

The old woman smiled. "All I know is when I looked in the mirror, it was many years ago. I saw myself at this age, far older and wiser than I ever believed I could be. I felt the aches in my knees and my back. I saw Death beckoning me. I also saw a life filled with richness and joy, and all those I love surrounding me."

She laughed, a surprisingly young laugh. "I'm not a soothsayer, child. The mystery of life is just that. It's a mystery given to each of us to solve. Who do we love? Who loves us? What is our destiny? The mirror doesn't give any answers. Nor do I. Even if I had the answers you seek, child, I'd not give them to you and thereby spoil your journey. It's enough the mirror gives you a sight of what might be if you wish it, if you're willing to do what's necessary."

Veronica studied their two hands, noting the stark differences of a few decades.

"I've looked in the mirror several times lately," she said. "I didn't see anything."

Old Mary offered her the mirror. "Go ahead, child. Look. See the future that lies before you."

Veronica stared at the mirror, realizing that it would either reveal something she wanted to see, or it wouldn't. She and Montgomery, together, should be responsible for the future they shared, not the Tulloch Sgàthán.

The old woman smiled, then slowly placed the mirror back on the table.

Mary turned and spoke to her granddaughter. "Go and fetch your husband to me. I'd see him again." After Elspeth left the cottage, the old woman turned to Veronica.

"Ask me your other question, child. I see it in your eyes."

"My parents told me I have a Gift," she said slowly. "I can feel what others feel." She glanced down at the scarred table, ran a finger over one particularly interesting gouge.

"Are you asking me if this is true?"

Veronica shook her head. She knew, despite what anyone said, that her Gift was real. "What I want to know is this. Can someone talk to the dead?"

Old Mary reached over, placed her hand over Veronica's again, and asked with genuine curiosity, "Why would you want to?" Her smile was a simple curve of closed lips, but her eyes were warm. "Life is for the living, my child. Not the dead." She pulled back her hand and sat back against the chair.

"In this land, ghosts are plentiful. We've kilted warriors, peddlers, Edinburgh dandies playing at war. We've young women swathed in plaid and children destined to be forever young." She stared off into the distance. "You would have enough to do if you spent your life seeking them out." Her smile faded. "You'd have none of your own life to live."

She leaned forward again, patting Veronica's hand. "Go and live your own life, child. Leave the dead to their graves."

Veronica didn't say anything for a moment and Old Mary allowed her the silence. When she did speak, it was softly, the words coming with difficulty.

"I want to see my parents," she said, feeling as if her throat were closing. "I want to say goodbye."

"Then say goodbye," Mary said, surprising her. "In your heart. Do you think they wouldn't know?" She reached over and patted her cheek. "In your heart, child. That's all you need to do."

Veronica smoothed her fingers over the cool surface of

the mirror, feeling the gold warm to her touch. She knew, coming there, what she would do.

Slowly, Veronica stood, then impulsively bent and kissed the old woman on the cheek.

"May I leave the mirror with you?" Veronica asked.

"I would be pleased to return it to where I found it," Mary said. "A full circle."

"Thank you," Veronica said softly, and left the cottage.

Her attention was caught by a figure on a nearby hill. As she watched, she realized it was Montgomery standing there. She raised her arm to signal him, and he responded in kind.

A borrowed Scot? Not that man. He looked at home, striding with confident steps as if he belonged in Scotland. He did, but would Montgomery realize it?

Chapter 30

Montgomery had left his carriage in Inverness, and when they arrived back in the city, he sent Veronica's coachman on an errand, to find Edmund Kerr and tell him he was needed at Doncaster Hall.

Instead of remaining overnight either at Perth or Inverness, they'd chosen to return home. Another dawn found them nearly there, his arm around Veronica's shoulders as she dozed.

She hadn't mentioned what she'd discussed with Old Mary, and her only comment about the mirror had been that it belonged with the Tullochs. He'd not disputed the claim or pressed her for more details. They'd said farewell to Elspeth and Robbie, who were going to stay with Elspeth's relatives another day or so before returning to Doncaster Hall.

"Won't you miss her help?" he'd asked, as they were leaving Perth.

She'd sent him a look that warned him it had been a foolish question.

"I never had a maid of my own until I married you."

"Many things have changed in the last two months."

She'd only smiled at that remark.

He gently cradled her as she slept, grateful beyond measure he'd gone to the Society of the Mercaii that night.

Once home, they slept for a few hours. He loved Veronica at dawn, slipping inside her, their bodies rising and falling in a slow, seductive, drugging rhythm. He'd wanted to pleasure her but pleased himself as well, lost in her. He slid one hand beneath her buttocks, lifted her, intent on giving her more, needing to give her more. She arched against him, a sound of surrender escaping her full and well-kissed lips.

Later that morning, he returned to the distillery to find Ralston had been busy in his absence.

The rest of the envelope had been retrieved and lay on the grass in strips. The silk was too damaged to be used again, but he thanked Ralston for his effort regardless.

"I'm going up tomorrow," he told Ralston, waiting for the other man's response.

"In what, Your Lordship?" Ralston asked, frowning. "The envelope is in shreds, and you've removed the baffles from your balloon to use on the ship."

He smiled, pleased at Ralston's knowledge. "You know that, and I know that, but no one else does. I'd like you to spread the word I'll be flying again tomorrow."

Ralston's brow furrowed. "Your Lordship, wide ears and short tongues are best, but I'm curious. Why?"

"Someone wanted my airship to fail, Ralston."

The other man nodded, suddenly understanding. "You're setting a trap, then, sir?"

"I am," he said.

"May I assist you, sir?"

He smiled. "Indeed you may. First, I'd like you to spread the word. Second, let me know when Edmund arrives, and third, join me back here once it's dark. Bring Tom. We'll need reinforcements. But no one else is to know."

Ralston nodded, looking pleased at his assignments.

Montgomery had taken the precaution of arming himself with the pistol he'd brought from Virginia. He hid it behind one of the abandoned whiskey kettles, studying the layout with an eye to tonight's performance. He'd settle himself into a depression in the earthen floor and wait.

First, however, he had another, even more important, task to perform.

He found Veronica an hour later, a good distance from Doncaster Hall, standing atop a knoll.

"What are you doing?" he asked when he reached her.

"Saying goodbye," she said, not turning.

"Goodbye?"

She nodded.

"To me?" Damned if his heart didn't skip a beat or two.

"No," she said, glancing over her shoulder at him. "To the past."

He stepped closer, wrapping his arms around her waist, pulling her back against him.

"Look around you, Montgomery Fairfax. What do you see?"

Green, rolling glens gave way to brushy hills covered by undulating flocks of sheep with black faces and shaggy coats. Beyond, the mountains were dark gray, the color of shale, punched into relief by black shadows, and highlighted by a midday sun. Even farther, the high peaks of mountains, already dusted with snow, poked at the sky.

Slashes of color brightened the landscape: a touch of purple, a soft blue, and here and there, a flavor of yellow in the form of an intrepid wildflower blooming brightly against a rock wall.

A soft wind blew from the west, ruffling the surface of

the river to the left. The scent was one he'd come to recognize as uniquely Scotland: a hint of chill in the air, the smell of moss, and a something he'd been told was peat.

In the distance, the ruins of a crofter's hut attested that someone had lived here once, braving the weather and the isolation with the same insouciance as the sheep still did.

"Scotland isn't just the scenery," she said, turning in his arms, curving her palms around his elbows. "It's a place. A feeling. Spirit, will, struggle, the essence of life itself. It's all here. There's power here, Montgomery, can't you feel it?"

He looked down at her. Her face was luminous, as if she were lit from within. She took his breath away.

He loved the sound of her voice, the way she pronounced words, the lilt of it, the flavor of Scotland in her speech.

"And sheep," he said, looking where she gestured. "Don't forget sheep. No wonder we eat so much mutton."

She laughed, the first time he'd ever heard her laugh like that, freely, completely. He found himself charmed by the sound, wishing she would laugh again. Perhaps she hadn't laughed before because he hadn't been amusing.

"Mr. Kerr called you a borrowed Scot," she said, startling him. "Will you prove him right or wrong?"

"A borrowed Scot?" He wasn't certain how he felt about that.

"Did you know he was a Fairfax?" she asked.

"I just discovered it."

To his surprise, she looked annoyed.

"There wasn't exactly time to tell you," he said. "I was occupied in chasing you all over Scotland."

Her eyes narrowed. "I wouldn't have left if you hadn't accused me of trying to kill you."

"Forgive me," he said, kissing her temple, then trailed his lips down her cheek. She deliberately turned her head away, and he smiled.

"I didn't think."

She slowly turned her head again.

She looked so desirable, he decided that it might be time to talk sternly to that part of him springing to attention. Instead, he drew her closer, in the grip of something he didn't quite understand. She melted against him as she always did, responsive, enticing, surrendering so easily and with such delight he was the one vanquished.

Need arrowed through him as he crushed his mouth to hers. She gripped his shirt, pulled him to her, wrapped her arms around his neck, and buried her face against his throat.

"I want you, now," he said, knowing damn well that *now* was not appropriate.

He kissed the curve of her ear, grabbed the lobe between his teeth, then trailed a heated path down her throat.

He forced himself to release her.

"How do you do that to me?" he asked, pulling away and staring into her face.

She blinked several times, as if trying to surface from a dream.

"I thought it was you," she said, her lips curving in a smile.

"Perhaps it's *us*," he said.

"Is that bad?"

"No," he said, leaning his forehead against hers. "It's not. But I'll be damned if I'll take my wife in the middle of a glen."

She sighed. "Really?" she asked, sounding disappointed.

"I came to tell you something," he said, stepping back from her. He couldn't touch her without wanting her. At her look, he smiled. "You'll hear I'm taking my airship up tomorrow."

Her expression was carefully expressionless, but he knew to look in her eyes.

"I came to tell you not to worry," he said, tracing his finger along her jaw.

She looked away, her view of the abandoned crofter's hut evidently of great interest. Finally, she turned to face him, her regard steady and unwavering.

"How do I do that?" she asked.

"Trust me to know what I'm doing," he said.

Again, that look.

She nodded, finally, almost a reluctant concession.

He didn't care how he protected Veronica but protect her he would. He wasn't a borrowed Scot, damn it. He was as stubborn, determined, and as Scots in his way as Veronica was in hers.

A few hours later, Veronica decided she was not going to tolerate this behavior from Montgomery anymore. He could not reveal the secret of his past in Virginia one moment and, in the next, retreat into silence. He'd not come to dinner. She hadn't seen him since this afternoon.

She was going to have to tell him exactly what she wanted. If, in time, she divulged her emotions, then so be it.

He would know she'd fallen in love with him.

Perhaps he wouldn't ridicule her, but he might get that look in his eyes, the one that said she confused him. But if he thought he was going to push her away again, however, she was having none of it.

She dressed in her new emerald dress, a shade that

brought out the green of her eyes and made them sparkle. Since Elspeth had not yet returned, and since she hadn't wanted to bother Mrs. Brody for a temporary replacement, she left her hair loose, spread over her shoulders.

She took the servants' stairs to the back of the house since she didn't want to be seen heading toward the distillery. They should call the building something different going forward. The Airship Building, perhaps.

The distillery was dark when she stood in the doorway, but before she could call out for Montgomery, she found herself grabbed and hauled bodily behind a kettle. She would have screamed if a hand hadn't suddenly clamped over her mouth.

"What are you doing here?" Montgomery whispered, relaxing his hand.

"Looking for you," she whispered back. She turned in his arms. "Why are we whispering? And why are we in the dark?"

When he didn't speak, she slapped her head against his chest. "Talk to me, Montgomery."

"I'm laying a trap."

"Why?"

"I know who sabotaged my airship," he said.

"Were you going to tell me?" she asked.

"No."

She took a step away from him. "You weren't?"

"Not until it was over," he said.

She folded her arms in front of her.

He grabbed her and pulled her close.

"I didn't want you involved," he said softly, "because you could get hurt. He's after me, not you."

"I don't want you hurt, either," she said, standing stiff within his embrace.

He lowered his head until his forehead touched hers.

"I'm supposed to protect you, Veronica," he said.

"You do. Without telling me, though?" She pulled back again. "He?" she asked, just now realizing what he'd said.

"Edmund Kerr."

"Mr. Kerr?"

"He's made no secret of the fact he thinks me a poor lord," Montgomery said. "Had it not been for my grand-father, he'd be the 11th Lord Fairfax."

She thought about his revelation for a moment. "I didn't like him when I first met him," she said. "I told myself I must be mistaken."

"You should have told me."

She placed her hands on her hips and regarded him. "When, Montgomery? As I remember, you didn't think much of my Gift."

Before he could answer, they heard a sound.

A shadow appeared on the wall: a creeping creature with a glowing heart.

"What is that?" she whispered.

Montgomery shook his head, placing one finger against her lips. She nodded her understanding as he moved to stand in front of her. She watched as the figure moved inside the old distillery, carrying a lantern, body curved over it to contain the light, and walking unerr-ingly to the corner.

Montgomery left the shelter of the kettle, advancing on the intruder as the figure lifted the lid of the blue-and-white barrel. She followed, fear chilling her.

The person lifted the lantern as Montgomery ap-proached. In the next instant, Veronica saw that it wasn't Edmund Kerr standing in front of the barrel of paraffin oil but a woman.

"Millicent?" she asked, startled. "What are you doing here?"

The next moments were a blur. Millicent pushed the barrel over, then threw the lantern down on the stream of paraffin oil. Montgomery whirled, pushing Veronica in front of him. Before she could question him, before she could even speak, he'd grabbed her, thrown her over his shoulder, and was racing for the door.

She didn't have time to protest.

A whoosh of air preceded the explosion. Billowing orange clouds limned in black rolled out of the doorway, carrying fire into the night sky. The air cracked open, deadened her hearing, and sucked the breath from her lungs.

She and Montgomery fell, thrown onto the graveled path by the force of the explosion. Pieces of roof, rendered almost molten by the blast, and shards of brick fell on them as Montgomery covered her with his body. She heard his groan of pain as something heavy struck his shoulder, and clutched him, wrapped her arms around his neck, and counted each screaming second.

Would they even survive to have a future?

Chapter 31

The ground shook, the air heated; Veronica was trembling beneath him. The explosion seemed to go on forever, forever being measured by minutes. The gradual slowing of the rain of pebbles was the first indication it was ending.

He got to his knees, helping Veronica up. They knelt there in the glow of the fire as he studied her carefully. Her dress had been singed on one sleeve. Her cheek was reddened where he'd probably been too rough in throwing her over his shoulder. A bruise, however, was a small price to pay for survival.

He finished his survey, just now realizing she was doing the same to him.

"Are you all right?" he asked.

She nodded, placing her palm against his cheek, her thumb gently brushing against the corner of his mouth.

"Are you? Your face is covered in soot."

He rotated his right shoulder, feeling the pain and discounting it in the same movement.

"I'm alive," he said. "That's all that matters."

He stood with some effort and pulled Veronica up. For a moment, they simply leaned together, each supporting the other. Together, they staggered to the bridge.

"What happened?" she asked, her voice faint.

"She set the paraffin oil on fire. It explodes," he said.

"What was she doing?"

He slung one arm around her shoulder. "It's why the burner failed," he said. "The oil was contaminated. Anything would have done it, but I suspected she was using dirt and grass."

"So, she was coming back to do it again?"

He nodded.

Suddenly, Ralston was there. Ralston, with his shirt half off his body and his face covered in red-and-black welts. His white hair was standing up in tufts, and for the first time in their acquaintance, Ralston looked angry.

"Are all right, sir?" he asked, voice quavering.

Montgomery nodded. "Where's Tom?"

"He's fine, sir. I had him by me watching."

"We need to find . . ." his words broke off as he turned to Veronica. "What's her name?"

"Millicent," she said.

"We need to find Millicent," he said. "If she's alive," he added. Ralston nodded, disappearing into the crowd of people from Doncaster Hall.

During the next several hours, Veronica's fire brigade performed admirably, arranging themselves in position within moments of the blaze. A line was formed leading to the river, and within two hours, the fire was extinguished. The distillery was reduced to rubble, nothing of the walls or roof remaining. Surprisingly, one of the last of the whiskey kettles still stood, a little battered, but remaining as a stubborn testament to the building's original purpose.

The location where the paraffin oil barrel had once stood was covered in earth, a preventive measure to ensure any remaining oil wouldn't be a hazard.

He and Veronica were surveying the damage when

Ralston and Tom approached, each holding the arm of a woman writhing between them.

"We found her, sir," Ralston said.

Millicent struggled, but the two men held her tight. Suddenly, she fell to her knees in front of Montgomery.

"Oh, sir," she said, raising a tear-streaked and scorched face to him. "It wasn't you, Your Lordship."

Ralston frowned. "Fair words won't make the pot boil, girl," he said.

Millicent's voice changed, grew rough as she sent Veronica a sweeping look of contempt. "It was her, sir."

"Explain yourself," Montgomery said.

Before the other woman could answer, Veronica stepped forward, grabbed his hand, and gripped it tightly. She didn't look in his direction, her attention on the maid.

"Did my cousin tell you to do such a thing? Was it Amanda?" Veronica asked, her voice emotionless. "Did she promise you a position in London?"

He squeezed her hand in wordless comfort, but she didn't look away from Millicent.

"I don't know your cousin," Millicent said.

"Then why?"

"I worked for that position," she said. "I deserved it. Five years I've worked here, and I do a better job than anyone."

Veronica couldn't find any words to respond to that shocking comment. Millicent and Amanda were separated by country, status, and appearance. Yet they were alike in their single-minded pursuit of what they felt was owed to them.

"What shall we do with her, sir?"

"Send her home," Montgomery said. "Send her anywhere but here."

Taking Veronica's hand, he turned and headed toward the bridge.

"You thought it was Amanda," he said.

She nodded. "It seemed like something Amanda would do. How very strange for two people to dislike me so much."

"I don't think Amanda likes anyone unless that person can serve her needs," he said. "As for Millicent, she's a twisted soul."

At the top of the bridge, Veronica turned and surveyed the damage.

"Will you rebuild the distillery?"

"We'll build a place for airships, instead."

She leaned on the edge of the bridge, gazing down at the water. Dawn was coloring the river orange and pink, shades strangely in keeping with the memory of a night filled with fire.

"How did she know fouling the paraffin oil would make the burner go out?"

"Who tends the lamps?" he asked. "Who filters the oil?"

"Millicent," she said. "Of course." A moment later, she asked another question. "She did it because she thought I'd be with you, didn't she?"

"You were on the first flight. Everyone at Doncaster Hall saw us, which probably gave her the idea."

"I wasn't on the second flight," she said. "Nor did she know I'd be on the one you let people know was planned. She'd have killed you, Montgomery."

She walked into his arms, clung to him.

"It's strange to make someone that angry at me," she said.

His silence earned him a quick look.

"I was never *that* angry," she said.

He smiled, and wordlessly they descended the other side of the bridge, taking the path back to Doncaster Hall, a journey interrupted each time someone wanted to speak with them.

Veronica was grateful to see no one seemed to blame her still for Montgomery's accident. Word of Millicent's confession had probably already circulated through the staff. Also, Montgomery was still holding her hand, and despite how many times they were stopped, refused to relinquish it.

"Why didn't you choose her?" he asked, when they had a moment alone.

"Millicent? I had a feeling about her," Veronica said.

"Your Gift?"

She glanced at him, but he only smiled.

"I'm beginning to think you can see into the hearts of others," he said. "God knows you have the ability to see into mine."

Her smile was a beautiful thing, alluring and tempting. He had no choice but to kiss her in full view of everyone.

Someone cheered, and he grinned when he pulled back.

Veronica laughed, tucked her hand in his, and together they continued toward the house.

Doncaster Hall commanded the knoll like a king upon his throne. Around it sat an emerald cloak of trees. The scepter of river ran close, the rays of a rising sun turning the surface gold.

The morning air was filled with scent, but unlike Virginia's heady magnolia and jasmine, this was a mix of burning wood and scorched earth. Overlying it was a breeze carrying the flavor of winter beneath the warmth.

As they approached the house, Montgomery realized the difference between Gleneagle and Doncaster Hall lay not solely in their locale. Gleneagle had offered an uncomplicated welcome to anyone who approached it. Doncaster Hall seemed to reserve judgment upon its occupants. Once measured and approved, however, a man never wanted to leave.

This was more than a home or a structure. Doncaster Hall was a heritage, a history, proof that the Fairfax family had existed.

That was what his grandfather had wanted to replicate.

People were depending on him at Doncaster Hall just as they had at Gleneagle. Decisions had to be made, decisions he'd pushed away, chosen not to address. He'd effectively escaped into his airships, into the minutiae of designing a baffle rather than thinking about the people who needed him.

How many were employed in various Fairfax industries? He was a little ashamed to realize he didn't know.

"I think, perhaps, that it's time I became the 11th Lord Fairfax of Doncaster in truth."

"Why not?" she asked. "You're no longer a borrowed Scot, Montgomery."

Surprised, he turned his head to look at her.

She nodded. "You're a real Scot," she said, picking up her skirts with both hands and walking several paces in front of him. She turned to face him, her skirts swinging, a smile lighting her face.

"How does one become a real Scot?"

She smiled, an enchanting expression that made him want to kiss her again.

"You're brave," she said. "You've proven that. Not only from being a soldier in your war but being a pilot in your airship."

She regarded him steadily, and he met her gaze head-on. "You're morally brave as well as physically brave."

"I doubt I'm as virtuous as all that," he said.

She ignored him, continuing. "You take responsibility. A Scot does that."

"Does he?"

Her smile was back, as was the sparkle in her eyes. "A Scot also has a certain knowledge of his own value."

"Arrogance, you mean."

She shook her head. "No, not at all. A Scot simply accepts that he's a better man than most." Her glance teased him to disagree.

"You've the same feeling for Doncaster Hall as you did Gleneagle," she said, looking toward the house. "Perhaps even more so. You have everything your grandfather wished and dreamed about."

"Does that include a wife who understands me?"

She renewed him, a stunning admission. She didn't just possess a Gift. She *was* a gift.

"Do I?"

Before he could answer, Edmund stepped on the path.

"Edmund," he said, nodding at his solicitor. "I've misjudged you."

"In what way, Your Lordship?"

Montgomery smiled, an expression that chilled Veronica. Mr. Kerr should be careful of his next words. Despite his smile, Montgomery wasn't feeling the least bit affable at the moment.

"I thought you behind the effort to sabotage my airship."

To his credit, Edmund appeared genuinely shocked.

"I would do no such thing, Your Lordship."

"I realize that, now," Montgomery said, taking a step

forward at the same time he drew back his arm, his fist slamming into the other man's jaw.

Montgomery watched as Edmund fell like a stone to the path. He stood over the man, shaking his hand as Veronica stared in shock.

"If you knew he was innocent, why did you hit him?"

"He's innocent of that deed, but you're not entirely innocent, are you, Edmund?"

He bent, hauled the man up by his collar, and held on until the solicitor blinked a few times.

"You were the one who told me about the Society of the Mercaii. You were the one who urged me to attend."

Edmund sputtered but said nothing coherent.

"You're a member, aren't you? I should have known the night of the séance."

She took a few steps away from Mr. Kerr.

"Was he there?" she asked. "That night, was he there?"

She stared at Edmund. She'd never known the identity of any of the members of the Society. Yet she'd sat in this man's company, had held his hand during the séance, and all this time, he'd been there. He'd seen her naked. Perhaps the feeling she'd had about the solicitor was based, not on her Gift, but because he'd made her uncomfortable in other ways.

Montgomery let go of Kerr's collar, and he fell back to the ground, remaining there and looking up at Montgomery warily.

"Are you going to hit him again?" she asked.

Montgomery turned to look at her. "Do you want me to?"

She'd never had such a champion. What a strange time to want to smile.

"No," she said. "I don't want you to hit him again."

"I got rid of Millicent. It's your choice what to do with him."

"Must you continue to employ him?"

"No," Montgomery said, stretching his hand to her. "Consider him no longer employed at Doncaster Hall."

He glanced down at Edmund. "I'll not be summoning you again," he said. "We'll just have to find a way to get along without you." He turned to Ralston. "If you would do away with that, please," he said, pointing in the solicitor's direction.

Ralston nodded as he and another man lifted Edmund to his feet.

Montgomery grinned at her, the expression changing his face to someone younger, less marred by memory, less filled with grief.

Her heart turned over in her chest.

She went to him and placed her hand on his cheek.

"I love you, Montgomery Fairfax," she said softly, giving him the truth.

He pulled her into his arms.

"Thank God for it," he said, pressing his cheek against her temple. "Thank God for that."

As they stood there, dawn approached shyly, banishing shadows, spreading over the landscape and setting it aglow.

For weeks, he'd questioned his decision to come to Scotland. As the first tentative rays of a renewed day stretched toward Doncaster Hall, Montgomery knew why his path had led him here. Not only to understand his past but to accept his future.

This moment, this instant, was the most perfect homecoming he'd ever had.

He could almost see the ghosts of his past, James and Alisdair on either side of Caroline, hands linked, arms swinging, walking into dawn's horizon. Their laughter caught at his heart, reminding him of days gone by and hinting at days to come.

"What about you, Montgomery Fairfax?"

He didn't even pretend to misunderstand her.

She pulled back, watching him, feeling her heartbeat escalate as he smiled at her. From the beginning, passion had linked them, leading to something stronger, more complete.

"I didn't want a wife," he said.

"Yes, I know," she said flatly, stepping back.

He pulled her into his arms again.

"Then Fate or Providence gave me you," he said.

Loneliness had once lived in his eyes, as well as pain. Now, however, another emotion was there, something that had her throat closing and tears washing to the surface.

Her head tipped back, her face offered up to his gaze. Her features were perfect, her eyes a pure green this morning, the soft rose of her cheeks and lips adding color to the ivory of her complexion. His lips hovered over hers, a mere breath away.

"Do I love you? How can I not? You're confusing, amusing, fascinating, and I suspect you'll lead me a merry race for the rest of my life."

"That was not the most romantic declaration of love I've ever heard, Montgomery Fairfax."

"Shall I agree to work on it?" he asked, bending his head to kiss her cheek. "Each day, in every way." He kissed the edge of her jaw.

He looked at her, not at Doncaster Hall. The sunlight struck her hair, lit her eyes, and illuminated her lovely face. Her beauty, face, feature, and soul, struck him and stole his breath.

In that instant, he realized Doncaster Hall was neither

more substantial nor blessed than any other building. It was, after all, only a structure, not capable of sentient thought or feeling.

Home was here, with this woman, with her courage and optimism, with her strength and resilience. Veronica was his home.

She stood on tiptoe, laid her cheek gently against his, feeling the abrasiveness of his unshaven skin. Turning her head slightly, she brushed her lips against the side of his nose, the corner of his mouth, his chin, before slowly trailing a path down his throat. Her lips rested against the pulse furiously beating there, placed the tip of her tongue there tenderly, breathed against the spot of moisture.

"Are you for seducing me, Veronica Fairfax?" he asked in the brogue of Scotland.

She smiled, feeling his lips against her temple as he spoke.

"I am, Montgomery Fairfax. Have you any objections?"

He pulled back, looked at her, amusement fading from his face.

"I love you, Veronica. There, is that better?"

Reaching up, she wrapped her arms around his neck and kissed him in response.

Epilogue

Mary Tulloch looked into the surface of the mirror. Her reflection was the same image she'd seen on that long-ago day when she was little more than a child.

She'd no complaints with life. She'd been loved and had loved; her children were healthy and a comfort. She'd been kind when she could and cruel when the occasion warranted it.

Now was time for it to end.

The reflection changed, as if the Tulloch Sgàthán had heard her thoughts, brown clouds boiling around the edge of the reflection.

A young girl, shockingly attired in faded blue trousers, stood there, her face twisted in an expression of irritation. A white pea was tucked into each ear, both peas connected by a white vine to something clutched in her fist. Behind her stood a crowd of people being led by a woman in a strange dress, consisting of a kilt and a man's jacket.

She could almost hear the derision in the girl's voice as she spoke to someone and wondered at the reasons for her anger. As she watched, the girl separated herself from the others, stomping away until she came to a plot of land so familiar Mary's heart clenched.

Her cottage was different, however, marked by placards and ropes. She tried to read one of the signs, but her vision had faded over the years. Instead, she concentrated on where the girl had gone, some distance behind the cottage.

She tripped on something laid into the earth, something existing even in this age. Her heart racing, Mary watched as the girl knelt, tucked the white beans and vine in her pocket, and lifted a rotting board. Slowly, the girl bent, her hand outstretched.

The image faded, but the purpose of it had been clear enough.

The day was blustery and threatening a storm as Mary Tulloch left her cottage. She took her time walking to the edge of her land, knowing that it might be the last time she made the journey. With some effort, she lifted the boards placed over an abandoned well, the very place she'd found the mirror all those years ago. Gently, she laid the Tulloch Sgàthán on a pillow of dirt for a girl in the future to discover again.

Author's Notes

An occult organization operated in London beginning in the 1830s. The actual group, on which the Society of the Mercaii was based, was discontinued in the 1840s, although some speculated it still functioned well into the 20th century, albeit under more secrecy.

John Contee Fairfax was born on a James River plantation in Virginia and became the 11th Lord Fairfax of Cameron. I've borrowed some of the Fairfax history for Montgomery's antecedents. Denton Hall was the seat of the Fairfax family in Scotland.

Lord Fairfax is a Lord of Parliament, a title created in Scotland before 1707. Its equivalent is close to a baron in the English peerage.

Early balloons were used to report troop movements on both sides in the Civil War. They were mainly tethered, the altitude enabling the pilots to overlook enemy lines. President Abraham Lincoln established a Balloon Corps that was disbanded in 1863. Once General George McClennan, one of the early supporters of balloons for aerial reconnaissance, was relieved of his command, little enthusiasm, and even less money, existed for the project. However, experimentation with aeronautics continued.

Paraffin oil is known as kerosene in the United States and Canada. In the early days of kerosene production, it was considered deadly because of its propensity for exploding. Today, because of the advances in the refining process, kerosene is a much safer product.

The topography of the Highlands and Perth is as realistic as I can make it. However, I've taken liberty with some geographical landmarks such as the River Tairn and Ben Wyllis. They're not to be found on any map.

The Royal George Hotel, visited by Queen Victoria and her retinue, was actually in Perth.

Turn the page for a sneak peek at
Eleven Scandals to Start to Win a Duke's Heart
by
New York Times bestselling author
Sarah MacLean
Coming in May 2011

In retrospect, there were four actions that Miss Juliana Fiori should have reconsidered that evening.

First, she likely should have ignored the impulse to leave her sister-in-law's Autumn ball in favor of the less-cloying, better-smelling and far more poorly-lit gardens of Ralston House.

Second, she very likely should have hesitated when that same impulse propelled her deeper along the darkened paths that marked the exterior of her brother's home.

Third, she almost certainly should have returned to the house the moment she stumbled upon Lord Grabeham, deep in his cups, half-falling down, and spouting entirely ungentlemanly things.

But, she definitely should not have hit him.

It didn't matter than he had pulled her close and breathed his hot, whiskey-laden breath upon her, or that his cold, moist lips had clumsily found their way to the high arch of one cheek, or that he suggested that she might *like it just as her mother had.*

Ladies did not hit people.

At least, English ladies didn't.

She watched as the not-so-much a gentleman howled in pain and yanked a handkerchief from his pocket, covering his nose and flooding the pristine white linen with scarlet. She froze, absentmindedly shaking the sting from her hand, dread consuming her.

This was bound to get out. It was bound to become an "issue."

It didn't matter that he deserved it.

What was she to have done? Allowed him to maul her while she waited for a savior to come crashing through the trees? Any man out in the gardens at this hour was certain to be less of a savior and more of the same.

But she had just proven the gossips right.

She'd never be one of them.

Juliana looked up into the dark canopy of trees. The rustle of leaves far overhead had only moments ago promised her respite from the unpleasantness of the ball. Now the sound taunted her—an echo of the whispers inside ballrooms throughout London whenever she passed.

"You hit me!" The fat man's cry was all-too-loud, nasal and outraged.

She lifted her throbbing hand and pushed a loose strand of hair back from her cheek. "Come near me again and you'll get more of the same."

His eyes did not leave her as he mopped the blood from his nose. The anger in his gaze was unmistakable.

She knew that anger. Knew what it meant.

Braced herself for what was coming.

It stung nonetheless.

"You shall regret this." He took a menacing step toward her. "I'll have everyone believing that you begged me for it. Here in your brother's gardens like the tart you are."

An ache began at her temple. She took one step back, shaking her head. "No," she said, flinching at the thickness of her Italian accent—the one she had been working so hard to tame. "They will not believe you."

The words sounded hollow even to her.

Of course they would believe him.

He read the thought and gave a bark of angry laughter. "You can't imagine they'd believe *you*. Barely legitimate. Tolerated only because your brother is a marquess. You can't believe *he'd* believe you. You are, after all, your mother's daughter."

Her mother's daughter. The words were a blow she could never escape. No matter how hard she tried.

She lifted her chin, squaring her shoulders. "They will not believe you," she repeated, willing her voice to remain steady, "because they will not believe I could possibly have wanted *you, porco.*"

It took a moment for him to translate the Italian into English, to hear the insult. But when he did, the word *pig* hanging between them in both languages, Grabeham reached for her, his fleshy hand grasping, fingers like sausages.

He was shorter than she was, but he made up for it in brute strength. He grabbed one wrist, fingers digging deep, promising to bruise, and Juliana attempted to wrench herself from his grip, her skin twisting and burning. She hissed her pain and acted on instinct, thanking her maker that she'd learned to fight from the boys on the Veronese riverfront.

Her knee came up. Made precise, vicious contact.

Grabeham howled, his grip loosening just enough for escape.

And Juliana did the only thing she could think of.

She ran.

Lifting the skirts of her shimmering green gown, she tore through the gardens, steering clear of the light pouring out of the enormous ballroom of Ralston House, knowing that being seen running from the darkness would have been just as damaging as being caught by the odious Grabeham . . . who had recovered with alarming speed. She could hear him lumbering behind her through a particularly prickly hedge, panting in great, heaving breaths.

The sound spurred her on, and she burst through the side gate of the garden into the mews that abutted Ralston House, where a collection of carriages waited in a long line for their lords and ladies to call for transport home. She stepped on something sharp and stumbled, catching herself on the cobblestones, scoring the palms of her bare hands as she struggled to right herself. She cursed her decision to remove the gloves that she had been wearing inside the ballroom—cloying or not, kidskin would have saved her a few drops of blood that evening. The iron gate swung shut behind her, and she hesitated for a fraction of a second, sure the noise would attract attention. A quick glance found a collection of coachmen engrossed in a game of dice at the far end of the alleyway, unaware of or uninterested in her. Looking back, she saw the great bulk of Grabeham making for the gate.

He was a bull charging a red cape; she had mere seconds before she was gored.

The carriages were her only hope.

With a low, soothing whisper of Italian, she slipped beneath the massive heads of two great black horses and crept quickly along the line of carriages. She heard the gate screech open and bang shut and she froze, listening for the telltale sound of predator approaching prey.

It was impossible to hear anything over the pounding of her heart.

Quietly, she opened the door to one of the great hulking vehicles and levered herself up and into the carriage without the aid of a stepping block. She heard a tear as the fabric of her dress caught on a sharp edge and ignored the pang of disappointment as she yanked her skirts into the coach and reached for the door, closing it behind her as quietly as she could.

The willow green satin had been a gift from her brother—a nod to her hatred of the pale, prim frocks worn by the rest of the unmarried ladies of the *ton*. And now it was ruined.

She sat stiffly on the floor just inside the carriage, knees pulled up to her chest, and let the blackness embrace her. Willing her panicked breath to calm, she strained to hear something, *anything* through the muffled silence. She resisted the urge to move, afraid to draw attention to her hiding place.

"*Tego, tegis, tegit*," she barely whispered, the soothing cadence of the Latin focusing her thoughts. "*Tégimus, tégitis, tegunt.*"

A faint shadow passed above, hiding the dim light that mottled the wall of the lushly upholstered carriage. Juliana froze briefly before pressing back into the corner of the coach, making herself as small as possible—a challenge considering her uncommon height. She waited, desperate, and when the barely-there light returned, she swallowed and closed her eyes tightly, letting out a long, slow breath.

In English, now.

"I hide. You hide. She hides—"

She held her breath as several masculine shouts broke through the silence, praying for them to move past her hiding place and leave her, for once, in peace. When the vehicle rocked under the movement of a coachman scrambling into his seat, she knew her prayers would go unanswered.

So much for hiding.

She swore once, the epithet one of the more colorful of her native tongue, and considered her options. Grabeham could be just outside, but even the daughter of an Italian merchant who had been in London for only a few months knew that she could not arrive at the main entrance of her brother's home in a carriage belonging to God knew whom without causing a scandal of epic proportions.

Her decision made, she reached for the handle on the door and shifted her weight, building up the courage to escape—to launch herself out of the vehicle, onto the cobblestones and into the nearest patch of darkness.

And then the carriage began to move.

And escape was no longer an option.

For a brief moment, she considered opening the door and leaping from the carriage anyway. But even she was not so reckless. She did not want to die. She just wanted the ground to open up and swallow her, and this carriage, whole. Was that so much to ask?

Taking in the interior of the vehicle, she realized that her best bet was to return to the floor and wait for the carriage to stop. Once it did, she would exit via the door farthest from the house and hope, desperately, that no one was there to see her.

Surely *something* had to go right for her tonight. Surely she had a few moments to escape before the aristocrats beyond descended.

She took a deep breath as the coach came to a stop. Levering herself up . . . reaching for the handle . . . ready to spring.

Before she could exit, however, the door on the opposite side of the carriage burst open, taking the air inside with it in a violent rush. Her eyes flew to the enormous man standing just beyond the coach door.

Oh, no.

The lights at the front of Ralston House blazed behind him, casting his face into shadow, but it was impossible to miss the way the warm, yellow light illuminated his mass of golden curls, turning him into a dark angel—cast from Paradise, refusing to return his halo.

She felt a subtle shift in him, a quiet, almost imperceptible tensing of his broad shoulders and knew that she had been discovered. Juliana knew that she should be thankful for his discretion when he pulled the door to him, eliminating any space through which others might see her, but when he stepped up into the carriage easily, with the aid of neither servant nor step, gratitude was far from what she was feeling.

Panic was a more accurate emotion.

She swallowed, a single thought screaming though her mind.

She should have taken her chances with Grabeham.

For there was certainly no one in the world she would like to face less at this particular moment than the unbearable, immovable Duke of Leighton.

Surely, the universe was conspiring against her.

The door closed behind him with a soft click, and they were alone.

Desperation surged, propelling her into movement, and she scrambled for the near door, eager for escape. Her fingers fumbled for the handle.

"I would not if I were you."

The calm, cool words rankled as they cut through the darkness.

There had been a time when he had not been at all aloof with her.

Before she had vowed never to speak to him again.

She took a quick, stabling breath, refusing to allow him the upper hand. "While I thank you for the suggestion, Your Grace. You will forgive me if I do not follow it."

She clasped the handle, ignoring the sting in her hand at the pressure of the wood, and shifted her weight to release the latch. He moved like lightning, leaning across the coach and holding the door shut with little effort.

"It was not advice."

He rapped the ceiling of the carriage twice, firmly and without hesitation. The vehicle moved instantly, as though his will alone steered its course, and Juliana cursed all well-trained coachmen as she fell backward, her foot catching in the skirt of her gown, further tearing the satin. She winced at the sound, all-too-loud in the heavy quiet, and ran one dirty palm wistfully down the lovely pale fabric.

"My dress is ruined." She took pleasure in implying that he had had something to do with it. He need not know the gown had been ruined long before she'd landed herself in his carriage.

"Yes. Well, I can think of any number of ways you could have avoided such a tragedy this evening." The words were void of contrition.

"I had little choice, you know." The words were soft and she immediately hated herself for saying them aloud.

Especially to him.

He snapped his head toward her just as a lamppost in the street beyond cast a shaft of silver light through the carriage window, throwing him into stark relief. She tried not to notice him. Tried not to notice how every inch of him bore the mark of his excellent breeding, of his aristocratic history—the long, straight patrician nose, the perfect square of his jaw, the high cheekbones that should have made him look feminine, but seemed only to make him more handsome.

She gave a little huff of indignation.

The man had ridiculous cheekbones.

She'd never known anyone so handsome.

"Yes," he fairly drawled, "I can imagine it is difficult attempting to live up to a reputation such as yours."

The light disappeared, replaced by the sting of his words.

She'd also never known anyone who was such a proper ass.

Juliana was thankful for her shadowy corner of coach as she recoiled from his insinuation. She was used to the insults, to the ignorant speculation that came with her being the daughter of an Italian merchant and a fallen English marchioness who had deserted her husband and sons . . . and dismissed London's elite.

The last was the only one of her mother's actions for which Juliana had even a hint of admiration.

She'd like to tell the entire lot of them where they could put their aristocratic rules.

Beginning with the Duke of Leighton. Who was the worst of the lot.

But he hadn't been at the start.

She pushed the thought aside. "I should like you to stop this carriage and let me out."

"I suppose this is not going the way that you had planned?"

She paused. "The way I had . . . planned?"

"Come now, Miss Fiori. You think I do not know how your little game was to have been played out? You, discovered in my empty carriage—the perfect location for a clandestine assignation—on the steps of your brother's ancestral home, during one of the best attended events in recent weeks?"

Her eyes went wide. "You think I am—"

"No. I *know* that you are attempting to trap me in marriage. And your little scheme, about which I assume your brother has no knowledge considering how asinine it is, might have worked on a lesser man with a lesser title. But I assure you it will not work on me. I am a *duke*. In a battle of reputation with you, I would most certainly win. In fact, I would have let you ruin yourself quite handily back at Ralston House if I were not unfortunately indebted to your brother at the moment. You would have deserved it for this little farce."

His voice was calm and unwavering, as though he'd had this particular conversation countless times before, and she was nothing but a minor inconvenience—a fly in his tepid, poorly-seasoned bisque, or whatever it was that aristocratic British snobs consumed with soup spoons.

Of all the arrogant, pompous. . .

Fury flared and Juliana gritted her teeth. "Had I known this was *your* vehicle, I would have avoided it at all costs."

"Amazing, then, that you somehow missed the large ducal seal on the outside of the door."

The man was infuriating. "It is amazing, indeed, because I'm sure the seal on the outside of your carriage rivals your conceit in size! I assure you, *Your Grace*," she spat the honorific like it were an epithet, "If I were after a husband, I would look for one who had more to recommend him than a fancy title and a false sense of importance." She heard the tremor in her voice, but could not stop the flood of words pouring from her. "You are so impressed with your title and station, it is a miracle you do not have the word 'Duke' embroidered in silver thread on all of your topcoats. The way you behave, one would think you'd actually done something to earn the respect these English fools afford you instead of having been conceived, entirely by chance, at the right time and by the right man, who I imagine performed the deed in exactly the same manner of all other men. Without finesse."

She stopped, the pounding of her heart loud in her ears as the words hung between them, their echo heavy in the darkness. *Senza finezza.* It was only then that she realized that, at some point during her tirade, she had switched to Italian.

She could only hope that he had not understood.

There was a long stretch of silence, a great, yawning void that threatened her sanity. And then the carriage stopped. They sat there for an interminable moment, him still as stone, her wondering if they might remain there in the vehicle for the rest of time, before she heard the shifting of fabric. He opened the door, swinging it wide.

She started at the sound of his voice, low and dark and much much closer than she was expecting.

"Get out of the carriage."

He spoke Italian.

Perfectly.

She swallowed. Well. She was not about to apologize. Not after all the terrible things that he'd said. If he was going to throw her from the carriage, so be it. She would walk home. Proudly.

Perhaps someone would be able to point her in the proper direction.

She scooted across the floor of the coach and outside, turning back and fully expecting to see the door swing shut behind her. Instead, he followed her out, ignoring her presence as he moved up the steps of the nearest townhouse. The door opened before he reached the top step.

As though doors, like everything else, bent to his will.

She watched as he entered the brightly lit foyer beyond, a large brown dog lumbering to greet him with cheerful exuberance.

Well. So much for the theory that animals could sense evil.

She smirked at the thought and he turned halfway back almost instantly, as though she had spoken aloud. His golden curls were once more cast into angelic relief as he said, "In or out, Miss Fiori. You are trying my patience."

She opened her mouth to speak, but he had already disappeared from view. And so she chose the path of least resistance.

Or, at least, the path that was least likely to end in her ruin on a London sidewalk in the middle of the night.

She followed him in.

As the door closed behind her and the footman hurried to follow his master to wherever masters and footmen went, Juliana paused in the brightly lit entryway, taking in the wide marble foyer and the gilded mirrors on the walls that only served to make the large space seem more enormous. There were half-a-dozen doors leading this way and that, and a long, dark corridor that stretched deeper into the townhouse.

The dog sat at the bottom of the wide stairway leading to the upper floors of the home, and under his silent canine scrutiny, Juliana was suddenly, embarrassingly aware of the fact that she was in a man's home.

Unescorted.

With the exception of a dog.

Who had already been revealed to be a poor judge of character.

Callie would not approve. Her sister-in-law had specifically cautioned her to avoid situations of this kind. She feared that men would take advantage of a young Italian female with little understanding of British stricture.

"I've sent word to Ralston to come and fetch you. You may wait in the—"

She looked up when he stopped short, and met his gaze, which was clouded with something that, if she did not know better, might be called concern.

She did, however, know better.

"In the—?" she prompted, wondering why he was moving toward her at an alarming pace.

"Dear God. What happened to you?"

"Someone attacked you."

Juliana watched as Leighton poured two fingers of scotch into a crystal tumbler and walked the drink to where she sat in one of the oversized leather chairs in his study. He thrust the drink toward her, and she shook her head. "No, thank you."

"You should take it. You'll find it calming."

She looked up at him, meeting his gaze without hesitation. "I am not in need of calming, Your Grace."

His gaze narrowed, and she refused to look away from the portrait of English nobility he made, tall and towering with nearly unbearable good looks and an expression of complete and utter confidence—as though he had never in his life been challenged.

Never, that was, until now.

"You deny that someone attacked you?"

She shrugged one shoulder idly, remaining quiet. What could she say? What could she tell him that he would not turn against her? He would claim, in that imperious, arrogant tone, that had she been more of a lady . . . had she had more of a care for her reputation . . . had she behaved more like an Englishwoman and less like an Italian . . . then all of this would not have happened.

He would treat her like all the rest.

Just as he had done since the moment he had discovered her identity.

"Does it matter? I'm sure you will decide that I staged the entire evening in order to ensnare a husband. Or something equally ridiculous."

She had intended the words to set him down. They did not.

Instead, he raked her with one long, cool look, taking in her face and arms, covered in scratches, her ruined dress, torn in two places, covered in dirt and streaked with blood from her scored palms.

One side of his mouth twitched in what she imagined was something akin to disgust, and she could not resist saying, "Once more, I prove myself less than worthy of your presence, do I not?"

She bit her tongue, wishing she had not spoken.

He met her gaze. "I did not say that."

"You did not have to."

He threw back the whiskey as a soft knock sounded on the half-open door to the room. Without looking away from her, the duke barked, "What is it?"

"I've brought the things you requested, Your Grace." A servant shuffled into the room with a tray laden with a basin, bandages and several small containers. He set the burden on a low, nearby table.

"That is all."

The servant bowed once, neatly, and took his leave as Leighton stalked toward the tray. She watched as he lifted a linen towel, dipping one edge into the basin. "You did not even thank him."

He cut a glance toward her at her peevish tone. "The evening has not exactly put me in a grateful frame of mind."

She stiffened at his tone, hearing the accusation there. Well. She could be difficult as well.

"Nevertheless, he did you a service." She paused for effect. "To not thank him makes you piggish."

There was a beat before her meaning became clear. "Boorish."

She waved one hand. "Whatever. A different man would have thanked him."

He moved toward her. "Don't you mean a better man?"

Her eyes widened in mock innocence. "Never. You are a duke, after all. Surely there are none better than you."

The words were a direct hit. And, after the terrible things he'd said to her in the carriage, a deserved one.

"A different woman would realize that she is squarely in my debt, and take more care with her words."

"Don't you mean a better woman?"

He did not reply, instead taking the seat across from her and extending his hand, palm up. "Give me your hands."

She clutched them close to her chest instead, wary. "Why?"

"They're bruised and bloody. They need cleaning."

She did not want him touching her. Did not trust herself.

"They are fine."

He gave a low, frustrated growl, the sound sending a shiver through her. "It is true what they say about Italians."

She stiffened at the words, dry with the promise of an insult. "That we are superior in all ways?"

"That it is impossible for you to admit defeat."

"A trait that served Caesar quite well."

"And how is the Roman Empire faring these days?"

The casual, superior tone made her want to scream. Epithets. In her native tongue.

Impossible man.

They stared at each other for a long minute, neither willing to back down until he finally spoke. "Your brother will be here any moment, Miss Fiori. And he is going to be livid enough as it is without seeing your bloody palms."

She narrowed her gaze on his hand, wide and long and oozing strength. He was right, of course. She had no choice but to relinquish.

"This is going to hurt." The words were her only warning before he ran his thumb over her palm softly, investigating the wounded skin there, now crusted in dried blood. She sucked in a breath at the touch.

He glanced up at the sound. "Apologies."

She did not reply, instead making a show of investigating her other hand.

She would not let him see that it was not pain that had her gasping for breath.

She had expected it, of course, the undeniable, unwelcome reaction that threatened whenever she saw him. That surged whenever he neared.

It was loathing. She was sure of it.

She would not even countenance the alternate possibility.

Attempting a clinical assessment of the situation, Juliana looked down at their hands, nearly entwined. The room grew instantly warmer. His hands were enormous, and she was transfixed by his fingers, long and manicured, dusted with fine golden hairs.

He ran one finger gently across the wicked bruise that had appeared on her wrist and she looked up to find him staring at the purpling skin. "You will tell me who did this to you."

There was a cool certainty in the words, as though she would do his bidding and he would, in turn, handle the situation. But Juliana knew better. This man was no knight. He was a dragon. The leader of them. "Tell me, Your Grace. What is it like to believe that your will exists only to be done?"

His gaze flew to hers, darkening with irritation. "You will tell me, Miss Fiori."

"No, I will not."

She returned her attention to their hands. It was not often that Juliana was made to feel dainty—she towered over nearly all of the women and many of the men in London—but this man made her feel small. Her thumb was barely larger than the smallest of his fingers, the one that bore the gold and onyx signet ring—proof of his title.

That reminded her of his stature.

And of how far beneath him he believed her to be.

She lifted her chin at the thought, anger and pride and hurt flaring in a hot rush of feeling, and at that precise moment, he touched the raw skin of her palm with the

wet linen cloth. She embraced the distraction of the stinging pain, hissing a wicked Italian curse.

He did not pause in his ministrations as he said, "I did not
know that those two animals could do such a thing together."

"It is rude of you to listen."

One golden brow rose at the words. "It is rather difficult not to listen if you are mere inches from me, shouting
your discomfort."

"Ladies do not shout."

"It appears that Italian ladies do. Particularly when
they are undergoing medical treatment."

She resisted the urge to smile.

He was not amusing.

He dipped his head and focused on the task at hand,
dipping the linen cloth in the basin of clean water once
more. She flinched as the cool fabric returned to her
scoured hand, and he hesitated briefly before continuing.

The momentary pause intrigued her. The Duke of
Leighton was not known for his compassion. He was
known for his arrogant indifference, and she was surprised he would stoop so low as to perform such a menial
task as cleaning the gravel from her hands.

"Why are you doing this?" She blurted at the next
stinging brush of linen.

He did not stop his ministrations. "I told you. Your
brother is going to be difficult enough to deal with without you bleeding all over yourself. And my furniture."

"No," she shook her head. "I mean why are *you* doing
this? Don't you have a battalion of servants just waiting
to perform such an unpleasant task?"

"I do."

"And so?"

"Servants talk, Miss Fiori. I would prefer as few people
as possible know that you are here, alone at this hour."

She was trouble for him. Nothing more.

After a long silence, he met her gaze. "You disagree?"

She recovered quickly. "Not at all. I am merely astounded that a man of your wealth and prominence would have servants who gossip. One would think you'd have divined a way to strip them of all desire to socialize."

One side of his mouth kicked up and he shook his head. "Even as I am helping you, you are seeking out ways to wound me."

When she replied, her tone was serious, her words true. "Forgive me if I am wary of your goodwill, Your Grace."

His lips pressed into a thin, straight line, and he reached for her other hand, repeating his actions. They both watched as he cleaned the dried blood and gravel from the heel of her palm, revealing tender pink flesh that would take several days to heal.

His movements were gentle but firm, and the stroke of the linen on the abraded skin grew more tolerable as he cleaned the wounds. Juliana watched as one golden curl fell over his brow. His countenance was, as always, stern and unmoving, like one of her brother's treasured marble statues.

She was flooded with a familiar desire, one that came over her whenever he was near.

The desire to crack the façade.

She had glimpsed him without it twice.

And then he had discovered who she was—the Italian half-sister of one of London's most notorious rakes, the barely legitimate daughter of a fallen marchioness and her merchant husband, raised far from London and its manners and traditions and rules.

The opposite of everything he represented.

The antithesis of everything he cared to have in his world.

"My only motive is to get you home in one piece, with none but your brother the wiser about your little adventure this evening."

He tossed the linen into the basin of now-pink water and lifted one of the small pots from the tray. He opened it, releasing the scent of rosemary and lemon and reached for her hands again.

She gave them up easily this time. "You don't really expect me to believe that you are concerned for my reputation?"

Leighton dipped the tip of one broad finger into the pot, concentrating on her wounds as he smoothed the salve across her skin. The medicine combated the burning sting, leaving a welcome, cool path where his fingers stroked. The result was the irresistible illusion that his touch was the harbinger of the soothing pleasure flooding her skin.

Which it wasn't.

Not at all.

She caught her sigh before it embarrassed her. He heard it nonetheless. That golden eyebrow rose again, leaving her wishing that she could shave it off.

She snatched her hand away. He did not try to stop her.

"No, Miss Fiori. I am not concerned for your reputation."

Of course he wasn't.

"I am concerned for my own."

The implication that being found with her—being linked to her—could damage his reputation stung, perhaps worse than her hands had earlier in the evening.

She took a deep breath, readying herself for their next verbal battle, when a furious voice sounded from the doorway.

"If you don't take your hands off of my sister this instant, Leighton, your precious reputation will be the least of your problems."

Next month, don't miss these exciting new love stories only from Avon Books

Midnight's Wild Passion by Anna Campbell

Blinded by vengeance for the man who destroyed his sister, the Marquess of Ranelaw plans to repay his foe in kind by seducing the man's daughter. But when her companion, Miss Antonia Smith, steps in to thwart his plans, Antonia finds herself fighting off his relentless charm. And she's always had a weakness for rakes…

Ascension by Sable Grace

When Kyana, half Vampyre, half Lychen, is entrusted by the Order of Ancients to find a key that will seal Hell forever and save the mortals she despises, she has no choice but to accept. But when she's assigned an escort, Ryker, a demigod who stirred her heart long ago, she knows that giving into temptation could mean the undoing of them both.

A Tale of Two Lovers by Maya Rodale

Lord Simon Roxbury has a choice: wed or be penniless. Surely finding a suitable miss should be simple enough? But then gossip columnist Lady Julianna threatens his reputation and a public battle ensues, leaving both in tatters. To rescue her good name and his fortune, they unite in a marriage of convenience. Will it be too late to stop tongues wagging or will it be a love match after all?

When Tempting a Rogue by Kathryn Smith

Gentleman club proprietress Vienne La Rieux has her eye on a prize that would make her England's richest woman when a former lover, the charming Lord Kane, disrupts her plans. Neither is prepared for the passion still between them, but with an enemy lurking in the shadows, any attempt to mix business with pleasure could have tragic consequences.

At Avon Books, we know your passion for romance—once you finish one of our novels, you find yourself wanting more.

May we tempt you with . . .

- **Excerpts** from our upcoming releases.

- Entertaining **extras**, including authors' personal photo albums and book lists.

- Behind-the-scenes **scoop** on your favorite characters and series.

- **Sweepstakes** for the chance to win free books, romantic getaways, and other fun prizes.

- Writing **tips** from our authors and editors.

- **Blog** with our authors and find out why they love to write romance.

- **Exclusive content** that's not contained within the pages of our novels.

Join us at
www.avonbooks.com

AVON

An Imprint of HarperCollins*Publishers*
www.avonromance.com